Praise for Janet Tronstad and her novels

"Janet Tronstad's quirky small town and witty characters will add warmth and joy to your holiday season."
—*RT Book Reviews* on *A Dry Creek Christmas*

"*Sugar Plums for Dry Creek* is another delightful holiday offering from Janet Tronstad."
—*RT Book Reviews*

"*Snowbound in Dry Creek* [is] an emotionally vibrant and totally satisfying read."
—*RT Book Reviews*

"Janet Tronstad delivers a heartwarming Christmas tale sure to be a keeper."
—*RT Book Reviews* on *Stranded With Santa*

JANET TRONSTAD

A Dry Creek Christmas
&
Sugar Plums for Dry Creek

HARLEQUIN® LOVE INSPIRED®CLASSICS

Recycling programs
for this product may
not exist in your area.

ISBN-13: 978-0-373-63292-3

A Dry Creek Christmas & Sugar Plums for Dry Creek

Copyright © 2016 by Harlequin Books S.A.

The publisher acknowledges the copyright holder
of the individual works as follows:

A Dry Creek Christmas
Copyright © 2004 by Janet Tronstad

Sugar Plums for Dry Creek
Copyright © 2005 by Janet Tronstad

HARLEQUIN®

www.Harlequin.com

Printed in U.S.A.

CONTENTS

Janet Tronstad grew up on her family's farm in central Montana and now lives in Pasadena, California, where she is always at work on her next book. She has written more than thirty books, many of them set in the fictitious town of Dry Creek, Montana, where the men spend the winters gathered around the potbellied stove in the hardware store and the women make jelly in the fall.

Visit the Author Profile page
at Harlequin.com for more titles.

A DRY CREEK CHRISTMAS

For every one that exalteth himself shall be abased; and he that humbleth himself shall be exalted.
—*Luke* 18:14

In memory of my dear friend
Judy Eslick

Chapter One

Millie Corwin squinted and pushed her eyeglasses back into place. The night was full of snow clouds and there were no stars to help her see along this long stretch of Highway 94. Millie was looking for the sign that marked the side road leading into Dry Creek, Montana. She could barely see with the snow flurries.

What had she been thinking? When she had told the chaplain at the prison that she would honor Forrest's request, she hadn't thought about the fact that Christmas was in the middle of winter and Dry Creek was in the middle of Montana so she would, of course, be in the middle of snow.

She hated snow. Not that it made much difference. Snow or no snow, she had to be here.

Millie saw a sign and peered down the dark road that led into Dry Creek. Only one set of car tracks disturbed the snow that was falling. Hopefully that meant most people were home and in bed at this time of night. She planned to arrive in Dry Creek, do what

she had to do, and then leave without anyone seeing her.

Millie turned the wheel of her car and inched her
way closer to the little town.

She wished, and not for the first time, that Forrest had made a different final request of her while
he was dying.

She met Forrest three years ago. He'd come into
Ruby's, the coffee shop where she worked near the
Seattle waterfront, and sat down at one of her tables.
Millie must have taken Forrest's order a dozen times
before he looked her in the eyes and smiled. There
was something sweet about Forrest. He seemed as
quiet and nondescript as she felt inside. He was rest-
ful compared with all of the tall, boisterous, loud men
she'd learned to ignore at Ruby's.

It wasn't until he had been arrested, however, that
she knew the whole truth about Forrest. He'd been a
criminal since he was a boy and had, over the years,
gotten deeper and deeper into crime until he'd eventually become a hit man. His last contract had been
for someone in Dry Creek.

When Millie got over the shock of what Forrest
was, she decided he still needed a friend. She had visited him while he was in prison, especially this past
year when he'd been diagnosed with cancer. The odd
thing was the sicker he got the more cheerful he became. He told her he'd found God in prison.

Millie was glad enough that Forrest had found re-
ligion if it made him happy. She smiled politely and

nodded when he explained what a miracle it was that God could love a man like him.

Personally, Millie thought it would be a miracle if God loved anyone, but that it had more to do with God than the people He was supposed to love. However, since Forrest was sick, she supposed it was good if Forrest thought God loved him and so she nodded pleasantly.

But when Forrest added that God loved her as well, she stopped nodding.

Of course, she kept smiling. Millie didn't want to offend either Forrest or God.

Then Forrest added that he was going to pray for her so she would know God's love, too. Millie could no longer keep smiling; she could barely keep quiet. She'd always kept a low profile with God and she figured that was the smart thing to do.

If God was anything like the other domineering males she'd seen—and there was no reason to think otherwise—then He looked out for His own interests first. If He noticed a person like her at all, it would only be to ask her to fetch Him a glass of water or another piece of toast or something else to make Him more comfortable.

Millie had grown up in a foster home where she was the one assigned to do chores. Usually, the chores consisted of cooking, doing laundry and taking care of the five boys in the home.

Millie didn't know if it was because she was easier to order around than the boys or if her foster mother really believed males were privileged, but—whatever the reason—she soon realized she was doing all of the work for everyone in the house and, instead of being grateful, the boys only became more demanding.

By the time Millie left that home, she'd had enough of dealing with loud, demanding males.

And those boys were mere mortals. She figured God would be even more demanding. No, it was best if God didn't even know her name. She didn't want anyone mentioning her to Him. She had no desire to be God's waitress.

Still, Millie wasn't good at telling people what to do or not to do, and she certainly couldn't tell a dying friend to stop praying. So she changed the subject with Forrest and asked what kind of pudding he had had for lunch. She would just have to hope Forrest came to his senses on his own.

He didn't. Every letter he wrote after that said he was praying for her.

When Forrest died, the chaplain at the prison forwarded a final letter Forrest had asked him to mail.

In the letter, Forrest said he had tried to right some of the wrongs in his life. He hadn't done anything about Dry Creek, however, and he asked Millie to go to the place and try to restore the little town's innocence.

"I fear I've made them distrust strangers and I regret it," he wrote and then added, "Please go there, without telling them who sent you, and do something to restore their faith in strangers. And when you go, go at Christmas."

Millie winced when she read that line in the letter.

Even though Forrest had gone to Dry Creek at Christmas himself, Millie knew it was more than that that made him suggest the holiday. Forrest knew Christmas was a lonely time for her.

Not that she didn't like Christmas. It was just that she always felt like she was on the outside looking in when it came to the holidays. She'd made Forrest tell her several times about the little town with the Christmas pageant and the decorations. It all sounded like a picture on one of those nostalgic calendars.

In the foster home where Millie grew up, they had never done much to celebrate Christmas. Her foster mother always said she was too busy for that kind of thing. Millie had tried to make a fake Christmas tree one year out of metal clothes hangers and tin foil, but the boys had laughed at it and knocked it down.

Millie had never had a Christmas like the one Forrest witnessed in Dry Creek and now, it appeared, he wanted her to have one.

Even though the thought of spending Christmas in Dry Creek held a kind of fatal attraction for Millie, she would never have agreed to Forrest's request if he were alive and she could tell him face-to-face why his idea wouldn't work.

For one thing, Forrest was asking her to make the little town trust strangers again, and she wasn't the kind of person who could do something that would make a whole town change its mind about anything. Forrest knew that.

Even more important, Millie suspected that if the people in Dry Creek knew who had sent her they wouldn't trust her even if she did manage to sound persuasive. After all, Forrest had tried to kill a woman in their town two years ago. The people certainly wouldn't welcome a friend of Forrest's, let alone want to celebrate Christmas with her.

But Millie couldn't tell Forrest any of those things when she got the letter, because—well, he was dead. So she did the next best thing. She called the chaplain who had mailed the letter and tried to explain why she wasn't the person to fulfill Forrest's last request. The chaplain listened and then told her Forrest had said she might call and that Forrest wanted her to know his request was important or he wouldn't have asked her to do it.

All of which was why Millie was here in the dark. She couldn't let Forrest down.

Of course, she couldn't do exactly what he wanted, either. Therefore, she made her own plan. She decided she would do what she could to restore Dry Creek's trust in strangers and she would do it at Christmas, but she would do it without actually talking to a single person. In fact, she'd do it without even seeing another person's face.

Forrest would have to be content with that.

Hopefully, she'd be able to do what she needed to do tonight, Millie told herself as she saw a few house lights ahead of her. She had gone down the road that led into Dry Creek. It was Saturday, December 22. If she left her presents in the café tonight, the people of Dry Creek would discover them on Monday, Christmas Eve Day.

By Christmas, the people of Dry Creek should all be talking about the kindness of the stranger who'd come to town in the middle of the night to bring them a wonderful surprise and who then left without even waiting to be thanked.

Maybe they'd call her the Christmas Stranger. Millie rolled her tongue over that phrase. Christmas Stranger. She rather liked the sound of that, she decided.

Brad Parker shoved his Stetson further down on his head and squinted as he tried to read his watch in the dark. Snow was falling outside and the heat from his old diesel engine barely kept the ice from forming on the windshield of his pickup. It was a sad night in Dry Creek, Montana when a thirty-four-year-old man ended his Saturday evening hiding out in his pickup without even a woman beside him to make it look like he had a reason for being there.

The worst part was, he'd already been parked behind the closed café for the past half hour, well off the road so no one could see him, and wondering when it would be safe to go back to the bunkhouse at the Elkton Ranch.

The last time he'd gotten back to the bunkhouse before dawn on a Saturday night was because of a tooth that was so infected Dr. Norris had insisted on opening the clinic to fix it even though it was Sunday—and everyone in the whole county knew Dr. Norris never missed a Sunday church service if he could help it.

Brad had been in enough pain at the time that he'd said yes when the good doctor asked him to come to church some Sunday morning. And, Brad told himself, he meant to do just that—someday. No one would be able to say Brad Parker didn't keep his word, even if they could say he was a fool to make a promise like that in the first place when he didn't own a tie and would rather have the root canal all over again than actually go to church.

Brad ran his tongue around his teeth. They all felt fine to him. He did an internal check for other pain and found none. He appeared to be in fine health. Which was a pity, in a way, because the guys would understand him making a short evening of it if he had reason to suspect he was dying or something.

If he wasn't dying, though, they were sure to guess the truth, and that was why Brad was sitting here in the cold. It was bad enough that he knew he always got depressed around Christmas. He didn't want to have to hear about it from the other guys in the bunkhouse, as well.

He'd left the poker party early because he was heading out to another game on the other side of town. He got halfway to the game and decided he didn't want to play anymore. All he wanted was to go home. Since he was already on the road, he just kept driving until he pulled into Dry Creek.

That's when Brad realized he couldn't show up at the bunkhouse yet. If Charlie hadn't stopped going to Billings on Saturday nights, no one would even be in the bunkhouse to hear him slip in early. But

Charlie fancied himself the grandfather of "his boys," and he was sure to make a big deal about Brad and Christmas.

Brad shook his head. He never should have told the guys that his parents had been killed in a car accident just before Christmas when he was small. It had been five years ago that he'd mentioned it, and every year he still caught one or two of them watching him with a certain look in their eyes just before Christmas. He didn't know why they made such a big deal about it.

It wasn't a crime to get depressed at Christmas anyway. Brad made it through the other fifty-one weeks of the year just fine. If he wanted to feel sorry for himself one week out of the year, the rest of the world should just let him.

Still, as long as he was going to bed early tonight, he might as well get up early tomorrow morning. Maybe, since his week was already shot because of Christmas, he should just keep his promise to Dr. Norris and show up in church.

Yeah, Brad thought to himself grimly as he tried to make himself comfortable on the old seat of his pickup, he'd just get all of the bad stuff out of the way and start the new year fresh. No point in wasting a good weekend next year by going to church.

That's what he'd do. Get rid of Christmas and church in one fell swoop. But first he'd give Charlie another half hour to go to bed just in case the old man might surprise Brad and actually be asleep when he got home.

It was sure going to be some Christmas, Brad said

to himself as he leaned back against the seat of his pickup and closed his eyes. Yeah, it was going to be some Christmas.

Chapter Two

Millie held her breath as the shadows of Dry Creek came into view. The little town was just as she had pictured it when Forrest told her about it. The clouds had parted and the moon was shining even though a few flakes of snow were still falling. There was one street lamp, and it gave off enough light that the flakes looked like glitter floating over the darkened town. A lone pair of tire tracks had packed down a thin path of snow on the road into town, but elsewhere snow sat soft and fluffy alongside the dozen or so buildings.

Millie could see the church with its steeple. The house next to the church had lights in the second floor windows and filmy white curtains. That must be the parsonage where the woman whom Forrest had been sent to kill lived. At the time, the woman had just been passing through Dry Creek when two little boys decided she must be an angel, and therefore just what they needed for the town's Christmas pageant.

Forrest always shook his head when he told Millie about the little boys who thought they'd found their own personal angel. Forrest had never known that kind of innocence in his own life. Of course, he hadn't been sent to kill the woman because the boys thought she was an angel. The woman had witnessed a crime, and that made some big guys nervous enough to want her out of the way.

Forrest was particularly glad he hadn't succeeded in that job.

The woman, Glory Beckett, was now married to Matthew Curtis, the man who was pastor at the church. The pastor also worked at the hardware store down the street, and Millie wished she could see that building more clearly. Millie's favorite memory of Forrest's Dry Creek stories was the part about the old men who sat around the woodstove in that building. If she were coming into town like a regular person, she would like to sit with those old men some morning and listen to them argue about cattle prices. It all sounded so peaceful. She truly wished—

Millie shook her head. She couldn't afford to dwell on those kind of wishes. A life around a cozy wood stove in Dry Creek wasn't meant for someone like her. She had her tables at Ruby's. They might be filled with scruffy men who wanted more coffee, but that was what she had for the time being.

Millie dimmed her lights when she pulled close to the café. No one was around, but she didn't want her lights to shine into the windows of any of the houses farther down the road. She didn't pull in too close, because the snow wasn't packed down that far off the road and she didn't want to get stuck. She checked the mirror behind her as she turned off her lights. No one was coming.

Millie opened her car's door. Forrest had told her stories about the café, and so she knew the spare key was sitting under a certain rock on the porch. With any luck, she would be in the café and have her surprises delivered in less than ten minutes.

Brad wasn't sure what woke him up. It might have been the lights on the car that was driving into Dry Creek. Not that the lights themselves would have woken him up. It was when the driver dimmed the lights that something stirred his sleeping brain. When he heard the thud of a car door quietly shutting, he opened his eyes. Even then half of his brain was thinking that Linda was coming in early to open up and maybe he could get a cup of coffee.

He discarded that theory as soon as he thought it. Linda had closed the café for Christmas week so that she could go visit that boyfriend of hers in Los Angeles. Linda had said the town could use the café if anyone wanted to cook a Christmas Eve dinner like she had in the past, but so far no one had agreed to do the cooking. In any event, Linda wasn't even in the state of Montana.

Brad slid open his pickup door and woke up completely. The cold air pushing into the pickup was enough to get a man's attention. He wished he didn't have to go and investigate, but he saw little choice.

Everyone knew Linda was gone, and if someone had mischief in mind, now was the time they would do it.

The snow softened Brad's footsteps as he walked along the side of the café. He looked in the corner of the window and saw a figure moving around inside. Whoever it was had thought to bring a flashlight, and the beam of the light was flickering around inside. The flashlight sealed the argument for Brad. No one who had any business being in there would bother with a flashlight when the light switch was right next to the door.

It must be some kid, Brad thought to himself. He could see the boy's shadow and judged him to be around eleven or twelve. Brad figured a boy that young would be more nuisance than trouble. Brad looked over at the car parked in front of the café. He didn't recognize it, but it was a kid's car all right— a beat-up old thing the color of crusty mustard. It looked like it was held together with rubber bands and bubble gum—but it was still a car. Which meant the boy was probably at least sixteen.

With any luck, Brad could deliver the boy back to his parents and that would be the end of it.

Millie's fingers were so cold she had a hard time keeping the flashlight steady. She had set the bag of flannel Santa socks at her feet and the other bag, the one with the hundred-dollar bills, on the table in front of her.

It was the perfect thing to do with the money Forrest had given her before he left for Dry Creek two years ago. Millie had tried to give the seventy-five hundred dollar bills to the police, but they didn't want them because they couldn't prove they were connected to a crime. She didn't want them because she couldn't prove they *weren't* connected to a crime. She had been poor all her life, but she'd never knowingly profited from the misery of others.

Millie had fretted about what to do with those bills until she'd realized they were the solution to her problem in Dry Creek. She'd give a bill to each person in Dry Creek along with a note saying the money was from a stranger. That would make them all trust strangers more, wouldn't it? A hundred dollars would do that to most people in Millie's opinion. It sure would have caused a stir with those boys in her old foster family.

Besides, she'd be able to get rid of the money and fulfill Forrest's request at the same time. It was brilliant. And the best part of all was, she wouldn't have to actually open her mouth and talk to anyone.

Millie supposed she should have pre-stuffed the socks and written her notes, but she had decided she would do that in the café. She wanted to think about how excited each person would be when they opened their socks and saw the money.

It had not been easy, but Millie had remembered the names of most of the people who lived in Dry Creek. Forrest had sprinkled his stories with a surprising number of names and, fortunately, they had stayed in her head. She'd written names on most of the socks. In her opinion, a present wasn't really a present unless it had a person's name on it.

Some of the names might be misspelled, but she was sure each stocking would find its owner. She even had a few labeled "Anyone," for those she might have missed. Most nights last month, after she finished at the coffee shop, she'd pick up the glue gun and personalize the Christmas socks. Before the glue dried, she sprinkled glitter on the writing.

She was proud of the socks. The money might be from Forrest, but the socks were from her.

Millie didn't know what made her think something was wrong. Maybe it was the fact that the air inside the café was suddenly a couple of degrees colder. Or maybe it was the darkness inside had grown just a shade deeper, like someone was blocking the moonlight that had been coming through the open door behind her. Whatever it was, she didn't have enough time to turn around before she felt the arms close around her.

Woosh. Millie felt her breath leave her as panic rose in her throat.

"What the—?" Brad revised his opinion of the juvenile delinquent he was apprehending. The boy might be small, but he wasn't puny. He had stomped on Brad's foot with all his might. The kid was wearing some kind of wool coat that made grabbing him difficult, but Brad had roped calves for the last twenty years and knew a thing or two about handling uncooperative creatures.

Brad grabbed the boy around the middle and

hoisted him up in the air where his feet could do less damage. The boy gasped in outrage, but Brad didn't let that stop him.

"If you want me to put you down, you have to stop kicking," Brad finally said as he shifted his arms so that the kid was hanging on Brad's hip like a bag of grain. Brad had his arm hooked around his captive's stomach, and the boy's head was facing toward the café door. He wore enough wool to clothe a small army, and it bunched up around his middle. Brad was having a hard time keeping the boy from wiggling out of his arm so he could walk back to the light switch.

The boy must be deaf, because he sure wasn't doing what Brad had politely suggested. Which was what Brad would expect, considering the whole night had gone from bad to worse. Well, Brad decided, he'd had enough.

He took his other hand and pushed the wool coat up high enough so he could get a firm grip on the boy's stomach. The boy's shirt had come untucked in the struggle, and Brad figured his hand was firmly anchored around the boy's stomach.

"That's better," Brad said. The boy had gone still in his arm.

Brad took a couple of steps over to the light switch even though something was beginning to make him think he'd got a few things wrong. The boy must be even younger than Brad had figured.

His stomach was softer than anything Brad imagined you'd find on a boy of fifteen who lived around these parts. Maybe that was the kid's problem. No one had taught him to ride horses or wrestle calves. Brad doubted the boy had even done any summer farm work. That belly had never been scratched by lifting a hay bale or sliding under a broken-down tractor.

The boy gasped again when Brad flipped the light switch, but Brad was ready for him. This time he tipped the kid upright so they could face each other.

"Oh." Brad still had the boy in his grip, or rather—he corrected himself—he still had her—*her*—in his grip.

"You're a girl!" Brad could see she was more like a woman, but he was only starting to sort things out, and "girl" would do for now. He never should have left those poker games tonight.

The girl-woman just glared at him. She had green eyes and wispy blond hair that settled in soft curls around her face. And her face—she looked solemn and scared all at the same time. The only muscles that moved on her face were her eyelids. She kept blinking.

"You dropped my glasses," she finally said.

Brad looked back and he saw where her glasses had fallen to the floor. He also saw a brown paper bag with a long tear in it on top of one of the tables. Through the tear he saw money.

Brad whistled. "I guess I don't need to ask what you're doing here."

The woman went even stiffer in his arms.

"I'm not one to judge people," Brad continued as he carried her over to the brown paper bag. He began to wonder if the woman had been getting enough to eat. She sure didn't weigh much. He could carry her around on his hip like this for hours without tiring. "I figure you're poor enough that stealing some money from a cash drawer is tempting, but you'd be much better off getting a job."

The woman relaxed some. "I have a job."

"Now, there's no need to lie to me," Brad continued patiently. "No one's blaming you for needing help. But in this town we ask for help, we don't steal from each other."

"I'm not stealing."

For such a little bit of a woman, she sure was stubborn. Brad looked at the bag more closely and frowned. Why had Linda kept that kind of money in the café? Even though break-ins were rare around here, there was no point in tempting folks.

"What's your name anyway?"

"You don't know me. I'm a stranger."

Something about the way the woman said that irked Brad. "I wasn't planning to sit down and socialize or anything—I just asked your name."

"Oh. My name's Millie."

"Millie what?"

"Just Millie."

Brad sat down in the chair next to the table. As he folded all six foot four of himself onto the chair, he shifted Millie so she sat on his knee.

Brad almost sighed. No wonder he had thought she was a kid. Even with her sitting on his lap, he still didn't meet her eye to eye. Which was a pity, because he'd been wondering if her eyes weren't more blue than green, and he'd been hoping to have another look. Of course, it wasn't because he was personally interested. It was just so he could answer the questions if he had to describe her for a police report. Looking down, he saw the top of her head. "How short are you anyway?"

That statement at least made Millie look up at him. Her face was no longer pale and scared. It was more pink and angry now. Of course, that was probably just because he'd been carrying her sideways.

"I'm just under five feet *tall*, not *short*," Millie said. "And I don't see what business it is of yours anyway."

Brad grinned. He'd always liked green eyes that threw spit darts at him. "Lady, everything about you is my business. At least until I can get the deputy sheriff to come pick you up."

That seemed to take Millie's attention away from him. She twisted around on his lap and looked at the door.

"Don't even think about making a run for it," Brad said. Until he said that, he had half a mind to give her a few dollars out of his own pocket and send her on her way. But he figured he should at least wait until she said she was sorry and promised to stop stealing from people.

"I don't run away," Millie announced.

Brad believed her. She sat as still as a stone on his lap, as if she was resigned to the worst. He didn't want to scare her. "Well, it's not like they'll probably lock you up or anything—you didn't even make a getaway."

Brad reached down and picked up Millie's glasses off of the floor, then gave them to her.

Millie took the glasses from him and settled them on her nose.

Brad frowned. Those glasses not only hid the golden tones in Millie's green eyes, they hid her face, as well. Without them, she was pretty in a quiet sort of a way. Her face was pale with freckles scattered across it. With her wispy blond hair and those solemn green eyes, she looked like pictures he'd seen of young girls living on the sun-bleached prairie a hundred years ago.

She didn't look like his ideal woman, of course. Her hair might be blond, but it didn't have any of the brazen look he preferred. He liked women with red lipstick and sexy laughs who knew how to flirt.

But still, for a quiet kind of a woman, she was pretty enough. Until she put those glasses on. The glasses made her look like a rabbit.

Of course, how the woman looked was not his problem. Brad stood up and wrapped Millie under his arm again. "Sorry I don't have any rope to tie you up with. So we'll just have to make do until I get the sheriff on the phone."

Brad sat down again once he reached the phone at the back of the café. He settled Millie back on his lap. This time it seemed more like she belonged there. Like he was getting used to her. "You don't really need those glasses, do you?"

"That's none of—"

"—my business," Brad finished for her. Well, she was right. She was too serious for the likes of him anyway. He needed a woman who liked a good time and would leave it at that. A woman like the one sitting on his lap would turn her green eyes on him and expect him to make a commitment to her. He didn't need any of that. Especially not when he was depressed anyway. He reached for the phone and dialed a number. The phone rang and rang. No one answered.

Brad sighed. It was time someone dragged Sheriff Carl Wall into the twenty-first century and got him a cell phone. What were law-abiding citizens supposed to do when they apprehended a thief in the middle of the night?

Brad looked back over at the bag of money on the table. The bag was small, more of a lunch bag than anything. Still, it was stuffed full. If she'd only been stealing twenty bucks to make it to the next town, he'd probably let her go.

But seeing that bag of money gave him pause. The side of the bag was split and he could see the bills. He wasn't close enough to see the denominations, but there were probably a few hundred dollars there. He wasn't doing anyone any favors if he let a thief like that loose in the night.

"I guess I'll just have to take you in," he said finally. The Elkton bunkhouse wasn't the fanciest place around, but it was built solid and all of the locks worked. He could just lock her in his room for the night, and get the sheriff to come out in the morning.

In the meantime, Brad would throw a tablecloth over that bag of money and lock the café door. It should be safe enough until morning when he and Sheriff Wall could come back and investigate. As he recalled, the sheriff was particular about the scene of the crime, and Brad wanted to be able to tell him that he hadn't touched anything.

For the first time that evening, Brad had a happy thought. He might not need to go to church tomorrow morning after all, not when he had to clean up after a crime. Even God and Dr. Norris had to understand that keeping the law was important.

And, Brad decided, because he had fully intended to go to church, that should count as keeping his promise even if he didn't actually get there. He told himself it wasn't his fault someone had been stealing from the café.

Chapter Three

"Get in," Brad said as he held the door of his pickup open. The passenger door had a tendency to stick, and he'd had to put Millie down so he could open it. He'd kept one arm hooked around her stomach while he'd swung the door open with his other hand. "Get in."

"I never ride with strangers," Millie said as she braced herself.

Brad sighed. He could feel the woman tense up. He never knew a thief could be so particular about the company she kept. "Don't worry. No one's a stranger for long in Dry Creek—"

Well, that made her relax, Brad thought.

"Really? So you're not worried about strangers around here?" she asked as she turned around to face him. "You trust them?"

The woman sounded downright cheerful. Brad wondered why for a moment before he remembered. "We're not so trusting that we don't lock our doors, of course."

Brad lifted the woman up into his pickup and settled her on the seat. He knew he was lying a little, but he figured it was allowed under the circumstances. Some people did lock their doors when they went away for a trip—if they could find their keys, of course.

Brad figured he should drive his point home just so she knew she wasn't in some nostalgic Rockwell painting where everyone was easy pickings for any thief who might come driving by. "We've had our share of crime here. Why, we had a hit man come to town two years ago at Christmas. He tried to kill the pastor's wife."

"Oh." The woman was looking straight ahead as if there was something to see out the windshield of his pickup.

"Of course, we took care of him. Had him arrested and sent to prison." Brad congratulated himself as he shut the door on his pickup. That should let her know that the people of Dry Creek knew how to handle bad guys.

Brad walked around to the driver's side and got in.

"I'm sure he must have been sorry," Millie said.

"Who?" Brad put the key in the ignition.

"The man who tried to kill your pastor's wife. I'm sure he was sorry."

The woman's voice sounded a little hurt. Brad looked over at her. That's just what he needed—a sensitive thief. Ah, well. "You don't need to worry. The people of Dry Creek are big on forgiveness once you say you're sorry. If you just explain that you tried to take the money because you were hungry—"

"I wasn't hungry." Millie lifted her chin and continued to stare straight ahead.

Brad gave up. "Fine. Have it your way."

"I wouldn't steal even if I *was* hungry," Millie added quietly.

"Fine." Brad looked in the rearview mirror as he put his foot on the gas and eased the truck forward. He really shouldn't feel sorry for a woman that determined to be unreasonable. "But if you were hungry, say real hungry, that might explain why you had broken into the café in the middle of the night."

There, Brad told himself, he'd given the woman an excuse for being at the scene of the crime. She could say the money was just sitting on the table and she'd only been looking for a piece of bread. He wasn't sure she was smart enough to use the story, but he'd done what he could for her.

Brad turned his pickup onto the road going through Dry Creek. The town sure was quiet at midnight.

After a few minutes of silence the woman said, "I'm not a thief."

Brad figured it was going to be a long night and an even longer morning with the sheriff. He was beginning to think maybe he wouldn't be getting such a good deal by skipping out on church to revisit the scene of the crime. What a night. He'd never imagined the day would come in the life of Brad Parker when church sounded like the better of two possibilities.

* * *

Millie's hands were cold. Ordinarily, she would put them in the pockets of her coat and they would be warm enough. But the man beside her made her nervous, and she wanted to keep her hands free. She didn't know exactly why, but it just seemed like a good idea. She'd never really liked big men, and this one had to be at least six feet tall. She could hardly see his face, not with the darkness and that Stetson he wore. Mostly, she could just see his chin. He needed a shave, but outside of that, his chin looked all right.

"I would think the jail would be back that way." Millie was trying to remember the map she'd studied before starting the drive from Seattle. The bigger towns were all west of Dry Creek. Going east, there weren't any towns of any size until you got to Minot, North Dakota. Leave it to a big man like that to have no sense of direction. Maybe he couldn't see very well with that hat on. If that was the case, she wouldn't criticize. She knew what it was like when a person couldn't see too well.

"I'm not going to the jail. I'm going home to the ranch."

"What?" Millie forgot all about being understanding. She knew she shouldn't have gotten into the man's pickup. That was a basic rule of survival. Never get into a car with a strange man. "You have to stop and let me out. Now!"

The man looked at her. "I told you I was holding you until I could get the sheriff."

Millie tried not to panic. The man was big, but he

didn't look malicious. Still, what did she know? The only part of him that she'd gotten a good look at was his chin. "Usually, suspects are taken to a jail to be held for the sheriff."

"We don't have a jail in Dry Creek."

Of course, Millie thought, she knew that. "There's one in Miles City."

The man grunted. "You'd freeze to death in there this time of year."

"I have a coat." Millie put her hands in her pockets. She did have a good warm coat, and she was glad she'd brought it with her. "I'd really prefer the jail."

The man just kept driving. "I'm not driving back that direction tonight. The sheriff can take you there tomorrow if he wants. He's the one that has to okay turning the heat on anyway."

"They don't heat it?"

The man shrugged. "Budget cutbacks. They only heat it when they have someone locked up, so the sheriff tries to keep it clear this time of year."

Millie looked out the window. The night was black. It was even too cloudy to see any stars. She didn't see lights ahead that might have signaled a ranch house, either. Not that she was anxious to get to this man's ranch. "Is your wife home?"

Millie told herself to breathe. The man must be a local rancher. That meant he had to have a wife. If there was a woman around, she'd be all right. She trusted women.

The man grunted. "I'm single."

"Oh."

"Not single in the sense that I'm looking for a wife." The man reached up and crunched his hat farther down on his head. "Of course, I enjoy a date just like the next man. I'm all in favor of dating. You know, casual dating."

"Oh." Millie was trying to count the fence posts outside. How was she going to find her way back to Dry Creek when he stopped this pickup? She really wished the man had a wife. "Do you have a sister?"

"Why do you want to know about a sister?" The man's voice sounded confused. "Are you into double-dating or something? If you are, I could set up a date with one of the other guys—Randy is seeing someone pretty regular."

"Will she be there?" Millie felt her hands tense up.

"Where?"

"At your ranch."

"My ranch? Oh, ah, yeah. My ranch. I think so."

Millie relaxed. "Good."

Brad told himself he hadn't been this stupid since he was sixteen. He'd just lied to a woman to impress her. Why had he allowed her to think he owned a ranch? Hadn't she seen his pickup? It was an old diesel one. Did he look like he owned a ranch? He should have corrected her and said he worked on a ranch. Worked, not owned. Of course, he dreamed of having his own ranch, and he hoped to make that dream come true before long, but still—

And, to make it worse, the woman was a thief. It stood to reason she would only date a man with property. Of course, it wasn't like she was a bad criminal. Maybe he should tell her he was close to owning his own ranch. His ranch wouldn't be as big and fancy as the Elkton Ranch, but it would do.

Brad shook his head. Was he nuts? The last thing he needed was to fantasize about dating a woman who was a criminal.

He usually didn't fall into the trap of lying about what he had in life. Of course, he usually didn't need to—women wanted to date him because he was fun to be with. There were lots of women who would like to date him—women, by the way, who didn't have a rap sheet.

Brad shook his head again. He didn't know what was wrong with him. He shouldn't even be having this conversation with himself. Maybe he was running a fever or something.

He looked at the woman out of the corner of his eye. She sat so close to the other door, Brad could have put two other women between them. Women, he might add, who would want to sit next to him. Millie, if that was her real name, sure wasn't the friendly type.

Besides, she had that little frown. He doubted she would recognize a good time if it came up and bit her on the backside. He shouldn't even care what she thought about him.

Brad turned the wheel of his pickup. The mailbox for the Elkton Ranch stood at the gravel road that led back to the ranch house. Fortunately, the boss was off spending Christmas with his wife's family in Seattle, so no one was home in the big house. The bunkhouse was just past the ranch house.

"I live here," Brad said as he eased the truck to a stop in front of the bunkhouse. Anyone with any sense would figure out from that that he didn't own any part of this ranch.

Brad expected some question about why he lived in the small house instead of the big house, but Millie didn't seem to notice.

"Someone's home inside," Millie said. The relief in her voice made her sound happier than if they had stopped at the big house.

Brad looked at the windows and, sure enough, Charlie stood in the window looking out to see who had driven up to the bunkhouse at midnight. It wasn't until Brad saw Charlie that he realized his plan had a small problem. The bunkhouse didn't have many rules. Actually, there were only two. No wet socks by the woodstove, because no one wanted to burn the place down. And no women allowed past the main living room of the bunkhouse.

Sometimes the rule on the socks was bent. But the one about women? Never.

Charlie would insist Brad turn around and go find Sheriff Wall and deliver the suspect to him. He wouldn't care that it was twenty degrees below zero outside and Brad didn't even know where the sheriff was right now, or that the suspect in question was unfriendly and uncooperative and looked at Brad, when she had those glasses of hers on, like he was the one who had committed a crime.

Brad decided he had had enough for one day.

"Here, you might want to wear my hat," Brad turned around and set his hat square on the woman's head. The woman's glasses were the only thing that kept the hat from falling halfway down her face. "And there's no need for the glasses."

"What?"

Brad plucked the glasses off the woman's nose and hooked the top button on her black wool coat. There, she looked like a juvenile delinquent again. "Just give me a minute of quiet and I'll have you safe inside."

"Safe inside from what?" The woman's voice was rising in panic.

"Ah." Brad thought. "Spiders. The man inside keeps pet spiders."

Brad congratulated himself. All women were afraid of spiders. But just in case. "He might have some snakes, too."

Brad could feel her stiffen up, and he felt a little bad. He pulled her across the seat to his side. "You don't need to worry, though. I'm going to carry you through to a safe place. You just need to be quiet for a little bit."

"Why?"

"Ah, the spiders go crazy when they hear any noise." Brad opened the door. The wind almost froze his ears now that he didn't have his hat.

Brad stepped out of the pickup and picked up Millie again. It didn't seem right to carry her like a bag of grain now that he knew she was a woman, but he didn't want to make Charlie any more suspicious than he'd naturally be. The truth was, those glasses of Millie's had reminded Brad that Charlie couldn't see so well at night anymore, and Brad figured there was a good chance he could slip Millie into his room without Charlie even seeing them. And he could do it, too, if he used the side door to the bunkhouse.

The door squeaked, and Brad tried to be as quiet as he could. The rooms for the ranch hands were all lined up in a row, and each had a door going off of this long hallway. At the end of the hallway was the main room where Charlie was standing by the window.

Brad held his breath. His room was only two doors down from the side door, and it would take only a little luck to reach it before Charlie figured out that he wasn't coming in the main door.

Brad put his hand on the doorknob leading into his room at the same time that he heard Charlie cough. Brad pushed the door open anyway and put Millie inside. "Stay there a minute."

Brad only waited long enough to be sure Millie was standing upright before he stepped out of the room and closed the door.

"That you, Brad? What's that you have?" Charlie asked as he peered down the long hallway.

Brad put on his best smile. "Nothing."

"Nothing?" The old man frowned.

Brad kept his smile going. "Well, Christmas is coming, you know."

"That's right." The old man relaxed and smiled as he walked down the hall toward Brad. "I forgot it's the time of year when a person shouldn't be too nosy."

"That's right. All those Christmas presents." Brad figured by now Charlie would be expecting more than the new pair of leather gloves Brad had tucked away in his drawer for the occasion. Brad figured he'd need to get Charlie a shovel or something big. Maybe a ladder would do.

"I'm glad to see you're in the Christmas spirit," the old man said slowly.

"It's a joy to give." Brad kept smiling. He wondered when lockjaw set in on a man's mouth. He figured it'd be coming any minute now.

"That's good to hear." Charlie was talking the same, but Brad noticed the old man wasn't looking at him anymore. Instead, he was looking over Brad's shoulder.

Brad turned around. Millie stood in the doorway of his room, and she wasn't wearing his hat or her glasses. She was wearing the coat buttoned up to her neck, which, with her blond curls and timid face, made her look like she was about twelve.

"I see we have company," the old man said gently.

"I thought you were going to stay in the room," Brad said.

"I'm not afraid of spiders," Millie said to no one in particular. Her face went white when she said it. "Unless they're black widows, and then anyone would be afraid."

Millie couldn't see much without her glasses. Mostly it just looked like a long tunnel with a white light at the end of it and several large rocks along the way. The closest large rock was the man Brad.

"If you have spiders, you really should make them stay out in the barn," Millie suggested. She'd taken off the hat he put on her head and looked for her glasses. "You forgot to leave me my glasses."

"Oh."

Millie didn't know why he needed to sound so annoyed. She hadn't made any fuss about the spiders. "I would imagine they'll have spiders in the jail."

"No, they won't. Too cold," Brad said as he held out her glasses.

Millie could see the arm outstretched, and she reached for the open palm. Ah, there were her glasses.

She blinked when she put them back on. Usually, she didn't blink so much. At first, she thought it was because of the light in the hallway. But that didn't make sense. Even though she couldn't see, her eyes had already adjusted to the brightness.

No, what was startling her eyes was the man. She hadn't had a good look at him until now. My goodness, he was handsome. Not that she was interested herself. The closest thing to a boyfriend she'd had in the last five years was Forrest, and he'd turned out to be a hit man. She didn't exactly have reliable sense when it came to men. But still, she'd have to remember what the man looked like so she could tell the other waitresses at Ruby's. They'd enjoy a story about a good-looking rancher who lived in a house full of spiders.

She took another good look at him so she'd remember. Brad's hair was dark as coal, she decided, and he kept it just long enough to curl a little at the ends.

The hair alone made him look like a movie star. But it didn't stop there. He had the blue eyes of the Irish. No wonder his chin was strong. The Irish always had strong chins. They also generally talked a lot, and that was what the man was doing right now.

Brad had stepped closer to the old man and was whispering something to him. The inside of the room was made out of oak logs. There were beige curtains on the window and long leather couches around the room. The old man nodded several times while Brad spoke.

Then both men looked up. Millie heard the noise, too. Even with all of the snow outside, it sounded like a dozen pickups had screeched to a stop out in front of the bunkhouse.

Brad didn't bother to leave the shadows of the hallway. He wondered what had made the other guys rush home from Billings. He looked at the clock on the opposite wall. It was only twelve-thirty. "There must have been a fight. There'll be a broken bone or two."

The door opened and eight other ranch hands stomped into the bunkhouse.

"Okay, who's hurt?" Charlie demanded as he stepped into the main room from the hallway.

All eight of the men who had entered the bunkhouse stopped. "We're worried about Brad."

Brad stepped from the hall into the main room. "Why? I'm right here."

"Oh." The men flashed each other guilty looks and then stared at the floor.

Finally, Howard, one of the older men, cleared his

throat and rubbed the beard on his chin. "We thought we'd check on you, that's all. Heard you hadn't made it over to the other game."

"Since when is it a crime to go to bed early on a Saturday night?" Brad was getting tired of apologizing for not spending his night gambling. Just because he didn't want to sit down with a bunch of smelly men and bet his week's salary against theirs, it didn't mean anything was wrong.

"It's just not like you," another of the men, Jeff, mumbled. Jeff was the only one who had taken his hat off when he came in the bunkhouse, and Brad could still see the snow melting on the man's shoulders.

"Whoa," Randy, the youngest ranch hand, said and then he whistled. "We take that back—it *is* like you. Going to bed early when you have company is an altogether different thing."

It took Brad a full ten seconds to realize what Randy was saying—or rather what he was seeing.

Brad turned around, but he already knew what he would see. Millie had left the hallway and was standing behind him. She was holding the neckline on her coat tight around her throat, and it made her look nervous and young. At least she had her glasses on so she didn't look as pretty as Brad knew she could.

"It's not what you think," Brad started.

"You don't need to say another word," Randy said as he grinned and backed up toward the door.

"Yes, he does," one of the other hands, William, spoke up. William had been an accountant before he became a ranch hand, and with his thinning blond hair and long face, he still looked like he was always trying to balance the books. William had known Brad for the past ten years. He was looking at Brad now like he'd never really known him, though. "Isn't she too young?"

"Of course she's too young," Brad snapped back.

"I'm twenty-three," Millie spoke up.

Brad groaned. How could the woman be twenty-three and be so dumb? "She's young for her age."

William nodded, no longer upset. "Still, it's the age that counts. Sorry we bothered you."

"You didn't bother me. Nothing's going on."

Brad could see the speculation in Randy's eyes. Randy was only twenty-two or so himself, and he looked like he was realizing Millie was more his age than Brad's.

Randy swallowed and spoke. "Well, if nothing's going on with the two of you, then maybe you wouldn't mind if I—"

Brad felt his arms tighten. It had been a while since he'd taken down any of the other guys with his fists, but he could still do it. "She's not in the market. Besides, you already have a girlfriend."

Charlie cleared his throat. "Now, there'll be none of that." He looked at Brad. "That's the reason why we have the rule—no women allowed."

"She's not here because she's a woman," Brad said. "She's here because she's a thief."

Brad expected his statement to bring some dignity to the situation. Instead, William looked at him like Brad was the one at fault.

"You don't need to lie. We're prepared to make some exceptions for you on account of—" William swallowed and stared at the floor "—on account of the time of year and all. If she eases the pain some, maybe we could let her stay with you for the night."

"What?" Brad was dumbfounded. Sometimes a man broke the bunkhouse rules, but never ever was anyone given *permission* to break them. How pathetic did they think he was?

"William's right," Charlie mumbled. "She could even stay with you through Christmas, since the boss isn't here. He'll never know. You've got your own bath and everything, so the two of you will be snug in your room. She'll make you happy."

Randy and the others just stared at the floor.

Brad snorted. "You're all hopeless. She doesn't make me happy. I caught her breaking into the café."

"Really?" William asked. He looked at Millie and smiled. "You're sure she wasn't just hungry? She's awfully small to be a thief."

"I'm not a thief," Millie said.

Brad looked over his shoulder. Millie stood in the hallway in that long wool coat of hers looking like a refugee. "Then what were you doing in the café with all that money?"

"I can't say."

Brad looked at the other men. "See?"

"Does anybody recognize her?" Charlie asked. He'd taken a step closer to Millie and was studying her. "Between all of you, I figure you know every woman over the age of sixteen in the whole county."

"Never seen her before," William said.

"I'd remember her if I had," Randy added.

"I'm a stranger," Millie said.

"A stranger who happens to be a thief," Brad added.

"Maybe," Charlie said thoughtfully. "She doesn't look like any thief I've ever seen, though."

"Well, we'll find out in the morning when I can get hold of the sheriff."

"The sheriff's not in his office tomorrow," William said. "It's Sunday—he'll be in church."

"Well, then," Brad said grimly, "that's where I'll need to go to talk to him."

There was silence in the room.

Finally Randy spoke. "You're going to church?"

Brad nodded. People went to church all the time around Dry Creek. What was the big deal?

There was more silence.

"Inside the building?" William finally asked. "Not just volunteering to shovel the steps like you sometimes do when it snows?"

Brad nodded. "Of course, inside the building—"

Randy whistled. "This'll be something to see."

"There's nothing to see. I'm going to just take Millie there to the sheriff and give her a chance to confess—"

"I didn't know they still did confessions in church," Randy said..

"I don't have anything to confess," Millie said. "Well, at least not about being a thief."

"Wow," Randy said. "This'll be something to see."

Brad was annoyed. "There's no reason to get all excited. There'll be nothing to see or hear in church tomorrow. I'm just going to tell the sheriff about the scene of the crime and—"

"You mean there's a crime scene?"

Brad shook his head. It was hopeless. "Anyone want to stay out here and chew the fat? Millie needs to go to bed and get her sleep, but I'll be sleeping on the couch out here and I'm happy to have some company for an hour or so."

"No, thanks." Randy grinned. "I think I'll be getting up early in the morning."

"Me, too," William added. "I haven't been to church in a while."

"You've *never* been to church," Brad said as he sat down on a folding chair. "You're as much of a heathen as I am."

"I was baptized as a baby," William protested as he turned to walk toward the hall. "That makes me a member."

Brad shook his head. "No, it doesn't."

"I think you need to pay dues to be a member," Randy added as he turned to the hallway, too.

"Just go to bed," Brad said.

Charlie nodded. "We all need our sleep."

Brad didn't know if it was sleep he needed. Maybe an aspirin would do him more good. He had a feeling he wasn't going to sleep at all tonight, and it wouldn't be because of the lumps in the sofa.

Chapter Four

Millie had been to church once when she was a child. Her foster mother had taken her to an Easter service because the child welfare representative was going to come the next day and there was always a question on the form the man filled out about church or other religious activity.

They had gone to an old church that had big stained-glass windows that showed pictures of Jesus in many different poses. Millie had been in awe. She liked the picture best of Jesus kneeling down beside a child. The child had been wearing a blue robe, and Millie had on a blue dress that day. She looked at the picture and pretended it was her that Jesus was smiling down at and talking to in such a friendly way.

When she left the church, Millie told her foster mother about pretending that she was in the picture with Jesus. Her foster mother said she was silly. She said those pictures of Jesus were from thousands of years ago and had nothing to do with today.

Millie still remembered the disappointment she felt. It was the first time she'd realized Jesus lived such a long time ago. Somehow she had the feeling he was supposed to still be alive today.

That was the last time Millie had been inside a church.

She was surprised that the church in Dry Creek didn't have any stained-glass windows. Of course, she remembered looking at the church last night in the dark and she hadn't seen any, but churches had always seemed mysterious places to her, and she expected to step into the church in Dry Creek and see something dramatic like a stained-glass window anyway.

Instead, the church was humble. The glass was frosted because of the cold outside, but not decorated in any other way.

There was a strip of brown carpet going down the middle of the church between the rows of wooden pews, but the flooring on both sides of the carpet was the kind of beige linoleum that she had seen frequently in coffee shops. The only problem with that kind of linoleum was that there was a special trick to getting off the black scuff marks. Millie looked down at the floor. Everything was scrubbed clean, but the black marks were still there. She could tell someone how to fix that.

Not that she was here to talk about the floor, Millie reminded herself. She was glad Brad didn't seem like he was in any hurry to actually go inside the church, either. They both just stood in the doorway.

There were quite a few people in the church already, but they weren't sitting down yet.

"Do I look all right?" Brad whispered down at her.

Millie looked up. She was getting used to Brad's face. Well, sort of.

Maybe it was because she'd spent the night on his pillow and grown accustomed to the warm scent of him that lingered in his room even as he slept in the other room on the sofa. When you've been in someone's bed like that, she thought, handsome didn't seem to matter so much.

Besides, he didn't seem to care that he was handsome, so that helped some more. He was mostly worried about the tie he had around his neck. He'd had to borrow it from Charlie this morning, and Charlie only had two ties and said he needed one for himself. Charlie kept the black one, the one he called his funeral tie.

Brad had had to settle for a red tie with elves on it that Charlie had won in some bingo game at the senior center in Billings last year.

Millie nodded. The elf tie did go, in a way, with the green shirt Brad had borrowed from William.

"I feel stupid wearing dancing elves around my neck," Brad said.

Millie wasn't used to men admitting they felt stupid. "They look a little like drunken mushrooms."

"Really?" Brad seemed cheered by the idea.

Millie nodded. "At least I have my coat to wear."

Millie had bought the black wool coat years ago because it covered everything. She could have her waitress uniform on and no one would know. She didn't always like people to know she was a waitress when she rode the bus to work. Too many men felt they could flirt with any woman who was a waitress. Of course, the men were usually harmless. But still, she didn't want to be bothered.

Brad was frowning down at her. Millie wondered if maybe the coat wasn't too protective. She didn't want men to scowl at her, either.

"I could hold your glasses for you," Brad said finally.

What was his problem with her glasses? That was the second time this morning that he had suggested she not wear them. "My glasses are fine."

Brad nodded. "I thought they might fog up so you couldn't see. You might not know that. Glasses do that in the cold."

"I'm fine."

Brad nodded again. "Well, we might as well go in then."

There was a double door that led into the Dry Creek church, but only one half of it was open this morning.

Millie felt Brad take her elbow at the same time that they took a step into the church.

"Oh." Millie wished she had given her glasses to Brad. At least then she wouldn't see all the people who had turned around to look at them. There were tall people, old people, short people, and children. They all seemed like they were talking—until she and Brad walked into the church.

"Well, welcome!" A ripple of excitement went around the people standing in the church.

"Why, Brad Parker!" An older man stepped forward and held out his hand. The man was wearing a tweed jacket, and he smelled of old-fashioned aftershave.

Brad shook the man's hand. "Good morning, Dr. Norris."

"I'm glad you came." The older man wasn't content with a handshake. He slapped Brad on the shoulder, as well.

"I told you I'd come," Brad said.

Millie was glad Brad didn't move. She was also glad he was so big. She could almost hide behind him as long as he stood just where he was. Maybe no one would notice she was there.

"And welcome to you as well, young lady," the doctor said as he stopped looking at Brad and looked over at Millie. "We're glad you've come to worship with us."

"Oh." Millie gave a tight little smile. "I don't know if we'll be staying for—"

"Of course you have to stay for the service." An older woman stepped forward and beamed at Millie. "We're singing Christmas carols, and the Curtis twins are going to practice their donkey song—you know, the donkey who carried Mary to the Inn?"

"You mean the twins—Josh and Joey?"

"Why, yes," the woman said. The woman had her gray hair twisted into a mass of curls on the top of her head, and she was wearing a green gingham dress with a red bell pin. Millie knew who the older woman was before she held out her hand.

"My name's Mrs. Hargrove," the woman said.

Millie nodded and took the woman's hand. She never thought she'd get to meet Mrs. Hargrove. Mrs. Hargrove had written to Forrest several times while he was in jail. That's why Forrest knew so much about Dry Creek. And to think, Millie would hear the twins sing. Oh, she hoped Brad didn't want to meet with the sheriff before she could do that. "My name's Millie."

"How did you know about the twins?" Brad asked quietly.

Millie looked up at him and saw the suspicion in his eyes. She'd have to be more careful. "I thought you mentioned them last night."

"Me?"

"Well, maybe it was William—he brought me an extra blanket in case I got cold and stayed to talk for a little bit. Did you know he used to do the books for a restaurant in Seattle?"

"William what? I thought you were going straight to bed. That's what everyone was going to do."

"Well, I couldn't go to sleep if I was cold, could I?"

Someone started to play the organ, and Millie was relieved to see everyone starting to sit down.

Brad was still scowling. But at least he'd stopped looking down at her, Millie thought.

"I don't see the sheriff here," Brad said.

"He'll be here any minute," the older man, Dr. Norris, said, as he gestured to the pews. "You're welcome to sit anywhere."

"I think we should sit at the back," Brad said. "In case Sheriff Wall gets here soon."

The doctor nodded.

Millie was glad that the sheriff wasn't there quite yet. She and Brad walked to the last pew and sat down. Brad seemed to relax. He even loosened his tie.

Now that Millie was getting a good look around, she noticed that someone had decorated the small church for Christmas. There was a short, stubby tree with tinfoil stars on it by the organ. Some of the stars were crooked, and they all looked like children had made them. Mixed in with the stars were some red lights that twinkled. Several poinsettia plants stood in front of the speaker's stand.

Some years at Ruby's they had poinsettia plants on the counter at Christmas. Once or twice the manager had given Millie one of the plants to take home after her shift ended on Christmas Day. They were hardy flowers and lasted almost till Easter.

"No one's wearing a tie, except for Pastor Curtis," Brad whispered in her ear. "I thought everyone wore a tie to church."

"This is sort of an informal church, I think," Millie whispered back.

Millie heard some sounds behind her and turned around. There stood all of the men from the Elkton Ranch bunkhouse, looking shy and out-of-place in the doorway.

"Welcome," the pastor said quietly from the front of the church. "Please take a seat anywhere."

The men filed into the back pew on the other side of the church, and the service started.

"I don't sing much," Brad whispered as everyone around them stood with a songbook in their hands.

"Me, neither," Millie said as she stood up. She figured it didn't matter if you sang or not as long as you stood up at the right time and were respectful.

Singing wasn't as hard as Millie had thought. Some of the songs were Christmas carols that she knew from the radio that played at Ruby's, and she joined in the singing of those—quietly, of course.

The church service reminded Millie of a roller coaster she'd ridden once. She was scared at every turn of the corner, but she found she enjoyed it if she sat back and didn't try to fight the experience. Being in church was kind of like that.

There was a light behind the wooden cross in the center of the church, and Millie decided she could stare at that. She wasn't sure she was supposed to be listening to the sermon since she was just here to wait for the sheriff, so she didn't want to keep her eyes on the preacher. Of course, she couldn't help but hear the sermon. It was something about grace.

Millie wasn't quite sure what it all meant. The pastor had said grace was when you got something for free, but the only time Millie had heard of grace was at Ruby's when sometimes a customer would pray before they ate. One of the other waitresses said the people were saying grace. Millie wondered now if the people had been hoping they would get their dinners for free and not have to pay. She was surprised Ruby hadn't put a stop to people saying grace if that was the case.

No one got a free meal at Ruby's unless they happened to be really down on their luck. Then Millie sometimes paid for their meal out of her tips for the evening. Millie wondered if grace was something like that. When she gave out a free meal because another person was hungry and couldn't buy the meal for themselves. She'd have to ask the pastor if that's what grace was.

Of course, she'd have to wait until Brad turned her over to the sheriff and the sheriff turned her loose. She didn't suppose the pastor would want to talk to a woman who was in the process of being arrested.

Millie's favorite part of the whole church service was when the Curtis twins put on their donkey faces and sang a song about taking Mary to the Inn. They walked up and down in front of the church like they were on a long journey. Once one of the twins brayed like a donkey and pretended to fly. That had to be Josh.

Millie hadn't thought about how difficult it must have been for Forrest to learn so much about the people of Dry Creek in the few days he was in the little town. Even with Mrs. Hargrove's letters, there was a lot he learned himself. He said he'd talked to people in the café and even stopped at a few houses to ask directions here or there and had stayed to chat.

"People will tell you anything if you get them talking," Forrest said to her once when she asked how he did it. "Everyone likes to talk."

Millie wished Forrest were here. He'd know what to do about the mess she was in. Of course, if he were here, he'd probably want her to continue on with her mission. She hoped Brad was right and that the people of Dry Creek did trust strangers. If they didn't, she sure didn't know how she'd get them to trust strangers now.

When the service was over, the pastor stood at the back door to shake hands. The men from the Elkton Ranch were the first ones in line. In fact, Millie suspected a few of them had tried to beat the pastor to the door so they could go through it before he even got there. But Charlie made them get in line.

Brad and Millie were right behind them.

"I'm glad you could join us this morning," Pastor Curtis said to Randy as he shook the younger man's hand.

Randy blushed and ran his finger around his necktie to loosen it. "We mostly came in to see the crime scene."

"What?" That was from Mrs. Hargrove. She was coming up to greet the men, too. "I know our singing isn't too good, but I'd hardly say it's a crime scene."

"No, ma'am." Randy turned even redder. "I mean the crime scene at the café."

A ripple of whispering went through the whole church until everything got silent.

"A crime! Has anyone seen a stranger?"

A gasp came from another corner. "Has anybody been shot this time?"

Millie looked around her. Forrest was right. He had taken away this little town's trust in strangers. She could see it in the faces around her. They were scared.

"It's nothing like that," Brad said gruffly. "Just a little bit of—well, maybe something was stolen."

"We have a thief?"

"I'm not a thief," Millie denied automatically. She wished she hadn't said anything when everyone turned to look at her.

"Well, of course you're not," Mrs. Hargrove agreed. "Anyone can see you're a nice young woman." The older woman smiled at Millie. "I was so pleased you were able to convince Brad to come to church with you."

Millie blushed. "Brad came to see the sheriff."

"Well, still—" Mrs. Hargrove kept smiling. "I can't believe you were stealing anything." The older woman looked up at Brad. "Are you sure she didn't just stop at the café thinking it was open and she could get something to eat? Maybe she was hoping to find a sandwich. Maybe she was hungry. Linda would have given her a sandwich if she had been there."

"That was a mighty green sandwich she was taking out of there. I was hoping to catch up with the sheriff so I could show him where I left everything." Brad looked around. "I thought he'd be in church this morning."

"He had something to do in Miles City," Pastor

Curtis said. "But he's planning to be at our house for lunch, so he should be here any minute."

Millie looked around. She saw skepticism on a lot of faces. "I wasn't taking the money. I was trying to give it away."

Brad nodded. "Give it away? Where'd you get it from in the first place?"

"I can't tell you where."

Brad snorted. "You're going to have to think of a better story than that if you expect Sheriff Wall to go easy on you."

"I think I hear the sheriff now," the pastor said. "Maybe we should go over to the café and get this settled."

Millie looked around. The faces that had been smiling weren't smiling at her anymore. They weren't exactly frowning, but she could see the caution in everyone's eyes. "I didn't do anything wrong."

"I'm sure you didn't," Mrs. Hargrove murmured as she patted Millie on the arm.

Millie noticed Mrs. Hargrove didn't look her in the eye when she said those words, however. Mrs. Hargrove had obviously reconsidered her confidence in Millie.

It wasn't the first time since Forrest died that Millie wished she could have a few words in private with him. If Forrest could see her now, he would have to agree that she wasn't the person to make everything better with the people of Dry Creek. She was going to make it worse. Even Mrs. Hargrove didn't believe her.

"He should have sent an angel," Millie muttered.

Dead people could do that, she figured. There were supposed to be lots of angels up there.

"What?" Mrs. Hargrove looked startled.

"Who's 'he'?" Brad bent down and asked. "Do you have an accomplice?"

"How many of them are there?" someone else asked.

"It's me. Just me," Millie said. She had never felt more alone in her life.

"It's best if you tell the truth." Brad frowned down at her. "I should have figured you had someone else in this with you. He probably sent you in as bait and—" Brad whistled "—I left the money right there for him."

Brad took Millie's elbow. "Let's go."

Millie had to almost run to keep up with Brad's long steps. The air outside was cold, and she hadn't had time to put the collar up on her coat. She could feel the air all the way down as she breathed it in. "You don't need to hurry."

Brad only snorted and kept walking. A dozen other people were trailing after them. "Don't know why it took me so long to figure it out—of course, a woman like you has a man around. Even Randy figured *that* out. With those eyes of yours, of course there's a man around."

"I don't—" Millie started to protest and then decided to save her breath. He wouldn't believe her anyway. They'd soon be inside the café, and he would see for himself that the money was still there and there was no man in sight.

Millie wondered how she had made such a muddle of Forrest's request. The people of Dry Creek would be even more suspicious of strangers after she left. Millie looked up at the determined set of Brad's chin and corrected herself. She should have said if she left. If she was able to.

The rancher didn't look like he'd let her leave anytime soon. She almost wished she did have some man someplace who would come get her. Although, as she looked at the rancher again, she didn't know what man she'd ever known in her life that she would put up against the one in front of her.

She looked at Brad again. Had she heard right? Did he think her eyes were pretty?

Chapter Five

Brad turned the handle on the door to the café before he remembered he had pushed the button on the other side of the handle and locked the door when he left last night.

"The key's under the rock," Mrs. Hargrove offered as she stood at the bottom of the steps. "The third rock on the porch there by your foot."

"But I have—" Millie said softly.

Brad didn't listen to Millie. Instead, he let go of her arm and bent down to turn over the rock. It was a piece of granite from the hills in the area, and snow was lodged in its crevices. It looked like Linda had hauled half of the mountain down here to place around her café. Some of the rocks outlined a dormant flower bed, but the rest of the rocks were just scattered here and there on the wide porch.

Brad decided that, when this was all over, he was going to ask the sheriff to do a public service talk on how to lock a door and keep it locked. Someone needed to pull Dry Creek into the modern age. What was the point of locking a door when a person left the key under a rock a mere four feet away? Except—

"There's no key here."

"—That's because I have it," Millie said as she put her hand in the pocket of her coat and pulled out the brass key.

"You have it." Of course, she had it, Brad told himself as he took the key she offered. He hadn't asked himself last night how Millie had gotten in. "I suppose you turned over every rock on this porch hoping to find a key."

Even as Brad said that, he looked at the other rocks. They were all covered with snow. No one had moved them in the last few days. Which meant Millie hadn't turned over every rock to find the key; she'd turned over only one. "How did you know which rock it was under?"

"Someone told me."

Brad didn't know how a voice as quiet as Millie's could give him such a splitting headache. He supposed he had begun to hope that she wasn't really the thief he had first thought her to be. That she was just going inside the café to get out of the cold and maybe to fix a sandwich for herself. He was even beginning to think that Linda might have left the money there in a brown paper bag and that Millie was just counting it.

The rock took away all of those comfortable illusions. "Someone must have scouted out the town. The whole thing was planned and premeditated."

Millie frowned. It wasn't much of a frown, but Brad noticed that the tiny lines in her forehead made her nose smaller, which made her glasses slip a little bit. When she spoke, her voice sounded hurt. "I wasn't going to do anything bad. 'Premeditated' makes it sound like murder or something."

Brad heard the gasp at the bottom of the stairs. He knew the whole congregation had followed him and Millie over to the café, so he wasn't surprised that everyone was listening. The gasp came from one of the Curtis twins. It was Josh. The boys were six years old and fascinated with the usual boy things. "Did she say murder?"

"Nobody is going to murder anyone," Brad said firmly, turning around. He didn't want the rest of the people to start thinking in that direction. "This is Dry Creek. We're not like Los Angeles, where they have murders on every street corner."

"We almost had a murder here," the Kelly girl reminded him as she twisted her ponytail. She stood off to the side of the porch in an old, worn parka.

Brad wished he could remember her first name. All he knew is that she had two older sisters that he sometimes saw in the bars in Miles City. He knew *their* names, not that it did him a lot of good with this girl. He'd just have to take a guess. "Now, Susie—"

"I'm Sarah," the girl corrected him. "Remember there was that hit man that came here? So you can't say it never happens." The girl turned her eyes from Brad and stared at Millie. "Maybe she's one, too."

Josh gasped again and turned his blue eyes up to Millie, as well. "Does she have a gun?"

"Of course she doesn't have a gun," Brad said automatically before he remembered that he hadn't really checked. "At least, I don't think she does—"

Brad was remembering that coat Millie wore. She could have a cannon tucked in the corner of that thing and the wool was so heavy it wouldn't even make a bulge. But she hadn't been wearing that coat the whole time, had she? Surely, he would have noticed if she was armed. She was too skinny to hide anything without the coat. Unless, of course, it was in the pocket of the coat.

Brad wished he'd just taken Millie to the jail last night. This was all getting out of hand. Where was the sheriff anyway? Brad ran his finger under his collar. It took him a minute to think of something to reassure the kids. "If she had a gun, she would have shot me by now."

"Some man came and tried to shoot my mom," Josh said to Millie. Josh was missing a front tooth, and he leaned toward Millie when he spoke. "That was before she was my mom."

"It happened at Christmas time, too," the Kelly girl insisted. "Right after the Christmas pageant. And we're having another pageant this year—I wonder if someone will be shot this year."

"I don't have a gun." Millie knelt down so she could look Josh in the eye. "You don't need to worry."

Brad snorted. He figured worrying was the only smart thing they *could* do, given the state of affairs.

He took a side step closer to Millie and looked down at her. He really should find out if she had a gun. "I should frisk you."

"What?" Millie said as her eyes looked up to meet his.

Brad had a sudden vision of running his hands up and down Millie's coat. The problem was, the coat was so bulky he'd have to run his hands under her coat. He wasn't sure he should do that in full view of everyone. At least not with the kids around. Maybe if she wasn't wearing that coat, he could see if she was armed. "You should take your coat off."

"But it's cold."

Brad nodded. He'd tried. "We'll leave it to the sheriff. Where is he anyway?"

"I hear him," Mrs. Hargrove said. "He's using the siren."

Millie cleared her throat and turned so she faced the people waiting at the bottom of the porch. The air was cold, but most of the coats she saw were unbuttoned and unzipped. Everyone was looking at her so intently; they didn't even seem to notice the cold. Millie wasn't sure this was an ideal moment to try to explain, but sometimes a woman had to deliver her message any way she could. "Just because a man's a hit man, it doesn't mean he's a bad man."

"What?"

Millie figured the bellow behind her came from Brad. It was close enough to cause her ear damage, but she continued. She smiled at Josh and Sarah both. "Maybe the hit man was real sorry for the things he did and wished he could do something to make it all better."

Millie stopped there. She'd done her best. She hadn't gone against Forrest's wishes and said she knew him, but she'd come close. Surely, someone in the crowd would read between the lines and understand what she was trying to say. Mrs. Hargrove was puzzling something out. Surely, *she* would understand.

Millie figured she'd been understood when Mrs. Hargrove stepped up on the porch looking like she'd puzzled her way to some conclusion and was ready to speak.

"Are you a reporter?" the older woman demanded to know.

"Me?" Millie asked, aghast. "I could never be a reporter." Millie could think of a hundred reasons why she wasn't a reporter. "I don't even know how to type."

Mrs. Hargrove bent over slightly and looked at Millie's hands. "You've got a tiny ink stain on one finger. Maybe you write in longhand."

"Well, I write, but it's not the news," Millie protested. Didn't Mrs. Hargrove know that shy people never became reporters? They would have to talk to people. All kinds of people. The woman could just as well have asked if Millie was an astronaut who flew to the moon. "It's more like—well, I take orders for things."

Millie could tell by the faraway look in Mrs. Hargrove eyes that she wasn't listening anymore. She was, however, thoughtful. "Now that I think of it, I'm surprised we haven't had more reporters snooping around doing some kind of a sequel to the story they did back then—they were quite interested in our hit man and the angel. I must admit it was a good angle. And here it is Christmas again. People might be interested in seeing what had happened to the town where it all took place."

"I swear I'm not a reporter." Millie raised her hand. She'd place her hand on one of those Bibles people were holding if they wanted her to. "I don't even know any reporters."

"Well, let's hope you know a lawyer or two," a man's voice came from the back of the crowd.

Millie looked up. That must be the sheriff. He wore the uniform and—everything. She gulped. He had a gun.

Millie blinked and pulled the collar of her coat closer around her neck. "I don't know any lawyers, either."

The sheriff nodded. "I expect the county will have to get you one then. Not that they'll be happy about it. They don't even want to pay for heating the jail this time of year."

The sheriff stepped in closer and looked at Millie intently. She felt like a bug under a microscope.

"Unless, of course, you have money to pay for your own attorney," the sheriff added hopefully. "That would be good. My cousin over in Miles City works cheap. You might be able to hire him."

Millie thought of the remaining tip money she had

in her purse and shook her head. "I used all my money driving here. I just have enough to get back."

"Where are you from?" the sheriff asked casually.

"Seattle."

"Lady, are you crazy?" Brad asked as he turned his back on everyone and jabbed the key into the lock on the door. "Driving all that way to rob us in Dry Creek? Let me tell you, the odds weren't great that you would find much money just lying around anywhere in town."

Brad shoved the door to the café open.

"I already told you. I didn't find the money here. I brought it with me."

Brad was tall enough that his shoulders filled out the doorway as he stood and turned on the light. "Yeah, and I'm the tooth fairy."

Millie took a deep breath. With a little bit of patience, she could explain everything to the sheriff. She could still keep Forrest's identity secret. She could just say that someone wanted to repay the people of Dry Creek, and she was the delivery person.

Millie heard Brad's low whistle before she stepped into the café, too.

"Don't touch the crime scene," the sheriff said as he stepped past Millie.

Brad had removed the tablecloth that he'd draped over the money last night.

"But look at these!" Brad had bent down and pulled one of the flannel Christmas stockings out of the sack on the floor. He had a look of horror on his face as he held it up. "I didn't get a good look at these last night."

Mrs. Hargrove and the pastor stepped ahead of Millie, too.

"Someone made them," Mrs. Hargrove said.

"I didn't have a pattern for the stockings," Millie said a little defensively. What did they expect? She'd relied on glue and hand-stitching to finish the stockings. Fortunately, she'd found several large remnants of red felt at a fabric store.

"It has Elmer's name on it," Mrs. Hargrove said, turning to tell everyone.

By now, half of the town of Dry Creek had come through the open door.

Mrs. Hargrove held another sock that Brad had pulled out of the sack. "This one says Jacob."

Millie could hear the murmur.

"I could see how a person might guess the name Jacob," someone in the back said. "But Elmer? I bet there's not fifty people left in the world with a name like Elmer."

"And here's Pastor Matthew and Glory." Mrs. Hargrove held up two more stockings.

The sheriff turned to Millie. "How do you know our names?"

Millie closed her eyes. "I was just doing a favor for a friend. He wanted to do something nice for Dry Creek, and he asked me to help him. That's all."

"We don't even have a phone directory anymore that lists everyone," Mrs. Hargrove said as she looked at all of the stockings on the table. "I'm not even sure

I could sit down and write out everyone's name—not without a picture or something in front of me."

"My friend had a very good memory," Millie said. "He knew everyone's name."

"Is your friend Santa Claus?"

Millie looked down at the last question. Little Josh was looking up at her with hope in his eyes.

"I want a train," he said. "One that runs on the tracks and has a whistle. My dad says they're expensive, but I'm sure Santa Claus has one."

"My friend's not Santa Claus," Millie said softly as she knelt down to look the boy in the eyes. "But if he knew you wanted to have a train, he would have sent one to you. My friend's dead."

"Is he in heaven?"

"I—ah, well, I—" Millie didn't believe in heaven, but the little boy was looking at her with such innocence that she couldn't tell him that. And who knew? Maybe he was right. She certainly didn't know anything about it.

"My mother's in heaven," the boy said. "It's real nice there. I bet they have lots of trains. Maybe your friend could send one down from there—a superduper flying train. Do you think they have flying trains in heaven?"

"I—ah—I wouldn't know," Millie finally managed to say.

"Me, neither," the boy agreed. "You have to die to go to heaven."

Millie nodded. "That's what I've been told."

"Looks like you've been told a lot of things," the

sheriff said. His voice was not friendly like the young boy's. "Mind if I ask some questions?"

Millie rose to her feet. She supposed it was too much to ask to be left alone so she could keep talking to Josh. "Go ahead."

"First, where are you from?"

"Seattle."

The sheriff wrote something in the black notebook he'd pulled out of his shirt pocket.

"That hit man was from Seattle," said an older man who had entered the café late.

"What brings you out this way?"

"I was doing a Christmas favor for a friend."

The sheriff looked a little interested in this, even though he didn't write anything in his notebook. "And who would that friend be?"

When Millie didn't answer, the sheriff looked over at Brad.

"Oh, no, it's not him," Millie protested. She didn't want anyone to suspect him of anything. "I don't even know him—not really. He was just doing his duty when he took me to his ranch last night—"

"His ranch?" The sheriff frowned. "You mean the Elkton place?"

"Is that your last name?" Millie turned to Brad. It was funny, she thought, that she hadn't heard his last name after all the time they had spent together. Of course, the time was hardly social, so she supposed it wasn't surprising. "I saw the name on the mailbox this morning."

The sheriff snorted and turned to Brad. "Did you tell her you owned the place?"

Millie saw the red creep up Brad's neck and said the only thing she could think of. "I think maybe I'm the one who assumed it was his place."

"But I didn't correct her," Brad said.

The sheriff shrugged. "Well, I suppose that doesn't matter. I guess it stands to reason you'd try to impress a pretty girl."

Millie pulled her coat a little tighter around her. She didn't much like it when Sheriff Wall said she was pretty. "We came to church this morning to see you."

The sheriff nodded. "Sorry I wasn't there. Now, answer me this—did you plan to take this money away from the café?"

Millie relaxed. "No."

The sheriff frowned. "So you're maintaining your innocence? You're saying you weren't in here last night planning to steal this money?"

"No, I was giving the money away."

Mrs. Hargrove gasped. "Don't tell me it's charity!"

Millie looked over at the older woman. She seemed more upset than she had been all morning.

"I bet it's that church in Miles City." Mrs. Hargrove was nodding emphatically as she turned to look at the rest of the townspeople. "Remember last year they wanted to give us food baskets? I told Pastor Hanks we didn't need their pity."

"Of course, we don't need any pity," the older man

at the edge of the group said. "We can take care of each other."

"It's not charity," Millie said softly. "It's a gift from someone who cares about each of you."

"Maybe it's from Doris June," the old man said as he looked over at Mrs. Hargrove. "You told me she was doing pretty good at that job of hers in Alaska now that they gave her that big raise. Isn't she making another ten grand a year now?"

"Even if she is, my daughter knows better than to throw her money away like this."

"I wasn't throwing it away," Millie protested. "I was trying to do the right thing."

Sheriff Wall put up his hand. "No sense in anyone getting all stirred up until we find out where the money came from. Mrs. Hargrove, do you have that telephone number for Linda down in Los Angeles?"

The older woman nodded. "It's at home."

"Well, would you mind calling Linda and asking her how much money she had in the cash register when she left?"

"I'll be back in a minute." Mrs. Hargrove turned around and started toward the café door. "And while I'm there, I'm going to call that Pastor Hanks and give him a piece of my mind. Charity—we don't need charity. The people of Dry Creek are doing just fine."

She slammed the screen door on her way out.

"Now—" the sheriff looked around at everyone in the room "—I'm going to ask everyone to step outside. Until we know otherwise, this is a crime scene in here, and I intend to keep it pure."

Millie looked around. The day was warming up, and sun streamed in through the windows. Most people kept their coats open, so they must be comfortable in the café even though it wasn't heated. They were all standing around the tables.

Millie thought the old man who was at the side of the room, the one who had been talking earlier, might be Elmer. And the couple sitting down at a table were probably the Redferns. The woman looked pretty enough to have been a cocktail waitress in Vegas, and she was holding a baby who looked like he was a year old. Forrest hadn't met her when he was in Dry Creek, but he'd heard about her in a letter Mrs. Hargrove had sent to him.

The people started walking toward the door. Millie turned to join them.

"Not you," the sheriff said as he put his hand on Millie's arm. "You stay with me. I need to ask you some more questions."

Millie nodded. She supposed she'd have to expect questions. At least until Mrs. Hargrove was able to talk to Linda and find out that the money hadn't been left in the café when Linda went away.

"In the meantime, why don't you count that money?" The sheriff nodded toward Brad. "Give us some idea of what we're talking about here. Misdemeanor or felony."

Millie was glad that Brad wasn't leaving with the others. She didn't feel exactly comfortable with the sheriff, not when he was asking her all of those questions. She wasn't sure that Brad believed that she wasn't a thief, but she did feel safer with him around.

Brad looked up. "They'd give her a hard time if it was a felony."

The sheriff nodded.

"I don't think she intended that much harm," Brad said as he walked over to the table that held the bills. "She probably just wanted some traveling money. That car of hers looks like it'd fall apart if someone sneezed in it. She probably needs to repair it, and I'd guess that'd take a fortune."

"There's nothing wrong with my car," Millie said before she remembered the ping in the engine. And the hiccup in the carburetor.

"That car needs to be taken out and given a decent burial," Brad muttered.

Millie frowned. She was slowly figuring out that the reason she felt safe with Brad was because he saw her as a kid instead of as a woman. Not that she wanted him to look at her like he wanted to kiss her or anything. But it was annoying to be around him and realize he was so totally immune to her charms.

Of course, she wasn't exactly swooning over him, either. Granted, he was tall and powerful. She supposed most women would fall at his feet. Fortunately, he wasn't her kind of man at all.

She'd always thought that if she was going to be attracted to a man it would be a man who was quieter. Someone who didn't always require attention and service. Someone who would be content to blend into the background with her. A man like Brad didn't blend at all. He stood out and demanded attention.

No, she shook her head, Brad wasn't even close to her ideal man. She should be grateful he didn't notice her. And if he wanted to treat her like a kid, so much the better. She'd just treat him like a—a— Millie sighed. She couldn't treat him like anything but what he was. The most gorgeous man she'd ever seen, with or without her glasses on.

Chapter Six

"Well, how much money is there?" the sheriff asked.

Millie had sat down on one of the chairs and loosened her coat. The sun was shining in through the windows and had warmed up the café considerably. The red-and-white floor gave the place a cozy feel. There were a dozen small tables in the place. Millie wouldn't mind working in a small place like this if she ever left Ruby's.

Brad grunted in answer to the sheriff's question. He had sat down at a different table and counted the bills.

Millie didn't need to hear Brad's answer to know that there were seventy-five hundred-dollar bills in that sack. She supposed that was more than enough to be a felony. She wondered how far she should carry Forrest's request to not let anyone in Dry Creek know she was his friend. Surely, he wouldn't want her to actually be arrested.

"It's not as much money as it looks like," Brad said slowly. He didn't look at either Millie or the sheriff. "I didn't quite get it all counted, so I don't have an exact count. But I'd guess it's under a thousand."

Millie sat up straight at Brad's answer. "There's more than that."

Brad wanted to put his head down and bang it against the table. Here he was trying to keep Millie out of jail, and she was doing nothing to help him. He clenched his teeth. "I'm sure there's not enough here to warrant felony charges."

"Oh," Millie said.

Finally, the woman looked like she was coming to her senses. At least she didn't argue with him again about the amount of money on the table. What was Linda doing with all that money anyway? Business at the café hadn't been *that* good.

Brad wondered if Linda and that boyfriend of hers had managed to sell the farm they had just bought. Brad rather hoped not. He had his eye on that place himself, and almost had enough saved to put a good down payment on it if it came on the market again.

"Well, it's fine with me if it's not a felony," the sheriff said. He'd picked up a few pieces of paper with tweezers and placed them in a bag. "I'd just as soon not do the extra paperwork."

Brad nodded. "Looking for fingerprints?"

Sheriff Carl Wall nodded without much enthusiasm. He was a decent sort of guy. He wouldn't be any more comfortable than Brad would be if they had to send Millie away on felony charges.

Brad looked over at Millie. The woman should sit in sunlight more often. The light filtered through her short blond hair and made her look almost angelic. She just didn't look dishonest, and that fact made Brad hesitant.

Brad had always thought he was a pretty good judge of people. A thief should look like a thief—at least when he looked in her eyes. Brad had been looking in Millie's green eyes and not seeing anything that made him think she was lying.

"Not that it'll do much good even if I do find fingerprints," Sheriff Wall continued. "This is a public place. People can have their fingerprints all over here and it's not a crime. Besides, Millie didn't actually take the money off the premises. Don't know if I'd have enough to ever get it to trial. Plus, there weren't any witnesses."

Brad nodded. "I sure didn't see anything."

Brad decided he'd done more than his share of good deeds for the day. He'd gone to church and stayed through the sermon. He'd even sung a hymn or two. Then he'd had mercy on a poor woman who obviously needed someone to take care of her. "I guess it's sort of like grace."

Millie looked up at him and blinked.

Brad stood up and walked over to where the woman sat. "You know, the pastor in church talked about grace. That's how it is for you—not having to go to prison and all. We'll just call your sins forgiven."

Brad sat down in a chair across the table from Millie. He was pleased with himself. Maybe he should go to church more often. He seemed to have a flair for making moral points.

"I didn't ask for forgiveness," Millie protested softly, and then bit her lip. "I don't have anything to be forgiven for—at least, not with the money. The money is mine to give away."

Brad frowned. Well, maybe he wasn't so good at making those points after all. But then the woman looked tired. Not that she wavered in what she said. He had to admire the fact that she had stuck with her story. She was tenacious for such a little thing. He was kind of growing to like her. "Do you ever flirt?"

Millie looked startled.

"I was just wondering. You're always so serious." Brad had never been attracted to a serious woman until now. He supposed it must have something to do with the Christmas season. He was all out of whack around Christmas.

"Men don't respect you when you flirt with them."

Brad shrugged. "Sometimes it's just a way of being friendly."

Millie was quiet for a moment, and then she looked down at the top of the table. "That's what some of the other waitresses said. And then they told me I'd get more tips that way."

"You're a waitress?" Brad was surprised. Usually waitresses did know how to flirt. Millie's co-workers were right—they did get more tips that way. He knew he always gave a little extra to someone who had entertained him with a joke or two.

Millie looked up at him. "What's wrong with me being a waitress?"

Brad spread his hands. "Nothing. Some of my favorite people are waitresses."

It was odd, Brad thought. When Millie looked so serious, those glasses somehow suited her face. She was as solemn as a Madonna, but she looked good. Maybe it was just the sun in her hair and the defiant look in those eyes of hers.

"I can flirt," Millie lied. What was it about that man that made her want to prove him wrong on everything? It was a good thing he didn't ask her if she could fly.

Maybe it was the arrogant way he sat there and seemed to assume someone should pay attention to him. He was the kind of man she usually didn't want sitting at one of her tables at Ruby's. Not that he'd probably be worried about that. He wouldn't starve. If he ever did get to Ruby's, the other waitresses would fight over bringing him his order.

"I just don't think it's honest to flirt with someone so they give you a bigger tip. A tip is for the service," Millie finished.

"And the smile," Brad said and paused. "I know a nice smile has cheered me up when I've been discouraged. I think that's worth something."

"Well, yes, of course. It's always good to be friendly."

Millie knew she sounded about as prim as a country schoolteacher. The truth was that she couldn't flirt with men because men, real men, scared her a little.

Of course, she couldn't admit that to someone like Brad. "I flirt with short men."

Brad frowned at that. "How short?"

"Shorter than me."

"But you're not even five feet tall."

Millie nodded. "Short men need encouragement, too."

"I'm pretty short," Sheriff Wall offered. He had been quiet, and Millie had forgotten he was there, but he had obviously been listening. "Maybe a bit more'n five feet, but short enough to need encouragement."

"You're the sheriff. That's encouragement enough," Brad said.

The sheriff walked over to the table. "Maybe, but if the lady likes short men, I thought I should put my hat in the ring. She's not going to find any men around here who are shorter than me."

"She doesn't like short men."

Sheriff Wall smiled. "Just because you're six-four, there's no reason to be cross. Plenty of women like tall men. You should leave a few for the rest of us, especially if they like short men."

Millie figured the sheriff was right. Plenty of women did like men as tall as Brad. Somehow the thought wasn't as comforting as it should have been. She looked over at Brad. "I suppose you have someone special anyway."

Brad grinned. "I'm free as a bird."

Millie blinked. She couldn't believe she actually cared.

Brad heard the knock on the café door before it became a pounding. He was enjoying the pink that was covering Millie's face, though, and he didn't much want to get up and answer the door.

It was slowly occurring to Brad that Millie might have cured his Christmas blues. He hadn't had a discouraging thought since he'd met her. Of course, that might be because he'd been busy trying to figure out whether or not she was a thief.

Maybe he should do something like this every Christmas. He didn't suppose, though, that he could count on the café to provide him with a thief just before Christmas every year.

"Are you going to answer that?" Millie finally asked.

Brad looked at Sheriff Wall. "You're the public servant."

Sheriff Wall snorted. "That doesn't mean I get the door."

Still, the sheriff stood up and walked over to the door. Halfway there, he stopped and looked back at Millie. "Just remember, Brad's too tall for you."

Millie blushed a bright red.

Brad smiled. Now she looked like a Madonna with a sunburn.

Millie turned to look at the door. Maybe if she ignored Brad and his teasing, he would stop looking at her like that—like he knew something that she didn't, and it was causing him to smile like a simpleton.

"I'm not really six-four," Brad whispered to Millie. "If I take my boots off, I'm only six-three. I'm shorter than you think."

"I don't care how tall you are."

Millie turned all of her attention to the doorway. It wasn't difficult to do, because Mrs. Hargrove was waving something at the sheriff and trying to talk.

"Let me get my breath," she finally said.

Mrs. Hargrove was standing in the doorway and taking deep breaths. She looked like she'd been running or, at least, walking fast. Her gray hair was a little disheveled and her coat was unbuttoned.

"You should have taken it easy getting back," Sheriff Wall said as he helped Mrs. Hargrove to a chair. "We're not in any rush."

"But—the money's—not Linda's," Mrs. Hargrove said as she sat down.

Millie could see the sheriff frown.

"Did you say it's not Linda's?"

Mrs. Hargrove took a deep breath. "No one left any money in the café. I talked to Linda, and she cleaned out the cash drawer to buy her plane ticket. She also said she wished she hadn't, but that's a different matter."

"So that means…" the sheriff began thoughtfully.

Everyone was silent for a moment.

"How about that church?" Brad asked. "You know, the one with the Christmas baskets."

Mrs. Hargrove shook her head. "I called Pastor Hanks. He thought I was nuts. He said they don't have that kind of money to give away in Christmas baskets, especially this year. They're giving canned green beans and some of those fried onion rings, so people can make a Christmas casserole. Then he said it had been a hard year and asked *me* for a donation. I told him I'd send him five dollars."

Everyone was silent for another moment. Millie kind of liked the silence she found in Dry Creek. There wasn't any traffic noise. There were no airplanes flying overhead. There weren't even any barking dogs, although she supposed that was only for the moment.

"So the money was hers," Brad said finally as he looked at Millie.

Mrs. Hargrove beamed. "That means she's innocent."

"Still, something's funny," the sheriff said as he scratched his head. "For one thing, she made an unlawful entry here even if it was because she was hungry or something."

Millie swallowed. She'd forgotten about using the key to get inside the café. That had seemed like the least of her worries.

"Not that that's worth locking her up over," the sheriff continued. "Not with the heating problems over at the jail and all. It costs fifty bucks a day just to keep a prisoner in jail this time of year, and the café is open to everyone."

"I'm sorry about the breaking and entering," Millie offered.

"See, she's sorry," Brad added.

Millie looked at Brad. He was looking at her like she'd just passed some sort of test and he'd guided her through it. If she wasn't mistaken, the man actually looked proud of her. Millie couldn't remember the last time anyone except Forrest had been proud of her.

The sheriff nodded. "Still, we have to do something. We can't have strangers thinking they can come into town and break into a place of business and nothing happens."

"I could pay a fine," Millie offered. Now that the money was hers again, she could use one of the hundred-dollar bills to pay the fine. She could take it from one of the extra stockings. "If it's a small fine, that is. I don't have too much extra."

"How far are you planning on driving?" Brad asked incredulously. "That money in there would take you to either coast."

"The money's not for me." Millie realized the people of Dry Creek had not suspected she was going to put the money in their stockings. Which meant that she just might pull off a Christmas surprise after all.

The sheriff shook his head. "I'm not doing some kind of fancy fine. It'd be one thing if it was a traffic fine, but I'd have to drive into Miles City just to get a form for a special-circumstance fine."

"Well, you give parking fines all the time," Brad said. "Charge her with one of those."

Sheriff Wall looked at Millie. "Might be better to just give her some community service to do."

Mrs. Hargrove brightened. "We do have a lot of work left to get ready for Christmas."

"Christmas?" Brad frowned. "I was thinking community service would involve something like picking the litter off the roads or something. I could help her with that. But Christmas—"

"No one can do litter removal with all this snow unless they have a bulldozer," Mrs. Hargrove said. "Besides, we've always done a good job of celebrating Christmas in Dry Creek." Mrs. Hargrove looked at Brad. "Just because you don't like Christmas, it doesn't mean it's not a good community-service project. Besides, it's time you got over your problems with Christmas anyway. It'll do you good."

Brad stared at her. "Who told you I have problems with Christmas?"

"Everybody knows." Mrs. Hargrove shrugged. "Why do you think we let you park behind the café last night and didn't bother you?"

"You knew I was there?"

Mrs. Hargrove looked at Brad. "Christmas can be a hard time when you have memories you would rather forget. But as far as I know, the only remedy is to make new memories."

"I don't have any memories," Brad protested, and realized it was true. And that's what bothered him most about Christmas. Other people could talk about the happy times they had shared with their families at Christmas. But he couldn't recall any. He was five when his parents were killed in the car accident, but he didn't remember any Christmases before that. Surely, he should have some memories of Christmas.

"What would I do for Christmas?" Millie asked.

Brad thought she looked a little too eager for someone facing community service. Brad turned to the sheriff. "It's not supposed to be fun, you know. She can't just decorate a Christmas tree or something."

"She could help get ready for the church service," Mrs. Hargrove said.

"I could help you get those black streaks off the floor," Millie offered.

"You know how to do that?" Mrs. Hargrove asked.

Millie nodded.

"Then you're an answer to my prayers."

"Well, I can't just let her run around free, either," the sheriff said as he looked at Mrs. Hargrove. "I don't suppose you would—"

"I'll be happy to keep an eye on her."

Brad snorted. "She'd sweet-talk her way around you in no time."

Mrs. Hargrove's eyes started to twinkle, and she nodded to Brad. "Maybe you should join us then."

"What?" The sheriff frowned. "Oh, I don't think that will be necessary. I planned to keep an eye on her myself."

Brad grinned. Mrs. Hargrove might be old, but she understood a young man's heart. It didn't always need to be the short man who got a break with the new woman in town. Brad turned to the sheriff. "Don't you have to be on duty?"

Sheriff Wall grunted. "No more than you do."

"Things are slow at the Elkton Ranch this time of year. I'm sure they can spare me for a little civic duty."

Millie was bewildered. It sounded like both of the men actually wanted to spend time with her. And they'd have to watch her mop a floor to do it. That didn't sound like any fun. "You'll get your shirt dirty standing around."

"I have some old shirts," Brad said.

"And I have some extra scrub brushes just waiting for a volunteer," Mrs. Hargrove said. "We've tried everything on those black streaks."

"I'll bring some coffee for a break when I come by in the morning," the sheriff said. "No point in anyone starting today. Besides, it's Sunday."

Brad turned to Millie. "I have some extra old shirts. You'll probably need one, too. I'll get you fixed up when we get back to the bunkhouse."

Sheriff Wall frowned. "I don't know if she should stay at the bunkhouse."

Millie agreed with the sheriff. "I don't mind the jail."

"Oh, you can't stay in the jail, dear," Mrs. Hargrove said. "It's cold this time of year. Besides, I think the bunkhouse might be just the place. Charlie will keep an eye on things."

"She can have my room. I don't mind sleeping on the couch."

"Well, it's all set then," Mrs. Hargrove said as she pointed to the money and then looked at Millie. "I guess that's all yours then. Keep it in a safe place."

"The bunkhouse is safe."

The sheriff nodded and looked at Millie. "Just don't go spending it too fast. I plan to make a couple of inquires just in case there've been any other thefts recently in the area. I should hear back today."

"Just as long as you know by Christmas," Millie said. She would want to have the stockings ready before Christmas Day. She was glad that things seemed to be working out. She didn't mind spending a couple of days in Dry Creek.

Millie looked at Brad. He was still smiling.

"Does everybody here drink the same water?" Millie asked. Maybe there was some kind of mineral in the water around here that made people smile a lot. She'd heard about places where the population was a little below average in intelligence because of a tainted water supply. She supposed a mineral that got into the water supply could have a similar effect on emotions.

"I guess we do," Mrs. Hargrove said. "We all have our own wells, but it comes from the same water table."

Millie nodded. "I was just curious."

Brad couldn't help but see the change that came over Sheriff Wall. The sheriff had been leaning against the wall by the door, and he straightened up. The smile left his face. His eyes narrowed like he was thinking.

"What kind of stuff do you figure you need to clean those black streaks off the floor?" he finally asked Millie.

Brad wondered why the sheriff was that interested in floor cleaners and then realized the man probably wasn't. Something else was going on here.

"I thought I'd get some baking soda," Millie said.

Mrs. Hargrove nodded. "That might work."

The sheriff was silent for a moment. "I've got baking soda at the office. I'll bring some out for you tomorrow. No point in buying any new."

"Oh, I don't mind," Millie said. "It won't take long to get some. And, if that doesn't work, I know another trick or two."

"Best to use county supplies since it is a public building."

"I wouldn't call the church a public building," Mrs. Hargrove protested. "I mean, it's open to the public, but we're independent."

"Still," the sheriff said, "I think it's best."

He turned toward the café door and motioned to Brad. "Mind if I have a word with you before we head out? You know, to explain your duties and all."

"Sure." Brad got up. He wasn't sure what was making the sheriff look older than his years, but he expected he would soon find out. He was pretty sure it was related to this floor-cleaning project.

Brad had scarcely stepped out onto the porch and closed the café door behind Sheriff Wall than the sheriff started to talk.

"I don't like it," Sheriff Wall said. "All them chemicals and cleaners—who knows what she's up to? Especially when she's asking about our water supply."

"You're not worried she's planning to do something to our water?"

"Well, not the water. It'd be hard to hit all the wells. But I didn't like the fact that she was asking," the sheriff said. "The way I figure it, that money could be payment for doing something—maybe the something just hasn't happened yet."

"Oh, I don't think—" Brad began to protest, but then he remembered. Dry Creek wasn't the same place that it had been before the hit man had come two years ago. He could no longer just assume that the only crimes in town were kids being mischievous.

Sheriff Wall nodded. "All I'm saying is that we need to keep an eye on her until we know how she came by that money."

"Maybe she saved it," Brad suggested. He didn't like to picture Millie as a criminal.

The sheriff shrugged. "Even if she saved it, what's she doing carrying it around in a brown paper bag? Most anyone I know who saves that kind of money keeps it in a bank or gets a cashier's check or something."

Brad had to admit the sheriff had a point. What would a waitress be doing with that kind of cash on her? And all in hundred-dollar bills. It wasn't her tip money, that was for sure.

"I'll keep a close eye on her," Brad said. He felt another headache coming on. The only good thing was that he figured this Christmas would be one he'd always remember.

Mrs. Hargrove thought he needed memories. Well, it looked like he was going to have them whether he wanted them or not.

He couldn't help smiling a little. He guessed he did want them, especially if the memories included a little bit of a woman with green eyes.

Chapter Seven

Millie drove her car back to the bunkhouse at the Elkton Ranch thinking the rest of the day would be spent in Brad's little room. Not that that was bad. She supposed it was better than a jail cell. The room was warm, and he had lots of books that she could read. She wouldn't mind dipping into a mystery novel or taking a nap.

Brad had driven his pickup right behind her all the way to the bunkhouse. He said it was so he'd be sure she didn't get stuck in a snowdrift, but she knew he was also making sure she didn't drive off now that she had the money.

Millie smiled to herself. All in all, it hadn't gone so badly. She hadn't been forced to tell anyone that she was in Dry Creek because of Forrest. Now if she could just avoid any other questions, she would do fine. The more she thought about it, a quiet afternoon all alone in Brad's room sounded perfect.

Millie hadn't stepped all the way into the bunk-house before Charlie came trotting over to the door.

"There you are!" Charlie said as he held out his hand for Millie's coat. "I was hoping you'd get back soon."

Millie looked up. Charlie was looking directly at her. "Me?"

Charlie nodded. "We need a woman's advice about the Christmas tree."

"Christmas tree?" Brad asked. He had followed right behind Millie through the bunkhouse door. "Since when do we put up a Christmas tree?"

"We decided this year should be different since we have company," Charlie said as he smiled at Millie. "Mrs. Hargrove called to tell you to dress in old clothes when you go down to clean the church to-morrow."

"Oh, I will." Millie slipped out of her coat and gave it to Charlie.

"Mrs. Hargrove is the one that said you'd be staying with us through Christmas," Charlie added as he turned to walk to the corner closet.

Brad decided the world had gone crazy. Charlie had shaved off his beard, and he usually didn't do that until spring. In addition, he was carrying Millie's coat to the corner closet as if they didn't always leave their coats in a pile on the one chair. And, unless Brad missed his guess, Charlie was also wearing his church shirt, and here it was the middle of the after-noon! Granted, it was still Sunday, but Charlie usually couldn't wait to change into his working clothes whenever he came back to the bunkhouse.

Plus, Brad took a tentative sniff, he could smell cinnamon.

Brad looked around. The smell was coming from the black woodstove that stood in the corner of the bunkhouse living area. He didn't have to walk over to see the tin can sitting on the stove. "Who's cooking cinnamon?"

Charlie was back from the closet and had the decency to blush. "I saw it on TV—you put a stick of cinnamon in some water and boil it. It makes the air fresh for holiday company."

Brad needed to sit down. He walked over to a straight-back chair that was sitting next to the stove. "I thought that's what coffee was for."

"I wasn't sure Millie liked coffee," Charlie said anxiously. "I didn't see her drink any at breakfast."

"Of course she likes coffee," Brad said. He had to move a bowl of popcorn so he could sit down. "She's a waitress."

Brad held the bowl of popcorn on his lap.

"Don't eat any of that!" Charlie ordered. "That's for the tree."

Brad looked down at the popcorn. "We're really having a tree? A live tree? Not just one of those tin-foil things that they sometimes give away at the diesel fuel place in Miles City?"

Charlie nodded emphatically. "Of course we're having a real tree. We've got to have a proper Christmas tree if we have company."

Millie blinked. She had never been someone's Christmas company. Charlie said it like it was an honor. A sliver of panic streaked through her. "I've never helped with a tree before."

Brad looked up from his popcorn and frowned. "Never?"

Millie shook her head. "I think they're pretty, of course. But I usually just got myself a poinsettia plant or something like that. A tinfoil thing would be just fine with me."

"Didn't your family celebrate Christmas?" Brad asked.

Millie blushed. "My foster mother was always too tired."

Brad gave a low sympathetic growl.

"Not that I minded," Millie said quickly. "I didn't need to have Christmas."

"Well, don't you worry about a thing, we're going to have just as much Christmas as we can right here," Charlie said. "And we're starting with a tree. How hard can it be to do a Christmas tree? That lady on television gave a few pointers. I'm sure we can figure it out."

"But there's a lot to having a tree. For one thing, you have to have decorations, and we don't have any," Brad said. "Everyone knows you need decorations."

"Well, Jeff's gone to Miles City to look for decorations," Charlie said. "All we need to do is get the stand ready for the tree, so that when he gets back we can go chop one down before it starts to snow again."

Brad frowned. "Where are you going to find pine trees this far down from the mountains?"

"We'll find something," Charlie said. "As I recall, there's a few pines on the north side of the ranch near that gully."

"But those trees are the windbreak for the north pasture," Brad protested. "The boss will have our hides if we chop them down. Besides, the cattle won't have any shelter then."

"Well, we wouldn't chop them all down. All we need is one little Christmas tree. The cows won't miss that. Then we'll get the popcorn strung and see what other decorations Jeff brings back."

Millie felt like she'd fallen down the rabbit hole and entered a whole new world. She was surprised she didn't have visions of sugarplums and reindeer dancing in her head. Actually, come to think of it, she did seem to have a little ringing in her ears. "Do you have any aspirin?"

Charlie looked over at her and thought a minute. "I think they'd be too small for decorations, but they are white, so maybe we could glue them on to something red."

"The aspirin's not for the tree," Millie said. She was beginning to feel the responsibility of being the Christmas company. No wonder so many people came to Ruby's for Christmas dinner. All they had to do then was pay for dinner. They didn't need to provide inspiration. "And—ah, speaking of the tree, I hope you're not doing anything special just because I'm here. I don't mind not having Christmas. Really. I usually don't do all the Christmas things anyway."

"Don't you worry about Christmas," the old man protested at the same time as he turned to scowl at Brad. "And don't think that we're going to let you mope around this Christmas, either. That's okay when it's just us guys here. But it's not okay when you have company."

Millie decided she really needed that aspirin. Or she would if she had to listen to Brad say one more time that she wasn't his company, wasn't his girl-friend, wasn't his date—wasn't his anything.

"You're right," Brad said simply. "I do need to cheer up and stop thinking about myself."

Millie looked at him skeptically.

Brad smiled at her slightly.

Millie looked at him and frowned a little.

Brad grinned and just kept looking at her.

"No one said where there was an aspirin," Millie finally said.

"I've got some right here." Brad handed her a small tin.

"I never take aspirin," Millie said as she snapped the tin open. Half of the eight tablets were already gone. She took out two of the remaining ones and handed it back to Brad.

"Neither do I," Brad said as he picked out two tablets for himself. "Neither do I."

Brad decided he was going to do Christmas right if it killed him—which, in this case, it just might. If he had a brain in his head, he would drive Millie back to town and let the sheriff take over guarding her. Let the county pay a few bucks to heat the jail. He'd even bring her a tinfoil tree to set in the window.

Brad no sooner thought of it than the picture of Millie spending Christmas in jail passed by his mind and he knew he couldn't do it, not even if he went in and sat in the cell with her and the little tree.

No, he had to make Christmas special for her. He had thought he was the only one who had never done any of the usual Christmas things, but it seemed like Millie might have him beat. She seemed more clueless about Christmas than he did. And he would have to be blind not to see the wistful look on her face when someone mentioned the Christmas tree.

"Can't we just tie the tree to that pole lamp or something? You know, the cast-iron one with the bear?" Millie asked as she watched him carefully select two pieces of lumber to make a Christmas tree stand. They were out in the barn and the wind was blowing in the open door. Millie was sitting on a bale of hay. Brad had the light on even though it wasn't more than three o'clock in the afternoon.

"The tree would be all crooked that way," Brad said. Ever since he'd decided to celebrate Christmas, he was determined to not take any shortcuts. Not that the lamp idea was a bad one. Charlie had won that lamp at some senior bingo party, and it would bear the weight of a tree—it just wouldn't keep it straight.

Still, it was kind of sweet of Millie to sit there with that little frown on her forehead and worry about how to save him the time and effort of building a stand. "Besides, it's not a problem. I can make a tree stand in no time."

Brad had built line shacks and corrals. He knew a little about engineering and carpentry. A tree stand wasn't even a challenge, but he wasn't in any particular hurry to finish the task and head back inside where all the other guys were sitting around stringing popcorn.

"Well, I guess if it's a small tree, it'll work," Millie said as she stood and walked over to look down at the lumber. "It will be a small tree, won't it?"

"It'll have to be. A large one will be too big for the horses to drag."

"Horses?" Millie stepped back. "Aren't we going in the pickup?"

Brad shook his head. "Too much snow this time of year. The horses are a better way to get there."

"But I've never ridden a horse."

Brad looked up at her. She looked a little scared and nervous and he decided that her look must be growing on him, because he didn't consider all of the other options that they had. "Then you'll have to ride double with me."

Brad held his breath. He wasn't at all sure that she would want to ride double with him. She might not know it, but riding a horse double was almost a date in Montana. After all her talk about short men and flirting, he'd gotten the distinct impression that she didn't want to date anyone and, if he was honest, she especially seemed not to want to date him.

"I don't know…isn't it cold?" Millie asked.

"You can wear my parka. It's down-filled and good for twenty below zero."

Brad didn't add that the lining was some kind of special silk and he'd spent a month's salary on it.

"But what about you?" Millie looked up at him, and her green eyes were full of concern.

"Don't worry about me. I'll keep warm," Brad promised. He was slowly realizing he'd like nothing better than to have Millie lean into him as they rode his horse back to the ranch. He'd ride without a shirt or a coat if he had to, just to have her trust him like he was picturing in his mind.

Millie still had that little frown on her forehead.

"I can borrow one of the spare coats," Brad added, and watched as her frown lifted. He congratulated himself that she cared about him and his comfort.

"You wouldn't be able to drive the horse if you got too cold," Millie said.

"Oh." Brad decided maybe she didn't care as much as he'd hoped. Brad drove a nail into the lumber he had set for the tree stand. There was no need to prolong the task. He drove in another nail. "You don't need to worry. The horse knows the way back to the ranch anyway. Even if I couldn't ride him, he'd make it back to his stall."

Millie nodded.

Brad hammered the final nail into the lumber and stood up. "Here. We've got us a tree stand."

Brad opened the barn door for Millie and followed her out into the yard of the ranch. Snow covered most of the ground, although it had been pretty well stamped down from all the feet that had walked over it. The air was cold, and Brad saw Millie put her hands in the pockets of her long black coat. "I'll lend you some gloves, too."

"I can just put my hands in the pockets of your coat," Millie said.

"Not if you plan to stay on the horse."

Brad regretted his words the moment they were out of his mouth. He could tell Millie was worried, so he added, "Don't worry. I won't let you fall off."

Millie knew something was wrong the minute she and Brad stepped inside the main room of the bunkhouse. There were two long strings of popcorn garland running between the bear lamp and green recliner. There were Christmas carols playing on a small CD player. What there wasn't any sign of was peace on earth and goodwill toward men.

All of the men in the room were hunched over something on the floor by the stove, and they were clearly arguing.

"I tell you it's wrong," Charlie said as he studied what looked like a large piece of white paper. "It doesn't look like any angel I've ever seen."

Millie walked over to the men. Someone had drawn a crayon picture of an angel—at least she thought it must be an angel. "Are those wings?"

"See, she can tell those are wings," Randy said triumphantly.

"She was *asking* if they were wings," Charlie protested. "That's a big difference."

Randy looked up at Millie. "It just didn't seem right putting wings on an angel like it was some big chicken or something. I mean, what's something like an angel doing with chicken wings? I think their wings should look more like a horse's mane. You know, rows and rows of curling hair. Now, hair is nice. It's got class. It's fitting for someone who lives in heaven."

"I notice the wings are blond," Brad said from behind Millie's shoulders. "You always were partial to blondes."

"That's an angel you're talking about," Charlie said. "Show some respect."

"Well, she's not an angel if she doesn't have wings," Brad said. "She's just a good-looking woman in a white nightgown with lots of blond hair. Lots and lots of hair."

"She kind of looks like that country-western singer with the big—" William began and then looked at Millie and blushed "—with the big hats."

Charlie cleared his throat. "I hope you're not planning on putting any—hats—on the angel. We run a respectable place here."

"We're a bunkhouse," Brad protested.

Charlie lifted his chin. "As long as we have Christmas company, we're a home, and a home has certain standards."

Brad was speechless.

"Wow, that's kind of nice," Randy said. "It's good to have a home at Christmas."

Brad looked over at Millie. How was it that one woman could make their bunkhouse a home for Christmas?

Come to think of it maybe that was why he got so depressed at Christmas. Christmas was a time for families, and every year when the holiday came around it reminded him that he was alone. All he had to do was listen to a song on the radio or pass by a display in a store to know that Christmas was for families. That must be it.

Brad was almost relieved. It was all because of decorations and ads that he was depressed. Everyone had to face the advertising world at some point and realize that just because someone in an ad had something it didn't mean he had to have it.

No, he just needed perspective. He certainly didn't need to change his being single. All he had to do was get through these few days each December.

He just needed to remember that Christmas was only one day. He still had the other 364 days left to enjoy his bachelorhood. The advertising world didn't make so much of families the other 364 days.

Yeah, he had the good life. Once he got past Christmas, his life would be normal again. He'd be worrying about a poker hand instead of popcorn garlands. It would all be fine. Christmas would be here and gone soon. Maybe even quicker if he could hurry it along. "We better go see about that tree."

"I rigged up a sled for the tree," Randy said as he

stood up and brushed his hands off on his jeans. "My horse can pull that easy enough."

"I figured I could bring the ax," William offered.

"But you can't just leave the Christmas drawing," Millie protested.

"Oh, yeah," Randy said as he bent down and rolled the paper up. "I'll need to finish it after we get the tree up so we can put it on top."

Brad nodded numbly. It shouldn't surprise him that they were going to have an angel who looked like a Vegas dancer sitting on top of their Christmas tree.

"I'll have some cocoa waiting for when you get back," Charlie said as they all started to look for their coats. It took a minute for everyone to realize Charlie had hung the coats up in the closet. No one ever hung up the coats.

Brad almost shook his head. He wasn't the only one who was going crazy at Christmas. Randy was drawing angels and Charlie was turning into Little Miss Homemaker.

It was going to be a miracle if they all survived this Christmas without turning into city gentlemen with manicured nails who refused to change the oil in their car. Before long, they'd all be useless.

And it was all her fault, Brad thought as he looked at Millie.

How could one woman who looked so small make such a big difference in this old bunkhouse?

Chapter Eight

Millie felt like she was in a snow globe as she rode behind Brad's saddle. The sun was setting, but there was still enough light to see the snowflakes fall. The air was so cold it felt brittle, but Millie found the steady sway of Brad's horse comforting. The landscape dipped into a long gully and then rose to small hills all around.

Millie couldn't remember the last time she'd been in a landscape with such openness. She didn't see any houses or roads or telephone poles. All she could see were stretches of white snow and the hoofprints the horses had made on their way into the gully where the pine trees stood.

Charlie was right. The cows wouldn't miss the small tree they had cut and strapped onto the sled that Randy pulled behind his horse.

They had debated which tree to cut until they saw the little tree. The branches on the tree were crooked, and William, after studying the ground around it, said they were doing the poor thing a favor by cutting it down. It was surrounded by taller trees and wasn't getting enough sunlight to grow properly.

The tree reminded Millie of that tree she'd tried to make long ago out of tinfoil and metal hangers. The tree was spindly and deformed, but somehow it tugged at her heart.

Millie turned her head around. It was getting dark, but she could still see Randy and William following behind them. She quickly turned her head back. The gap between her and Brad's back when she turned let cold air between them. Millie shivered. She was glad she had Brad's back to block the wind that came with the snow flurries.

"Sorry," Millie whispered. She suspected the borrowed coat Brad was wearing wasn't nearly as warm as the parka he had lent her, so she leaned against him as closely as she could so that at least his back would be warm.

"No problem," Brad mumbled.

All of the horses kept their heads down as they walked into the wind, and Millie knew Brad kept his head down and had his wool scarf tied around his mouth. A bandanna kept his hat tied down and his ears warm.

Millie settled into her place on Brad's back. She rested her cheek against his one shoulder and wrapped her arms more securely around his waist. She had to lift the edge of his coat in order to hold tight to his waist, and she worried that in doing so she left room for a draft of cold air. She had offered earlier to put her hands on the outside of his coat, but he had declined, saying she'd freeze her fingers.

Millie could feel the snaps on Brad's shirt, and she kept her hands clasped around the snap just above his brass belt buckle. Her hands had made a warm spot against his stomach, and they were cozy there.

Millie wondered why she felt so comfortable pressed against Brad's back this way. Well, maybe "comfortable" was the wrong word. It was more a feeling of belonging than comfort. It must be because, with her hands clasped around his stomach, they had started breathing to the same rhythm. Or maybe it was because she could be so close to him and she didn't have to worry that he was going to turn around and want to talk or anything.

Millie sighed. It wasn't easy when you were a shy woman to spend any time around an outgoing man like Brad. She'd been a waitress long enough to know men like him weren't happy with simple conversation; they wanted witty remarks and flirtatious comments. The few times Millie had gone out with men like that she'd learned she wasn't what they were looking for in a date. Those dates had been disastrous, and she wouldn't care to repeat them.

It was too bad, she thought. There was something about Brad that she was growing to like, especially now as they rode through the darkening night. If only they could ride like this forever and not have to talk.

"You can see the lights of the bunkhouse," Brad said through his muffled scarf. "We're almost home."

Millie nodded and snuggled a little closer. Brad

pulled on the horse's reins and she could feel his muscles ripple down his back. She thought for a second that she would have to remember to tell the other waitresses about this ride, but then she realized she never would. This night belonged only to her. Even though she could hear the hooves of the other horses behind them stepping on the snow, it felt like she and Brad were alone outside.

"I don't mind if you take it slow getting back," Millie whispered.

She felt Brad's muscles tense. He probably thought she was crazy.

"It'll be easier on the horses," she added. She didn't want to be pushy. "They must be cold."

"They're fine," Brad said.

Millie nodded.

Brad had never been so glad to see the shape of the Elkton Ranch barn come into view. And that was counting the time he'd almost frozen to death rounding up strays during the bad winter about ten years back. Brad needed to end this ride and he needed to end it soon.

If it didn't, he was going to go way over the deep end. He didn't know what was wrong. Millie wasn't the kind of woman he should be thinking about dating. Who was he kidding? He'd stopped thinking about dating a mile back there and had gone right on to thinking of the big time.

He needed to end the ride. For one thing, she deserved someone more permanent than him. He wasn't ready for the *big* time. He was the kind of guy women looked to if they wanted a *good* time. And that was the way he liked it. He steered clear of women like Millie who made a man think of settling down and having babies.

He didn't know what was wrong. Millie didn't even wear lipstick, and yet he'd been one breath away from starting to whistle the wedding march. He barely knew the wedding march and, besides that, his lips were near frozen from the cold.

Brad shook his head. It must be something about the way she laid her cheek against his back that made him want to take care of her.

Of course, he knew it was only the Christmas craziness, but if he started whistling some wedding song, he'd make a fool of himself for sure.

"Yeah, we're almost there," Brad repeated himself as his horse walked into the edge of the ranch yard.

Millie thought she must be frozen to the back of Brad's saddle. "I can't move."

Brad had ridden into the barn and swung out of the saddle easily enough himself. But Millie was stuck. Her legs felt like they were permanently glued to the saddle.

The air was warmer inside the barn and the horse was standing politely beside the feed trough waiting to be given some oats. Randy and William had ridden over to the bunkhouse so they could unload the tree from the sled, but Brad and Millie had gone straight to the barn to dismount.

Millie tried to move her toes, and she felt the muscles tighten in her boots. At least she didn't have frost-bite.

Brad took the reins of his horse and led the animal over to a small pile of hay. "You're just sore from all that riding. I didn't know we'd be gone that long."

"I'm never going riding again," Millie said, and then gave an exaggerated groan for emphasis.

Brad chuckled.

Oh, my word, Millie thought, *I almost made a joke. And he laughed.* She couldn't remember the last time she'd joked with a handsome man. Usually she only felt relaxed enough to joke with her women friends and men like Forrest who were shy themselves.

"It might help if you take the coat off," Brad said. "That'll help you move easier."

Millie pulled her left arm out of the parka and then finished pulling it off her right arm. She handed the coat down to Brad, and he set it on a hay bale. Millie shivered. It was cold, but she could move easier.

"Here," Brad said as he held his arms up to her. "Now let me swing you down, and you can sit on these bales."

Millie pushed against the back of Brad's saddle and tried to get her leg to properly swing itself over the horse. It didn't work. Finally, she just tilted her whole self over and let the leg come if it wanted.

Brad held his arms out to catch Millie. She fell into his arms and grabbed him around the neck. Usually when a woman had her arms around his neck, Brad recalled she also had a certain inviting look in her eyes.

Brad could only see one of Millie's eyes because he was actually facing her ear instead of her face, but he was pretty sure the look he hoped for wasn't there. Her eyes showed panic.

"Don't worry. I've got you," Brad whispered.

If it was possible, she looked even more alarmed.

"I can stand," Millie said.

Brad noted she didn't relax her grip on his neck, and her glasses were perched precariously on her nose.

"I think my leg just went to sleep, but it'll be fine when I put some weight on it," Millie added.

Since Millie wanted to stand, Brad shifted her, hoping to get her in a position where she could. He regretted it the minute he did it.

Instead of looking at her ear, Brad was now looking at those green eyes of hers. Both of them. Her glasses had fallen completely off, and he saw them resting on her shoulder. Without glasses, Millie's eyes went soft and dreamy. She relaxed in his arms.

Brad supposed Millie might have become calm because she couldn't see, but he told himself it was just possible that it was because she was caught up in the magic of the moment, as he was—and that she was thinking how close they were to kissing, and if he just moved an inch or two this way and she moved an inch or two that way, they would meet in a kiss.

Brad took a deep breath just like the one he took every time he climbed into the chute at the Billings rodeo. He was an amateur at bull riding, just like he was an amateur at kissing. He'd never realized before, though, that a kiss could take every bit as much courage as climbing on the back of a two-thousand-pound bull.

"Oh," Millie said softly as Brad moved a little closer.

"May I?" Brad asked. He looked carefully at Millie's eyes. He didn't expect her to give him a verbal okay, but he did expect to see in her eyes if she was okay with a kiss.

"Oh," Millie repeated even softer.

Brad didn't see any refusal in her eyes. He looked twice to be sure. Then he took a deep breath and kissed her.

Millie thought her heart was going to stop. Failing that, her brain was going to melt. And it was all because her glasses had fallen off and in all the surrounding blur Brad was kissing her like he thought she was a fragile china doll.

Millie had been kissed before, but never like she was precious.

"Oh," Millie said when he pulled away a little bit.

Brad was smiling and, for some reason, he didn't look nearly as tall as he had before. It must be because his face was a little blurry and fuzzy. Millie decided she should go without her glasses more often if it made men like Brad look so very nice.

Millie heard the barn door open even though she couldn't actually see the door open. She could, however, see the big blocks of gray color that moved inside, and then she heard the neighing of a horse.

"Hey, there."

Millie recognized Randy's voice.

"What's happening here?" That was William. He sounded suspicious—like he'd added up the columns and wasn't sure they matched.

"I need my glasses," Millie said. If she was going to answer questions, she needed to be able to see.

Brad handed her the glasses.

"I was just helping Millie get off the horse," Brad said. His arms were still around Millie's shoulders.

William snorted. "Looked to me like you were helping her with a whole lot more than that."

Millie put her glasses on, and everything became clear. She could see through the open barn door that the night was almost fully dark now. The light Brad had turned on inside the barn gave the walls a yellow glow. Hay bales were stacked in one corner of the barn and horse stalls lined another wall.

William and Randy were both sitting on top of their horses and leaning forward as they looked at her and Brad. Randy was grinning, but William was looking stern and worried.

"My leg went to sleep," Millie explained. "I couldn't get off the horse, and Brad was helping me."

William looked directly at Millie. "You just be careful of him. He's a heartbreaker, he is."

"Oh." Millie blinked. Of course. She knew Brad was a flirt even if she had forgotten it for a moment. Men like him kissed women all the time for no good reason.

To be fair, women probably kissed Brad all the time for no good reason, too. He was certainly worth kissing if all of his kisses were like the last one. It wasn't his fault that Millie was the kind of woman who liked a reason for a kiss. A reason being maybe she was becoming a little special to the man kissing her.

Brad looked up at the other two ranch hands in astonishment. "Since when am I a heartbreaker?"

Brad always made very sure the women he was dating had no illusions about him. No one's heart had ever been cracked as far as he knew. Certainly, none had been broken. He didn't date the kind of woman who would be serious. "Besides, last night you were willing to let her sleep in my room with me because I was feeling a little down about Christmas. And now I can't kiss her!"

"That was different," William said firmly. "We didn't know Millie back then. Now, well—anyone can see she's the kind of woman who deserves a guy who's going to make a commitment."

Brad wanted to argue with that, but he couldn't. He didn't know much about Millie. He didn't even know for sure that she wasn't a thief or that she wouldn't leave tomorrow without saying goodbye. But one thing he did know: she did deserve one of those husbands mothers always wanted for their daughters. She deserved a man who could give her a home and financial security. Brad might have that someday, but today he didn't. He had nothing to offer a woman like Millie except his diesel pickup, and he had a feeling that wouldn't do.

"Well, then, we'd best get to the bunkhouse," Brad

said. William sure knew how to bring a man down to earth. "It's cold enough out here to spit ice."

William nodded and smiled. "Charlie wasn't kidding about the cocoa. That'll warm you up. We could smell it when we took the tree inside."

Brad nodded. He supposed he would have to be content with that.

"Does he have marshmallows?" Millie asked.

Brad looked down at her. Her short blond hair was sticking out in all directions because she'd pulled off the wool cap he'd given her earlier. Her glasses were still a little crooked on her face. Her cheeks were red from the cold, and her lips were warm from his kiss.

Brad would have promised Millie the moon—the least he could do was get her some marshmallows. "If he doesn't, I'll go get some."

"Where?" William stopped midway through stepping down off his horse and turned to stare at Brad. "Where would you get marshmallows way out here in the middle of the night? And it's Sunday. Even the stores in Miles City are closed by now."

From the expression on William's face, Brad would have thought he'd offered to bring Millie the moon after all. "I could borrow some marshmallows from Mrs. Hargrove. She always keeps things like that on hand."

William finished stepping to the ground before he gave Brad another peculiar look.

"She's a well-prepared woman—Mrs. Hargrove is," Brad said for no reason other than to try and stop the look that was growing and growing on William's face.

"You don't have a temperature, do you?" William finally asked as he took a step closer to Brad. "I hear the flu this season makes people a little light-headed."

"I don't have a fever," Brad said. He couldn't swear that he wasn't light-headed, but he was pretty sure his temperature would log in at a normal 98.6 degrees.

"Well, we should get these horses taken care of and get inside anyway," William said. He gave Brad another curious look before he turned back to his horse. "No sense in hanging out here in the cold when we can be inside decorating the Christmas tree."

Brad nodded. He had forgotten about the Christmas tree. He had the whole Christmas thing yet to do. There would be the tree and more cinnamon on the stove. And that was only tonight. Tomorrow night would be Christmas Eve, and that would be even worse. He wondered if Charlie would want them all to go to the Christmas pageant at church. Brad had a feeling this was one holiday he would never forget.

At least when he thought of Christmas in the future, he could look back to this evening ride with Millie. If that wasn't Christmas magic, he didn't know what was.

Chapter Nine

The warm air in the bunkhouse made Millie's glasses fog up.

She stepped to the side of the doorway so that she wouldn't block the way as Brad and the other two men came inside the bunkhouse. The air inside smelled of chocolate and fresh pine. Empty cups ready for cocoa were sitting on a small table by one wall. The ranch hands were gathered around the small tree that was lying on the floor next to the black stove.

Millie rubbed her hands. The wood burning in the stove kept the large room heated. Her fingers had stung a little from the cold when she first stepped inside the room, but they were already starting to warm up. She was grateful for the prickly feeling in her hands as the heat reached them. That small tingling distracted her from The Kiss.

Millie stole a look up at Brad. He might be accustomed to a kiss like the one they had just shared, but she sure wasn't.

Brad was looking over at the group of men inside the room so Millie took her time and studied him carefully. He was handsome as usual. He still wore his hat, but she could see his face beneath it and it all looked normal. He wasn't wearing any tiny smile or dreamy expression on his face.

Millie frowned. She knew William had said Brad was a heartbreaker and she supposed she shouldn't be surprised that he didn't look any different, but she had secretly hoped he would. Not that she'd expected him to be smiling like an idiot or anything, but shouldn't he have some sort of funny look on his face after a kiss like that? He didn't look like he was affected at all. He certainly didn't have the stunned look she knew she was wearing.

She watched as Brad said a quick hello to the guys in the bunkhouse and then as he wiped his boots lightly on the rug by the door. He took his hat off and brushed the snow off it before he put it on a rack next to the door. He still had a few snowflakes melting on his cheek and his face was a little red from the cold.

Outside of that, Millie couldn't detect anything different about him. There was no sign Brad's heart had been beating in an irregular rhythm or that he was remembering a particularly sweet moment. In fact, he had paid more attention to his hat than he had to her since they'd come inside.

If Millie had been wearing a hat, she wouldn't even have remembered she had it on after that kiss. She felt like her own heart had been dipping and fluttering as if it belonged to a crazy woman. She'd even been

trying to remember all she'd ever heard about flirting so that she'd know what to say next.

But now, seeing Brad, she hoped the sputtering
happiness she felt inside hadn't shown on the outside.
She was grateful she hadn't tried to say anything on
the walk back to the bunkhouse. She didn't want to
embarrass Brad by gushing over him when the kiss
seemed like it was just routine to him. He probably
kissed every woman who couldn't manage to get off
a horse by herself. Maybe he meant it to be kind, like
kissing backward children on the forehead to console
them for their clumsiness.

Millie blinked and told herself it wasn't a tear that
she felt in the corner of her eye. It was just moisture
from the sudden heat of the room.

"I'm a little tired," she said as she gave a small
yawn and an apologetic shrug. That should get rid of
any doubt that she was still excited about a kiss that
had happened a full five minutes ago. She didn't want
anyone to think she was gullible enough to think that
kiss mattered.

"Here, let me look at you," Brad said as he turned
his full attention toward her. He bent his head and
peered at her critically.

"I'm fine, though," Millie hastened to add. She
didn't want to overplay being tired. Charlie would
insist she go lie down, and she didn't want to miss
any of this time taking a nap. Even if the kiss was
nothing to remember, she wanted to remember every
minute about this evening.

"How tired?" Brad asked as he took hold of her wrist and began to raise her hand up.

Millie blinked. Was he going to kiss her hand?

Brad stopped raising her hand and put his thumb on her wrist to feel her pulse.

"Being tired can be a sign you got too cold out there," he said. His blue eyes had deepened with worry. Millie started to hope maybe he did care, until he added. "People usually go to sleep just before they freeze to death."

"I wasn't that cold—and I'm not really that tired." Millie decided Brad was looking at her now like she was a sick bug at the bottom of a microscope. That wasn't the kind of attention she wanted. "I'm just— fine."

There had been many times in her life when Millie wished she were clever, but during none of those times did she wish it as fiercely as she did now. She felt as if she only knew how to flirt and be bold, she would know how to capture Brad's interest. Even a bug that knew how to flirt could capture his attention when he was standing so close.

Well, Millie guessed that technically she had his attention, but it was only because he thought she might be overly cold and on the verge of death. Brad probably didn't want to deal with the sheriff, which he'd have to do if he let her die while he was supposed to be watching her.

Unfortunately, all of the advice on flirting from other waitresses that she had listened to at Ruby's hadn't left her with a clue on how to flirt with a man when he was standing right in front of her counting out her pulse to make sure her heart was beating normally so she'd be able to pay for any crime she might have committed.

Of course, Millie thought optimistically, a woman didn't need to know how to flirt to be friendly. And the first step in being friendly was to find out more about the other person.

"You know, I never did get your last name," Millie said as she looked up at Brad. She smiled a little to show she was friendly, but not so much that he would think she was *too* friendly. It was the best she could do.

Brad looked down at Millie. She was smiling politely at him like she was a cashier at the grocery store and was asking him whether he wanted a plastic bag or a paper bag to carry home his potatoes. He had just kissed the woman. Shouldn't she at least look a little moved by the experience? "It's Parker. Brad Parker."

Millie nodded at him.

Brad expected her to ask about the weather next, and he didn't think he could hold his temper if she did. It was downright humbling to a man to know his kiss could have so little effect on a woman.

If he wasn't a little off-center because of everything that was going on, he would be able to think of something to say to make Millie smile at him like a woman ought to smile at a man who had just kissed her.

He could tell her that her eyes looked like emeralds when she laughed or that her skin was as soft as velvet, but Millie didn't look like the kind of woman who would like any of those words. Even he knew they were clichés. Unfortunately, in her case they were also true. Not that that would matter. Women always liked something that they hadn't heard before. Brad couldn't think of one thing to say that didn't sound like it had been said a thousand times already.

How did a man describe a woman like Millie?

"I see Charlie has the tree all ready to go," Brad said finally as he finished taking her pulse. "Your heart rate seems healthy."

At least her heart seemed to be doing better than *his,* Brad said to himself as he turned to face the other men in the bunkhouse, who were all gathered around the little tree they had chopped down.

Brad was glad none of the men were paying any attention to him and Millie. He suspected that wasn't because of good manners but because they'd finally gotten a steady look at the tree. It had been half dark when Randy cut it down, and sometimes things looked different when they had some light on them.

"It's kind of small," William said as he tipped the tree upright. The tree barely made it to William's belt buckle. "And it's got a bald spot where it didn't get enough sun. At least, I think that's its problem."

William turned the tree around so everyone could see the place where there were no branches.

"It's beautiful," Millie declared as she reached out and tried to coax a nearby branch into covering the bare spot. "It just needs a little help, that's all."

Millie didn't get the branch to cooperate and she stepped back.

"I guess we could stick it in the corner behind the lamp—if we angle it just right no one will see the bald spot," Charlie said hesitantly as he measured the tree with his hand. "And then maybe if we put some extra lights on it right there—"

"I only got one string of lights," Jeff interrupted as he handed a plastic bag to Charlie. Jeff had been leaning against the wall, but he stood up straight to deliver his lights. "And I was lucky to get those—the stores in Miles City are all sold out. Vicki at the grocery store had to get that strand from the back room. I owe her dinner some night next week."

Charlie reached into the bag and pulled the strand of lights out. He looked at them for a moment. "But these are pink."

Jeff nodded. "Well, Vicki said they were Easter lights—they used them around the store windows in April—but I figure lights are lights. There's no reason Christmas trees can't have pink lights."

There was silence for a moment.

"Maybe they'll turn sort of red when we get them on," Millie finally said. "Sometimes things look different when they're on a tree."

Brad didn't care if the lights were purple. Millie was looking at the tree the way he wanted her to look at him. "They'll look just fine. The thing is that they're lights."

Millie turned and looked at him gratefully. "That's right, and I've always liked lights."

Millie still wasn't looking at him with quite the adoration that she had for the tree, but Brad felt he was making progress. It was a sad day when he had to compete with a tree for the affection of a woman. Brad looked at the tree. To make it even worse that was one pathetic tree. He'd swear it had two bald spots instead of just one.

Brad reached up and patted his own hair just to reassure himself. It was damp, but all there. No bald spots for him.

"Did you get any ornaments?" Millie asked Jeff as she walked over to where the man stood.

Brad followed Millie over. He'd compete with the tree if he had to, but he wasn't about to compete with Jeff just because the man had a few fancy ornaments in his hand.

"Wait, let me get my camera," Charlie called out as he limped across the floor to the shelf on the wall. "I want to get pictures of the tree decorating from start to finish."

"Since when do you have a camera?" Brad asked.

Charlie never took pictures. Not even the time William rode the calf backward down the loading chute. Charlie always said a man should rely on his memory when it came to things he'd seen in his life.

"Jeff brought me back one of them box cameras— you know, they're made out of cardboard so if a cow steps on them or something you're not out a lot of money," Charlie explained as he picked up the disposable camera from the shelf. "I'm thinking of starting a Christmas memory scrapbook for the bunkhouse here."

Brad wasn't even stunned anymore. If the truth were told, he wasn't even listening. "That sounds nice."

Brad had stopped listening and just concentrated on looking. He wished he had a camera of his own, so he could take a picture of Millie. How did she manage to look twelve and twenty-three all at the same time? She had her head tilted to the side and was watching Jeff reach into the bag in front of him just like he was Santa Claus and the bag held the treasures of the world.

"Didn't your mother ever take you to see Santa?" Brad stepped a little closer so he could ask her the question and not risk it being heard by everyone in the room. He thought all mothers took their kids to see Santa Claus. He'd always imagined that, if his mother had lived, she would have taken him.

Millie looked up at him. Her eyes held on to the excitement of the tree as she shook her head. "I had a foster mother."

Somehow, Millie let him know all about her foster mother just by the flatness of her voice.

"I'm sorry." Brad was surprised by how much it disturbed him to know that someone had neglected Millie. She would have been the kind of little girl who should have had a mother who cared about her.

"It's all right," Millie said.

Brad scowled. No, it wasn't all right, but there was nothing he could do about it. Except perhaps get those ornaments for her. "If we need more things for the tree, I can drive to Billings tonight."

Charlie frowned and looked at his watch. "Even if the roads were good, the stores would be closed by the time you get there."

"They have that new place that's open twenty-four hours," Brad said. "What's it called—the something Mart?"

"Isn't that too far to drive?" Millie asked softly.

"It is when it's starting to snow like this." Charlie frowned again and shot Brad an incredulous look. "You've driven that road enough to know about that one place where it always drifts closed in a few hours after this kind of snow—now, I know you'd get to Billings, but you wouldn't get back before Christmas."

There was a moment of silence. Charlie stood holding his cardboard camera. He hadn't even taken one picture yet. William was still holding up the pathetic tree by its top branch. Jeff held the bag with whatever ornaments he'd found. Randy sat on the floor with a string of popcorn in front of him. They had all stopped what they were doing to look at Brad.

"Unless that's what you want," Charlie finally said quietly. "Not to be here for Christmas."

Brad was speechless. He had been ten kinds of a fool. Here he had spent years mourning the fact that he'd never had a family Christmas, and he'd had family who wanted to celebrate with him all that time. The guys in the bunkhouse weren't worried about his Christmas depression because it meant he wasn't his usual cheerful self. They were worried because they cared about him.

"There's no place I'd rather be for Christmas than right here with all of you," Brad said. His voice sounded heavy, so he gave a cough at the end of his speech. He wouldn't want anyone to think he was sentimental. It would be better if they thought he was coming down with something.

"Well, good then," Charlie said with a cough of his own. He set his camera down on a chair and pulled a big red handkerchief out of his jeans pocket to wipe at his eyes. "I think someone must have put some green wood in that stove—it's started to smoke a little and it's getting in my eyes."

"I don't see any—" Randy began, then stopped when William jabbed him in the ribs with an elbow. "Well, maybe a little smoke—"

Everyone was silent for a moment.

Finally, Millie spoke. "The tree doesn't really need decorations. It can still be a Christmas tree."

Brad could have hugged her for bringing them back to a safe topic.

"But I have some decorations," Jeff offered as he pulled a package of shiny red balls out of the plastic bag. There were six ornaments. "It might not be enough, but that's all they had left on the shelf."

"Well—" Charlie cleared his throat and put his handkerchief back in his pocket "—I don't want anyone worrying about decorations. I've been watching that television show, and that woman said you could make Christmas decorations out of anything you have around—old hair curlers or those cardboard things from toilet paper."

Randy frowned. "It doesn't seem right to have toilet paper on a Christmas tree."

"It's not the paper, it's the cardboard rolls."

"Oh." Randy still looked unconvinced. "I guess I just can't quite picture it."

"Well, do you have any old hair curlers lying around?" Charlie asked in exasperation.

Randy shook his head. "I guess toilet rolls are all right."

Everyone took a minute to look at the tree.

Brad was the first to hear the sound of a car— or maybe it was two cars—driving up to the bunkhouse. Charlie was the one who limped over to the window, however, and opened the curtains a little so he could see.

"Looks like we got company," Charlie announced. "Good thing I made lots of cocoa."

Millie walked over to the window, and Brad followed.

"Who'd be coming to see us?" Randy asked.

Brad had asked the same question. He knew every one of the men in the bunkhouse knew lots of people and went lots of places. But most of the places they went were bars, and the kind of people they met there weren't the type to come calling on a Sunday evening, especially when it was a long drive from the highway to the Elkton Ranch bunkhouse. When it was snowing, a person had to have a reason to come calling to the bunkhouse.

"Maybe it's Christmas carolers," Charlie said. "It looks like they've got a red light going—"

"It's the sheriff," Brad said. He doubted Sheriff Wall was coming to bring them a Christmas fruitcake.

Brad moved closer to Millie until he stood directly behind her as she looked out the window. The sheriff wouldn't be able to see Millie when he came in the door if Millie stayed right where she was. Brad knew he couldn't hide Millie from Sheriff Wall if she was wanted for a string of crimes, but that didn't stop him from wanting to try anyway. He told himself it was just because she was so little that he felt so protective of her. He didn't know why he had to get all mixed up with a woman who was probably a thief—and not a very good thief at that.

"What's the sheriff doing here?" Charlie said. Brad noticed the older man wasn't moving over to the door to open it.

"Maybe he found out something about Millie's money," William said with a frown. He wasn't moving toward the door, either.

No one was moving. Everyone just stood there worrying.

"Maybe it's not the sheriff," Jeff finally said. "Maybe he lent his car out to someone for the night and they got low on gas."

Brad snorted. "He wouldn't lend that car to his mother. No, he's here about the money."

"There's nothing he can say about the money," Millie protested softly. "It's just regular money."

Brad didn't even bother to answer her. There was nothing regular about a stack of hundred-dollar bills in this part of the country. He suspected there was nothing regular about it in Millie's life, either.

Chapter Ten

Millie had never seen so many silent men standing and looking at each other. Brad stood in front of her, and she wouldn't have even been able to see anything but his shirt if she hadn't moved to the side. She had no sooner moved than William stepped in front of her, and so all she saw was William's back.

Even Charlie, who had just opened the door, was still standing beside the open door like he was waiting for the sheriff to turn around and head back out of the bunkhouse. It took Charlie two minutes to close the door. By then the temperature inside the bunkhouse had fallen ten degrees.

Even when the door was closed, no one moved.

Finally, the sheriff spoke. "I thought I should check in."

He stood on the mat just inside the door, and the snow on his tennis shoes had not begun to melt. He hadn't smiled since he stepped inside. "Just doing my duty, you know."

No one answered.

"Well, you've checked in," Brad said finally.

Millie had never been a chatty waitress, but she knew that many fights had been avoided by a few friendly words, and sometimes it was as simple as finding a safe topic of conversation. She quietly stepped out from behind William and looked toward the sheriff. "Did you have an easy drive out from town?"

The sheriff turned to look at her. For her, he smiled. It was quick and humorless, but it was a smile. "Yes, I did."

Millie tried to smile back. "Good."

Brad shifted himself so he was in front of Millie again, but Millie didn't care. She had done what she could to start a regular conversation.

No one else offered any topics of conversation. Millie swore she could hear the frost growing on the windowpanes. Finally, she decided she needed to make one more attempt. She moved out from behind Brad again. "We've got a tree to decorate."

"I heard." The sheriff grunted. "That's why I'm here."

"You came to decorate our tree?" Brad asked in amazement.

Millie was glad she wasn't still standing behind Brad. She wouldn't have been able to see the astonishment on Brad's face if she had been. He was cute when he was dumbfounded.

"Not exactly," Sheriff Wall said. He finally took his cap off and held it in his hands. "I came to check out the story I heard that you rode horses back into the gullies to get the tree."

"Of course we rode horses," Brad said. "None of the pickups would have made it in all the snow back there."

The sheriff nodded. "I'm afraid I'll have to ask you to keep the barn locked then."

"What?"

Millie wasn't sure which of the men had asked that question. Maybe it didn't matter. They were all looking at the sheriff like he had forgotten where he was. Or maybe who he was.

"The barn doesn't have a lock," Charlie finally spoke.

"Oh," Sheriff Wall said as he looked at Millie and then studied the floor. "Well, then, I guess you'll just need to be sure that you keep a good eye on the—ah—the suspect so she doesn't steal a horse and ride out of here while she's under surveillance. I can keep an eye on the road through Dry Creek. But if she steals a horse and rides across the land, I'd miss her."

"Me?" Millie figured she was as astonished as the men now. "Steal a horse and ride it away? Across fields and everything?"

"She can't even get off a horse by herself," Randy said from the sidelines. "Probably can't get on one, either."

"She did just fine for a beginner," Brad said. "Nobody knows how to do anything the first time they try it."

"Me?" Millie still couldn't quite believe it. No one

had ever accused her of doing something that adventurous before. "Do you really think I could do that?"

Brad figured he must have had a premonition about his life and that was why he never truly liked Christmas. People sure weren't themselves today, and the only thing that was different was that Christmas was the day after tomorrow. He couldn't believe Millie stood there looking at the sheriff like he had handed her a prize compliment.

"He's saying you would be running from the law," Brad said so she would understand there was nothing complimentary about it.

"Well, technically, it would be *riding* from the law," Sheriff Wall said. He'd stopped looking at the floor, and now, when he talked, he flashed a quick grin at Millie that made him look ten years younger.

Brad snorted. He could see the sheriff liked the look in Millie's eyes. She was looking at him like he had said something very clever. Brad would have been the first to congratulate Sheriff Wall if he had said something useful. But he hadn't. And it didn't matter how young he looked at the moment, the sheriff was too old for Millie.

"Could I learn how to ride a horse that quick?" Millie asked.

Brad started to feel uneasy. Millie looked a little too eager for his comfort.

"It's not about learning anything fast," Brad said. He looked at the sheriff. "You don't have to worry about Millie. Even if she knew how to ride a horse, she'd have more sense than to ride off by herself at this time of year across the fields. It's freezing out there."

"It's not so bad out," Sheriff Wall said as he started to take his jacket off. He still hadn't stopped grinning.

Brad frowned. He was finally getting a good look at the sheriff, and he was realizing what was wrong. He was wearing tennis shoes. That was part of the reason he looked so young. "What happened to your boots?"

"No sense in wearing them today in all the snow."

Brad snorted. "You've worn them in snowdrifts up to your hips. You're not wearing them now because they make you look taller—that's why. They add a good two inches to your height."

The sheriff shrugged. "There's nothing wrong with being short. I'm just being who I am."

Brad grunted. Who did Sheriff Wall think he was kidding? "I don't think many people are going to vote for a sheriff who doesn't wear boots."

"It's not election year for another two years."

"Time goes fast around here."

Millie figured Brad had that all wrong. Time didn't go fast at all. It fact it didn't even seem to crawl. It was frozen now that all the silence had come back.

"Maybe we should have some cocoa," Charlie finally said. He looked at the sheriff. "You're welcome to stay now that we know you've really come courting and not to make things difficult for Millie."

The sheriff looked like he was going to protest, but finally ducked his head in a nod. "Thanks."

"Courting!" Brad protested until Charlie cut in.

"A man's got a right to go courting," Charlie said firmly. "And the sheriff here is a good prospect for some woman. He's got a home—"

"He lives in the Collinses' basement," Brad said. "And that's only in the winter. I don't even know what he does in the summer when the water table rises and the basement's too damp."

"I'm looking around to buy a house," the sheriff said.

"And he's got a good public service job," Charlie continued, just as if Brad had not even spoken.

"A badge doesn't make a man any better," Brad said.

"I'm ready to get married," the sheriff said. "I'm not just looking for a good time, like some men."

Brad figured he was beat. Sheriff Wall was ready to make a commitment. Brad knew most mothers would look at a man like the sheriff and hope their daughters had sense enough to be interested.

Brad didn't like to be rushed. If he ever did get married, he wanted the marriage to be because he wanted to live with that particular woman and not because he had just arrived at some time in his life when he wanted a wife. But that kind of decision took time. The sheriff was as ready to marry as Brad was to date. Brad could never compete with Sheriff Wall if a woman was anxious to get married. And Millie, if she had any sense, would have to see that marriage to a man like the sheriff would solve all her problems.

Brad looked over at Millie. The smile on her face

hadn't changed much since the sheriff started talking. Still, if she was smiling, that had to mean she was interested. Brad wondered if maybe he hadn't been too cautious about marriage in his life.

Millie didn't know why Brad had turned polite. He'd been arguing away with the best of them, and then he stopped and put a tight smile on his face and became quiet.

"Well, how many want cocoa?" Charlie said as he started walking to the small room off the back of the main room. That was Charlie's kitchen.

"I'd like some," Millie said. She turned toward Charlie. "And let me help you."

"No." Charlie shook his head. "You're our company, and the day I put company to work in the kitchen is the day that I retire as cook." Charlie looked around at the men in the room before looking back at Millie. "You sit and visit with the sheriff. Brad can help me."

Millie would have rather helped Charlie with the cocoa than sit and talk with a strange man. She didn't have anything in particular to say to the sheriff, especially since he had announced he was looking for a wife. He might be a little shorter than the other men in the room, but Millie couldn't picture herself being married to him all the same.

Of course, she still had to talk to him. The sheriff had walked over to the tree with her, and they were both looking at it.

"It's not always how big the tree is that counts," Millie remarked. That tree was looking shorter and shorter to her each time she saw it. She looked over at Randy. "You're not cutting more off the bottom, are you?"

"I'm not cutting anything off anywhere," Randy said.

"Maybe the branches are drooping when they thaw," William said as he walked over to look at the tree, too.

"Maybe we can set the stand on a box," Millie suggested. "I'm sure it'll look fine as long as it's up higher."

"And we don't have the decorations on it yet," Jeff chipped in as he carried his plastic bag over to the tree. He pulled out the string of lights again. "I tested these, and they're ready to go."

"But they're pink," the sheriff said as he looked at the lights. "Aren't you worried they'll make everything look a little strange?"

"The lights might look red when they're on the tree," Millie said. "You need to give them a chance."

Sheriff Wall looked at Millie. "You're right. That's the way we do it in Dry Creek. We always give everyone a chance."

Millie thought she might be turning a little pink herself. Not because she was embarrassed, but because she was annoyed. "You don't need to give me a chance. I didn't do anything wrong."

Brad held the mugs of cocoa a little higher. Good for Millie. She wasn't falling for the sheriff. She just stood there beside the tree looking a little fierce, like she was ready to defend something.

"Cocoa?" Brad offered one mug to Millie. "I put extra marshmallows in it for you."

Brad would have dumped the whole bag of miniature marshmallows in the cup if he could have. As it was, the melting tower of marshmallows only stood a half inch over the rim of the mug.

"Thanks." Millie took the cup and gave him a shy smile. "That's the way I like it."

Brad felt like he might be in the running after all. Just to make sure, he added, "That tree is looking pretty good."

"Do you really think so?" Millie looked up at him anxiously. "I'm hoping the decorations will make it look better."

"We've only got six ornaments," Jeff reminded everyone as he pulled one of the shiny red balls from the bag. "There won't be enough to cover the tree."

Everyone looked at the ornament Jeff held up. It had a scratch on one side of the ball, and silver showed through. The ornament was about two inches in diameter and hung a little lopsided from Jeff's fingers.

"I'll make some ornaments," Brad said. He regretted his words the minute they left his mouth. How was he going to make ornaments? Then he remembered a glimpse of a long-forgotten scene. He was with his father, and his father was showing him how to make cowboy ornaments for the Christmas tree. Brad must have been only four years old at the time.

"You will?" Millie's face was lit up. "You'll make ornaments?"

The look on Millie's face must have been what

his own face looked like all those years ago, Brad thought.

"No one's getting me to make anything out of toilet-paper rolls," Jeff muttered. "I don't care what they call those ornaments."

"And this popcorn has too many kernels to string right," Randy added. "I keep poking myself with the needle."

Brad kept looking down at Millie. "All we need is a whole bunch of empty tin cans."

Brad thought he was looking at the prettiest Christmas ornament there was. Millie's smile lit up her whole face, and Brad stopped noticing her glasses altogether. She was beautiful.

"That's one thing we've got is tin cans," Charlie said. He was holding two more mugs of cocoa and gave one each to Randy and Jeff. "We can empty more if we need them."

"We have some old paint in the barn, too." Brad was reluctant to stop looking at Millie, but he figured he'd better. He knew she didn't like a lot of attention coming her way, and he didn't want to spook her off just when he was beginning to think the two of them might have a chance.

"I'm planning to buy a farm in the spring," Brad said, only half realizing he had spoken his words instead of just thinking them.

Everyone turned to Brad and looked puzzled.

Brad cleared his throat. "I had thought some of that old paint might come in handy when I buy my place, but it's better to use what we can now."

Brad was relieved that his explanation seemed to make enough sense to everyone that they didn't pester him anymore about what he had meant. He wasn't ready to answer questions about anything. He hardly knew himself what the tumble of emotions inside of him was about. He was forgetting who he was. He was Brad Parker. He liked women who liked a good time. He wasn't the kind of a man to make a commitment.

Brad stopped for a moment. He'd forgotten the most important thing: Millie. He didn't know much about her, but he did know that she hadn't had an easy life. She deserved a man who was better than Brad Parker and the sheriff combined. She deserved to marry a saint.

Brad looked at her. Everyone in the room had turned their attention back to the Christmas tree. Millie was frowning slightly at it.

"Maybe if we just move this branch," she finally said as she reached out and gently bent one of the branches.

Brad knew the tree was a hopeless cause. He also knew that it was a cause that was important to Millie. He might not be saint enough to marry her, but he sure could do his best with that tree of hers. "I've got some twine we can use if we need it."

Millie smiled gratefully up at him. "Do you think it will work?"

Brad nodded his head. He'd make it work even

if he had to nail more branches on that tree. He was
going to give Millie a good Christmas if he had to use
every nail and tin can on the Elkton ranch.

Chapter Eleven

Millie let go of the sigh she was carrying. Randy had tied his picture angel to the top of the tree, and Charlie had turned off the last of the lamps in the bunkhouse. Everyone was standing in a circle around the tree. Millie decided there was no doubt the scraggly pine was a Christmas tree now that it was all dressed up.

Brad had used a hammer and a nail to pound holes into the sides of dozens of tin cans, and when he put a small candle in the middle of each tin, the candlelight shone through the holes and made hundreds of tiny twinkling stars. The cans themselves had been painted dark red, and some of them had white trim.

Jeff and William had tied the cans to the tree with haying twine before adding the decorations Jeff had bought. The strand of pink lights circled the tree a couple of times, and with the red of the tin cans, the lights actually looked like they belonged.

"It's beautiful," Millie said.

Brad let go of the sigh he was carrying. It had occurred to him when he was halfway through emptying out all of the soup cans in the kitchen that the tree would look homemade with the ornaments he was making. Tin cans couldn't really compete with ornaments a person could buy in the store. He didn't want Millie to be disappointed in the tree. If it wasn't too late to get to Billings and back, he would have dug his way past the drift that usually stopped people and gone out to buy more ornaments right then. Even now he wasn't sure. "You really like it?"

Brad wondered how it could be that, with five other men hovering around the tree, Millie smiled up at him like those tin cans were filled with diamonds instead of holes and it was all due to him.

"It's just like I've always pictured a Christmas tree should look," Millie said softly. "It reminds me of a starry night."

Brad swallowed. The light from the candles flickered over Millie's face in the darkness and then left her in shadow. "I'm glad you like it."

The other men were silent except for the sounds of swallowing or coughing or clearing their throats. Charlie was the only one brave enough to bring out his handkerchief and dab at his eyes.

"That smoke's still hanging around," Charlie muttered after he put his handkerchief back into the pocket of his overalls.

Each of the men had their faces turned toward the Christmas tree. The tree itself was standing on a wooden crate that Jeff had pulled in from the barn.

Charlie had donated a few white dishtowels to cover the tree stand and the crate. Millie had arranged the towels so they looked almost like snowdrifts.

The clock was ticking in the corner of the room, and the fire was crackling a little as it burned in the corner stove, but otherwise it was a silent night.

"It's too bad Mrs. Hargrove isn't here," William said finally. "She'd have us all singing a carol or two—"

Brad wished the older woman were here with them. She'd enjoy the tree.

"Oh, that reminds me," the sheriff said as his hand went to his shirt pocket. Sheriff Wall was wearing a white shirt with broad gray stripes and a black leather vest. "She asked me to give you something when she heard I was coming out here tonight."

The sheriff pulled several blue index cards with printing on them out of his shirt pocket. "These are the visitor forms for the church. In all the commotion, she forgot to have you fill them out this morning, and she felt bad about it."

Charlie frowned. "I didn't know you had to fill out a form to go to church. Is it like voter registration?"

"Nah," Sheriff Wall said as he fanned the cards out and held them out to everyone. "It's just a new program Mrs. Hargrove volunteered to do. I don't really know much about it—I've only gone to church the past month or so, and they didn't have them back then. I think it's just to give Mrs. Hargrove your address or something so she can send you another postcard."

"Mrs. Hargrove knows where we live," Charlie

said, but he took one of the cards anyway. "Still, I guess it's only polite to thank the church for having us, so I guess I'll be filling one out."

After Charlie took a card, he gave a stern look to those around him. Finally, William took a card. Then Randy and Jeff each took one. Brad held his breath when he put his hand out and took one. Millie even took one.

Everyone just looked at his or her card.

"Mrs. Hargrove said something about handing them back to her when Millie comes to town tomorrow to do her community service," the sheriff said. He looked pleased with himself that he had delivered all of the cards. "I'll be happy to come by tomorrow and pick Millie up so she can get started."

"Millie and I will be in town at eight," Brad said. He put the card in his shirt pocket. He was perfectly able to see to Millie. "There's no need for you to drive all the way out here."

"I don't mind," the sheriff said before he shrugged his shoulders and looked at Brad. "Don't suppose it matters, though—I will see you and Millie at eight. I thought maybe we should meet in the café."

"I thought we were going to the church," Millie said. "To take care of the black marks on the floor."

"We'll start out at the café," the sheriff said as he walked toward the closet that held his coat. "We'll be wanting some coffee and the county runs a tab there. Linda showed me where everything was before she left—even her flavored creamers."

"Linda trusted you with the stuff in her café?" Charlie asked. The older man was frowning.

"Yeah," Sheriff Wall said as he opened the closet door and reached for his coat. "Of course she trusts me. I'm sworn to uphold the law."

"That wouldn't have made any difference to Linda a year or so ago," Charlie commented as he walked over to the door. "I guess she's finally growing up. She always struck me as someone who'd rather put poison in a lawman's coffee than creamer. I don't suppose she sits down with you while you drink it, though, does she?"

The sheriff grinned. "Now that you mention it, she does. I guess we all grow up sooner or later."

Sheriff Wall he put his coat on and walked toward the door before turning to the others in the room. "We'll see some of you tomorrow."

Millie smiled. "We'll be there."

"I'll wish the rest of you a Merry Christmas then," the sheriff said as he tipped his hat to the group. "Be sure and watch that tree of yours, or you'll burn the bunkhouse down."

"We'll be fine," Brad said. He had seen the flicker of worry in Millie's eyes. "There's enough snow outside to stop a forest fire anyway."

"That's true," Millie said.

Brad didn't bother to wave to the sheriff as the man opened the door and stepped into the night darkness. Sheriff Wall could find his way home all right. Brad was much more interested in Millie.

"I could bring some snow in if you're worried,"

he offered. He figured the candles would burn for another half hour or so. He wanted Millie relaxed while she watched it. "Just so it's handy if we need it for anything."

Millie was happy. She was having the kind of Norman Rockwell Christmas that she'd imagined. Granted, Christmas Eve wasn't until tomorrow, but she was sitting here with a group of people who had actually decorated a tree.

Millie had always known she could decorate a tree for herself when she was in Seattle. One year she'd even bought some tinsel and lights. But when it came time to get a tree, she didn't. Part of her Christmas dream was to decorate a tree with other people.

"We've got more cocoa," Charlie said as he sat down on one of the leather couches that Jeff had pulled closer to the tree. "It's self-serve in the kitchen."

Millie walked over and sat down on the couch next to Charlie. "You make great cocoa."

Charlie beamed as though she'd handed him a hundred-dollar bill. For the first time that night, Millie remembered what she was doing in Dry Creek. She had a mission, and it had nothing to do with tin-can lights and cocoa.

Millie looked around the room. She didn't feel like a stranger anymore. She wondered how she could fulfill Forrest's request or if it was really necessary.

"The community service won't be hard," Brad said as he sat down on the couch next to Millie. "No one really expects you to work."

Millie had to stop herself from scooting over to sit pressed against Brad.

"*I* expect me to work," Millie said. Her voice was a little sterner than she had intended. She didn't care what Sheriff Wall thought about her and her community service, but Millie hadn't been a slacker before she came to Dry Creek, so there was no reason to start now.

Brad smiled slightly. "I guess I'm not surprised at that."

"We can't all be prima donnas," Millie continued. She didn't want Brad to think she was boring, but she just couldn't summon up the effort to pretend to be carefree. She was a person who obeyed the rules in life, and that was just the way it was.

Brad smiled wider. "No chance of that happening. You won't even let me wait on you."

"You got me cocoa," Millie protested. She wasn't used to a man wanting to help her with her coat and that kind of thing. She was used to doing this for herself *and* a table of other people at the same time. "Besides, I don't need help with much."

Brad stopped smiling. "I scared you with all my talk of spiders before. I'm sorry I did that."

Millie didn't know who had moved, but she was sitting closer to Brad on the sofa than she had been before. She looked around the room. Charlie had gotten up from the sofa and was over by the table. Jeff and Randy had left the room, and she could hear them in the kitchen. William alone sat near the tree.

If Brad only knew, it wasn't spiders she was scared of right now.

"It's okay," Millie said as she tried to move away from Brad without being obvious about it. She was afraid she had been the one to move closer in the first place, and she didn't want him to think she was—

"Oh." Millie realized that as she moved away, Brad moved closer. Maybe she wasn't the one who had moved on the sofa after all.

William got up and left his place beside the tree. Millie looked around. She and Brad were alone in the room. "Everyone's in the kitchen."

"Probably more cocoa." Brad doubted it was a sudden thirst for cocoa that had made the other men give them some privacy, but Brad was glad for the kindness they were showing him.

He wasn't sure if it was good news or bad news that Millie looked so nervous around him all of a sudden. He wished he had another month or two to get to know her before he kissed her again. But he didn't have a month. She would be gone by then for sure. He tried to slide down into the sofa cushions a little more. Maybe she really *didn't* like tall men.

Brad pulled the blue form out of his shirt pocket, more for something to do than because he even remembered what the form was for.

"I wonder what they send you," Millie said. She was looking down at her own form intently.

The Welcome Visitors form was as basic as they came, Brad figured, but he was grateful for it. Even with all of the lamps in the room off, there was enough light from the tree to see what was on the card. There was a graphic of a church on one corner and several printed questions in the middle of the card. One question asked if you would like someone from the church to visit you. The other asked if you had a prayer request. At the bottom, the church said they'd send a special gift to anyone who returned the card with his or her address. That must be what Millie had just read.

"It can't be much," Brad said. "The church doesn't have money to buy people anything. They've been raising money for the past year just to get a new organ for the place."

"Money's tight around here, isn't it?"

"Not so tight that we don't get by," Brad said. He didn't want Millie to think they were poor in Dry Creek. "And when money *is* tight—or someone has a health problem or something—we all chip in and help them over the hump."

Brad wished he'd paid more attention to the accountant he'd paid to do his taxes last year. Brad was so close to having enough to buy a place of his own that he had wanted to ask the man a few questions about buying property in addition to the usual questions about his taxes. "We're not rich by any means, but no one has lost their place or not had enough for some medical care—at least, no one that I've known of, and I've lived here for ten years."

"You mean you haven't always lived here?" Millie asked.

Brad could swear she was surprised. He tried real

hard not to be offended. He knew some women put great stock in men who had traveled and been lots of places. Some of the waitresses he'd known thought travel was the measure of a man. Of course, that might be because they were used to truckers, and a trucker wasn't really a trucker until he'd been to both coasts a few times. But Brad had never had any desire to move around.

"I was born in Illinois," Brad said, "but I like Dry Creek. I don't expect I'll be moving from here."

"But surely you travel?" Millie insisted.

"Not if I don't have to," Brad said. He figured the woman might as well know him. He was a basic kind of a guy. No particular flash. He wasn't one to fly a woman over to Paris for her birthday. Now, he *might* drive her to the coast or up to Canada for a long weekend or something.

Millie didn't seem to have anything to say in response to him not traveling so Brad just sat there on the sofa. He figured his chances were about zero.

"Does anyone in Dry Creek travel?" Millie asked. She was suddenly realizing that she would need to leave in a couple of days. After she completed her community service, there would be no reason to stay in Dry Creek. And she couldn't stay. Once she gave out her Christmas presents, she would be broke. She'd have to go back to work. She accepted that, but she'd hoped that she might see some of the people in Dry Creek again. She'd hoped at least some of them occasionally went to Seattle.

"Mrs. Hargrove flew up to Alaska to see Doris

June a couple of years ago," Brad said. "She liked the moose—they walked right down the streets in Anchorage just like they owned the place."

"Does anyone else go anywhere?"

Brad was silent a minute. "The sheriff goes to conventions every year—he gets around pretty good."

"Oh." Millie blinked and looked down at the card in her hand so that Brad wouldn't see the tears in her eyes. She supposed she was silly to have gotten so attached to the people in this town. Millie looked out of the corner of her eye at Brad. He was sitting a little awkwardly, like he was trying to push himself into the sofa cushions. He had a frown on his face, and he was staring straight ahead at the tree. But Millie wished he was the one who went to conventions. If he went to conventions, he was bound to come to Seattle once in a while.

"I went to a rodeo once," Brad offered.

"Really? Where?"

"Cheyenne."

"Oh." Millie realized that she had never heard of anyone having a rodeo in Seattle.

Brad swore he didn't know how to please a woman. He'd finally realized he could offer a wife some excitement, and Millie sat there looking like it was nothing to her. Of course, he supposed it didn't matter to her where he took any future wife. "Rodeos can be good entertainment."

Millie nodded. "Now that I know more about riding a horse, I can appreciate them more."

Her response certainly didn't ring with enthusiasm. Brad figured he could have suggested a trip to the dentist and gotten the same response. He told himself it was probably just as well. If excitement and travel were important to Millie, it was good that he knew it now.

"I should have gone and gotten some better decorations for the tree," Brad said. The poor thing looked a little forlorn to him just now, even though the candles were all still burning brightly and he had arranged branches so that he'd covered the bald spots on the tree. Why had he thought that tin-can ornaments could compete with the shiny new balls that people expected on their trees these days?

"I love that tree," Millie said fiercely.

"Really?"

Millie nodded firmly. "It's beautiful."

"Yes," Brad agreed, even though he'd stopped watching the tree and was watching Millie watch the tree. The candlelight reflected off her glasses and cast a golden glow all over her face. When had her face become the only one he wanted to look at? Her hair still didn't have any more brass in it, and she still didn't wear any of the makeup that he'd thought looked so good on most women. But she was beautiful.

Brad moved a little closer on the sofa. Millie didn't move away. He took that as a sign of encouragement and moved closer still. Millie did look up at him when he did that. But she didn't move away. Instead, she gave him a shy smile.

Brad moved all the way closer and put his arm on the sofa behind Millie.

Millie forgot about how much she would miss Brad when she left. She forgot about the fact that she was a cautious woman and not at all the kind of woman men like Brad wanted to date. All she could think about was the moment she was living.

Brad had his arm around her, and they were looking at the most beautiful Christmas tree she had ever seen. The light from the candles danced between the pine branches of the tree and reflected off the bottoms of the tin cans. The pink lights added a softness to the shadows the branches cast.

Millie was having her Christmas. The Norman Rockwell one Forrest had wanted her to have.

"I owe him an apology," Millie spoke without thinking.

"Who?" Brad said as he moved his arm from the back of the sofa to her shoulders.

Millie felt enclosed and happy. "Just a friend."

Millie took a good look around her. She wanted to remember this Christmas for the rest of her life. She hoped she'd remember the feel of Brad's arm around her as well as the flickering light of the candles on the Christmas tree. She'd never experienced anything like it yet in her life, and she wasn't hopeful enough to expect another one to come along. But she sure would be grateful if it ever did.

Chapter Twelve

Millie could smell the coffee the minute she stepped out of her car in front of the café in Dry Creek. It was only eight o'clock in the morning, but she felt like she had been up for hours already. She hadn't slept well and had to admit she was feeling annoyed with life in general. She didn't know what was wrong with her today.

Well, maybe she did know, she thought as she shut her car door. But there was nothing to be done about it. Last night had shown her what Christmas was all about, and the experience had made her feel more alone than she'd ever felt in her life.

No wonder her foster mother had never bothered with Christmas.

A sentimental Christmas wasn't worth it when a person had to go back to her real life. And for her, Millie thought, real life consisted of waiting on tables of complaining, demanding people at Ruby's cafe.

"I guess the sheriff is here."

Millie looked up at Brad when he spoke. He had driven behind her into Dry Creek after she had refused his offer to ride in his pickup with him. For some reason, she wanted to be alone in her old car. She certainly didn't want to be sitting next to Brad. The wind made his lips white and his face red, but he didn't seem in any hurry to step past her and go into the café.

The morning itself was dreary. The sun was hidden behind thick gray clouds, which probably meant snow was coming later today. The snow that had fallen yesterday was tramped down around the café and didn't look as clean as it had yesterday. A film of dirt had settled over everything.

"I hate snow," Millie announced.

Brad only grunted. "Everybody can't live at the beach."

"I don't live at the beach," Millie protested. She rented a small apartment so close to the docks that she perpetually smelled fish. She tried hard to convince herself the neighborhood was charming. "It's the waterfront, and that's altogether different."

Now that Millie thought about it, she didn't know what she had against snow. The weather on the docks in Seattle could be just as wet and almost as cold as Montana in winter. Maybe she had just always hated snow because it reminded her of all those days she'd spent with her foster family in Minnesota. She had moved to Seattle five years ago to start a new life. Some days, though, it felt like her new life was just a repeat of her old life. All that had changed were the people sitting around the tables that she waited on.

"It's all by the water," Brad said. His lips were pressed into a line that could not be mistaken for even the smallest of smiles. "I know there's fancy prices at the coast, but living by the water doesn't make a man a better man. There's nothing wrong with a bit of snow. Lots of good men live in the snow."

Millie didn't have a chance to answer because Brad started walking up the steps to the café. His boots stomped on each step, one at a time, until he reached the top.

Brad figured he had ruined any chance he'd ever had with Millie. But, he said to himself as he opened the door, it was probably just as well. There was no point in imagining how much fun he and Millie would have on a real date when he knew the price he'd have to pay when she left. The simple fact was, they had no future and he was wise to realize that.

Brad stood to the side and held the door for Millie.

He smelled cinnamon on her when she walked by. Millie had helped Charlie prepare an early breakfast this morning, and Brad couldn't help but notice she had been not only civil, but downright nice to Charlie. In fact, Millie had had a smile for all of the men in the bunkhouse…except for him.

Brad wondered when everything had changed with him and Millie. She'd seemed to like his arm around her last night. She had even snuggled up against him the little while they sat and looked at that tree.

It was the tree's fault, Brad decided. No good ever

came from taking a pathetic little pine tree and dressing it up like it was something to stare at. It gave rise to all kinds of hopes in a man's chest that just simply weren't going to come true. Maybe there was a good reason he'd never liked Christmas, Brad told himself as he followed Millie into the café. Maybe he didn't like Christmas because he had the sense to be content with his lot in life and wasn't given to empty dreaming.

Christmas was nothing but a promise that hadn't come true in his life. Maybe it did for some people, but it hadn't for him.

"Good morning," the sheriff called out in greeting to Brad and Millie, just as if he were blind and not able to see they were miserable. "Looks like it'll be a good day."

"It's overcast," Brad said. "It'll probably snow later, unless it's too warm to snow—then it'll be some kind of icy slush."

Brad didn't know how any man could be optimistic with the thought of slush falling on him later in the day, though the sheriff seemed like he could be. At least he didn't flinch when Brad informed him of the prospect.

"I got the coffee ready for you, but I'm going to need to go into Miles City. I have some official work to get done," Sheriff Wall said as he started to put his coat back on.

Brad could see that several cups, napkins and spoons had been set out on one of the tables. Someone had even folded the napkins, and Brad was sure it hadn't been the café owner, Linda, because the corners were all crooked. When Linda bothered to fold napkins, she got them straight.

"Thanks," Brad said, even though he figured the sheriff wasn't listening to him since he was looking at Millie. Sheriff Wall was as pathetic as he was, Brad figured by looking at him. Maybe the sheriff was worse, Brad decided. At least Brad hadn't tried folding napkins to impress Millie.

"Did you sleep all right last night?" the sheriff asked Millie just as though he cared.

Millie nodded. Brad had to give her points for knowing to be cautious about the sheriff. Of course, he then took some points away when she smiled at Sheriff Wall as she said thank-you. A simple thank-you would have been enough. She didn't need to smile at the man. The lawman would be out folding more than napkins if Millie didn't tone down those smiles.

"I'll be back in a few hours," the sheriff continued. "Might even make it back for lunch. Mrs. Hargrove promised to make us her special meat loaf with black olives—it's her Christmas special."

Millie longed with all her heart to have a special Christmas recipe that people knew about. Since she usually worked on all of the holidays, her Christmas special was whatever the chef had made for the day. And the only reason people asked her for it was because she was their waitress. Most of them didn't even know her name.

"Maybe I'll ask for her recipe—unless it's a secret." Millie looked at Brad. "Do you think it's a secret?"

"I doubt it. It's hard to keep anything a secret in Dry Creek."

Millie didn't point out that *she* still had a secret. Maybe that's why she was feeling so cranky today. She had a secret and she didn't want to keep it a secret. She wanted to tell Brad what she was doing and why she was in Dry Creek.

"Well, I guess I better get going," the sheriff said as he nodded his head at Millie. "Besides, I see Mrs. Hargrove coming, so you guys will be getting down to work in no time."

Millie smiled goodbye to the sheriff. She guessed the spilling of secrets would have to wait until she got the floors in the church all scrubbed.

Thinking of the floors made Millie feel more cheerful. There was nothing like getting rid of black marks to make a person feel like they had accomplished something in a day. She might not have a special Christmas recipe, but she did have a special cleaning method.

"Aren't you worried about what she's going to put on those floors?" Brad asked the sheriff, just to remind the man that it hadn't been that long ago that he thought Millie was planning some kind of a crime. The sheriff had made that remark about the water supply and hadn't followed up. Brad wondered what kind of a lawman the sheriff was.

"Naw," the sheriff said as he waved goodbye. "I ran her through the system and got enough information on her to put my mind at ease. Besides, I have a buddy on the Seattle police force."

"Does that mean I don't have to do the floors?" Millie asked.

The sheriff stopped with his hand on the door. "Well, you still broke into the place…"

Brad held his breath. If Millie didn't have to do the floors, she didn't have to stay at all. He thought he at least had today to convince her to stay. He was glad she had the community service. If there was one thing he knew about Millie, it was that she didn't take the easy road anywhere.

Millie nodded. "I would do them anyway. I just wanted to know if anything was going on my official record."

The sheriff went a little pink at this.

"Don't worry," Brad said. "Unless I miss my guess, the sheriff didn't even file the report. He hates paperwork."

Sheriff Wall left the café as Mrs. Hargrove entered it, and they nodded to each other.

"Good, the coffee's on," the older woman said as she unwound a wool scarf that she'd worn around her head. "There's nothing like a cup of coffee to get me going in the morning."

Mrs. Hargrove drank her cup of coffee while she was standing on the welcome mat in the front of the café. "I got snow on my boots coming over here, and I don't want to track up this clean floor. We have enough to do with getting one floor clean. No point in adding another floor to the list."

Millie looked at Mrs. Hargrove. She was wearing a navy parka over a pink gingham dress. Forrest had told Millie that Mrs. Hargrove usually wore a gingham dress in some color or another.

"You don't want to get your dress dirty," Millie said. "Brad and I brought lots of old clothes if you'd like to borrow some."

When Millie left the bunkhouse, Charlie had insisted on giving her old flannel shirts to take with her and several pairs of men's overalls.

"They're full of holes," Charlie had said when he handed the two bags to Millie. "So you might want to wear a couple of the shirts at the same time—mostly the holes aren't in the same places."

Millie looked at the older woman. "I've got the old clothes in the trunk of my car. I thought I'd take them over to the church and put them on there."

"Makes sense, since the church is heated. Pastor Matthew said he went over and turned the heat on at seven this morning, so it should be comfortable by now. And don't you worry about these dresses of mine—they all wash up fine," Mrs. Hargrove said. "I haven't met the stain yet that I couldn't figure out— except for the black marks on the church's floor. I'm anxious to see how this baking soda idea of yours works."

"Oh," Millie remembered. "The sheriff didn't leave me the box of baking soda he said he had in his office."

"Don't worry," Mrs. Hargrove said as she patted the pocket of her parka. "I brought a small box that I had. It's brand-new—never been opened. Don't know if that makes a difference or not, but I'm not taking any chances. Those black marks have been bothering me for years now."

Millie knew how easily water splashed, and that was why she had worried about Mrs. Hargrove's clothing. She'd never once expected the woman to help her clean the floor. But it was clear when she, Brad and Mrs. Hargrove walked up the steps of the church ten minutes later that the older woman expected to scrub.

"Oh, no," Millie said as she took the final step up to the church. She had her purse strapped around her neck, and her hands were free. Her long wool coat kept her warm even though the air was cold. Millie stopped to take a breath. "You don't need to get down on your knees or anything. There's plenty of cleaning you can do without that."

"Maybe you could dust the rails of some of the pews," Brad suggested. He had carried up both bags of old clothes even though Millie had protested.

"You mean sit down while the real work is going on?" Mrs. Hargrove asked as she turned the doorknob on the church's outer door. "Nothing ever got cleaned by someone sitting down and taking a swipe at a little bit of dust. Besides, the pews will be cleaned later this morning. The twins do that when it's the Curtis family's turn at cleaning. I think they pretend the pews are dragons."

Millie knew the twins liked dragons. What she

didn't know was that they cleaned the church. "Aren't they too young?"

"Too young. Too old," Mrs. Hargrove said as they stepped into the church. "Sometimes it seems that all of the work at the church is being done by the people you wouldn't expect."

Millie and Brad followed Mrs. Hargrove into the church.

"Of course, that's the beauty of it," Mrs. Hargrove said as she stood in the entryway to the church and unwound the scarf from her head again. "The Bible talks about the weak being made strong and the slave being made free. I figure that since the very beginning, the church has been surprised by what people can do and be."

"But that was a long time ago, wasn't it? The beginning, that is." Millie was remembering the time when she'd gone to church with her foster mother and the woman had told her that Jesus lived thousands of years ago and so had no meaning for today.

Mrs. Hargrove shrugged her shoulders. "God says a thousand years are but a day to Him. The way I see it, we're still in the early days with God and will be for a long time at that rate."

"You said there were scrub brushes around?" Brad asked. Just because God had all day didn't mean Brad did. He figured if he got the floor cleaned in the church before lunch, then maybe Millie would agree to go riding horseback again with him this afternoon. If he could get her leaning into him on the horse again, maybe he could talk to her and he could ask her to stay in Dry Creek for a little longer.

Brad decided he needed his head examined. Women didn't just stay in Dry Creek while they waited for some man to get to know them. No, he needed a better plan than that.

"Brad?" Millie asked for the second time. Brad was standing there, muttering to himself and frowning. He hadn't even heard her the first time she said his name.

"Huh?"

Brad focused on her, but she couldn't help but notice that his face turned a little pink at the same time.

"Mrs. Hargrove said the brushes are on the shelf above the sink in the kitchen. Do you know where that is?"

"Yeah, sure," Brad said as he started to walk toward the small room on the side of the church. "I was just going to get them."

When Brad stepped into the kitchen, Millie turned to Mrs. Hargrove. "I hope he's okay."

The older woman chuckled. "Oh, he's okay, all right."

"He seems a little distracted."

The older woman chuckled even harder. "I'd say that's a fair bet."

Millie frowned. She'd hoped to have another conversation with Brad like the one she'd had yesterday, and that didn't seem too likely if he was going to be distracted by something as simple as brushes.

"Is there a restroom where I can change?"

"Right through there, dear. The second door on your left."

Millie ended up wearing two flannel shirts and one of Charlie's old coveralls. She needed some twine to belt the overalls tight to her waist so they didn't flap around too much, but outside of that, everything had adjusted to her.

Millie decided it was a good thing she'd changed when she first got to the church. If she'd waited ten minutes, she never would have changed. That's when Pastor Matthew and his two boys came over to the church.

Millie had already started to scrub the first black mark. If she hadn't already been on her knees, the sight of Pastor Matthew would have put her there.

The minister wore an apron. Well, maybe it wasn't so much an apron as it was a dishtowel tied around his waist. But Millie could hardly believe what she was seeing. "He's going to start cleaning."

"I thought I told you it was the Curtis family's turn to clean the church this week," Mrs. Hargrove said. The older woman was sitting on one of the pews near Millie sorting through a box of crayons from one of the Sunday School classrooms. She had finally agreed to observe instead of scrub, since there were only two scrub brushes and Brad insisted he was going to take one and scrub beside Millie.

Millie had her scrub brush in one hand and water stains on her overalls. She'd clipped her hair back as best she could with the barrettes she had in her purse. She still couldn't believe it when she saw Pastor Matthew go into the kitchen with a mop. "But he's the minister!"

"I hope you're not saying that men can't scrub floors," Brad said. Millie looked over at him. He had speckles of black on his face and his forehead was damp. He had been working on some black marks about ten feet away from her, and Millie had to admit he was doing a good job.

"Well, ah, no, I wasn't saying that exactly." Millie wondered what she *had* been meaning to say. Of course, she knew that some men worked at cleaning. She'd seen janitors before. But, somehow, even with the janitors, she'd always assumed that they never cleaned or helped out at home.

"I'm just surprised that a minister would be doing the cleaning," Millie finally said. "Isn't he the boss?"

Mrs. Hargrove chuckled. "He'd be the first to tell you that he's not."

Millie couldn't figure it all out.

"When was the last time you did this?" Millie demanded as she sat back and looked straight at Brad. Even he must not clean regularly.

Brad stopped scrubbing. "Me?"

Millie nodded.

"I've never done this before," Brad said.

Ah, Millie thought to herself, she was right.

"At least not here," Brad continued. "But I do my share of cleaning up after other people. Just ask Charlie. We all take turns."

Millie frowned. This isn't what she expected. But

even if Brad was willing to clean something on occasion, that didn't explain why the minister would.

"I thought ministers told people what to do," Millie said finally. She was puzzled. She had always thought that getting close to God would mean that she'd be run ragged doing errands for Him. He was powerful and He was male. That meant there would be no end to doing things for Him. "He should tell somebody to scrub the floor."

Mrs. Hargrove nodded. "I know it seems like that's the way it would work. But God has turned everything upside down."

Millie felt like she was the one who'd been turned upside down. Why would someone who could order others around do anything? "And where's Glory?"

"I think she's painting a scene for the pageant," Mrs. Hargrove said as she put the blue crayons in a plastic bag and tied a knot in the bag. "Everyone decided to try a simpler pageant this year, but we still wanted it to be nice."

Millie wasn't so sure she wanted to talk about God, but she wanted to talk about the Christmas pageant even less. It seemed like every time anyone brought up the Christmas pageant, they also brought up Forrest. When Millie thought of Forrest, she remembered those Christmas stockings in her trunk and wondered if she'd ever be able to fulfill Forrest's final request.

"But who does all the praying if the minister scrubs the floor?" Millie asked. She remembered the blue card in her pocket and pulled it out. "It asks for things to pray about here—I thought the minister would do all that."

Millie figured the church must pull in lots of prayer requests each week. It would keep the minister busy praying for all of them.

"Well, he certainly does some of it. But we all pray," Mrs. Hargrove said as she looked at the blue card. "I'm glad to see the sheriff got the cards to you. Have you filled one out yet? I'm happy to take yours and put it with the others."

"I'll do it when I finish scrubbing." Millie put the card back in her pocket. She hadn't been going to fill one out. She had told herself there was no point. She thought God didn't care about her or the things that worried her. But now she was beginning to wonder if she had been wrong. Maybe He did care.

"Can I put down a secret request?" Millie asked. She didn't know how to name some of the longings she was starting to feel. But if God were as smart as everyone seemed to think, He would know what she meant.

"Of course." Mrs. Hargrove nodded. "That sounds fine."

Millie went back to scrubbing.

"The baking soda is working," Millie said as she rinsed off the piece of floor she'd just scrubbed. Millie leaned back on her heels and stretched her back.

Mrs. Hargrove stood up and walked over to where Millie had scrubbed. "Why—my goodness—it sure is! What a blessing!"

"I'm glad it's working."

Millie liked looking around the church when it was almost empty like this. Brad had moved over by the pulpit to scrub the floor there, and Mrs. Hargrove still stood next to where Millie was scrubbing. The Christmas tree Millie had noticed on Sunday looked even more humble as it stood beside the pulpit.

"We decorated a tree last night, too," Millie told Mrs. Hargrove. "It's a homemade one like the one here. It's beautiful."

Mrs. Hargrove nodded. "Sometimes they're the best ones. The Sunday school classes made the decorations for the tree here."

"Brad made our decorations."

Brad looked up from where he was scrubbing. His knees ached, and they felt stuck to the wet floor. But even with all that, his knees went weak when he saw the look on Millie's face as she talked about the decorations. She was describing their tree to Mrs. Hargrove, and it was apparent that any annoyance she might have felt toward him this morning was not felt toward the Christmas tree back at the bunkhouse.

Millie loved that old pathetic Christmas tree.

Brad was watching Millie and didn't pay any attention to the shadow that was passing beside him.

"So, that's the way it is," Pastor Matthew said quietly.

Brad looked up. "It's the tree she likes. She doesn't have much use for me."

Pastor Matthew smiled. "Well, we don't know that for sure, do we?"

Brad figured he did know, but he didn't want to

contradict the man. Brad just waited for what he was sure was coming next. A minister was supposed to say something about faith and God and how everyone should reach for the impossible. But the minister didn't say anything, so finally Brad added, "I wouldn't think there's any point in praying about something like this."

Brad waited a minute for the pastor to disagree with him. Finally, Brad could no longer contain his feeling of hope. "Is there?"

Pastor Matthew smiled. "God cares about love, if that's what you're asking."

"I wasn't thinking that—" Brad swallowed and then stopped. "I mean it wouldn't be right to ask God something like this—I mean, He doesn't cast love spells or anything, does He? Something that would make Millie stay around awhile so she could get to know me."

Pastor Matthew smiled. "Maybe not love spells, but He can work miracles, and less than that seems to be required here. After we finish, stop by my house for a few minutes, and we'll pray about it. Glory's over painting the scenery for the pageant and we can have some privacy. That is, if you want it to be private."

Brad glanced at Millie. He sure did want it to be private. He didn't know what she would think if he said a prayer about her staying in Dry Creek. Come to think of it, he didn't know what he thought about it himself. He'd never prayed about anything before that he could remember.

"God might not know me." Brad thought he should mention the fact to the minister. "We don't exactly talk."

Pastor Matthew nodded. "I figured that might be the way it is."

Brad looked around the church. It wasn't just Millie who might find it odd if he decided to pray. The guys in the bunkhouse would never understand. Brad looked back at the minister. "This is confidential, right? I mean, seeing a minister is like seeing a lawyer, isn't it? You can't tell anyone, can you?"

Pastor Matthew smiled. "My lips are sealed."

Brad nodded. That was good. He didn't need a rumor going around that Brad Parker was in such deep trouble with his love life that he had to ask God to help him. Because, of course, he wasn't in deep trouble. Not really. Was he?

Chapter Thirteen

Millie had heard about the old barn that the town of Dry Creek had turned into a community center. There hadn't been cows in the barn for years, and someone had added heaters to the building when they had the Christmas pageant inside it a couple of years ago. The wood plank floor of the barn was scrubbed clean, and the unfinished wood had a weathered look to it.

The middle of the barn was the stage, and chairs had been set up all around the walls of the barn. High, tall windows let light into the area and several bales of hay were pushed against the far wall. The faint scent of paint thinner filled the cold, moist air inside the barn.

Millie looked up and saw the pulleys on the rafters that allowed the angel to swing down over the audience during the pageant. When Forrest had tried to kill the angel, he had waited until after she made her swing out and back. In fact, the pageant was over when he'd pulled out his gun. Forrest had been able to hide behind some tall screens that had been placed around and, at first, no one had seen that he had his gun pointed at the angel.

There were no screens anymore. In fact, as Millie looked around, she saw a shiny new lock on the back door to the barn and there were no places to hide behind screens or curtains or large chairs. Even the hay was pushed firmly against the wall.

Forrest would have been saddened to see how his actions had made the people of Dry Creek feel unsafe. The lock on the barn wasn't the only new lock Millie had seen as she walked over to the barn from the church.

The day was still cold and Millie didn't have any snow boots to wear, so she had walked in the path of several tire tracks to avoid the loose snow that was lying on the ground. Brad had said he needed to discuss something with the minister and had gone off with him, telling Millie he would meet her later over at the barn.

Millie was glad to have a few minutes alone and lingered in the doorway to the barn for just a minute. The snow that was predicted for today was still not falling. The clouds had gotten grayer, though, and the air felt weighted. Something about the day matched her restlessness—like she was carrying around something cold and heavy inside of herself and she needed to let go of it just like the clouds needed to let go of their moisture.

It was those Christmas stockings, she said to herself. When she put the money in them and delivered them, she would have done all she could in memory of Forrest. She would be released from the guilt she felt on behalf of him.

When that was done, she would be able to leave Dry Creek, she told herself. The tie she felt holding her here would be gone. Her life would go back to the way it was, and she would have to try and be content.

Millie stepped all of the way inside the barn and quietly closed the door. The day was so overcast that someone had turned on the electrical lights that were attached to some of the rafters.

The pastor's wife, Glory, was kneeling in the middle of the stage area and painting what looked like a trellis. Old newspapers were spread around underneath wooden figures. Several open cans of paint sat around on the newspapers.

"May I take a look?" Millie asked.

Glory looked up from her paints and smiled. "You can take more than a look. You're welcome to pick up a brush and join me."

Millie walked over to where Glory was painting.

Large wooden cutout figures were lying on the floor beside Glory. Some of them had been painted and some of them were still raw wood. Millie counted three sheep.

"Is that a dog?" If the cutout had been any less like a dog, Millie would have assumed it was supposed to be a sheep.

Glory nodded. "I'm afraid that over the years, our pageant has picked up some additional characters that you won't find in the Biblical account of the Nativity.

One of them is a dog named Chester. He's supposed to be a sheepdog, but everyone knows Chester just shows up anywhere in the pageant."

Millie knelt down and sat the same way Glory was sitting with her legs crossed. "I thought Chester was a real dog."

Millie remembered Forrest telling her about the dog that chased the chicken in the Christmas pageant he had seen two years ago.

Glory nodded. "He is. This is the committee's way of compromising. They decided not to have any live animals in the pageant this year, but they did ask that we make a cutout of Chester just like we have a cutout of the sheep. It's to keep the children happy. They all like having Chester in the pageant."

"It seems like in a barn you would have real animals," Millie said.

Glory nodded. "It was a difficult decision to cut back this year. But people just didn't seem to have the heart to put on a full-scale pageant. Usually we invite some of the area churches, but this year we're just doing it simple and for ourselves."

Millie didn't want to ask why the people of Dry Creek were having a difficult time. She was afraid she knew.

"It's the economy," Glory added. "Everybody just seems a little more worried this year than last."

"Oh, the economy," Millie said. That wasn't so bad. "It's tough all over."

Glory looked up from her painting and smiled. "Is that what happened to you? Did you lose your job?"

Glory was friendly and her questions didn't have any sting in them.

Millie shook her head. "I still have my job. I'm on a break. It might not be much of a job, but it's waiting there for me when I go back in a few days."

"Well, that's good," Glory said as she picked up a brush and dipped it into a small can of black paint. "It seems like around here everyone is looking for work. It's always worse at Christmas. My husband keeps thinking about adding another part-time person to the staff at the hardware store just to give someone a little help."

"That's nice of him," Millie said as she looked over the brushes. If she wasn't careful, she would be telling all of her worries to Glory, and she didn't want to do that. She would keep Forrest's secret until she could fulfill his request.

Millie nodded her head at the cutout animals. "Would you like me to paint one of the figures? If there's something simple, that is."

"Take any one of the sheep," Glory said. "Just paint it all white, and then we'll go back and paint on the hooves and the face."

Millie ran out of white paint after she painted two of the sheep.

"I think they had black sheep back then," Glory said as she passed the black can of paint. "At least it's a better color than the brown we're using for the donkey."

"There wouldn't be a black sheep at the Nativity scene, would there?" Millie asked dubiously.

Glory chuckled. "I don't know why not—the church always seems to specialize in black sheep."

Millie picked up a brush and dipped it into the black paint. She was beginning to think that the church was nothing like she had ever thought it would be.

The afternoon light had darkened by the time Millie finished all of the sheep.

"This one looks a little hungry," Millie said. Glory had given her suggestions on how to paint the sheep's faces, but then had left it up to Millie. "I hope the children don't mind."

Each of the cutout animals had straps on the back where a child was going to hold it during the pageant.

"The twins have already suffered their own disappointment. They wanted me to make some dragons, but I drew the line. I said I'd do Chester, but that was it. No dragons." Glory gave Millie a rueful look. "I think they wanted to surprise the angel when she comes out and says 'Behold, I bring you glad tidings.'"

Millie had never actually read the Bible. "There aren't…?"

Glory shook her head. "No. But the twins swear there should have been. I think they figure if Mary and Joseph had come in riding a dragon, the innkeeper would have given them better accommodations."

"That's kind of cute."

Glory sighed and stood up. "Yeah, they're hard to say no to. In fact—" Glory walked over to the bales and picked up two cutout figures that had been lying on top of them "—I made them these little ones for later—after the pageant."

Millie smiled at the two little dragon figures Glory had made. They were both still unpainted.

"Mrs. Hargrove is going to flunk us all in Sunday school if they use these in the pageant," Glory said.

Both Millie and Glory heard the voices of the men and looked toward the entrance of the barn. Pastor Matthew and Brad opened the door and stepped inside the barn.

"How's it coming?" Pastor Matthew asked.

"Good," Glory said.

Millie nodded and smiled.

Pastor Matthew walked over to Glory and gave her a kiss. Brad walked over to Millie, and she had a moment's panic that he meant to kiss her, as well.

"I painted a black sheep," Millie blurted out, and turned to walk back to where the animal cutouts were.

Well, Brad thought to himself, he guessed Pastor Matthew was right when he said God didn't hand out any love potions to people. Millie hadn't gazed up to him with anything near the look of adoration that Glory had on her face when she turned toward her husband.

Of course, Brad decided, it might be too soon for Millie to feel that settled, married love that Glory seemed to feel. Maybe a love potion would start out different—maybe there'd be a tingling sensation or something.

"Are you feeling okay?" Brad asked as Millie walked away from him. "Not dizzy or anything?"

"My one leg has a cramp in it," Millie said as she turned to him and then sat down. "It must be the way I was sitting. How did you know?"

"Oh, ah, there's a lot of paint fumes in here. I figured they might be affecting everyone."

"I don't think they'd give me a leg cramp," Millie said and stretched her leg out in front of her. "Unless it's some kind of slow-acting poison or something."

Brad had to congratulate himself. He'd just witnessed the opposite of a love potion. Millie wasn't even smiling at him now. In fact, she was frowning at him. He couldn't have done a worse job of it if he'd tried.

Brad sighed. He wasn't the kind of man who could be subtle. He'd just have to plough forward and hope that Pastor Matthew's God would have mercy on him.

"I wouldn't worry about it—the fumes aren't poisonous. I'm sure they haven't affected you at all. And that's good you're able to be around the paint fumes and not get sick," Brad said. He needed to get it out there before she started thinking she had the plague. "You know there's a job that's going to be opening up soon at the hardware store. Probably working with paint some. It might be a natural fit for you."

Brad decided Millie was looking at him like he'd sprouted another ear. "Some people really enjoy working in the hardware store."

"I've always worked in restaurants."

"Well, maybe Linda needs someone to help her

out in the café," Brad said. She wasn't making this easy for him.

"The café's closed."

"Well, now it is, sure—but it'll open again when Linda gets back from Los Angeles."

Brad didn't know how a man could break a sweat when the air in the barn was cold. Maybe he was the one getting sick from the fumes.

"Do you think she'd hire me?" Millie asked. Brad swore he saw a flare of hope in her eyes before it died. "After all this fuss about me breaking in and all. I mean, she might think I was planning to rob her."

"Oh."

"Of course I wasn't robbing her," Millie added. "It's just that—"

Brad nodded. He needed another prayer session with the pastor. After they'd talked and prayed, Brad had begun to have hope that Millie would stay in Dry Creek long enough for the two of them to have a proper courtship. He didn't think Millie was the kind of woman who would get engaged after knowing a man for only a day or two.

No, he needed some time to show her they would be good together. It didn't seem like it was such a big miracle for God to perform. It didn't require bringing someone back to life from the dead or parting a sea or anything. All Brad needed was a little time.

"How's your car doing?" Brad asked. That car might be his best hope. If the thing broke down, Millie would be around for at least a week while they sent away for parts.

"Fine," Millie said.

Brad nodded. He'd pray about that car of hers. He wasn't even sure you could call it a miracle if the car broke down before she left Dry Creek. In fact, it would probably be a miracle if it *didn't* break down. All he needed to do was have her drive it around until it died. He might not even need any prayer to pull this off. A full tank of gas might be all he needed.

Millie decided Brad was right about the paint fumes. They certainly seemed to be affecting him. One minute he was frowning, and the next minute he looked perfectly happy.

"I'll go open the door," Millie said as she stood up. The air outside was cold, but it was better to be a little cold than to be affected by those fumes.

When Millie opened the door, she saw that it was starting to snow. Tiny flakes were drifting to the ground. "It's snowing."

"We should get your car back to the ranch before the roads get slippery," Brad said as he walked over and stood behind her.

"I could ride back with you," Millie said.

"Really?" Brad looked happy and then he looked stern. "No, it's better if you drive your car back. Wouldn't want to leave it in Dry Creek. And your tank is almost full, isn't it?"

Millie nodded. She knew to fill her tank in Miles City. Brad was right. She did like to have her car close by just in case. Besides, she still had those stockings in the trunk.

"You might want to drive it out to the barn when

you get back to the ranch, too. Get some more practice driving in the snow. And then you'll want to drive it back tonight for the pageant."

Millie nodded again. She definitely needed her car tonight. It was nice of Brad to realize that, especially since he'd seemed so intent this morning on keeping her car off of the roads.

Chapter Fourteen

Millie stood outside the bunkhouse of the Elkton Ranch and stared down at the contents of her car's trunk. The sun was setting and light snow was still falling. It had been snowing for several hours, but Charlie had said the roads were not in danger of being blocked.

Charlie seemed particularly pleased that there was no reason to worry about the roads. He'd already convinced all of the men in the bunkhouse to drive into Dry Creek tonight to see the Christmas pageant.

It was the Christmas pageant that was causing Millie's frown. She had just slipped a hundred-dollar bill into each of the red stockings she'd made, and she'd stacked the stockings alphabetically in two neat piles in the trunk of her car. She was all ready to deliver the stockings, but she didn't know how to do it now.

At first, she had thought she would go to the barn before the pageant and lay the stockings around the room on the chairs. But then she realized it would create a lot of fuss, and she didn't want to take anything away from the pageant.

No, she decided, she'd have to deliver the stockings after the pageant. Maybe she could just leave them inside the barn door on the bench where people sat when they needed to take off their snow boots. Everyone would see them on their way out of the barn.

When Millie made her decision, she expected the heavy feeling inside of her to lift. She had almost completed her task. It hadn't gone as Forrest probably thought it would, but she would be able to deliver the hundred-dollar bills and finish what she had started. She should feel good, not sad.

After all, things were working out. Millie figured she was still a stranger to most people in Dry Creek—at least as much of a stranger as Forrest had been when he had been here. He'd only been in the little town a few days, as well. When she left, even the people she had met would eventually forget her name and what she looked like.

She would truly be a Christmas stranger.

And that, Millie finally admitted, was why she was sad. The people of Dry Creek might forget her, but she would never forget them. Not Glory, or Charlie, or Mrs. Hargrove. And especially not Brad.

Of course, Brad would forget her, Millie decided in a burst of irritation. The man couldn't wait for her to get in her car and drive off somewhere. He didn't even seem to care where she was going. She could have suggested she drive to the moon, and he would have encouraged her to do it. Just to please him, she'd already driven up and down the driveway into the Elkton ranch several times this afternoon.

Millie looked over toward the bunkhouse. The last time she'd parked her car this afternoon, she'd deliberately parked so she could see in the big window in the living room. Frost had edged the window, but she could still see the little Christmas tree on the opposite wall.

That tree would always be her favorite Christmas tree, even though Millie vowed she would decorate one for herself next Christmas. Something about this Christmas had changed the feeling she had inside that she needed to be on the outside looking in at Christmas.

Maybe it was going to church here and seeing the people all work together. Or being Christmas company at the bunkhouse. Or even riding out to get the Christmas tree with Brad.

Maybe it was all of it. She supposed it didn't matter. What mattered was that she no longer felt so alone. Not even, she swallowed, when she was leaving.

There, she thought to herself, she'd said it. She was leaving Dry Creek.

She really had no choice. She knew the job at the hardware store was a charity job and was meant for someone in Dry Creek. The pastor hadn't created the job to give it to someone who had just come into town. It might be an option to work at the café, but Linda was gone and there was no one to ask about working there.

It wasn't the stockings in the trunk that were bothering her, Millie finally admitted. It was her small suitcase that was sitting next to them. Millie had slipped the suitcase out of the bunkhouse earlier this afternoon without anyone seeing her.

She needed to be ready to leave Dry Creek. The longer she stayed, the harder it would be to leave.

Millie wondered if Forrest was looking down from heaven and seeing what a mess she'd made of her version of the plan. She knew now that Forrest had wanted her to meet the people of Dry Creek.

She had wanted to sneak into town and leave before anyone saw her. She would have succeeded, too, if Brad hadn't been parked behind the café.

For the first time it struck her just how odd that was. What had Brad been doing parked there? He couldn't have been having trouble with his pickup, because the old thing had started right up when he turned the ignition. And, if he'd had a flat tire, he wouldn't have been parked behind the café. Brad must have been sitting there for a long time, because she knew he hadn't driven back there while she was inside.

There was only one reason Millie could think of for Brad to be there, and she didn't like it.

Millie slammed the trunk of her car and headed back to the bunkhouse.

The main room of the bunkhouse was empty, but Millie heard someone in the kitchen.

Charlie stood at the stove stirring a big pot of

something. Whatever it was, it smelled good, but Millie hardly noticed.

"I have a question for you," Millie said. She couldn't think of a subtle way to ask what she needed to know. "Around here, when you see a car that's pulled off the road at night, what do you think?"

Charlie looked up from his stirring. "Car trouble."

Millie shook her head. "There was no car trouble."

"Maybe it's late and no one's in the car," Charlie suggested.

Millie shook her head again. "Oh, someone was in the car all right."

Charlie smiled. "Well, if there's two someones in the car, then you have your answer. There's nothing quite as romantic as sitting together under the stars."

Millie nodded her head. She didn't know what had happened to the woman that had been in the pickup with Brad. "Do people around here ever drive into Dry Creek and leave their cars at the café before they go into Miles City?"

"Sure, if they're going to drive together most of the way." Charlie looked at her quizzically. "You worried about your car dying or something? If you are, anyone would be happy to give you a lift anywhere you need to go."

Millie shook her head. "No, my car is fine. Thanks."

Charlie shrugged. "Well, if you need anything, let me know."

Millie nodded. What she needed wasn't something Charlie could give her.

Millie walked back into the main room of the bunkhouse and sat down on a sofa. What she needed was to leave Dry Creek and Brad Parker before the cracks that were starting in her heart caused it to break in two.

Brad stopped and scraped his feet before he entered the bunkhouse. He'd been forced to drive back from Miles City all by himself. You'd think the other guys had never smelled women's perfume before. Brad had been determined to find the perfume that suited Millie best, and how was he supposed to tell what each one smelled like if he didn't have the sales clerk spray the air in front of him?

The other guys had gone together and bought Millie a wool scarf and some mittens, but Brad wanted a special gift, and that was a challenge in the small department store in Miles City.

Finally, Brad had settled on something called "Snow Angel" that the salesclerk swore was light and sounded, from everything he had told her, like it would be perfect for Millie.

Brad saw that Millie had been looking at the Christmas tree before he came in. When she heard him, she turned around.

"Sorry to let the cold air in," Brad said. When he had opened the door to the bunkhouse, a gust of wind had followed him in. "The wind's blowing out there."

"You must be cold," Millie said as she stood up. "I could start the coffeepot."

Brad shook his head. "I'll just warm up by the fire."

Brad had the bottle of perfume in his pocket. The clerk had wrapped the perfume for him, but he decided to wait until after the pageant to put the box under the tree. He didn't want Millie to think she needed to give him a present, so he didn't want her to know about the box.

Millie sniffed the air. The closer she walked to Brad, the more she could smell the perfume. It wasn't some kind of cologne for a man, either. No, the perfume was definitely the kind a woman would wear.

"I thought you were out with the other guys," Millie said.

"Oh, I was," Brad said. Millie thought he looked a little guilty, but he continued, "We had some business to take care of."

Millie wondered what the woman's name was. Not that it was any of her business, she reminded herself. "Well, that's good then, I guess."

Just then the rest of the ranch hands came into the bunkhouse. Millie noticed as each one filed through the door that none of them smelled of perfume. Which meant that, wherever Brad had been, he hadn't been with them.

Millie decided, as she blinked a few times, that it was just as well that she was leaving tonight after the pageant.

Chapter Fifteen

The pageant was scheduled to begin at seven o'clock, and by then the sky was completely dark. The snow flurries had stopped an hour earlier, and the clouds had parted enough to allow a few stars to shine through the blackness. The lights inside the barn showed through the high windows, and Millie could see into the barn each time someone opened the main door.

Millie parked her car as close to the barn as she could. She was surprised that Brad had offered to give her a ride to the pageant. She almost asked him why he wasn't giving a ride to Miss Perfume. But she didn't. She couldn't ride with him anyway, because she had the Christmas stockings. The Christmas stockings were supposed to be a surprise, and she no longer felt any desire to tell Brad all her secrets.

Brad would know soon enough anyway. Millie had decided the town of Dry Creek should know that Forrest was sorry, and so she'd enclosed a note in Mrs. Hargrove's stocking explaining everything.

The air was chilly when Millie opened the door to her car, and she walked quickly to the barn. She'd come back later and get the stockings.

The light inside the barn was dim, and Millie could see the trellis in the middle of the floor that had a sign hanging from it saying Bethlehem Inn. From the sounds of the shuffling feet and giggles coming from behind a makeshift curtain at the end of the barn, the animals were getting ready to play their parts.

A stereo was set up in the barn and Millie could hear the muted sounds of Christmas carols. She also heard the sound of Brad's voice and saw him talking with a group of men gathered near a coffeepot in one corner of the barn. There was no one standing near him who might be Miss Perfume, but then, Millie reasoned, the woman might be one of the ones she saw helping the children get into their costumes.

Millie walked over to a place where there were several empty chairs. Walking through the people of Dry Creek wasn't as easy as it sounded. People smiled at her and greeted her every step of the way. She'd refused several offers of a chair by the time she reached the one she wanted.

Millie picked a chair that had empty chairs on both sides of it. She didn't want to get to know any more people in Dry Creek. She'd just be leaving soon anyway.

Someone turned the music up louder and flicked the light switches. That must be the signal that the pageant was ready to begin. The people who weren't already seated started to move to the sides of the barn where the chairs were positioned.

"May I?"

Millie heard Brad's low question as he sat down in the chair next to her.

Brad didn't know why Millie had such a surprised look on her face. He'd followed her car into Dry Creek to be sure she didn't have any mechanical trouble on the way. He'd even sat in his pickup for a little bit after they both parked until it became clear that she was not going to go inside right away. The only reason he'd gone in ahead of her was because he was beginning to feel like a stalker.

She should have figured out by now that he was planning to sit beside her.

"You're wearing perfume." Brad noticed the fact as everyone around them was sitting down. He hadn't thought she had been wearing perfume before. The scent she was wearing now was light and fruity. Maybe she wouldn't like the perfume he had bought for her. He should have asked if she had a preference. "What kind is it?"

"It's not perfume. It's peach soap."

"Ah, soap." Brad didn't know if that meant she would like perfume or not. Well, it was too late now anyway. He planned to give her the perfume tonight when they got back to the bunkhouse. He could only hope for the best.

The lights were dimmed almost completely for a minute.

Brad assumed by the sounds that the children were getting in place for the pageant.

The donkey was the first thing to come out from behind the curtain. The donkey was followed by nine-year-old Angie Loden wearing a blue table-cloth wrapped sari-style around her. A pillow made her look awkwardly pregnant, but the look in her eye made her look like a schoolteacher.

Millie smiled when she saw the little girl in blue. She wondered if girls playing at being Mary always wore blue because they had all seen the same stained glass picture of Jesus talking to the little girl in the blue robe.

Millie heard the choked-back laughter as the girl started her walk. She obviously wasn't as worried about talking to Jesus as she was about correcting the boy who was playing Joseph. Millie could almost hear the girl scolding him in a low whisper as the boy tried to keep up with the girl and the donkey. The boy was having a hard time not tripping on the hem of his robe, until finally Mary reached over and adjusted the belt around the robe so that material bunched up around the boy's waist, making the robe shorter.

One of the Curtis twins was carrying the cutout figure of the donkey, and he was leading the girl along the path toward the makeshift inn.

The Christmas music was turned almost completely off, and another voice came from the loudspeakers. Millie decided the voice was from a tape, because she didn't recognize it from the voices she'd heard in Dry Creek.

"At that time, Augustus Caesar sent an order that all people in the countries under Roman rule must list their names in the register," the voice said, as Mary, Joseph and the donkey slowly walked toward the inn.

Millie had not realized the whole Nativity scene started because someone wanted to collect everyone's name. She thought of the stockings in her trunk. They made a more appropriate Christmas gift than she had thought. She'd had to collect all the names of the people, as well. She knew how much trouble that could be. It gave her a certain empathy with Augustus Caesar.

Millie sat back and decided to enjoy the pageant. She chuckled along with everyone else when the innkeeper looked uncertain about whether or not he had any rooms. Finally, Mary looked down some imaginary hall and said she could see his inn was filled with tourists, and so there were no rooms for those people who really needed a place to stay.

The angel didn't fly overhead like she had in other pageants, but a blond girl climbed a ladder and flapped her wings while shouting out "Behold!" with as much enthusiasm as the original angel must have had.

Chester, the real dog, chose this moment to run inside and shake the snow off of his coat.

Millie expected the adults to scold and ask who had let Chester into the barn, but they all just seemed to shrug their shoulders and turn their attention back to the unfolding pageant.

It must have been when the shepherds were coming in from their fields that Brad put his arm on the back of her chair. Millie could feel it on her shoulders. She'd been laughing at Chester's efforts to herd the wooden sheep, and she looked up at Brad.

Brad was happy. He'd moved his arm from the back of Millie's chair to her shoulders and she'd smiled up at him. Her face was still glowing from the laughter, and even though he wasn't the reason for her laughter, the delight she was feeling spilled over onto him.

Brad began to wonder if he was wrong about how long it took for a man to fall in love. He'd thought he needed to get to know Millie. But he was beginning to think he knew all he needed to know right now.

If the sheep hadn't arrived at the inn just then, Brad would have whispered something silly in Millie's ear. But she'd turned her gaze back to the pageant, and he wanted her to remember every single moment of this night. He'd wait and whisper in her ear tonight after he'd given her the perfume.

Millie sighed when the wise men started walking toward the inn. The littlest of the boys had trouble keeping his crown on his head and had to set his golden box of spices down on the floor so he could adjust his crown. Chester, of course, had to come over and sniff at the spices until he sneezed. Whatever it was that was supposed to be myrrh scattered across the floor.

All in all, Millie thought when the lights were dimmed for the last time, the pageant had been delightful. It had also gone much too fast.

Millie looked over at Brad. She'd have to say good-bye to him later. Maybe she wouldn't have to leave right after she delivered the stockings. But, for now, she should make her move while the children all came back on stage to sing "Silent Night."

The air outside the barn felt sharply cold to Millie after she had been inside. Brad had thought she was leaving to use the restroom, or he would have come with her. Setting the stockings out for everyone was something she had to do by herself. Forrest had been her friend, and she would help him do what he could to make his actions up to the people of Dry Creek. She had left Mrs. Hargrove's stocking on top of all the others, since it had the note inside it.

Millie could barely hold all of the stockings in her arms, but she didn't want to make two trips. She planned to leave them on the bench inside the door. Now that the pageant was almost over, it wouldn't be long before someone turned and saw the stockings.

Millie had left the door slightly open so that she could just push it completely open with her arms. She managed to come back inside the barn and stand by the door without anyone noticing her.

Everyone inside the barn was looking at the children singing in the middle of the floor, and Millie could see why. With their crooked angel wings and dragging shepherd robes, the children were charming. Even Chester was sitting calmly beside the wooden sheep while they sang.

Millie set the stack of stockings down on the

bench. There were mittens and scarves on the shelf above the bench and some rubber boots under the bench. But the bench itself was clear until Millie set down her stockings.

When children finished their last notes of "Silent Night," Millie stepped back outside the door. She left the door cracked open so she could hear people's excitement. Within minutes, she heard the first exclamation.

"Look at these!" a woman's voice said.

"Don't touch them," a man's voice answered.

"Why, they're Millie's stockings," Mrs. Hargrove said.

Millie smiled. The older woman would convince everyone to trust that the stockings were okay.

"Look what's inside them!" That voice sounded like it came from a teenage boy. "It's hundred-dollar bills!"

"What's money like that doing here?" the man who had spoken earlier said.

"I wonder if the stores are still open. I'd love to get the kids real presents for Christmas and not just new mittens," a woman said.

"Maybe I'll get my train set," a little voice said.

Millie heard a chorus of excited whispers until the man spoke again.

"But what's the money doing here?" the man insisted loudly. "If we don't know what it's doing here, we shouldn't touch it."

"It's from Millie," Mrs. Hargrove said. "She left a note."

Millie could hear the people crowding next to Mrs. Hargrove.

"Is it counterfeit?" someone asked.

"No," Mrs. Hargrove said slowly. "It's money from Forrest."

"Who's Forrest?" someone else asked.

"That's the name of the hit man," someone else answered. "But what's that got to do with that woman?"

"Millie was his friend," Mrs. Hargrove said. "And she writes that Forrest wanted us to know he was sorry for what he did here."

There was almost total silence on the other side of the door.

Finally, Brad spoke. His voice was low, but Millie could hear it clearly.

"She was friends with a hit man?" Brad's voice contained a world of confusion and disbelief. "What kind of person is friends with a hit man?"

Millie turned to walk down the stairs. She'd heard enough. It was time to leave.

The air was just as cold when Millie walked back to her car, but she didn't notice a thing. The cold outside didn't begin to compare with the cold inside of her.

She opened the door to her car and was grateful that the car started right up when she turned the ignition. She backed the car away from the barn before she turned on the headlights. She didn't want her car lights to shine into the windows of the barn. She would leave Dry Creek as quietly as she had come.

Millie rolled down the window as she pulled away

from the barn. She wanted to hear any last music that might be coming from the pageant. She thought they would turn the stereo on again with the Christmas carols, but she didn't hear anything.

Finally, she rolled her window back up. She'd have to listen to her radio instead.

Chapter Sixteen

Brad sat down on the steps outside the church. He wasn't planning to go to church this morning, but it had snowed last night, and he figured he'd shovel off the steps just to show God and Mrs. Hargrove that he didn't hold any hard feelings toward them. Well, not many hard feelings anyway. Which wasn't bad considering he had met the woman of his dreams and neither one of them had helped him to keep track of her.

Millie had slipped away from the barn on Christmas Eve, and Brad hadn't even known it for a full fifteen minutes. She'd said she was going to the restroom, and he'd believed her. By the time he realized she wasn't inside the barn, he'd gone racing outside only to see that her car was gone.

He'd gotten into his pickup and followed the road all of the way into Miles City thinking he would find her. When he didn't see her, he figured she had gone the other direction out of Dry Creek, and he came barreling back and drove all the way into North Dakota before he turned around.

That old car of hers went faster than he'd thought possible.

Brad stopped shoveling and leaned on his shovel. The days had been gloomy ever since Christmas. He'd always dreaded Christmas. But now he knew it wasn't Christmas that was his problem. It was all of the rest of the days that stretched out after Christmas was gone that were going to give him grief.

Even with all of the excitement in Dry Creek these days, Brad was miserable. Every time someone talked about what they had spent their hundred dollars on, Brad thought of Millie. He'd thought of her through conversations about toy dolls and new tennis shoes. Mrs. Hargrove even informed him about the new ice-crushing blender she'd bought with part of her money.

Brad still had his hundred-dollar bill in his shirt pocket next to his heart.

Brad had wished a million times since that night that he hadn't been shocked Millie had been friends with a hit man. He shouldn't have even been surprised. He knew Millie would be loyal to her friends, and that she took up with the underdogs. It only made sense that she would stand by her friends if they were arrested.

He wished he could tell her, though, that it was her note that made the difference to the people of Dry Creek, and not the money. Just hearing that the hit man had been deeply sorry allowed people to start trusting in strangers again.

Brad started moving his shovel again. The thing he really regretted, however, was that he'd never asked Millie for her address. He was sitting here with his heart full of things to tell her, and he didn't even know how to find her. All he really knew was that she lived somewhere around the waterfront in Seattle.

Brad had finished shoveling all of the steps when he saw the pastor come out of the parsonage and start walking toward the church.

"Good morning," Pastor Matthew called out. "You're joining us this morning for church, aren't you?"

Brad grimaced as the minister came closer. "I'm not fit for polite company these days."

Brad ran his hand over his face. He hadn't shaved for a couple of days, and he figured he looked pretty rough.

"Having a hard time?" the pastor asked as he came closer to Brad.

Brad nodded. "Not much I can do about it though."

The pastor looked at Brad for a minute. "If you want to come to my office with me, I think I have something that might cheer you up."

"No offense," Brad said as he leaned against his shovel, "but this is something prayer can't fix."

"God might surprise you," the pastor said as he started climbing the steps.

Brad figured God had already had His chance to work on Millie and had missed His opportunity completely.

"What you might not understand is that I need concrete help," Brad said as he started to follow the pastor. "I mean prayer is nice, but I need, well, real help."

The pastor had walked up the steps to the church and opened the main door. Brad still followed him as the minister crossed the back of the church and opened a door into a small room.

Pastor Matthew went to his desk, picked something up and turned around to face Brad.

"Is this concrete enough for you?" the pastor held out a blue card.

"Millie filled out a visitor's form?"

The tightness Brad had felt in his chest all week started to loosen.

The pastor nodded. "Of course, it wouldn't be right for me to give the information on this card to just anyone."

"Oh."

"However, I figure that a representative from the church should be allowed to call on Millie, since she did mark the box that asked for a visit from someone from the church."

"I've been to the church twice now—if the Christmas pageant counts."

Pastor Matthew grinned as he held the card out to Brad. "All you really need to do is invite Millie to next Sunday's service. I can even send a church bulletin along with you, so you have all the information."

Brad understood why people throughout the ages had kissed the feet of holy men when they got their prayers answered. "Thank you."

Ruby's café was on the Seattle waterfront, and

most mornings in January the air was cold. The floor at Ruby's was made of thick wooden planks and the walls were filled with large paned glass windows. Ruby believed in natural light, plants and strong coffee. It was the coffee that brought the customers in, but Millie suspected it was the plants that made them want to linger over their meals.

Not that Millie was worried about customers who wouldn't leave.

She had just mixed up the order on table seven. Instead of bringing the man coffee with cream, she had brought him tea with sugar. In all of her years at Ruby's she'd never made a mistake on an order until after she got back from Dry Creek. Since she'd gotten back eight days ago, however, she'd made thirty-two mistakes. The reason she knew the exact number was because the other waitresses were trying to guess the limit of Ruby's patience and they were counting.

Of course, the waitresses all knew Millie's job was safe because they were running shorthanded. The dishwasher had quit, and Ruby had no sooner put the Help Wanted—Dishwasher sign in the window than one of the waitresses had quit, as well.

Not that the other waitresses weren't also sympathetic. They'd cooed and fussed over Millie that first day back until she thought she would have to take to her bed and have herself a good rest just to get some peace from people's good intentions.

Millie had distracted the other waitresses from their sympathy by telling them about the Christmas pageant at Dry Creek. When she left Montana, she fully intended to entertain them all with stories about Brad. But she found the stories she had thought were so funny when they happened now only made her feel sad. Even the story about the spiders would have made her cry if she tried to tell it.

Millie had slipped once when she was talking to Louise and had mentioned that she'd stayed in the bunkhouse in the room of a nice man.

The waitresses at Ruby's weren't usually impressed with someone who was just nice, but they seemed to know there was more to Millie's stories than she was telling.

The door to Ruby's buzzed whenever anyone opened it and came inside. Ruby said the buzzer allowed them to have good customer control. No customer was ever supposed to wait more than five minutes at Ruby's before he or she was seated and offered a cup of coffee.

So it was only natural that all of the waitresses looked up when the buzzer sounded.

Millie's mouth dropped open. In all of the days since she'd left Dry Creek, she never thought she'd look up at Ruby's and see Brad Parker walk into the café.

"What are you doing here?" Millie walked over to the man and asked.

For the hundredth time that day, Brad wondered if his plan was a good one. It was a long drive from Dry Creek to Seattle, and he'd thought of a million clever things to say to Millie when he saw her. But then he'd decided to just be himself and be honest.

When he saw how white Millie's face was, however, he wished he had thought of something to tell her that didn't contain the words "I came because of you."

"I came for the job," Brad blurted out. He'd seen the sign in the window of the diner, and he was only beginning to see the advantages it offered.

"What job?" Millie frowned.

"Dishwasher," Brad guessed. He was almost sure that was what the sign said.

That seemed to leave Millie speechless. Finally, she swallowed. "Here?"

Brad nodded. "I think that's where the job is."

Millie just stared at him.

"I'm hoping they'll take me temporarily. For a few weeks," Brad added. "I could use a break from moving cattle."

Millie might be speechless, but Brad could hear the other waitresses start to chatter. Finally, one of them walked over to him.

Brad saw by the woman's badge that her name was Sherry. Ordinarily, she would be the kind of woman who would catch his eye. Her hair was all highlights and curls. Her fingernails were deep red and slightly pointed. Her smile was friendly and her uniform not buttoned up tight.

"I'm sure Ruby will hire you on the spot," the waitress said as she stepped closer to Brad. "I sure would."

"Back off, Sherry," an older waitress said. "This is a *nice* man."

Brad thought she said the word "nice" like it was a code.

"A *nice* man from Dry Creek, I believe," the older woman said as she gave Sherry a stern look.

Sherry shrugged her shoulders and turned away. "Can't blame a girl for trying."

Millie decided she better set down the coffeepot that she was holding. Come to think of it, she should just sit her whole self down.

Louise seemed to agree. She looked at Millie and said, "Now's a good time to take your break. We're not busy. There's no one on the patio."

Millie nodded as she turned toward the patio.

"Take your time. I'll send out some of those fresh donuts for you and your friend."

Millie walked out to the patio, and even though she heard his footsteps behind her, she was still surprised to see Brad himself behind her there when she came to the table and sat down.

"Mind if I join you?" Brad said.

Millie blinked. She hadn't noticed how nervous he seemed. She had always thought she was the only one who got nervous. "Please do."

Brad sat down at the small table across from Millie.

"What brings you to Seattle?" Millie finally asked.

"You."

Brad knew he'd been clumsy. He hadn't meant to rush Millie like that. "I mean, I came to see you because you asked for a visit from someone from the church."

Brad pulled out the blue visitor's card that Millie had filled out when she was in Dry Creek. The corners were bent because he'd kept it on the dash of his pickup all the way from Montana to Seattle.

"You came to invite me back to church?" Millie sounded incredulous.

"I came to invite you back to Dry Creek," Brad said quietly.

Millie didn't answer right away so he just kept on explaining. "I know it's too big of a decision to make right away. I know you've only known me for a couple of days. But you aren't going to get to know me better unless you're in Dry Creek or I'm here." Brad took a deep breath. "So I thought I'd stay here for a while so we can get to know each other."

Millie started to smile. She felt like someone had turned the sunshine on in the middle of an overcast day. "We're going to get to know each other?"

Brad nodded and started to smile himself.

"You're willing to wash dishes so you can get to know me better?" Millie still couldn't believe it. Most men she knew wouldn't wash dishes for any reason. "You know Ruby throws in the pots and pans, too. It's not just the easy stuff like glasses and silverware."

"I'd figured as much," Brad said as his smile turned into a full grin.

"You do get a share of the tips though," Millie added. "And meals—you get meals."

"I'd settle for a kiss or two from the right waitress," Brad said, and then he remembered something and reached in his pocket. "And I have a Christmas present for you."

Millie looked at the silver box with the red ribbon on it. No one had ever given her such a pretty gift.

Brad handed her the box.

"Go ahead, open it," Brad said.

Millie had half of the paper off when she started to smell the perfume. She recognized it from the fragrance that had surrounded Brad on the night of the Christmas pageant. *She* was the perfume woman in Brad's life! She had to blink a little to keep the tears away.

"You're not allergic, are you?" Brad asked.

Millie shook her head. She only had one problem at the moment. "I don't have a present for you."

Millie figured the hundred-dollar bill didn't count because that was really from Forrest. She hadn't expected to meet Brad when she went to Dry Creek, so she hadn't taken a present with her. And she hadn't expected to ever see him again when she left, so there was no reason to buy him one later.

There was only one gift she could think of that might please him, and she couldn't think about it too long or she'd decide it wasn't grand enough.

Millie stood up and leaned across the table. Then she bent down and kissed Brad square on the lips.

Millie had to swallow a chuckle, because she knew she had startled Brad for a second. But the man adapted quick. Before she knew it, the kiss was making her head spin and her knees buckle.

"Oh, my," Millie said when the kiss had ended. She was leaning into Brad and she was halfway into his arms. He moved around the table and settled her on his lap.

"You know, I have a feeling I'm not going to mind washing all those dishes at all," Brad said.

Millie just smiled. She had a feeling she wouldn't mind him washing all those dishes, either.

Epilogue

Four Months Later

Millie smiled as she looked at her bridal dress in the mirror. She had been staying at Mrs. Hargrove's for the past two weeks while she and Brad received marriage counseling from Pastor Matthew and made final plans for their wedding.

She and Brad had been going to a church in Seattle, but they both wanted to be married in the church in Dry Creek, especially after Millie started receiving the notes of thanks from the people in town. She was pleased that the notes were as likely to thank her for letting them know that the hit man was sorry as they were to thank her for the money.

The people in Dry Creek were good, solid people.

Millie and Brad intended to live their lives in Dry Creek and wanted to make the church their home. Since neither one of them had ideal childhoods, they knew that church would be their family.

Millie marveled at how much her understanding

of God could change in just a few months. She and Brad had both asked God to help them understand more about Him, and they'd been astonished at what they were learning.

Millie fingered the lace on her veil. She had never thought she would know a man who wanted to take care of her as much as she wanted to take care of him. Brad had put a down payment on a ranch just outside of Dry Creek, and that would be where they would raise their family.

"Are you ready?" Mrs. Hargrove called up the stairs. "The carriage is here to pick you up."

When the ranch hands had heard that she and Brad were going to get married, they had rigged up one of the ranch wagons as a wedding carriage. Millie had seen the wagon this morning. It was covered with cascades of spring flowers. Pinks. Lavenders. And blues.

Millie refused to ride in the wagon without Brad, even for the short distance to the church, so everyone had decided to forget all the usual traditions, and she and Brad were riding to the church together. After the reception, they'd ride to their new home in the wagon, as well.

It would be a good start for them, Millie thought as she gave her face a final glance in the mirror and then headed down the stairs to her own true love.

* * * * *

Dear Reader,

Do you ever feel like God is asking you to do something that is just too difficult? I do. Like Millie in the book, I sometimes feel as if I am a humble waitress and am being asked to do something that God should know requires being a king—or at least an elder statesman. The peculiar thing about God, however, is that He does mix it up. He uses the most unlikely people to do what He wants done.

Of course, while this is sometimes alarming and often frustrating, it is also what makes life with God unique. He isn't impressed with your credentials or stature; He is impressed with your heart. If you are willing, He will lead you—and heap blessings upon you in the process.

Sincerely,

Janet Tronstad

SUGAR PLUMS
FOR DRY CREEK

I can do all things through Christ
which strengtheneth me.
—*Philippians* 4:13

This book is dedicated to my grandfather,
Harold Norris,
who shared his love of a good book with me.

Chapter One

Lizette Baker wished her mother had worried less about showing her the perfect way to pirouette and more about teaching her a few practical things, like how to coax more warm air out of her old car's heating system and how to put snow chains on tires so smooth they slipped on every icy patch she found as she drove east on Interstate 94 in southern Montana.

A colder, frostier place Lizette had never seen. Even with a wool scarf wrapped around her neck and mittens on her hands, she couldn't stay warm. It was only mid-November and it was already less than ten degrees Fahrenheit outside. No wonder hers was the only car in sight as she drove along this road hoping to reach Dry Creek, Montana, before her heater gave out completely.

The attendant in the gas station she'd stopped at back in Forsyth had offered to call a mechanic to repair her heater. Another man, with a dirty blond beard and a snake tattooed on his arm, had made a different suggestion.

"Why put out good money for a mechanic?" he'd asked in an artificially friendly voice. Lizette hadn't liked the way he was looking at her. "I'll keep you warm if you give me a ride down the road a bit. I'm looking for my kids." He'd reached into his pocket and pulled out a worn snapshot, which he'd then shoved at her. "Kids need to see their old man. You haven't seen them, have you?"

Lizette would have rather given the snake on the man's arm a ride than the man himself, but she hadn't wanted any trouble, so she'd politely looked at the picture of his two children.

"No, but they're beautiful children." And the children probably would have been beautiful, she thought, if they hadn't looked so skinny and scared. "Sorry about the ride, but I have a car full of boxes. Moving, you know."

Lizette hoped the man hadn't looked at her car too closely. If she'd shifted the boxes around a little, she could have cleared enough room in the front seat for a passenger.

The tattooed man hadn't said anything more, but he'd put the picture back in his pocket.

After a moment's silence, the attendant had finally asked, "So do you want the mechanic to come over to fix that heater? He doesn't keep regular hours, but he can get down here in fifteen minutes flat."

Lizette had shaken her head. "Thanks though."

She barely had enough money left to get her ballet school going; she couldn't afford to fix anything that wasn't actually falling off the car. The heater was spitting out just enough warm air to keep her from freezing to death, so it would have to do for now.

She'd looked out her rearview mirror as she'd pulled away from the gas station and had seen the man with the snake on his arm watching her leave.

It wasn't the first time since she'd left Seattle that Lizette had wondered if she was making a mistake.

Her whole life had changed in the last few months though, and she needed a new beginning. Besides, where else could she get free rent to start her own business? Lizette had learned to be frugal from her mother, Jacqueline. Indeed, it had been Jacqueline who'd found the ad for free space.

Lizette had not known until recently that her mother had saved for years with the hope that they could open their own ballet school someday. When Lizette's father had died, years ago, Jacqueline had given up the fledgling ballet school she and her husband had started and had taken a steady job in a bakery. At the time, Lizette had not realized the sacrifice her mother was making to keep them secure, probably because Jacqueline never complained about giving up the school. When she'd first tied on her bakery apron, she'd even managed to joke. She said she wished her husband could see her. He'd say she was really a Baker at last.

Her mother had made the job sound as though it was exactly what she wanted, and Lizette had believed her back then. Maybe that was because Lizette herself was happy. The bakery was a playground to her. She loved the warm smells and all of the chatter of customers. The bakers even got into the habit of asking Lizette to try out their new recipes. They said she had a taste for what the customers would like.

Giving up that ballet school was only one of the many sacrifices Jacqueline Baker had made for Lizette over the years. Lizette hadn't even known about some of them until her mother had been diagnosed with terminal cancer. That's when she'd started giving instructions to Lizette.

"You'll find fifteen thousand dollars in this safety deposit box," Jacqueline told her as she handed Lizette a key. "I wanted it to be more, but it'll get that school of ours started if we're careful. Then there'll be no need for you to work at the bakery—you'll be free to dance. The money should cover everything for a year. We don't need anything expensive—just something with good floors and lots of room for practice."

Lizette was amazed and touched. So that was why her mother'd never spent much money on herself, not even after she became the manager of the bakery and started earning a better salary. Lizette could see how important it was to her mother to start what she was calling the Baker School of Ballet.

As the pain increased and Jacqueline went into the hospital, she talked more and more about the school. She worried that Lizette had not been able to find an affordable space to rent even though she'd gone out to look at several places. Jacqueline even asked the hospital chaplain to come and pray about it.

Lizette was surprised her mother was interested in praying. Jacqueline had shown little use for God over the years, saying she could not understand a God who took a man away in his prime. Unspoken was the complaint that He had also robbed her of her beloved ballet school at the same time.

But now, at the end, who did her mother want to talk to? The chaplain.

If they hadn't been in a hospital when her mother asked to speak to a minister, Lizette wouldn't even have known how to find one. She herself had never been to church in her life. Sunday was the one day she could spend with her mother, and Jacqueline made it clear she didn't want to go to church, so Lizette never even suggested it.

Yet on her deathbed Lizette's mother spent hours talking to the chaplain about her hopes for a ballet school. Lizette quietly apologized to the man one afternoon when the two of them had left the room so the nurse could give Jacqueline an injection. Lizette knew the chaplain was a busy man, and she doubted he was interested in ballet schools—especially ones that didn't even exist except in a dying woman's dreams.

The chaplain waved Lizette's apology aside, "Your mother's talking about her life when she talks about that school. That's what I'm here for. It's important."

In the last days, the soft sound of the chaplain's praying was all that quieted Jacqueline. Well, Lizette acknowledged, toward the end it was also those expensive injections that kept her mother comfortable.

Lizette never did tell Jacqueline that those injections weren't covered by their insurance plan.

It didn't take much money to open a ballet school, Lizette told herself when her mother kept asking about sites. By then, the extra hospital bills had used up the entire fifteen thousand dollars, and Lizette's small savings account as well. Lizette said a prayer of her own when she promised to open the school in the fall.

"You're right. Fall is the best time of the year to start a ballet school," Jacqueline said as she lay in her hospital bed. "We can start our students right out on our simplified version of the Nutcracker ballet, and they'll be hooked. Every young girl wants to be Clara. Plus we already have all of those costumes we made for you and the other girls when you were in dance school."

Part of the deal in the sale of her parents' ballet school had been that the new owner, Madame Aprele, would give Lizette free lessons. Lizette had studied ballet for years, and even though she didn't have her mother's natural grace, she still did very well.

"And you'll be there to watch." Lizette dreamed a little dream of her own. "You've always loved the Nutcracker."

Her mother smiled. "I can almost see it now. I remember the first time I danced Clara as a five-year-old. And later, the Sugar Plum Fairy. What I wouldn't give to dance it all again!"

Lizette vowed she'd find a way to open a school even without money. Then maybe her mother would get stronger and they could run that school together. With all of the praying the chaplain was doing, Lizette figured they were due a miracle.

Later that week Jacqueline claimed she'd found a miracle—right in the middle of the classified section of *The Seattle Times*. The ad offering free rent for new businesses had been buried in the used furniture section of the paper. Lizette called the phone number from the hospital room so her mother could listen to her end of the conversation.

Free rent would solve all of their problems for the school, and Lizette wanted Jacqueline to share the excitement of the phone call. Lizette hadn't realized until she was halfway through the conversation that the free rent was in a small town in Montana.

Jacqueline kept nodding at her during the conversation, so Lizette found herself agreeing to take the town of Dry Creek up on their offer. She couldn't disappoint her mother by telling her that the free rent wasn't in Seattle.

Of course, Lizette had no intention of actually going to Dry Creek, Montana. She knew nothing about the place. Something about the phone call calmed Jacqueline, however, and she seemed truly satisfied. The chaplain said she made her peace with God the next afternoon. After that, nothing Lizette did could stop her mother from slipping away.

After Jacqueline was gone, Lizette remembered the small town in Montana. Seattle seemed the emptiest city in the world without her mother. Lizette couldn't stay at the bakery, even though she'd worked there for the past six years. Lizette enjoyed the job, but she knew her mother would have scolded her for hiding away there.

Besides baking, the only other skill Lizette had was her expertise in ballet and there were no jobs for young ballet teachers in Seattle. Oh, Madame Aprele offered her a job, but Lizette knew the small school didn't need another teacher, and she wasn't desperate enough to take charity.

No, she had to go somewhere else, and she didn't much care where.

So, here she was—moving to Dry Creek, Montana, and all because of a phone conversation with an old man and an offer of free rent. Lizette wasn't sure the school would work. A small town in eastern Montana wasn't the place she would have chosen to open the Baker School of Ballet.

Not that it was absolutely the worst place to start, Lizette assured herself. So few people appreciated ballet these days, and it gladdened her heart to remember the enthusiasm in the old man's voice when she had called in response to the ad. The man she'd talked to on the phone was gruff, and she couldn't always hear him because of the static, but he seemed excited that she was taking the town up on their offer of six months' free rent. He kept talking about how large the area was that they could set aside for her.

The old man had mentioned tables and chairs and counters, so he might not be too familiar with ballet, but Lizette wouldn't let that discourage her. It was the enthusiasm in his heart that counted. She'd be happy to educate this little town on the finer points of ballet.

Lizette was going to go ahead with a modified Nutcracker ballet. Her mother had been right that it was a great way to start. Lizette decided she would even make Sugar Plum pastries for a little reception after the performance. Stuffed with dried plums and vanilla custard, they were a Christmas favorite with many of the customers at the bakery.

The people of Dry Creek would like them as well.

Yes, Lizette thought to herself. A little music, a little ballet and a cream-filled pastry—the people of Dry Creek would be glad she'd opened her school in their town.

Chapter Two

Judd Bowman was standing at the back of the hardware store in Dry Creek counting nails. He figured he needed about fifty nails, but every time he got to thirty or so, one of the kids would interrupt him because they had to go to the bathroom or they wanted a drink of water or they thought they heard a kitten meowing. Judd sighed. Trying to take care of a six-year-old boy and a five-year-old girl was no picnic. Fortunately, the hardware store had a heater going, and it took the edge off the cold.

"Just sit down until I finish," Judd said when he felt Amanda's arm brush against his leg. He'd gotten to thirty-seven, and he repeated the number to himself. He knew the kids needed reassurance, so he tried to speak two sentences when one would have done him fine. "I won't be long and then we can go over to the café and have some cocoa. You like cocoa, don't you?"

Judd felt Amanda nod against his knee. He looked

over to see that Bobby was still drawing a picture on the piece of paper that the man who ran the hardware store had given him earlier.

Amanda seemed to squeeze even closer to his knee, and Judd looked down. She was pale and clutching his pant leg in earnest now as she stared around his leg at the men in the middle of the hardware store.

Judd looked over at them, wondering what had stirred up the old men who sat around the potbellied stove. Usually, when he came into the store, the men were dozing quietly in their chairs around the fire or playing a slow game of chess.

Today, with the cold seeping into the store, the fire was almost out. There was wood in the basket nearby, so there was no excuse for anyone not to put another log in the stove.

But the men weren't paying any attention to the cold or the fire.

Instead, they were all looking out the window of the hardware store and across the street into the window of what had been an old abandoned store that stood next to the café. The store wasn't abandoned any longer. Judd could see the woman as she tried to hang what looked like a sign on the inside of her window.

Judd didn't usually pay much attention to women, but he'd have remembered this one if he'd seen her before. She was tall and graceful, with her black hair twisted into a knot on the top of head. He could see why men would be looking at her.

"They're just talking," Judd said as he rested his hand on Amanda's shoulder.

Judd had little use for idle conversation, but even he had heard a week ago that a new woman was moving to town. Several months ago the town had placed an ad in *The Seattle Times* inviting businesses to move to Dry Creek. The town had sweetened the deal by offering six months of free rent. Even at that, the woman was the only one to actually agree to come, so the town had given her the best of the old buildings they owned.

Judd squeezed Amanda's shoulder as Bobby walked over to stand beside them as well. The boy had become attuned to his sister's moods, and it never took him long to know when Amanda was frightened.

Judd spoke softly. "They're just talking about the new woman who moved here."

"Remember I told you about her?" Bobby added as he leaned down to look his sister in the eye. "She's going to make doughnuts."

"I'm not sure about the doughnuts," Judd said. He worked hard to keep his voice even. Amanda picked up too easily on the emotion in men's voices, and even though Judd was angry at the man who had made her so sensitive and not at *her,* he knew she'd think he was upset with her if he let his voice be anything but neutral.

Getting involved in the problems of Dry Creek was the last thing Judd wanted to do, but if that's what it took to help Amanda realize all anger wasn't directed at her, then that's what he'd have to do. "Let's go see what it's all about."

Judd walked slowly enough so Amanda could keep her fingers wrapped around his leg. She had her other hand in Bobby's small hand.

"How's it going?" Judd asked when they arrived at the group around the stove.

Judd had seen these men a dozen times since he'd rented the Jenkins farm this past spring, but he'd been so busy all summer with farm work and then with the kids that this was the first time he'd done more than nod in their direction.

Fortunately, the men were all too steamed up to wonder why he chose to talk now.

"Charley here is going deaf," Jacob muttered as he leaned back with his fingers in his suspenders.

"I am not," Charley said as he looked up at Judd through his bifocals. "I had a bad connection on that new fangled cell phone. Don't know what's wrong with it. Some of the words don't come through too clear."

"That's when you ask the person to repeat themselves," Jacob said.

The two men had obviously had this conversation before.

"I was being friendly," Charley protested as he stood up and looked straight at Judd. "Everyone kept telling me to be friendly if anyone called. Now, do you think it sounds friendly to keep asking someone to repeat what they've just said?"

"Well, I guess that depends." Judd hesitated. He

didn't want to get involved in the argument. He just wanted Amanda to hear that it wasn't about her.

"You know, I got that phone because everybody said people would be calling about the ad at all times of the night and day," Charley complained as he sat back down. "I even carried it to bed with me. And this is the thanks I get."

"So you're all angry because of the phone." Judd nodded. There. That should satisfy Amanda that the argument had nothing to do with her.

"It isn't the phone," Jacob said as he shook his head. "It's what he was supposed to do with the phone. He was supposed to make sure that businesses were suitable for Dry Creek."

"He said she was a baker!" another old man protested.

"I had my mouth all set for a doughnut," Jacob admitted. "One of those long maple ones."

"Well, she kept saying Baker," Charley defended himself. "How was I supposed to know that was just her name? Dry Creek could use a good bakery."

"But she's not a baker. She runs a dance school!" Jacob protested.

"And that's the problem?" Judd tried again. He could feel Amanda's hold on his leg lessen. She was listening to the men.

"Of course that's the problem," Jacob continued. "She doesn't even teach *real* dancing, like the stomp-and-holler stuff they have at the senior center up by Miles City. This here is ballet. Who around here wants to learn ballet? You have to wear tights."

"Or a tutu," another old man added. "Pink fluffy stuff."

"It isn't decent, if you ask me," still another man muttered. "Don't know where she'll buy all that netting around here anyway."

"The store here started carrying bug netting since the mosquitoes were so bad over the summer. They still have some left. Maybe she could use that," the first old man offered.

"She can't use bug netting," Charley said. "Not for ballet. Besides, she probably wants it to be pink, and that bug netting is black."

"Well, of course it's black," another old man said. "Mosquitoes don't care if it's some fancy color."

"Netting is the least of her worries. She isn't going to have any students, so she won't need any netting," Jacob finally said.

There was a moment's silence.

"Maybe she *will* take up baking—to keep herself busy if she doesn't have any students," Charley offered. "I heard she was trying to make some kind of cookies."

"They burnt," another man said mournfully. "The smoke came clear over here. I went over and asked if maybe a pie would be easier to bake."

"She's not going to be making pies. She's going to go around trying to change the people of Dry Creek into something we're not. It's like trying to turn a pig into a silk purse. I say just let a pig be a pig—the way God intended," Jacob said.

Judd looked down at Amanda. She'd stopped holding on to his pants leg and was listening intently to the men. He was glad she was listening even if she wasn't talking yet. In the three months that Judd had been taking care of the two kids, Amanda occasionally whispered something to her brother, but she never said anything to anyone else, not even Judd.

Amanda leaned over to whisper in Bobby's ear now.

The boy smiled and nodded. "Yeah, she *is* awfully pretty."

Bobby looked up at the men. "Amanda thinks the woman looks like our mama."

Judd's breath caught. Both kids had stopped talking about their mother a month ago. Barbara was his second cousin, but Judd hadn't known her until she showed up on his doorstep one morning. She'd paid an agency to find him because she wanted to ask him to take care of her kids while she got settled in a place. She was on the run from an abusive husband and had the court papers to prove it.

Judd had refused Barbara's request at first. Sheer disbelief had cleared his mind of anything else. Judd had never known his mother, and the uncle who had raised him had been more interested in having a hired hand that he didn't need to pay than in parenting an orphan. The stray dog Judd had taken in earlier in the summer probably knew more about family life than Judd did. Judd wasn't someone anyone had ever thought to leave kids with before this. And one look at the kids showed him that they were still in the napping years.

"You must have taken care of little ones before—" Barbara had said.

"Not unless they had four feet and a tail," Judd told her firmly. He'd nursed calves and stray dogs and even a pony or two. But kids? Never.

No, Judd wasn't the one his cousin needed. "You'll need to find someone else. Believe me, it's best."

"But—" Barbara said and then swallowed.

Judd didn't like the look of desperation he saw in her eyes.

"You're our only family," she finally finished.

Judd figured she probably had that about right. The Bowman family tree had always been more of a stump than anything. Ever since his uncle had died, Judd had thought he was the last of the line.

Still, he hesitated.

He thought of suggesting she turn to the state for help, but he knew what kind of trouble that could get her into. Once children were in the state system, it wasn't all that easy to get them out again, and he could see by the way she kept looking at the kids that she loved them.

He might not know much about a mother's love himself, but he could at least recognize it when he saw it.

"Maybe you could get a babysitter," Judd finally offered. "Some nice grandmother or something."

"You know someone like that?"

Judd had to admit he didn't. He'd only moved to Dry Creek this past spring. He'd been working long and hard plowing and then seeding the alfalfa and wheat crops. He hadn't taken time to get to know any of his neighbors yet.

He wished now that he had accepted one of the invitations to church he'd received since he'd been here. An older woman, Mrs. Hargrove, had even driven out to the ranch one day and invited him. She'd looked so friendly he'd almost promised to go, but he didn't.

What would a man like him do in church anyway? He wouldn't know when to kneel or when to sing or when to bow his head. No, church wasn't for him.

Now he wished he had gone to church anyway, even if he'd made a fool of himself doing so. Mrs. Hargrove would probably help someone who went to her church. She wasn't likely to help a stranger though. Who would be?

"Maybe we could put an ad in the paper."

Barbara just looked at him. "We don't have time for that."

Judd had to admit she was right.

"Besides, this is something big—the kind of thing family members do to help each other," Barbara said with such conviction that Judd believed her.

Not that he was an expert on what family members did to help each other. He couldn't remember his uncle ever doing him a kindness, and the man was the only family Judd had ever known. His uncle had lost all contact with his cousin who was Barbara's father.

He had to admit he had been excited at first when Barbara had come to his doorstep. It was nice to think he had family somewhere in this world.

He looked over at the kids and saw that they were sitting still as stones. Kids shouldn't be so quiet.

"Are they trained?" he asked.

Barbara looked at him blankly for a moment. "You mean potty-trained?"

He nodded.

"Of course! Amanda here is five years old. And Bobby is six. They practically take care of themselves."

Barbara didn't pause before she continued. "And it might only be for a few days. Just enough time for me to drive down to Denver and check out that women's shelter. I want to be sure they'll take us before I drag the kids all that way."

Barbara had arrived in an old car that had seen better days, but it had gotten her here, so Judd figured it would get her to Denver.

Still, if she had car trouble, he knew it would be hard to take care of the kids while she saw to getting the thing fixed. He supposed—maybe—

"I guess things will be slow for the next few days," Judd said. He'd finished putting up the hay, and he had enough of the fence built so his thirty head of cattle could graze in the pasture by the creek. He meant to spend the next few days working on the inside of the house anyway before he turned back to building the rest of the fence. He supposed two trained kids wouldn't be too much trouble.

Judd didn't exactly say he'd keep the kids, but he guessed Barbara could tell he'd lowered his resistance, because she turned her attention to the kids, telling them they were going to stay with Cousin Judd and she'd be back in a few days. That was at the end of August. It was mid-November now.

Judd still hadn't finished all of the fencing, and it was already starting to snow some. If he waited any longer, the ground would be frozen too far down to dig fence holes. That's why he was at the hardware store today getting nails and talking to the old men by the stove.

Judd watched the old men as they smiled at the kids now.

Jacob nodded slowly as he looked at Amanda. "I saw your mama when she brought you and your brother here. She stopped to ask directions. You're right, she was pretty, too."

"My mama's going to come back and get us real soon," Bobby said.

Jacob nodded. "I expect she will."

Judd gave him a curt nod of thanks. Barbara had asked for a few days, but Judd had figured he'd give her a week. By now, she was at least two months overdue to pick up the kids.

Judd hadn't told the kids he'd contacted the court that had issued the restraining order their mother had flashed in front of him and asked them to help find her. Fortunately Barbara had listed him as her next of kin on some paper they had. The court clerk had called every women's shelter between here and Denver and hadn't located Judd's cousin.

Judd had had to do some persuasive talking to the clerk, because he didn't want to mention the kids. He figured his cousin needed a chance to come back for them on her own.

"She's just hurt her hand so she can't write and tell us when," Bobby added confidently.

"I expect that's right. Mail sometimes takes a while," Jacob agreed, and then added, "but then it only makes the letter more special when you do get it."

The older men shifted in their seats. Judd knew they were all aware of the troubles Amanda and Bobby were having. They might not know the details, but he had told his landlady, Linda, back in the beginning of September that he was watching the children for his cousin for a couple of weeks. By now, everyone in Dry Creek probably knew there was something wrong.

Even if he was a newcomer, he would be foolish to think they hadn't asked each other why the kids were still here. Of course, the old men were polite and wouldn't ask a direct question, at least not in front of the kids, so they probably didn't know how bad it all was. They probably thought Barbara had called and made arrangements for the kids to stay longer.

"Speaking of letters, maybe we could write a letter to the new woman and tell her we all want a bakery more than a ballet school." Charley finally broke the silence with a suggestion.

"We can't do that," Jacob said with a sigh. "You don't write a letter to someone who's right across the street. No, we need to be neighborly and tell her to her face. It isn't fair that we let her think she'll make a go of it here with that school of hers."

"Well, I can't talk to her," Charley said. "I'm the one who promised her everything would be fine."

"Too bad *she* wasn't the one who was deaf," one of the other men muttered.

"I'm not deaf. I had a bad connection is all," Charley said. "It could happen to anyone."

"Maybe *he* could go talk to her," the other man said, looking up at Judd. "He seems to hear all right."

Judd felt his stomach knot up at the idea. "I got to count me out some nails. I'm building a fence."

He walked back to the shelves that held the boxes of nails. Amanda and Bobby trailed along after him. Judd looked down at Bobby. "Why don't you take your sister and go across to the café and put your order in for some of that cocoa? Tell Linda I'll be along in a minute."

The Linda who ran the café was also his landlady. She was renting him the Jenkins place, with an option to buy come next spring. Judd had saved the few thousand dollars the state had given him when it settled his uncle's estate and added most of the other money he'd gotten to it for the past six years.

He'd started out working as a ranch hand, but the wages added up too slowly for him, and so he'd spent the next couple of years on the rodeo circuit. He'd earned enough in prize money to set himself up nicely. Right now, he had enough money in the bank to buy the Jenkins place, and he'd already stocked it with some purebred breeding cattle. He could have bought the place outright, but he wanted to take his time and be sure he liked it well enough before he made the final deal. So far, the ground had been fertile and the place quiet enough to suit him.

Judd watched Amanda and Bobby leave the hardware store before he reached into the nail bin and pulled out another nail. Fortunately, the older men had given up on the idea that he should talk to the new woman. They probably realized he'd botch the job.

Outside of talking with Linda at the café and smiling politely when Mrs. Hargrove had delivered the books the school had sent him when he'd decided to homeschool the kids, Judd hadn't had a conversation with a woman since his cousin had left the kids with him. Well, unless you counted the court clerk he'd talked to on the phone.

Judd never had been much good at talking to women, at least not women who weren't rodeo followers. He had no problem with women at rodeos, probably because *they* did most of the talking and he always knew what they wanted; they wanted a rodeo winner to escort them around town for the evening. That didn't exactly require conversation, not with the yelling that spilled out of most rodeo hangouts in the evening.

As long as his boots were polished and his hat on straight, the rodeo women didn't care if he was quiet. He was mostly for show anyway—if he was winning. If he wasn't winning, they weren't that interested in talking to him, or even interested in being with him.

The few temporary affairs he'd had with rodeo followers didn't leave him feeling good about himself, so eventually he just declined invitations to party. By then he was counting up his prize money after every rodeo anyway, with an eye to when he could leave the circuit and set himself up on his own ranch.

In those years, Judd hadn't known any women outside of rodeo circles, and he thought that was best. Judd never seemed to know what those women were thinking, and he didn't even try to sort it all out. He liked things straightforward and to the point. The other kind of women—the kind that made wives—always seemed to say things in circles and then expect a man to know what they meant. For all Judd knew, they could be speaking Greek.

Judd had a feeling the new woman in Dry Creek was one of that kind of women.

No, he wasn't the one to talk to her about what she was doing here, even though he had to admit he was curious. She sure knew how to hang a sign in that window.

Chapter Three

Lizette shifted the sign with her left hand and took a deep breath. It had taken her the better part of three days to get the practice bar in place along the left side of the room and the floor waxed to a smooth shine. She still had the costumes hanging on a rack near the door waiting to be sorted by size, but she'd decided this morning it was time to put the sign she'd made in her window and start advertising for students.

She could still smell the floor wax, so she'd opened the door to air out the room even though it was cold outside. At least it wasn't snowing today.

Lizette had bought a large piece of metal at the hardware store yesterday and some paint so she could make her sign. The old men sitting around the stove in the store had obviously heard she was setting up a business, because they were full of suggestions on how she should make her sign.

Of course, most of the words centered on the Baker part of the school's name, but she couldn't fault them for that. She was heartened to see they had so much enthusiasm for a ballet school. If this was any indication of the interest of the rest of the people in the community, she just might get enough students to pull off a modified Nutcracker ballet for Christmas after all. She'd even assured the men in the hardware store that no one was too old to learn some ballet steps. In fact, she'd told them that lots of athletes used ballet as a way to exercise.

The old men had looked a little dismayed at her comments, and she wasn't surprised. At their age, they probably didn't want to take up *any* exercise program, especially not one as rigorous as ballet. "You'd want to check with your doctor first, of course," Lizette added. "You should do that before you take up any new exercise program."

The men nodded as she left the hardware store. All in all, they'd been friendly, and she wasn't so sure she wouldn't get a student or two out of the bunch. And if she didn't get any students, at least she'd gotten some good neighbors. One of them had already been over to check on the smoke coming out of the small kitchen off the main room when she'd been baking some cookies earlier and had forgotten they were in the oven. He'd even offered to bring her over some more flour if she was inclined to continue baking. He'd expressed some hope of a cherry pie.

The chair Lizette stood on gave her enough height so she could lift the sign and hook it into the chain she'd put up to hang it with. The sign had a white background with navy script lettering.

Lizette planned to take a picture of the sign later and send it to Madame Aprele. She wasn't sure she'd tell her old teacher that she didn't have any students yet, but she could tell her that the school was almost ready for classes now that the practice bar was in place. Lizette had planned to use a makeshift practice bar at first, because she couldn't afford a real one. Madame Aprele had surprised her by sending her one of her own mahogany bars. Her old teacher had shipped it before Lizette left Seattle, and Linda, next door in the café, had kept it for Lizette until she arrived.

Lizette had called Madame Aprele, thanking her and insisting that she accept payment for the equipment. It would help enough, Lizette explained, if she could just pay for the bar over time. She didn't add that she had no need of charity. Madame Aprele agreed to let Lizette make payments if Lizette promised to call her with weekly updates on her school.

At first Lizette was uncomfortable promising to call Madame Aprele, because she knew her mother would disapprove. But then Lizette decided that whatever problem there had been between her mother and Madame Aprele, there was no need for *her* to continue the coldness.

Twenty years ago when Madame Aprele had bought the school from Lizette's mother, the two women had been friends. But, over the years, Jacqueline spoke less and less to Madame Aprele until, finally, her mother wouldn't even greet the other women when she picked Lizette up after ballet class.

At the time, Lizette didn't understand why. Now she wondered if her mother didn't look at Madame Aprele and wish her own life had turned out like the other woman's.

Not that there was anything in Jacqueline's life to suggest she wished for a different one. Madame Aprele had been born in France in the same village as Lizette's mother. Both women had studied ballet together and had left France together. Lizette's mother had become more Americanized over the years, however, especially after she'd started working in the bakery.

As Lizette's mother became more conservative in her dress, Madame Aprele became more outrageous, until, in the end, Lizette's mother looked almost dowdy and Madame Aprele looked like an old-fashioned movie star with her lavender feather boas and dramatic eye makeup.

Lizette stepped down from the chair just as she saw two little children cross the street from the hardware store. The sun was shining on the window so Lizette could not see the children clearly, but she could tell from their size that they were both good prospects for ballet.

Lizette didn't know how to advertise in a small town like Dry Creek, but she supposed she could ask about the children at the hardware store, find out who their parents were and send them a flyer.

When the children passed her door, they stopped. The little girl was staring at something, and it didn't take long for Lizette to figure out what it was. The sunlight was streaming in, making the Sugar Plum Fairy costume sparkle even more than usual. Lizette's mother had used both gold and metallic pink on the costume when she'd made it, and many a young girl mistook it for a princess costume.

"If you go ask your mother if it's okay, you can come in and look at the costumes," Lizette said. She doubted things were so casual in Dry Creek that parents wanted their children going into strange stores without their knowledge.

The girl whispered something in the boy's ear. He nodded.

Lizette had walked closer to the children and was starting to feel uneasy. If you added a few pounds and took away the scared look in their eyes, those two kids looked very similar to that snapshot she'd seen several days ago. She looked up and down the snow-covered street. There were the usual cars and pickups parked beside the hardware store and the café, but there were no people outside except for the two children. "Does your mother know where you are?"

Both children solemnly nodded their heads yes.

Lizette was relieved to know the children had a mother. Their father hadn't looked like much of a parent, but hopefully their mother was better.

"Our mother won't mind if we look at the dress," the boy politely said after a moment and pointed inside. "That one."

The rack was very close to the door and Lizette decided she could leave the door open so the children's mother could see them if she looked down the street. Really, if she moved the rack closer, the children could touch the costumes while they stood outside on the sidewalk.

Lizette pushed the costume rack so it was just inside the door. "The pink one is my favorite, too."

Lizette watched as the little girl reached out her hand and gently touched the costume.

"That's the dress for the Sugar Plum Fairy in the Nutcracker ballet," Lizette said.

"What's a ballet?" the boy asked.

Lizette thought a moment. "It's like a play with lots of costumes and people moving."

"So someone wears that dress in a play?" the boy asked.

The boy and Lizette were both seeing the same thing. The little girl's face was starting to glow. One moment she had been pale and quiet, and the next her face started to show traces of pink and her eyes started to sparkle.

For the first time, Lizette decided she had made the right decision to come to Dry Creek to open her school. If there were more little girls and boys like this in the community, she'd have a wonderful time teaching them to love ballet.

Chapter Four

Lizette heard a sound and looked up to see a half-dozen men stomping down the steps of the hardware store and heading straight toward her new school. She wasn't sure, but she thought every one of the men was frowning, especially the one who was at the back of the group. That man had to be forty years younger than the other men, but he looked the most annoyed of them all.

"The children are still just on the sidewalk," Lizette said when the men were close enough to hear. While she hadn't thought anyone would want children to go into a building alone, she certainly hadn't expected there would be a problem with them standing on the sidewalk and looking at something inside. If the citizens of Dry Creek were that protective of their children, she'd never have any young students in her classes.

Lizette braced herself, but when the men reached

her, they stood silent. Finally, one of them cleared his throat. "About this—ah—school—"

"The children will all have permission from their parents, of course," Lizette rushed to assure them. "And parents can watch the classes any time they want. They can even attend if they want. I'd love to have some older students."

The younger man, the one who had hung back on the walk over, moved closer to the open door. He seemed intent on the two children and did not stop until he stood beside them protectively. Lizette noticed that the young boy relaxed a little when the man stood beside him, and the girl reached out her hand to touch the man's leg. She knew the man wasn't the children's father because she'd met that man already. Maybe he was their stepfather. That would explain why the father hadn't known where the children lived.

"Well, about the students—" The older man cleared his throat and began again. "You see, there might be a problem with students."

"No one has to audition or anything to be in the performances," Lizette said. She wasn't sure what was bothering the men, but she wanted them to know she was willing to work with the town. "And public performance is good for children, especially if it's not competitive."

"Anyone can be in the play," the boy said softly.

The men had all stopped talking to listen to the boy, so they all heard the next words very clearly.

"I'm going to be a Sugar Plum Fairy," the girl said, and pointed to the costume she'd been admiring.

Judd swallowed. Amanda never talked to anyone but Bobby, and then only in whispers. Who knew all it would take was a sparkly costume to make her want to talk?

"How much is the costume?" Judd asked the woman in the doorway. He didn't care what figure she named—he'd buy it for Amanda.

"Oh, the costumes aren't for sale," the woman said. "I'll need them for the performance, especially if I want to have something ready for Christmas. I won't have time to make many more costumes."

"About this performance—" the older man said, then cleared his throat.

Lizette wondered what was bothering the old man, but she didn't have time to ask him because the younger man was scowling at her.

"So the only way Amanda can wear this costume is if she's in your performance?" he asked.

"I wouldn't say it was *my* performance." Lizette felt her patience starting to grow thin. "All of the students will see it as *their* performance. We work together."

"About the students—" The older man began again and cleared his throat for what must have been the fourth time.

"I'll sign Amanda up," the younger man said decisively. "If she signs up first, she should get her pick of the parts, shouldn't she?"

"Well, I don't see why she can't be the Sugar Plum Fairy," Lizette agreed. After all, Lizette herself would be choreographing the part for the children's ballet, and could tailor it to Amanda's skills. She'd just gotten her first student. "She'll have to practice, of course. And we'll have to have a few more students to do even a shortened version of the Nutcracker."

The younger man squeezed the boy on his shoulder.

"I'll sign up, too," the boy offered reluctantly.

"There—I have two students!" Lizette announced triumphantly. "And I only just hung up my sign."

The older man cleared his throat again, but this time he had nothing to say. All of the older men were looking a little stunned. Maybe they were as taken aback as she was by the fierce scowl the younger man was giving them.

"You might want to see a doctor about the cold you're getting," Lizette finally said to the man who had been trying to talk. "Usually when you have to clear your throat so often, it means a cold is coming on."

The older man nodded silently.

"And you might ask him about taking up ballet while you're there," Lizette said. "Just to see if the exercise would be all right for you. Now that I have two students, I can begin classes, and you'd be more than welcome."

Lizette decided the older man definitely had a cold coming on. He had just gone pale. He even looked a little dizzy.

"You'll want to wait until you're feeling better before you start though," Lizette said to him. That seemed to make him feel better. At least his color returned.

"I'll think about it," he mumbled.

Lizette nodded. She knew she couldn't manage for long on the income she'd get from two students, but just look how much people wanted to talk about her school. With all of that talk, she'd get more students before long.

Lizette smiled up at the younger man. He might scowl a lot, but she was grateful to him for her first two students. "Your wife must be happy you take such good care of the children."

The young man looked down at her. "I don't have a wife."

Lizette faltered. "Oh, I just thought that because their father showed me their picture that—"

"You know the kids' father, Neal Strong?"

If Lizette thought the men had been quiet before, they were even more silent now.

"No, I don't know him. Some man just showed me their picture in Forsyth when he asked me to give him a ride out this way. He said they were his kids and he was trying to find them. He probably didn't know the address or something."

Judd felt Amanda move closer to his leg, and suddenly he had as great a need to be close to her as she had to be close to him, so he reached down and lifted her up even though he had his heavy farm coat on and it probably had grease on it from when he'd last worked on the tractor.

"Don't worry," Judd whispered into Amanda's hair when she snuggled into his shoulder.

Judd reminded himself that the papers Barbara had shown him when she left the children with him included a court order forbidding the children's father from being within one hundred yards of them.

Judd knew the court clerk well enough now that he could ask for a copy of the court order if he needed one. Of course, that would mean the clerk would guess that the children were with him. No, there had to be another way. Besides, he didn't actually need a copy of the order for the court to enforce it.

"You're sure it was him?" Judd turned to ask the woman. He didn't know how the children's father would even know where they were unless Barbara had told him.

"He had a picture and he said he was their father," Lizette said. "He had a snake on his arm."

Amanda went still in Judd's arm. The kids had told him about the snake.

Judd nodded. He should have figured something like this would happen. He wondered if his cousin had gotten back with her husband, after all. Generally, Judd was a supporter of married folks staying together. But some of the things Bobby had let slip while he was at Judd's place would make anyone advise Barbara to forget her husband.

The one thing Judd knew was that he didn't want that man to come within shouting distance of the children.

"You have a lock on this place, I suppose," Judd

said as he looked inside the building the woman was going to use for her school. If he brought the kids to the lessons and then came back to pick them up, they should be safe.

"I could put a lock on," one of the older men spoke up. "It's no trouble. They have some heavy-duty ones over at the hardware store."

"And it wouldn't hurt Charley here to come over and sit while the kids have their lessons," another older man offered. "He always complains that the chairs at the hardware store are too hard anyway. Now that he's got his fancy phone, he can call the sheriff any time, night or day."

Judd nodded. It felt good to have neighbors, even if he hadn't been very neighborly himself. He wasn't sure what he could do to repay them, but he intended to try. "I'll be watching, too."

"Is something wrong?" Lizette looked at the men's faces.

"Their father isn't fit to be near these kids—even the court says so," Judd said quietly. He could see the alarm grow on Lizette's face. "Not that you have to worry about it. We'll take care of the guarding. You won't even know we're here. We can even sit outside."

"In the snow?" Charley protested.

"Of course you can't sit outside in the cold," Lizette said. "I'll put some chairs along the side of the practice area. And I'll be careful about who else I accept as students. I'll check references on any grown man who wants to join the class."

Charley snorted. "Ain't no grown man hereabouts that'll sign up. Not if he wants to keep his boots—"

One of the other older men interrupted him. "I thought you was gonna sign up yourself, Charley. You can't just sit and watch everyone else practice. That wouldn't be right."

"Why, I can't do no ballet," Charley said, and then looked around at the faces of his friends. "I got me that stiff knee, remember—from the time I was loading that heifer and it pinned me against the corral?"

"The exercises might even help you then," Lizette said. "We do a lot of stretching and bending to warm up."

If Judd hadn't still been thinking about the children's father, he would have laughed at Charley's trapped expression. As it was, he was just glad Charley would be inside with the children. For himself, Judd thought, he'd set up a chair outside the door, so he could keep his eyes on who was driving into Dry Creek.

Judd didn't trust the children's father and was determined to keep the man as far away from Dry Creek as possible. First thing in the morning Judd decided he'd tell Sheriff Wall all about the court order.

Judd had only met the sheriff once, but he trusted the man. Sheriff Wall might not be one of those big-city sheriffs who solved complicated crimes, but he had the persistence and instincts of a guard dog. And the man knew every road coming near Dry Creek, even the ones that were just pasture trails. The kids would be safer with Sheriff Wall on the job.

"I can pay in advance for the lessons," Judd announced. He didn't like the sympathetic look the ballet woman was giving the kids now that Charley had accepted his fate. Judd didn't want the woman to think they couldn't pay their way, especially not when she'd have to give special attention to the security of her classroom.

"There's no need to pay now," the woman protested.

But Judd already had two twenty-dollar bills in his hand and he held them out to her. "Let me know if it costs more."

"That should cover their first couple of lessons," Lizette said as she took the money and turned to a desk in a corner of the large room. "Just let me get a receipt for you."

Judd watched the woman walk over to the desk. He couldn't help but notice that she didn't just walk— she actually glided. He supposed that was what all of that ballet did for a body.

Judd tried not to gawk at the woman. The fact that she moved like poetry in motion was no excuse for staring at her.

Judd heard a soft collective sigh and turned to see all the old men watching the woman as if they'd never seen anyone like her before. Charley had obviously forgotten all about his reluctance to be in the class.

"There's no need for a receipt," Judd said.

The woman looked up from the desk. Even from across the room he could see she was relieved. "But you should have one anyway. Just as soon as I get all my desk things organized, I'll see that you get one. I could mail it to you, if you leave me your address."

"I'm at the Jenkins place south of town. Just write *Jenkins* on the envelope and leave it on the counter in the hardware store."

It had taken Judd two weeks to figure out the mail system in town. The first part was simple. The mail carrier left all of the Dry Creek mail at the hardware store, and the ranchers picked it up when they came into town. The second part still had Judd confused. For some reason, if he wanted to get his mail sooner rather than later, he still had to have it addressed to the Jenkins place even though no one by the name of Jenkins had lived on the ranch for two years now.

When Judd finally bought the Jenkins place, he told himself he'd get the name changed. He'd asked the mail carrier about it, and the man had just looked at him blankly and said that's what everyone called the place.

Judd vowed that once he had the children taken care of and the deed to the place signed, he'd take a one-page ad out in that Billings paper everyone around here read. He'd make sure people knew it wasn't the Jenkins place anymore.

But, in the meantime, he didn't want to have the woman's envelope returned to her, so he'd go along with saying he lived at the Jenkins place.

The woman nodded. "I know about the hardware store. I've been meaning to post an announcement about the school so everyone will know that we're currently taking students."

"About the students—" one of the old men said and then cleared his throat. "You see, the students—well, we're not sure how many students you'll have."

"Of course," Lizette assured him. She knew she needed a few more students to do the ballet, but surely three or four more would come. "No one knows how many people will answer the flyer I put up. But I need to start the classes anyway if we're going to perform the Nutcracker ballet before Christmas."

Lizette figured the students who came later could do the parts that involved less practice.

"Christmas is only five weeks away," Judd said and frowned. He knew when Christmas was coming because he figured his cousin would surely come for the children before Christmas.

Judd had gone ahead and ordered toys for the kids when he'd put in a catalog order last week, but he thought he'd be sending the presents along with them when their mother picked them up. Thanksgiving was next week, and it was likely the only holiday he'd have to worry about. He figured he could cope with a turkey if he could get Linda to give him some more basic instructions. She'd already told him about some cooking bag that practically guaranteed success with a turkey.

"I don't suppose you have a real nutcracker in that ballet?" one of the older men asked hopefully. "I wouldn't say no to some chopped walnuts—especially if they were on some maple doughnuts."

"You know there's no doughnuts, so there's no point in going on about them," Charley said firmly as he frowned at the man who had spoken. "There's more to life than your stomach."

"But you like doughnuts, too," the older man protested. "You were hoping for some, too—just like me."

"Maybe at first," Charley admitted. "But I can't be eating doughnuts if I'm going to learn this here ballet."

Lizette smiled as she looked at the two men. "Well, I do generally make some sort of cookies or something for the students to eat after we practice. I guess I could make doughnuts one of these days."

"You mean you can bake doughnuts?" Charley asked. "I didn't know anyone around here could bake doughnuts."

Lizette nodded. "I'll need to get a large Dutch oven, but I have a fry basket I can use."

"Hallelujah!" Charley beamed.

"And, of course, I'd need to have some spare time," Lizette added.

"And she's not likely to have any time to bake now that she's starting classes," Judd said, frowning. It would be harder to guard the kids if every stray man in the county was lined up at the ballet school eating doughnuts.

Judd told himself that it was only his concern for the safety of the kids that made him worry about who was likely to be visiting the ballet school. He'd been in Dry Creek long enough to know about all the cowboys on the outlying ranches.

A woman like Lizette Baker was bound to attract

enough attention just being herself without adding doughnuts to the equation.

Not that, he reminded himself, it should matter to him how many men gawked at the ballet teacher. He certainly wasn't going to cause any awkwardness by being overly friendly himself. He was just hoping to get to know her a little better.

She was, after all, the kids' teacher, and he was, for the time being, their parent. He really was obligated to be somewhat friendly to her, wasn't he? It was his duty. He was as close to a PTA as Dry Creek had, since he was the almost-parent of the only two kids in her class right now. If Bobby and Amanda were still with him in a few months, he'd have to enroll them in the regular school in Miles City instead of home-schooling them. But, until then, it was practically his civic duty to be friendly to their ballet teacher. And he didn't need a doughnut to make him realize it.

Chapter Five

Lizette worried there was something wrong with her. She thought she had been working through the grief of her mother's death, but maybe she was wrong. After all, she hadn't had that much experience with mourning, and the chaplain at the hospital had talked about going through different stages of grief.

Lizette wondered if one of those stages of grief was twitching.

Here she was wrapping up the day's dance lesson, and her mind wasn't concentrated on the three people who were her students or the five more students she needed if she was going to pull off even a modified version of the Nutcracker ballet. Instead, she was all jumpy inside, and her gaze kept going to the window, where she could see Judd sitting on the steps of her school and looking out to the street with a scowl on his face.

If she didn't get a firm hold on herself, she'd be actually twitching when she looked at that man.

Lizette had had three days of lessons now, and for the better part of all of those days Judd had had his back turned toward her and the students. The first day she didn't notice his silence and his scowls. The second day she noticed, but she didn't feel the need to do anything about it. Today, she felt obsessed by the man.

She kept fighting the urge to go out and talk to him—and that was after she'd already been outside five times today to ask him questions. She didn't have much to talk about either, except for the weather, and how many times could she ask if it looked like it was going to snow? He'd think she was dim-witted. There wasn't even a cloud in the sky anymore.

She kept expecting each time she went out and asked the man a question that she would then be able to move on with her lessons with a focused mind.

She was still waiting for that to happen.

The really odd thing was that nothing had changed in those three days.

She didn't need to see his face to know he wore the same scowl he'd worn every day so far. Every time today she'd found an excuse to slip outside and ask him a question, she'd known he'd have the same fierce look on his face even before she opened the door.

Lizette wondered if Judd thought his look would keep strange cars off the street in front of the school. Actually, he might be right about that one. That scowl of his would stop an army tank from approaching him.

With all of the frowning, Lizette knew there was

no sane reason she should feel drawn to go up and talk to him. But she was.

She thought it might be his shoulders. For as hard as his face scowled, his shoulders told a different story. It wasn't anger he was feeling, but worry. Anxiety hung on his shoulders. It was there in the way he angled his head when he heard a sound and the way he stood to take a look down the road every half hour or so.

Judd was taking his duty seriously, and he was worried.

That's it, Lizette thought to herself in relief. She found him compelling because he was protecting the children. She'd just lost her mother, and the man was obviously doing everything he could to guard the children in his care. That made him an unconscious picture to her of her mother, she told herself. She'd be as attracted to a chicken if it sat there guarding its eggs. It had nothing to do with the fact that he was a man. He was simply a concerned parent.

Lizette felt better having figured that out. Not that she would have been opposed to finding the man attractive as a *man,* she just didn't have time for that kind of distraction right now. She only had three students—Amanda, Bobby and Charley. She needed to worry about getting more students instead of thinking about some man's shoulders.

And, yet, she let herself walk over to the doorway. Bobby and Amanda were sitting on the wooden floor untying their dance shoes. Since Charley wore socks instead of dance shoes, he didn't have to worry about ties. Instead, he was pulling in his stomach and admiring himself in the mirror she'd hung behind the exercise bar. None of her students needed her immediate attention.

"They're almost done," Lizette said as she walked out on the porch and crossed her arms in the chill. At least she wasn't asking about snow this time, even though the air felt cold enough for it. She always wore black tights and a black wrap-around dress when she practiced. Unfortunately, the dress was sleeveless. "Aren't you cold out here waiting for the kids?"

Judd looked up at Lizette and forgot to frown. He almost forgot to breathe. She was standing in front of the sun, and although the temperature was low enough outside to make his fingers ache if he didn't keep them in his pockets, the sun was shining brightly and she looked as though she was rimmed with gold. Her black hair was pulled back into a bun, and the smooth lines of her head made him think of an exotic princess. Her face was smooth and, even without lipstick, she looked like a picture he'd once seen of Cleopatra. The flimsy black thing she had draped over her made her look as if she was in constant motion. No wonder there had been so many wars fought back in Cleopatra's day.

Judd was outclassed and he had sense enough to know it. All he asked was that he not embarrass himself around her. "It's not that cold. Forty-six, last I checked."

"Yes, well." Lizette smiled.

"And no snow," Judd added.

He'd already figured out that it wasn't snow she was worried about. The few clouds that had been in the sky this morning were long gone. No, it was the kids' father she was fretting about. She didn't know Judd well enough to know that she didn't have to worry about him leaving his post.

Not that he minded her coming out to check on him. He knew he hadn't been around many women in his life, but he didn't remember women being this naturally beautiful. He almost smiled in return. "So the kids are almost finished? Did they do all right?"

Lizette smiled even wider. "You do make a good mother."

"What?" Judd choked on the smile that didn't happen. Had he heard her right? She thought he made a good *mother?* A mother?

"I mean with all of your concern and all," Lizette continued.

Judd grunted. He'd known he was out of her class, but he hadn't realized he was that far out of it. A man didn't get further away from date material than having a woman think of him as a mother.

"I used to ride rodeo." Judd thought he owed it to himself to speak up. "Won my share of ribbons, too. Bronc riding and steer wrestling. They're not easy events. I placed first in 2003 in bronc riding at the state fair in Great Falls."

"Is that where you got your scar?"

Judd had forgotten he had a scar on the right side of his forehead. The scar hadn't made any difference to his life, and he no longer even really saw it when he shaved. "No, I got that in a fight."

Judd didn't add that it had been a snowball fight when he was eight years old. He'd been dodging a snowball and hadn't seen the low-hanging branch of the tree. He wasn't going to admit he had got the scar playing, however—not when he was talking to a woman who thought of him as a mother.

"I'll bet you're strong," Lizette said, and almost shook herself. That was the most obvious come-hither line a woman had ever uttered, and she felt foolish saying it. Unfortunately, it either wasn't obvious enough for Judd, or he was just not interested. It didn't even make his scowl go away. "I mean, of course you're strong. You'd have to be with the way you swing Amanda around."

Lizette had watched the way Amanda ran to Judd after classes. The little girl would run straight at him, and he'd bend down to scoop her up. While Amanda giggled, he'd gently toss her up in the air.

"You don't need to worry about Amanda and Bobby's father. I can take him in a fight if need be," Judd said. He figured that was what all the talk about how strong he was came from.

Neither one of them heard the two kids come out on the porch.

"He has a gun—my dad does," Bobby said.

"You don't need to worry about your father either," Judd said gently as he put his hand on the boy's head.

It had taken Judd a full month to calm the nightmares that woke Bobby up. The boy still wanted to sleep in a cot at the bottom of Judd's bed. Judd had figured he might as well let him, since Amanda was already sleeping on a cot on the right side of his bed. If he wasn't worried about them rolling out of his bed, Judd would have let the two children share it, and he would have rolled his sleeping bag out on the floor. But the cots were closer to the floor, and the kids seemed to like them.

"But if he has a gun," Lizette said, "shouldn't we let the sheriff know?"

"The sheriff already knows."

Judd had given a complete report. He had even given the sheriff a photo of the kids' father that had been in one of the suitcases Barbara left with them.

That photo had given Judd many an uneasy moment. The photo was a picture of the two children, Barbara and her husband. He knew it had been taken a couple of years ago because a date was handwritten at the bottom of the picture. It had been one of those pictures from a photo booth like the kind you find in an amusement park. Judd had a feeling the family didn't have many photos. The fact that Barbara had left it for the kids might mean she knew she wasn't coming back.

But, right now, the photo was the least of his worries. Judd didn't like the pale look of both of the kids' faces. Of course, that might be because they were outside without their mittens on.

"Where'd you put your mittens?" Judd asked them as he stood up and herded the two children back into the warm room. He'd ordered the mittens from the back of the seed catalog, and he'd since wished he'd gotten three pairs for each of them instead of only two.

"I'm afraid that might be my fault," Lizette said as she followed them inside and closed the door behind herself. "I told them they could have a doughnut after class today."

"We didn't want to get our mittens dirty," Bobby explained. "The doughnuts have sugar on them."

"You don't need to give them doughnuts," Judd said, even though he could smell the doughnuts and didn't blame the kids for leaving their mittens off. The ballet practice room smelled of home. The only smell they usually had in his kitchen was the aroma of his morning coffee. Everything else was canned or microwaved or put between slices of bread in a sandwich. Judd didn't know much about cooking, and he'd never met anyone who actually baked. Even Linda at the café didn't do that kind of baking.

"Of course she needs to give us doughnuts." Charley joined them from his perch on one of the chairs spaced around a work table. "I had to drive up to the Elkton ranch to borrow that Dutch oven. I would have driven further for homemade doughnuts. I mean to have one if it's offered."

"Did anyone see you borrow the Dutch oven?" Jake asked.

"Of course they saw me!" Charley said indignantly. "I didn't steal it."

"I mean, did any of the ranch hands see you borrow it? Or did you just talk to the cook?"

"Pete Denning saw me. He told the cook not to give it to me—said I'd be using the thing to soak my feet! I told him we were using it to make doughnuts."

Jake's worse fears were confirmed. "I don't suppose you told him the doughnuts weren't going to be anything more exciting than flapjacks."

"Now, why would I do that?"

"To avoid a stampede."

"Oh," Charley said as he considered the matter. "I didn't think of that."

Both men looked down the road.

"I don't see anyone though," Charley said. "Maybe Pete forgot."

"Not likely."

"Maybe we should eat our doughnuts now," Bobby said. He'd been standing beside Judd.

"And I'm sure you don't need to worry about someone else coming for doughnuts," Lizette added. "There are plenty of doughnuts to share with a few other people."

Judd grunted. Maybe they were all right. Maybe he didn't need to worry about a stampede of cowboys coming for doughnuts. They probably thought Charley was doing the cooking anyway, and Charley wasn't known for his skills in the kitchen.

Lizette came back with a platter of doughnuts and some white paper napkins. There were powdered doughnuts and maple doughnuts. Twisted cruller doughnuts and apple doughnuts. Even jelly doughnuts.

Lizette tucked a napkin into the neckline of Amanda's dress and then put one into Bobby's shirt before spreading white napkins on the table in front of each of them.

"You made these?" Judd asked. He felt as wide-eyed as those cowboys he was worried about. He knew Lizette had said she made doughnuts, but he'd never expected that she could make doughnuts like these. He'd expected something more like biscuits. But these doughnuts were so perfect they glistened.

"I used to work in a bakery," Lizette said as she held the platter out to Charley. "Part of that time as a baker."

"There must be two dozen doughnuts here," the older man marveled as he took a jelly doughnut and eyed the rest longingly. "Maybe three dozen."

"Well, if you're making doughnuts, you can't just make a few." Lizette passed the platter to the children next. "The recipes all make about five dozen."

Amanda took an apple doughnut and Bobby took a maple one.

Judd was still standing, but Lizette turned the platter toward him anyway. "I know you're not a student, but you're working, too."

Lizette gave him a small, hopeful smile. Judd would have taken a burnt stick off a platter if she'd offered it to him with that smile. As it was, he picked up the first doughnut he touched—it was a cruller.

"Don't you need a machine or something to make doughnuts?" Judd said after he ate his first bite of pure heaven. "I didn't know regular people could even make doughnuts like these."

Lizette laughed. "All you really need is something to make the holes. Oh, and a Dutch oven, of course, unless you have a deep fryer."

Charley took a bite out of his doughnut and started to purr. "I could put in an extra practice session this afternoon if you want."

"I don't think that will be necessary," Lizette said. "But if that's a hint that you'd like a second dough-nut, you can have one anyway."

"Ah, well, then," Charley said as he took another bite out of his doughnut. "Too bad the boys over at the hardware store don't know you're giving these to your students. They'd be signed up in no time."

Judd stopped eating his doughnut. He'd just looked out the window and had seen several of the ranch hands from the Elkton place go into the hardware store. He supposed it was too optimistic to think they'd come to town to buy nails.

"Well, I could take the tray over to the hardware store," Lizette said as she looked out the window in her studio and into the big window in the hardware store. "We certainly won't be able to eat all of these doughnuts, and we do need a few more dancers to do the Nutcracker."

"Jacob would appreciate a doughnut," Charley said. "He's been eating his own cooking for weeks now."

"Why don't you go get Jacob and invite him over," Judd suggested. So far the hardware store door was still shut. Maybe the cowboys really had come in for nails. "Just don't tell him there's doughnuts here."

"I know how to keep a secret," Charley said as he slowly stood up. "Although the pastor might want a doughnut, too, and I wouldn't feel right overlooking those two little boys of his if they're there."

"Oh, please invite the children," Lizette said. "I heard the pastor had two boys. I just haven't had a chance to invite them to ballet class yet."

"I'm not sure you'll want them in your class," Charley said doubtfully. "They have a tendency to be hard on the furniture."

"That's perfect then, because I don't have any furniture—at least not in the practice area," Lizette said. So far she had just fixed up the main room in her building. The building had been a grocery store years ago, and it had a nice backroom with a kitchen area that she was using as a small apartment for herself. "And if they're the kind of boys that like to move a lot, I'll just make them be mice."

Amanda giggled. "You can't turn boys into mice."

"Oh, yes, I can," Lizette said as she tousled Amanda's hair. "If I can turn a little girl into the Sugar Plum Fairy, I can turn little boys into mice or snowflakes or flowers."

"I'd rather be a mouse than a flower," Bobby said.

"Well, we'll see," Lizette said as her hand rested on Bobby's head, too. "Maybe you can even be something more exciting than either one."

Judd wasn't so sure about Lizette's powers to turn little boys into mice, but watching her casual affection with the children sure turned him into something else.

"I'm surprised you don't have children," Judd said. "Of your own, I mean."

Lizette looked up at him. "I do hope to have children some day."

Judd could only nod. He didn't really even have any good reason to feel so disappointed. Of course she wanted children. She had to be ten years younger than him, which would only make her twenty-three or twenty-four. A woman like her would want the whole family thing.

Judd didn't know where the thought had come from in the past few days that maybe he could marry if he just limited himself to a wife and didn't think of children. Children were what made a family anyway. He wouldn't have a clue about how to be a father. Sure, he'd gotten along fine with Bobby and Amanda. But they weren't like other kids. They'd been frightened so badly that they clung to him for safety. If he hadn't been there, they would have clung to that stray dog of his as long as the dog defended them from their nightmares.

Other children would expect more. No, a man like him had no business thinking about raising children. Maybe someday he'd meet a woman who didn't want to have children either, and the two of them could marry.

Suddenly the doughnut Judd was eating didn't taste so good. It was too bad about Lizette.

Chapter Six

Lizette heard the sound of boots crunching in the snow. Lots of boots.

"Better hide those doughnuts," Charley said as he stood and looked out the window. "Another couple of pickups from the Elkton ranch are parked in front of the hardware store. Wonder when they got here."

"It's too late," Judd said. He'd eaten the last of his doughnut, and he pushed his chair away from the table.

The door to the ballet school was closed, and there were a dozen knocks on it all at the same time. Lizette could see, just by looking out the side window, that a lot of men were standing on her porch.

"I don't suppose they want to sign up for class," Lizette said as she stood to go to the door.

"No, I can't imagine they want to be mice," Judd agreed.

Lizette looked over her shoulder at the platter of doughnuts she had on the table. It still had five doughnuts on it. She had the rest of the doughnuts in the back room.

She opened the door and saw a sea of cowboy hats nod at her. "Come in."

"Thank you, ma'am," the man who stepped over the threshold first said.

"My, it does smell like heaven in here," the second man said as he walked into the room.

Each man who stepped into the room craned his neck to see the doughnuts sitting on the platter that was on the table. There was a black mat next to the door, but none of the ranch hands paused to let their wet feet dry there.

"We just stopped by to say a neighborly hello," one of the cowboys said as he craned his neck to look around her at the doughnuts.

"That's nice," Lizette said. She decided that if they didn't notice her standing there, it was futile to point out the black mat. Besides, the mat wouldn't make much difference. If a couple of men stopped to let their boots dry, the others would just keep the door open and the floor would eventually get wet anyway. In addition, the air in the room would be cold.

"The doughnuts are for the ballet students," Charley said before anyone could carry the conversation further. Then he sat back down at the table. "And for the men who have been guarding the school, of course."

Several of the older men stepped forward through the pack of cowboys.

"We're the guards," Jacob said as he stepped forward. Two other older men followed him. "We've been keeping a watch out the windows for strangers."

"That ain't a fair way to decide who gets the doughnuts—they haven't had to do anything but sit where they always sit," one of the cowboys said before he turned to Lizette and swept off his hat. "Begging your pardon, miss. I don't think I've had the pleasure of meeting you. My name's Pete Denning. The boys and I heard you were making doughnuts. What a fine thing to do on such a nice day."

Judd could see that the longer Pete talked to Lizette, the less concerned he'd become about the doughnuts. By the time the man had stopped introducing himself, he had a grin on his face that Judd would wager had nothing to do with baked goods.

"Of course, I'm not asking for any doughnuts for myself," Pete continued, confirming Judd's suspicions. "I just wanted to come over and see if I could do any chores for you—you know, something to welcome you to Dry Creek."

Judd grunted. "She's probably got some dishes to wash now that she's made the doughnuts."

Pete's smile wavered. "I was thinking more along the lines of chopping firewood or something. You know, one of those chores that single women need a man to help them out with."

"I have an electric stove," Lizette said. "And the dishes are all done. All I need is someone to dance for me."

Pete's smile brightened. "I can do that."

"She means the ballet," Charley muttered from

where he sat at the table. "She's not talking about line dancing or anything fun."

"She's not?" Pete looked at Lizette. "You're sure? There's a place in Miles City that sets up a mean line dance."

"What place is that?" Jacob asked as he joined Charley at the table. "You're not thinking of the senior center, are you?"

"No, I'm not thinking of the senior center. How romantic would that be? No, I've got my own kind of places," Pete said.

"In Miles City?" Charley asked. "What kind of places are there that we don't all know about?"

There was a moment of tense silence.

"Thanksgiving is almost here, and that's no time for quarreling," Jacob finally said. "It's a time for lighting our candles at church instead." Jacob turned and addressed his words to Lizette. "That's been the tradition here since before the town started. Everyone lights a candle and says why they're grateful. It helps us all be thankful for what we've got."

"What we've got right now is doughnuts," one of the older men said as Lizette started passing the plate of doughnuts to the men who were the regulars in the hardware store. The man who spoke took a maple doughnut off the plate. "And I'm sure enough grateful for having one."

"I have more in back, so there's enough for everyone," Lizette said as the plate made its way around.

By now all of the cowboys were standing with their hats off. Lizette knew she should say something about going back to wipe their wet boots, but she didn't have the heart. They were all gazing at her with hope in their eyes, looking more like little boys than grown men.

Lizette went into the back room and brought out another full tray of doughnuts. She had a row of chocolate frosted ones, a row of powdered doughnuts, a few jelly ones, a row of apple ones and a section of maple bars. She'd even shaken red and green sprinkles over a couple of sugar-glazed doughnuts just to see what they'd look like when Christmas came. She was almost glad the ranch hands had stopped by. What would she have done with all of these doughnuts otherwise?

The men all sighed when Lizette carried the full tray over to where they stood.

"Of course, these doughnuts are to help advertise my ballet classes." Lizette felt she did owe it to herself to say that much as several hands reached for doughnuts. "And, remember, no one is too old for ballet."

One cowboy who was still reaching stopped with his hand midway to the doughnut. "We don't need to do this ballet stuff if we take one, do we?"

Another ranch hand who had already taken a bite of his doughnut sighed. "It would be worth it if we did."

"No, you don't need to sign up," Lizette said. Half of the doughnuts were already gone from the tray. She looked around and saw that everyone had a doughnut. "You could help by spreading the word though. We're hoping to do the Nutcracker ballet before Christmas, and I still need a minimum of five more students."

"The pastor has twin boys that are about six years old," Pete Denning said as he licked his fingers. He'd had a jelly doughnut from the plate earlier and was now eyeing the tray. "I think the pastor went to get them when we heard about the doughnuts."

"Well, we'll have to save some doughnuts for them then," Lizette said as she turned to take the tray out of the room.

"They might not want doughnuts," Pete said as he saw Lizette turn to leave.

Judd snorted. At least *he* knew kids better than that.

Pete heard him. "Well, maybe they'll want a doughnut, but their mother might not let them have one since it's so close to lunchtime and she'll be worried they won't eat their vegetables."

Judd flinched. He probably shouldn't have let Bobby and Amanda have doughnuts, either. This being a parent seemed to have lots of rules that he didn't know. He looked over at the two kids. They both had frosting on their chins and happy gleams in their eyes. It was likely they wouldn't want lunch.

Judd doubted the kids would eat any vegetables either if he put any in front of them at this point. He'd have to be sure they took a vitamin pill when they got home. He'd bought a big jar of children's vitamins when Bobby and Amanda first came. He didn't want his cousin to accuse him of stunting her kids' growth when she came to pick them up.

He wondered if he should take the kids to the dentist, too. When did kids start going to the dentist anyway?

Just then someone knocked on the door.

Lizette started to walk toward the door, but one of the ranch hands opened it before she got there.

Mrs. Hargrove came into the room and looked around with surprise showing on her face. Or at least what Judd could see of her face seemed to show surprise. The older woman had a red wool scarf wrapped around her neck, and she started to unwind it. She was wearing a long pink parka with a green gingham housedress under it. Her gray hair was clipped back with a red barrette. Mrs. Hargrove was always colorful.

"You must have gotten the news then?" Mrs. Hargrove said as she looked around the room. She still stood on the small black mat that was beside the door. "Looks like I'm interrupting the celebration. Sheriff Wall always did say the rumor line beat the phone line in this part of the country any day."

"What news?" Judd asked since she seemed to be looking at him.

"They're just here for the doughnuts," Charley said as he jerked his head at the ranch hands. "They didn't bring anything but their appetites with them."

Mrs. Hargrove looked over at the group of cowboys and frowned. "Don't tell me you came to beg doughnuts off of Lizette when she's hardly even settled in yet? What's she going to think of us?"

"Oh, that's all right," Lizette said. "I'd already made the doughnuts when they came."

"Still, these boys know better than to come in and eat up your food supplies like this. What if you were on short rations yourself?" Mrs. Hargrove looked at the men. "I'll bet each of you have been short a time or two in your lives."

"They're only doughnuts," Lizette said.

"No, she's right, Miss," Pete said as he pulled a dollar bill out of his pocket. "We sure don't expect you to feed us without getting something in return for it."

Pete put the dollar bill on the tray where the powdered doughnuts had been. He hadn't even finished putting the bill there before a dozen other bills joined the one he had placed there. She even saw a five dollar bill sticking out. There must be twenty dollars there.

"You really don't need to—" Lizette protested.

"We're happy to do it, Miss," Pete said. "Those were real fine doughnuts."

"The best I've ever eaten," another man said.

"I'd be willing to buy a whole tray of them if you want to make them," another man said. "It's my turn to bring something to eat when the guys get together on Friday night in the bunkhouse."

"Well, I guess I could make another batch," Lizette said. Now that she had the Dutch oven for the oil, all she would need was a few more eggs.

"I'll pay you a dollar a doughnut," the man said.

"Oh, that's too much," Lizette said. She could use the extra income, but she didn't want to overcharge her new neighbors. "Especially if you buy a few dozen."

"It's worth it to me, Miss," the man said. "Last time it was my turn to bring the dessert, I tried to make an angel food cake myself."

"It came out flatter than a pancake," another man said as he gave Lizette a pleading look. "You'd be doing us all a favor if you let him buy the doughnuts. We ended up eating crackers the last time he was in charge of refreshments. And even those were stale."

"Well, all right," Lizette said. "But you'll get a bulk discount on the price. How does eight dollars a dozen sound?"

Lizette knew that was somewhere between what a doughnut shop and a bakery would charge for a dozen doughnuts.

"You've got yourself a deal," the man said.

"So you don't know the news?" Mrs. Hargrove said now that she had unwound her scarf and finished scraping her shoes on the black mat. "About the—" Mrs. Hargrove stopped and looked at the children. "Well, the news will keep for a little bit I guess— what with the kids here."

"Are there some more kids who are going to be in the ballet?" Amanda asked Mrs. Hargrove. "We need more kids."

Judd watched as Mrs. Hargrove bent down until she was on the same eye level as Amanda. Judd could see why the older woman was such a popular Sunday-school teacher. She smiled at Amanda.

"I heard you're going to be the Sugar Plum Fairy," Mrs. Hargrove said.

Amanda's eyes shone as she nodded her head. "And I get to wear the fairy-princess dress. Want to see it?"

"Why don't you ask your teacher if you can bring it over and show it to me?" Mrs. Hargrove said.

Amanda ran over to talk to Lizette.

Judd wondered if Mrs. Hargrove was going to invite him to church again. He almost hoped so. He could use an excuse to talk with the older woman some more. She seemed to know all about children and she could probably answer some of his questions—like was Amanda too old to still suck her thumb occasionally and, even if she was, was it better to just let her be or should he try to do something about it?

He wondered what the news was that Mrs. Hargrove had come over to tell. Maybe she'd just heard that they were taking precautions to be sure the children's father didn't come near them. If that was it, he could put her mind at ease. "Jacob and Charley have been keeping the streets of Dry Creek safe. Well, technically, the *street* of Dry Creek."

There was just one main street that ran through the town.

"I understand you have been keeping watch, too," Mrs. Hargrove said with a nod to Judd. She then looked down at Bobby. "And I expect you have a little helper here."

Bobby smiled up at the woman. "We're guarding the ballet."

"So you're in the ballet, too," Mrs. Hargrove said with an approving nod. "What part are you going to play?"

"I don't know yet. I might have to be a snowflake if we can't get any other kids to be in it with us."

"Ah," Mrs. Hargrove murmured. "Snowflakes are wonderful things. Especially at Christmas. Each one is different."

"Yes, ma'am," Bobby said without much enthusiasm.

"Why don't you go help your sister with that costume?" Judd said to Bobby. Judd had a feeling that Mrs. Hargrove wasn't going to tell him the news she had as long as either of the children were around to hear it.

Bobby pushed his chair back from the table and left to follow Amanda.

Mrs. Hargrove sat down in the chair Bobby had left. She didn't waste time but got straight to the point. "Have you heard from the sheriff this morning?"

Judd shook his head. "The kids have had lessons this morning, and I come in with them. I've been here."

"That's what the sheriff thought. That's why he called me. He wanted you to know that they think they've arrested the kids' father over in Miles City. The man won't say who he is, but he had that picture Lizette described with him."

"Did the man have a tattoo of a snake on his arm?"

Mrs. Hargrove nodded. "The sheriff said it was a cobra."

"That sounds like it's him, all right. Did he have a woman with him when he was arrested?"

Mrs. Hargrove shook her head. "No, it was just him. Are you thinking your cousin is hooked back up with him?"

"I don't know what to think," Judd admitted. "She should have been back here weeks ago, even if she'd had car trouble on the way to Denver. Besides, I don't know how he would know where to find the kids if he hadn't gotten the information from my cousin. Though I can't understand why she'd be foolish enough even to talk to the man."

"She must have had her reasons," Mrs. Hargrove said.

"Well, I hope they were good ones."

Mrs. Hargrove nodded. "The sheriff said they caught the man breaking into a gas station in the middle of the night."

"How long will he be in jail?"

"Long enough. They took him to the jail in Miles City for the time being. In a week or so they'll take him to the jail in Billings. If he is the children's father, apparently there's another warrant out for his arrest from the state of Colorado, so when they finish with him here, they're going to ship him down there."

"He's a popular guy."

"I'd say so. The sheriff figures they'll be sending him to Colorado sometime after Christmas."

Judd nodded. "That'll be some Christmas present for the kids."

Amanda and Bobby were starting to walk back toward them with the fairy costume in their hands. Even from here, Judd could see the excitement on Amanda's face.

"Do you think it will upset them to know their father's in jail?"

"I wish I knew," Judd said. "On the one hand, he is their father. But on the other hand, they're afraid of him. Knowing he's in jail might make them more comfortable even coming into town here. They seem a little nervous when they're not at my place."

Mrs. Hargrove nodded. "I wondered if that's why you haven't brought them to Sunday school yet." She didn't leave time for Judd to think of the real reason he hadn't brought the children. "But now that it's cleared up, I'll hope to see you this Sunday. It's the last Sunday before Thanksgiving, and the kids will be decorating candles and thinking about what they're going to say at the service we have the night of Thanksgiving."

"I heard about that—"

"It's a wonderful thing for families to do together," Mrs. Hargrove said as she turned to smile at Bobby and Amanda, who had just reached them.

Amanda was holding the pink costume out for Mrs. Hargrove to see.

"Oh, that's beautiful," Mrs. Hargrove told the little girl.

Watching Amanda talk with the older woman

made Judd decide he would take the kids to Sunday school this Sunday. It would do Amanda good to talk to more people, and she certainly seemed to have no trouble chatting with Mrs. Hargrove. It would be good for Bobby, too, to meet some more kids.

The only one it might not be good for, Judd decided, was himself. He would be a fish out of water in church. Maybe he could leave the kids at the church and then walk over to the café and have a cup of coffee. Now that sounded like the way to do this. Although, now that he thought of it, he couldn't remember if the café was open on Sundays. He thought Linda went to the church in Dry Creek, too, so she probably didn't open the café that day.

For the first time, Judd wished Dry Creek were a bigger town. In a place like Billings, or even Miles City, no one would notice who was going to church and who wasn't. They probably had coffee shops that were open on Sunday mornings as well.

Maybe he'd just have to sit in his pickup for the hour or so that the kids were inside. Yeah, he could do that.

Chapter Seven

Judd still hadn't talked to the sheriff about it all, but it was Saturday, and it had been two days since Judd had learned that the kid's father had been arrested. Hearing that news had surprised Judd enough. But what he was looking at now made that surprise go clear out of his head. He figured pigs were going to start flying down the street of Dry Creek pretty soon. He couldn't believe his eyes. Right there, in the middle of Lizette's practice room, was Pete Denning trying to do a pirouette.

The man's Stetson hat was thrown on the floor, and his boots were next to it. He wore one white sock and one gray sock, but both of his feet were arched up in an effort to hold him on his tiptoes.

"We should start with something simpler," Lizette was saying. She was dressed in her usual black practice leggings and T-shirt and had stopped her stretching on the practice bar to watch Pete.

"No, I saw this on TV and I know I can do it," Pete said as he tried again to stand on his tiptoes.

The man looked like a pretzel that had come out of the machine wrong.

"I see you got another student," Judd said. The kids and Charley were in the other room getting out of their coats and into their dancing slippers. Judd should have positioned himself in his usual chair outside on the porch, but he'd seen Pete, and that had changed everything.

"It's a free country," Pete said.

Judd lifted his hands up in surrender. "I didn't say anything."

"Yeah, but I know what you're thinking."

Judd chanced a quick look at Lizette. She'd paused midway through a stretch, and the curve of her back was the most beautiful thing he'd ever seen. He certainly hoped the cowboy didn't know what he was thinking.

Pete didn't wait for Judd to answer. "You're thinking that a Montana man like me wouldn't know what to do with a little culture."

"I didn't say that."

"But you would be wrong even to think it," Pete continued without listening. Pete was looking at Lizette, too, now. Lizette had stopped bending and was stretching her arm along the practice bar. A faint sheen of perspiration made her face glow, and tiny wisps of black hair had escaped the braid she wore.

Pete sighed. "A true man can appreciate fine art."

Judd didn't like Pete looking at Lizette. The cowboy didn't have fine art on his mind. Judd knew that much at least.

"You might have to wear tights," Judd said. That got the other man's attention away from Lizette, so Judd added, "Pink tights."

Now he had the cowboy's full attention.

Pete wasn't looking at anyone but Judd. He looked horrified. "Nobody said anything about tights."

"I said there would be costumes," Lizette said as she lifted her leg onto the practice bar and made another curve with her body.

"But 'costumes' doesn't mean tights," Pete said as he watched Lizette.

For a moment, neither man spoke.

Pete breathed out slowly. "Well, maybe if they're not *pink* tights."

Lizette finished her ballet move and turned to look at the two men. "Don't discourage him, Judd."

Judd felt that odd sensation in his stomach again. The last day or so Lizette had started calling him Judd, and he liked the sound of his name coming from her lips. Of course, it *was* his name, so it shouldn't be any big deal. It was just that he wasn't used to people saying it all of the time. If he was on the phone with someone, he was usually called "Mr. Bowman." In the rodeo, people had just called him "Bowman." His uncle had called him "You," if he called him anything at all. Judd guessed first names were more of a woman's thing.

"I won't discourage him," Judd finally said. "I'm looking forward to seeing him prance around up on stage." He could see the panic return to the other man's eyes.

"If he backs out, Judd Bowman," Lizette warned. "You're going to have to take his place."

"Me? Up there?"

"It would do you good," Lizette said. "Especially if you scare away any of my students. I don't know what the phobia is about tights anyway. They're really no tighter than football uniforms."

"Yes, but with f-football—" Pete stuttered. "Well, with football, you get to knock people around."

"I'm hoping you're not going to say that that makes you more of a man than ballet does," Lizette said to Pete.

Judd felt a little sorry for the cowboy. The two of them both knew that, of course, football made a man more of a man. And real men wore boots and not ballet slippers. They just couldn't tell any of that to Lizette.

"No, ma'am," Pete finally said. "I'm not going to say that."

"Good, because I'm expecting three more new students today, and with any luck, we can start some serious practicing for the Nutcracker."

Judd almost groaned. He hoped she wasn't expecting three more of Pete's cowboy friends. He couldn't stay out on the porch with all of those cowboys in here practicing their moves. And he didn't know what excuse he would give Lizette for guarding her classroom from inside the room, especially now that they all knew the kids' father was in jail in Miles City.

"This Nutcracker you want me to play," Pete said. "Does the Nutcracker wear tights?"

Lizette smiled at the cowboy. "Usually, he does."

Pete nodded glumly. "The guy sounds like some kind of a nut all right." Another look of alarm crossed Pete's face. "He is a guy, isn't he?"

Lizette laughed. "Yes, he's a guy. He wears a tall red hat with a black band under the chin."

"And tights," Pete said.

"Yes."

Pete shook his head.

"I suppose if you insisted, you could be a snowflake. It's just that I was saving those parts for the little kids."

"Maybe I could be an usher," Pete offered. "They get to wear clothes, don't they?"

"Of course they wear clothes," Lizette said. "Everyone wears clothes. All dancers are fully clothed at all times. What made you think they weren't? I can't afford for that rumor to get around. I won't even keep the students I have if people hear that."

"Maybe you need some help with the scenery," Pete finally offered. "Something with hammering."

Judd watched the disappointment settle on Lizette's face.

"Charley has already offered to build the fireplace that we need. Mrs. Hargrove has offered us her artificial Christmas tree. And we won't have enough dancers to do even a small version of the Nutcracker if you back out now," Lizette said.

Judd was a fool. He just couldn't stand that look on Lizette's face. "I could do something."

"Charley already offered to build the fireplace," Lizette said.

"No, I mean, I could do a dance part."

Judd wished he'd offered sooner. Lizette looked at him like he'd just hung the stars in the sky.

"You would? Dance a part?"

"Now, just wait a minute," Pete said. "I haven't said I *won't* do any dancing. I was just offering some extra help. Besides, I thought the deal was that the first people to sign up got their pick of the parts. Isn't that why your little girl gets to be the Sugar Plum Fairy?"

Judd nodded. He guessed those were the rules.

"So I pick the meanest dancer in the whole thing," Pete said. "Someone who commands respect on the street. Is there a part like that?"

"Well, if you're sure you don't want to be the Nutcracker, you can be the Mouse King," Lizette said, and then added quickly as Pete started to frown, "he's not a furry little mouse. He's really a rat. He comes charging out of the fireplace and tries to take down the Nutcracker."

"Kind of like in football?" Pete said with a smile. "And I bet he doesn't have to wear tights."

"Well, he does usually wear tights," Lizette admitted. "But the rest of the costume covers them up pretty much."

"So Judd here's going to be the Nut guy?" Pete asked.

Lizette raised a hopeful eyebrow at Judd.

"I guess so," Judd admitted. He only hoped the Nutcracker got to fight back when the Mouse King tackled him. Judd didn't relish going down without a fight.

"Good," Pete said with satisfaction as he looked at Judd. "Let's hope that little black band keeps the hat on your head when I come after you."

Judd hoped the little black band kept his head on his shoulders when Pete tackled him. "This Nutcracker guy, he's not a coward or anything, is he?"

Judd had just realized he might be required to run away from Pete. He'd decided to make this little community his home, and he didn't want to get a reputation for running away from trouble.

"Oh, no, the Nutcracker fights him back," Lizette assured them both. "It's a glorious battle. All done in ballet, of course. The audience doesn't know until the last minute who wins."

Judd wondered how he was going to defend himself if he had to do it on tiptoes.

Just then the outside door to the dance classroom opened, and in walked Mrs. Hargrove and the pastor's twin boys.

"Well, we're here to learn to dance," Mrs. Hargrove said as Lizette moved to greet them.

Judd had to admit he was relieved. At least the new students weren't more cowboys.

"Oh, we're going to have such fun," Lizette said as she led Mrs. Hargrove and the twins back to the area where they could take off their coats.

Judd was less enthusiastic. His only consolation

was that Pete didn't seem any happier about the arrangements than he was.

"I hope you've got room in those tights for some knee pads," Pete finally said, but he said it like the fight had already gone out of him. "I'd hate to bang up your knees too bad when I bring you down."

"My knees will do just fine," Judd said.

Pete was silent for a moment. "You don't suppose the guys are going to come to see this ballet thing, do you?"

Judd grunted. He figured there was about as much chance of the guys not coming to see this particular ballet production as there was of those pigs deciding to fly down the main street of Dry Creek. No, he and Pete were doomed to be everyone's merry entertainment for the holidays.

"You'd be welcome to come over to my place and hang out for a couple of days after the show if you want," Judd offered. He knew what a bunkhouse could be like when it came to teasing. "You could tell people you'd gone on a trip or something."

"I've been wanting to go to Hawaii."

"Well, maybe you could take that trip then. Winter's a slow time in ranching," Judd said.

"Can't afford to really go," Pete said.

"Well, then I'll just put some Hawaiian music on and turn up the heat in the spare room."

"I appreciate that," Pete said. "That doesn't mean I won't hit you hard when I can, but I do appreciate it."

Judd understood. Pete could no more take it easy on him than Judd could run away when Pete came after him. Even though Lizette had not told them how the fight turned out, Judd figured anyone who was named King, even if it was Mouse King, was the one who won the battle. Judd supposed Pete figured it the same way; the cowboy sure didn't look worried that he'd lose.

When the rest of the dancers came back to begin practice, Judd and Pete were both ready. Judd wondered what kind of nonsense he'd let himself in for. But he was a man of his word, and one thing he knew for sure—Lizette was counting on him to dance a part. His might not be the best part in the whole ballet, but it was the part she needed and he was willing to play it for her.

Judd only hoped Lizette thought he was doing it for the kids. He wouldn't want her to know he'd taken one look at her disappointed face and agreed to make a fool of himself. No, a man had to have some pride, even if he was a nutcracker.

Chapter Eight

Judd ached. It was Sunday morning, and he'd gotten the kids up and dressed for Sunday school like he'd promised them, but his body ached all over. Just a few months ago, he'd loaded two tons of hay bales by hand with nothing more than leather gloves and a metal hook. He hadn't felt a single ache in his body then. He was a man in the prime of his life. He was a rancher. But one day of ballet practice had about done him in.

And they hadn't even started practicing their parts yet. Lizette had just shown them some basic ballet steps. She said she was going to wait to practice the individual steps when she got the costumes she was borrowing from her old teacher and made sure they all fit.

Lizette had taken a moment to tell both Judd and Pete that she was sure both of their costumes would fit. And if not, she said, she'd improvise. Judd figured it was her way of telling them they had no hope of escaping.

After about an hour of ballet practice, Judd had stopped worrying about wearing tights. He didn't care what he wore. He just hoped that the Nutcracker guy stood in one place and let the Mouse King plow into him. His body would hurt less that way than if he had to keep practicing.

"Can you braid my hair?" Amanda stood in front of him after breakfast with a blue ribbon in her hand.

"Oh, but it'll look pretty if we just brush it and tie the ribbon around it," Judd said. He'd never braided hair in his life.

"No, I want it to look like Miss Lizette's," Amanda said. "She's awfully pretty."

"That she is, sweetheart," Judd said as he picked up the ribbon. He supposed he could try to braid hair. He was good at tying knots; he should be able to figure out hair braids.

Judd did a cross between a sailor's knot and a square knot.

"It doesn't look like Miss Lizette's," Amanda said as she stood up to look in the driver's mirror of his pickup. Judd had just pulled into a parking place near the church and was unfastening the seatbelts the children wore.

"The ribbon's pretty," Judd said reassuringly.

Judd looked at the braid again. Amanda was right. It didn't look at all like the one Lizette wore. "Maybe if you keep your head tilted to the right."

Judd wondered how many times he needed to bring the kids to Sunday school before he could throw himself on the mercy of Mrs. Hargrove. If he could just spend an afternoon with her asking questions, he knew he could do a better job with Amanda and Bobby. There should be some kind of a book or something that people could buy when they inherited kids all of a sudden like he had. Something that covered nightmares and braids and the other questions he had.

"You're coming with us, aren't you?" Bobby asked anxiously after he and Amanda had both climbed out of the passenger side of the pickup.

Judd looked over at them. They looked like little refugee children, frightened of a new experience and excited all at the same time. They'd asked so many questions this morning about church and Sunday school that he knew they'd never gone to either in their short lives. They didn't know what to expect any more than he did.

"Sure. I'm coming," Judd said as he opened his door. He hoped this wasn't one of those churches that required ties, because he didn't own one. It had always seemed pointless to have a tie when he didn't have a suit. Judd wished he'd screwed up his courage and visited this little church before the children came. At least then he could tell them what it looked like inside.

"It might have windows with pictures," Judd had said this morning. He couldn't remember actually looking that closely at the church in Dry Creek, but churches had those stained-glass windows, didn't they?

Judd looked down the side of the church now. He didn't see any stained-glass windows showing from the outside. "Even if there's no pictures, Mrs. Hargrove will be there."

The last seemed to reassure Bobby and Amanda. Judd wished he had thought to remind them of that fact earlier.

"She's going to be the Snow Queen," Amanda said. "But her costume won't be as pretty as mine."

"I think you're going to have the prettiest costume of all," Judd agreed as they started walking up the steps of the church. He put his hand on top of Amanda's head.

"There's Miss Lizette," Amanda said when they reached the bottom of the steps.

Judd looked down the street. Sure enough, Lizette was walking toward them. She wore a red wool coat and had a small black hat on her head. She looked more uptown than anything Judd had ever seen in Dry Creek.

"Good morning," Judd said. He couldn't think of one good reason why he'd never bought a suit and a tie in his life. A man should be prepared for days like this.

"Hello," Lizette said as she smiled at them. "Are you going to church, too?"

Amanda nodded. "And we're going to sit in a pew," Amanda leaned over and confided to Lizette. "But that's not a stinky thing. Cousin Judd says it's a long chair and we've got to share it."

Judd figured even a tie wouldn't save him now. "The children were curious about church."

"Of course," Lizette said.

All four of them had come to a stop at the bottom of the church stairs. There were only seven steps to the landing, but Judd didn't feel inclined to step forward and, apparently, neither did anyone else.

"Have you been to church here before?" Lizette finally asked as she stood looking up at the door.

It was a perfectly ordinary door, Judd decided. A good solid-wood double door. It was winter so the door wasn't wide open, but it was open a good six inches or so and he could hear the sounds of people talking inside.

"No, I've never been," Judd admitted.

"Oh," Lizette said, and then looked at him instead of the door. "But you've been to other churches, right?"

Judd shook his head. "I don't know a thing about them."

"Me neither," Lizette said.

"I thought I should bring the children," Judd finally said.

Both Judd and Lizette looked down at the children and then looked at each other.

Lizette nodded. "Yes, the children should go to church."

Lizette held out her hand to Amanda. Judd held out his hand to Bobby. The four of them walked into church just like they were a family.

Yes, Judd thought. The next time he went to Billings he was definitely going to buy himself a suit and a tie.

* * *

Lizette looked around the church the minute she and Amanda stepped through the door. She'd searched through her costume trunk to find the French fedora she wore, and not another man or woman in the church was wearing a hat. She'd tried so hard to blend in that she was sticking out.

"Well, welcome," Mrs. Hargrove said as she walked over from another group of people. She had her hand extended out to Lizette. "I can't tell you how happy I am that you decided to join us this morning."

"I thought the children should come to church," Lizette said, and then blushed. She wasn't the one who was related to the children. It wasn't her place to see that they went to church.

"Oh, we have something for all ages," Mrs. Hargrove said as she extended her hand to Judd as well. "And you made it, too. I'm so glad."

Judd nodded.

"The children are going to decorate candles this morning," Mrs. Hargrove said as she leaned down to the level of Amanda and Bobby. "And you're going to talk about the light of the world."

"Can I make a blue candle?" Amanda asked. "I like blue."

"They have all colors of candles and sequins and all kinds of things to put on them," Mrs. Hargrove said as she motioned for another woman to come over. "Glory Curtis, the pastor's wife, will take you back to the Sunday-school room and get you settled."

Lizette watched the two children walk away with the pastor's wife.

"I can just wait outside until—" Judd began.

"Nonsense," Mrs. Hargrove said as she took them both by the arm. "The pastor has an adult Sunday-school class, and today's topic is how to have a happy marriage."

"Oh, but I'm not—" Lizette began.

"Nonsense," Mrs. Hargrove said as she walked them forward. "What he's going to say will apply to many relationships in life."

Judd decided that Mrs. Hargrove was wrong within five minutes of the pastor starting to talk. Judd had never had a relationship in his life that sounded like what the pastor described. His uncle certainly hadn't acted that way toward him. He'd never had a friend who was like that. Certainly none of the women he'd met on the rodeo circuits had cared about him that way.

He'd never even heard things like the pastor read from the Bible. What kind of person did good things to the people who wanted to do bad things to them? That would be like if the Nutcracker guy just lay down and let the Mouse King dance all over him and then got up and thanked him for it. The world would be all lopsided if that kind of stuff started happening. A man could get all confused about who his enemies really were.

"Inspiring," was all Judd could think of to say when the pastor finished the lesson and came over to greet him and Lizette.

"Very inspiring," Lizette added.

The pastor chuckled. "I'll admit it doesn't make a whole lot of sense at first. The one thing you'll learn about God though is that He turns things upside down a lot."

Judd nodded. He wasn't sure he wanted to be standing here talking with the pastor about God. What he knew about God wouldn't fill an old lady's thimble, and he didn't want to appear ignorant in front of Lizette, especially not now that she'd taken his arm by the elbow. He doubted she even realized she was leaning into him a little. He liked the faint lilac perfume she was wearing. He wondered if it was okay to notice a woman's perfume in church. He supposed it was a sin. Of course, he couldn't ask. A man should already know something like that.

"We've got coffee out back in the kitchen," the pastor said. "We've got some tables set up, and you're welcome to sit and have a cup while you wait for the kids to finish. We'll be starting church services in about fifteen minutes."

Judd hadn't realized there was more to this church business than what he'd just sat through, but he wasn't about to say anything.

"I could use a cup of coffee," Lizette said.

The church kitchen was painted yellow and smelled like strong coffee. Mugs sat on the counter next to a big urn of coffee. Next to the coffee was another urn that held hot water. A basket of various tea bags sat next to the hot-water urn. Several card tables were set up on the wall opposite the cabinets. Folding chairs rested against the wall.

Judd and Lizette were the first ones in to get coffee. They both moved toward the urn as if they were dying of thirst.

"I don't belong here," Lizette burst out before she even got to the coffee mugs.

"*You* don't belong? I don't even have a tie," Judd muttered as he reached for a mug.

"Nobody here is wearing a tie—or a hat," Lizette said. "There should be a book telling people what to expect in church."

"I guess they just assume most people know those things," Judd said as he held the mug. "Would you like coffee or tea?"

"Tea, please. And how would we know what to expect in church? I've never been to church before."

Judd turned to fill the mug with hot water. "When you say you've never been to church, you just mean recently, don't you? I mean, I know you had a mother and a reasonable family life—I thought all families went to church at some point."

"Not ours."

Judd handed Lizette the mug of hot water. "I'll let you pick the tea you want."

Lizette pulled a lemon spice packet out of the basket and tore the paper wrapping off the tea bag. She put the bag in the hot water. "My mother was always mad at God. I don't think she had ever heard about any of the kinds of things the pastor was talking about back there."

"I wonder if he knows what he's talking about," Judd said as he poured himself a cup of coffee. Then he flushed. He might not know much about church etiquette, but he was pretty sure a visitor wasn't supposed to call the pastor a liar. "I mean, maybe something is translated wrong."

Lizette nodded. "It is pretty odd, isn't it? But I imagine he knows what he's talking about. Mrs. Hargrove seems to trust him, and I noticed she carries a Bible around with her. She must read it and agree with the man."

Judd nodded as they both walked over to one of the card tables. He had a tendency to trust Mrs. Hargrove. "It just must be that church is one of those things people like me don't understand."

They both sat down.

"What do you mean by that?" Lizette had wrapped her hands around her cup of tea, but she was making no move to lift the cup and drink any of it. Her face looked serious.

Judd's heart stopped. Here he had been muttering to himself, never expecting anyone to listen. It looked like Lizette had been listening.

"You keep saying 'people like me' like you were raised on Mars or something," Lizette said with a smile. "You don't look that different to me."

Judd swallowed. There had to be a lot of clever things to say to that kind of question. Pete would know something brash to say that would turn the moment into a chuckle. But Judd realized he didn't want to avoid the question. "I'm different because I was raised by an uncle who didn't care about me. He never once celebrated my birthday. What am I saying? He never even said 'Good morning' or 'How was your day?' or 'Do you feel all right?' I could have laid down and died and he wouldn't have noticed except for the fact that the chores hadn't gotten done."

"Oh."

Judd plowed on. "I'm not saying that to say I had it worse than everyone else, it's just that I'm different. A lot of things other men know—things like how to be part of a family—those are things I don't know."

There. Judd had made his speech. It wasn't fancy, but it was the first time in his life he'd come out and said why he was so different.

"I do know how to work, though." Judd felt he needed to add something positive. "That's one thing I learned living with my uncle. I learned how to work."

"Oh."

Judd didn't add that he'd also learned not to trust anyone and not to expect anything from anyone else.

There was a moment of silence.

And then Lizette took a sip of tea. "My mother always wanted me to be a ballet dancer."

"But you *are* a ballet dancer."

"Yes, but don't you wonder what would have happened if I hadn't been able to dance?" Lizette asked. "What would have happened between my mother and me then? I think part of me always wondered about that, but I was afraid to ask her—I was even afraid to ask myself the question."

Judd had never thought that someone who had a family still might have had problems.

"Well," Judd said. He didn't know what else to say, so he just put his hand over Lizette's hand and patted it like he would have patted Amanda's hand if she had been there.

Judd guessed that maybe there was something to this going to church after all. Before he knew it, he wasn't patting Lizette's hand but was holding it instead.

"The tea's kind of hot," Lizette said as she blinked.

"Yeah, so is the coffee," Judd said as he pulled out a handkerchief and gave it to Lizette. He might not have a tie, but he'd started carrying one or two extra handkerchiefs since Amanda and Bobby had come into his life. It seemed like a lot of things were changing since those kids had come into his life.

Chapter Nine

Lizette wasn't ready for her students to come for practice. Oh, she was ready. She'd received the box of costumes and props from Madame Aprele and she had them laid out in the back room. She had the stage book marked for Charley, the narrator, so he could read aloud the abbreviated story of the Nutcracker and direct some of the scenes. What she wasn't ready for was to see Judd.

How did you explain to a man that you aren't crazy? Especially when he's seen your mood swing with his own eyes. She still didn't know what had happened. One minute, she was sitting there drinking tea with Judd and, before she knew it, she was sniffling into his handkerchief and talking about her mother. Lizette hadn't even known all of those questions about whether or not she measured up to her mother's hopes were inside her until they came spilling out to Judd. She was a mess.

It was the pastor's fault, of course. All of the talk

about love and family and forgiveness—well, anyone would start to thinking about their life, wouldn't they?

It's just that it couldn't have happened at a worse time. She'd wanted to impress Judd. He was sort of the parent of the first two real students she'd ever had in her life, and she wanted him to see her as a professional.

After listening to her cry yesterday, he probably saw her as someone who *needed* a professional instead of someone who *was* a professional.

And he hadn't even had a choice but to listen to her. He'd patted her hand after her first few tears and told her that it would be all right. She should have stopped then. But she didn't. She'd gone on and on, telling him about this and that, and he'd kept patiently patting her hand. Then he'd held her hand for a bit, and it was the sweetest thing. Most men would have used the whole thing to make a move on a woman, but Judd didn't. Which, when Lizette thought about it, was the most embarrassing thing of all.

She'd been vulnerable and he'd been a gentleman. She'd been around enough to know what that meant— he wasn't interested. Plain and simple. No chemistry.

Not that she cared if he was interested. It was really best that he wasn't. After all, she was the teacher of the children under his care. He certainly wasn't obligated to think of her as anything but a teacher. She didn't *want* him to think of her as anything but a teacher.

And, to make things even worse, when it was all over and she'd cried her fill, he'd taken pity on her and asked her to sit with him and the children in church. Of course, she couldn't say no, because by then other people were coming in behind them for coffee, and she didn't want to turn around and have to face the others. So she had to keep sitting at the table with Judd until she'd blinked away some of the redness in her eyes.

In the meantime, Judd kept enough conversation going with the others so that no one noticed she wasn't turning around and talking. And he'd done it all so naturally, as though he was used to taking care of someone.

Lizette was never going to go to church again.

Judd wouldn't have believed that Lizette had cried in one of his handkerchiefs yesterday morning. Amanda had asked over breakfast if she could invite Lizette over for Thanksgiving dinner, and Judd had actually agreed it was a good idea. He'd thought they'd all had a nice time together yesterday. Now, he wasn't so sure. It was practice time for the ballet, and the woman whose soft hands he'd held yesterday had turned into a drill sergeant today, and she apparently saw him as nothing more than a raw recruit.

"I can march or I can ballet," he finally said. "I can't do both."

Well, Judd admitted, that was an exaggeration. He could march, but he wasn't so sure anyone could call his tortured steps ballet. People couldn't walk like that, could they? Lizette insisted she wasn't trying any advanced moves, but they sure seemed advanced to him.

Mrs. Hargrove and Charley were sitting on two folding chairs at the back of the practice room talking intensely until they both happened to look at him doing his ballet moves. Judd couldn't decide if it was encouragement or astonishment that he saw in their eyes, and he wasn't about to ask. At least they had stopped their conversation and bothered to look at him.

Which was more than he could say for Lizette. She didn't even look at him to see how he was doing when he complained. The only students she looked at this morning were the children. His sole consolation was that Pete looked even more bewildered than he was.

"My toes don't bend backward," Pete said.

"Of course not," Lizette said with some alarm in her voice as she left the children and went to Pete's side. "You must have your feet placed wrong. Here, let me help you."

Lizette put her arm around Pete and stood at his side. "Now, do this."

Judd grunted. Pete wasn't even looking at Lizette's feet as she showed him how to move his big feet. Instead, the cowboy was grinning triumphantly over at Judd. Well, Judd had to admit that the cowboy knew how to get a lady's attention better than he did even if he was just as bad at ballet.

"Now you try it," Lizette said to Pete.

"Ah." Pete looked around in alarm. "I think I need to see it all again."

"You put your foot like this," Lizette began again.

Judd wondered why she needed to keep her arm around the cowboy when all she was doing was showing him how to stand on his tiptoes. "Shouldn't he be practicing at the bar over there?"

Judd knew the bar was for practicing. He didn't much like looking in the big mirror behind the bar, but he did know what it was for.

"I'm learning just fine here," Pete said. "It's not easy being a rat."

Judd grunted. He thought the other man was doing a particularly fine job of being a rat.

"I think a rat would move his feet like this," Pete said as he danced a little.

Fine, Judd thought, now the cowboy was doing interpretive dance.

"That looks a little like the tango," Lizette said with a frown. "That's good, but it's more like the steps the mice would take. You're the leader. You need more power in your moves. You play a huge king rat."

"Think big and fat," Judd offered. "All of that cholesterol from the cheese."

Pete scowled at him. "I'm sure I'm a very fit rat."

"I don't see you eating any cottage cheese in this role," Judd said. If anyone should have power in their moves, it should be the Nutcracker. Judd had a feeling he was going to need some power.

"At least no one's going to be staring at my legs like they will be at the Nutcracker's," Pete said smugly. "I have a costume that covers my legs."

"Oh, that's right," Lizette said. She moved away

from Pete and stood in the middle of the room. "Let's take a break and try on the costumes. Then we'll do a quick read through with the narration so people get familiar with the story. We'll do the actions, but not worry about all of the dance steps yet."

"Good." Judd could do action.

The children and Pete went into the back room first to look at the costumes. Judd wanted to talk with Mrs. Hargrove.

"Good morning," Judd said as he walked over to her and sat down in the chair that Charley had just vacated. Charley decided to go into the back room to see the costumes, too.

Mrs. Hargrove smiled and nodded. Then she waited.

"I enjoyed church yesterday," Judd lied. It was true that he'd found church very interesting, but he could hardly say that. It made the whole experience sound scientific and cold, and it hadn't been, either. Lizette had been right that there should be some advice book about churchgoing.

"I thought you might think it was a bit too personal," Mrs. Hargrove said.

"Oh, no," Judd lied again. Now that he thought about it, that was exactly what had been wrong with all those things the pastor was saying. Whose business was it anyway how he wanted to treat his enemies? Enemies shouldn't expect nice treatment. Maybe people wouldn't have so many enemies if everyone just stayed with their own business.

"I'm glad you feel that way," Mrs. Hargrove said. "I'll look for you to become a regular at church then."

"Ah," Judd stammered. He didn't want to give that impression. "I'll certainly come when I can, but I'm building a fence, you know."

Mrs. Hargrove smiled. "Well, I'll pray you finish it quickly then."

"It might be more than one fence."

Judd stopped before the heavens opened and God struck him dead. He'd already told three lies, and it wasn't even noon. He'd better get to the point. "I was wondering if sometime—it doesn't have to be now— if you'd have a few minutes to talk about raising children? I mean, you seem so good at it."

Mrs. Hargrove chuckled. "You haven't talked to my daughter lately if you think that."

"I didn't know you had a daughter."

Mrs. Hargrove nodded. "I do. A more stubborn, opinionated woman you're not likely to meet than Doris June Hargrove."

"Have I met her?" Judd tried to think of the women of Dry Creek. He couldn't remember any of them who were named Doris.

"She doesn't live around here. She insists on staying up in Anchorage even though her heart is back here where the rest of her belongs. And Charley's son knows she belongs here, too. The two of them are just too stubborn to do anything about it."

"Well, some people take longer to get to know each other."

"Humph," Mrs. Hargrove said. "Those two know

each other just fine. Give either one a pencil and paper and they could list every fault of the other in a minute. They'd enjoy doing it, too."

"Well, then, maybe they're happier being apart."

"They're miserable and it's time someone did something about it."

"Well—" Judd started and stopped. He hoped she didn't mean *he* should do anything. He didn't even know either one of them. There hardly seemed anything to say. "Maybe someone will."

Mrs. Hargrove nodded. "That's the first thing you need to learn about being a parent. Sometimes you need to step into your child's business and make it your own."

"Bobby and Amanda are both still a little young for love problems," Judd said. He didn't mention his own problems with the opposite sex. He wasn't sure he'd want Mrs. Hargrove to fix his love life. She looked unstoppable.

"Of course they are. This is information for the future."

"I'm looking more at the next few months," Judd said. "You know, things like nightmares and missing their mother and braids."

"Braids?"

Judd nodded. "I don't know how to braid hair, and Amanda wants her hair to look like Lizette's."

"Oh, of course," Mrs. Hargrove nodded. "It's perfectly obvious that Amanda wants some motherly affection from Lizette."

"It is?"

Mrs. Hargrove nodded. "And it's a good thing. Spending time with Lizette will make her feel better."

"She wants to invite Lizette over for Thanksgiving dinner, but—"

"You're not one of those men who think women are the only ones who should cook, are you?"

Judd shook his head. "I'm not opposed to cooking; I'm just not sure how good I am at it."

"Oh, you'll do fine with cooking a turkey dinner. You just get a bag for the turkey, and I can give you some simple recipes to see you through. You might need to buy a pie though."

"Got a couple in the freezer."

"Well, then, you're all set. I just wish a broken heart was as easy to mend."

Judd looked up in alarm. It was a bit extreme to say his heart was broken. Dented a little maybe, especially after the cool way Lizette was acting toward him today, but not broken. Not at all. "People make too much of broken hearts."

"So you think I shouldn't do anything to make Doris realize she's still in love with Charley's son?" Mrs. Hargrove looked worried.

"Don't listen to me," Judd rushed to say. "I don't know anything about this kind of stuff."

He hadn't even known she was talking about someone else, that's how much he didn't know.

"I'm sure she'll appreciate whatever you do for her," Judd added.

Mrs. Hargrove chuckled. "I wouldn't go that far,

but we'll see. In the meantime, why don't I teach you to braid hair after class today?"

Judd nodded in gratitude just as he heard his name being called from the back room.

"Excuse me," he said to Mrs. Hargrove. "That's Amanda calling."

"Look at your hat," Amanda said with a squeal when Judd entered the back room.

Lizette had found an old sofa for the back room and a mound of colorful costumes were spread out on it. It looked as though some of the accessories were sitting on the square table in one corner as well. There was a curtain at one end of the room, and Judd figured the bed was behind it.

He wondered how anyone could make an old room look so inviting. Then he took a good look at the hat Amanda was pointing at.

"It's real red," Judd said. He figured that was an understatement. Some reds could be dignified. This one wasn't. It was bright enough to light up the darkness. "And it's so big."

The hat was two feet tall.

"Well, you are a nutcracker," Lizette said patiently.

"But I didn't know I was a *giant* nutcracker."

Judd didn't need to look over at Pete to know the man was snickering. He could hear the cowboy trying to contain his laughter even if he didn't look at him.

"Remember, the Nutcracker fights back," Judd said as he looked over at Pete.

"What? Are you going to slap me with your top hat?" Pete said as he chuckled.

"Oh, no, you can't damage the costumes," Lizette said. "We're going to need to return them when we finish."

"I'll be careful," Judd said. He wouldn't need a hat anyway to fight back against the cowboy.

"And, Pete, you'll be careful too, won't you?" Lizette asked, turning to the cowboy. "Your tail is a little fragile."

Judd started to grin. "His tail?"

Pete stopped laughing. "My tail?"

"Well, you are a mouse," Lizette said.

Amanda and Bobby both giggled. Judd thought he heard Charley give a snort or two as well.

"Rat," Pete corrected. "You said I was a rat."

"Mouse. Rat. They both have tails," Lizette said as she reached into a bag.

Judd grinned even wider. The tail Lizette pulled out of the bag had to be five feet long. And it was pink.

"I can't wear pink," Pete said.

Lizette frowned as she looked at the tail. "It's not exactly pink. It's more puce than anything. Your whole costume is puce."

Judd could see that the costume was pink.

"Maybe I could have my tail chopped off," Pete said. "I bet there are rats that've run into trouble and are missing part of their tail. You know, the fighter kind of rats, like I will be."

"But the tail balances out the ears," Lizette said as she pulled two pink ears out of the bag.

Pete was speechless.

Judd decided his hat wasn't such a bad thing. "If you don't like the look of your ears, maybe you should get a hat."

"Well, at least I have to have something to fight with, don't I?" Pete finally said. "I mean, I have to have something to fight with—like a knife or something."

"You have teeth," Lizette said as she also pulled out a rat's head.

Judd had to admit the head looked like a fighter rat. An uglier mask he'd never seen.

"That's more like it," Pete said as he picked up the mask and turned it around.

"Well, everyone try on their hats and heads. I want to be sure everything fits," Lizette said.

Judd looked around him at all of the other dancers. Mrs. Hargrove had come into the room and was fingering a billowing white dress that must be the Snow Queen outfit. Charley was trying on an old tweed bathrobe that was the costume for the narrator. Judd wished *he'd* been the narrator. The bathrobe looked comfortable. Amanda was, of course, eyeing the Sugar Plum Fairy costume that was over in the corner. Even Bobby and the twins looked happy, since they were going to be either mice or toy soldiers in the first part of the ballet and snowflakes at the end.

Judd realized he'd never been in anything like this in his life. His uncle had thought school itself was a waste of time, so Judd had never tried out for any school plays. There were always chores to do. The closest thing to costumes he'd ever seen were the clown costumes at the rodeo and everyone knew those clowns were not for fun.

Judd decided he liked the thought of playing a part in something like this ballet. Especially now that he'd seen the tail Pete had to wear and realized he wasn't going to be the only man who was wearing a ridiculous costume.

Besides, Judd thought as he saw Amanda and Bobby, he'd never seen the two of them so excited, and it was worth making a fool of himself to see them having such a good time.

Chapter Ten

The first official rehearsal of the Dry Creek Nutcracker ballet was underway. An X was taped to the floor where the artificial tree would be. Charley was sitting on a folding chair next to the fireplace he had built out of cardboard. Mrs. Hargrove was backstage helping the Sugar Plum Fairy adjust her wings. The Curtis twins were being good little mice and sitting in the corner until it was time for them to run across the stage. Bobby was sitting next to the twins in his tin soldier costume. Pete was looking at his new mouse head in the mirror by the practice bars. Judd was holding his hat and frowning at it.

Yes, Lizette thought to herself, they were really going to be able to do this. Even though this was the first time on stage for all of her performers, they already looked like a typical group of ballet students. The only thing that was missing was for one of the performers to be sick.

Lizette had changed into her Clara costume—with

Amanda choosing the Sugar Plum Fairy part and no other young girls clamoring for the role, Lizette had decided to adapt it for herself. For the first time today, she felt as if she was the teacher and had everything under control. Generally, Clara had several different costumes during the performance, but Lizette had decided to keep her costume simple. It was a yellow dress with a short skirt. Clara was a young girl, so Lizette had braided her hair into a single braid down her back and tied the end with a big yellow ribbon.

"Let me get the narrator's book and we'll begin," Lizette said.

Madame Aprele said the book she'd sent was a condensed story of the Nutcracker that she had used for one of her own productions years ago when she was first starting her school. She'd eliminated some of the scenes and changed others. She'd promised Lizette that it was a very simple rendition of the classic ballet. Lizette had briefly reviewed the narration and was ready to begin.

"Everyone take your places," Lizette said as she gave Mrs. Hargrove the audiocassette tape to put into the small stereo system Lizette had set up earlier.

Judd knew ballerinas were supposed to glide, but seeing Lizette dance the first dance left him breathless. She was dipping and bowing and soaring all over the practice floor. And while Lizette was moving, Charley kept reading from the narration about a young girl and her brother who were given special gifts at Christmas time.

The sun was starting to set, and Charley asked Mrs. Hargrove to bring him a lamp that was along the side of the room.

Once the lamp was there, Lizette danced in the circle of light it gave.

Judd was watching Lizette so closely that he didn't notice when his cue came.

"The Nutcracker," Charley cleared his throat and repeated a little louder. "When Clara opened her present, she saw the Nutcracker."

"Just walk into the circle of light," Lizette directed. "You're not alive at this point, so no one will expect you to move."

Judd moved into the circle of light.

"You mean I'm your present?" Judd whispered to Lizette in dismay. "Your Christmas present?"

Judd had gotten Amanda a doll for Christmas with eyes that lit up depending on what kind of eye makeup the girl put on the doll. Judd didn't pretend to know much about little girls, but he was willing to bet that very few of them would be excited about getting a nutcracker for a Christmas present. "Do I at least come with a few walnuts or something?"

"Way to go, Nutcracker," Pete said as he stood by the fireplace holding his rat-king head. "I'd at least bring her some cheese."

"Clara was very excited to open her present and see the Nutcracker," Charley read from the book.

Lizette danced some more, and Judd would swear that the movements of her arms and legs did remind him of an excited little girl. The background music for this part of the ballet was very light and fanciful.

Maybe it wasn't so bad being Lizette's present, Judd thought as he looked over at Pete. The cowboy was still leaning against the wall, only now he was frowning.

"Clara's brother was also given a gift—some toy soldiers," Charley read as Bobby marched forward in a toy soldier costume. "But, even though he liked the toy soldiers, he was jealous of Clara's nutcracker and broke it just when it was time for everyone to go to bed."

Lizette danced into the shadows as the narrator said, "everyone went to bed," leaving the Nutcracker and the toy soldiers in the living room.

"That night after everyone was asleep," Charley kept reading, "Clara and her brother went back downstairs."

"Mice gather over by the fireplace," Lizette whispered, and the Curtis twins hurried over to the fireplace.

"Clara and her brother start playing with the mice," Charley read. Then he reached into the prop bag and pulled out a large wind-up alarm clock. "But then the clock strikes midnight."

Charley pulled a button so the alarm clock would ring.

"When the clock strikes midnight, the mice stop playing. The room becomes darker and is no longer a friendly place. The mice start attacking Clara and her brother. The toy soldiers try to fight back, but they are outnumbered."

The Curtis twins ran up and started flinging their arms around Bobby, who was the toy soldier.

In the middle of the action, Lizette danced around the stage like a wounded bird.

"Seeing that Clara is in trouble, the Nutcracker comes to life and starts to defend her from the mice."

"From the mice?" Judd said. "I thought I was going to fight that Rat King."

Judd figured he shouldn't even have worried. The day he wasn't equal to two little kids was the day he'd give up ballet.

Judd spun around on his tiptoes and pulled the cardboard sword out of the sheath on his belt. Then he tried to dance to the music while he fought back the mice. Of course, he was careful not to fight too hard. He didn't want to discourage the Curtis twins in their mice roles.

"Gradually, it looks like the toy soldiers and the nutcracker are pushing back the mice, and then a giant rat comes bursting out of the fireplace."

Pete crawled out of the front of the fireplace. Of course, the cowboy was on his knees and it took a moment for him to stand. It took another second for him to roar.

Judd took a deep breath so he wouldn't laugh. Pete's tail was twisted around his shoulders, and his ears were as lopsided as a rabbit's.

Pete put his rat head down and charged toward Judd.

"Stop," Lizette commanded. "I have to show you how to stage a fight."

Judd figured it was too late to stage anything. So he moved to the side and let Pete catch him on the shoulder.

Charley kept reading. "The giant rat keeps fighting the Nutcracker until the Nutcracker is weary."

Judd didn't feel the least tired. He rather liked the look of concern he saw on Lizette's face. It might take a charging rat for her to worry about his well-being, but it was nice to know that she could do so with the proper encouragement.

"But we need to stage the action," Lizette said. "There shouldn't be any physical contact."

"How am I going to hit him if I can't touch him?" Pete said as he raised his head.

"You pretend. We all pretend," Lizette said.

"It's okay. He can touch me," Judd said.

Pete lowered his head. "Let the story continue—"

Charley cleared his throat. "The Mouse King gets ready for one final attack. The toy soldier is lying on the floor. Only the Nutcracker is left, and he is wounded."

Pete pawed the floor like a bull would do before it charged.

Judd figured this was the final act for him.

"Clara sees the Mouse King get ready to attack and puts herself between the rat and the Nutcracker," Charley reads.

"What?" Judd said.

"What?" the rat echoed.

"I can fight my own battles," Judd said. He'd thought there was nothing worse than dying in this battle. He was wrong. He'd never live it down if the Nutcracker hid behind a woman's skirts.

"I'd never hit a lady," the rat said.

"You don't have to hit me," Lizette hissed. "Remember, there's no physical contact. Everything is staged."

"B-but, still—" Pete stammered.

"Besides, you don't hit me in the story," Lizette whispered. "I hit you."

Charley turned a page in the book and continued. "Clara takes off one of her shoes and throws it at the Mouse King."

Lizette threw her dance slipper at the rat.

"The shoe hits the Mouse King and topples him," Charley continued.

Pete still stood in astonishment.

"Lie down," the Curtis twins whispered to him. They were both already lying on the floor where they had fallen in battle. "You're dead."

"From a shoe?" Pete asked. "I get beat by a shoe?"

Judd shook his head. He supposed he should be happy that the Mouse King was defeated, but he had to wish right along with Pete that it had happened another way. It didn't do Judd's image any good either to be rescued by a woman and her shoe.

Pete reluctantly slid to the floor. "Even if I'm dead, I'm not closing my eyes."

Charley was fumbling in the bag and the music was starting to soar.

"Because of the bravery of Clara and the Nutcracker, the Nutcracker comes to life and becomes a man," Charley read.

Judd liked the sound of that.

The music soared even further.

"When Clara sees that her beloved Nutcracker is alive, she kisses him," Charley read.

"She what?" Lizette said.

"She does?" Judd grinned.

"Well, nobody told *me* that," the Mouse King said, and it looked like he was going to rise again.

Charley looked up. "That's what it says right here."

"Madame Aprele must have changed the text," Lizette said as she walked over to Charley and looked at the book for herself.

"I think a kiss would be nice," Mrs. Hargrove said from the sidelines. "Everybody likes a little romance in a ballet."

"Well, I guess it could be a stage kiss," Lizette said as she walked back to Judd.

"And you need to take his hat off for when he turns into a prince," Charley whispered. "Those are the directions."

Judd forgot all about the room that was around them. He forgot about the dead mice lying on the floor and the live rat looking ready to pounce. He forgot about the Sugar Plum Fairy sitting on the sidelines watching him. All Judd could think about was the green eyes staring straight at him.

Why, she's nervous, Judd thought to himself. The woman who had been treating him all morning like he was a raw recruit and she was the drill sergeant was actually nervous to be this close to him.

"It'll be okay," he said softly.

"It's just a stage kiss," Lizette reminded him.

Judd wasn't even going to ask what a stage kiss was. He figured a raw recruit should be able to plead ignorance.

Judd took the tall hat off his head and set it on the floor beside them. He'd never yet kissed a woman with his hat still on his head, and he wasn't going to start now.

The background music dipped, and the green in Lizette's eyes deepened. She must have guessed his intent, because she gave a soft gasp and her mouth formed a perfect O.

Judd kissed her. He'd meant to satisfy his curiosity with the kiss. He'd been wanting to kiss Lizette since he saw her hanging that sign in her window. When he kissed her, though, he forgot all about the reasons he wanted to kiss her. He just needed to kiss her. That was all there was to it.

Judd finally heard Charley clearing his throat. Judd wasn't sure how long the man had been sitting there doing that, but he figured it must have been for some time. The others were looking at them in astonishment.

Somehow Judd's arms had gotten around Lizette and she was nestled in the curve of his shoulder. She still had her face turned into him, and Judd felt protective of her.

"We were just doing this stage kiss," Judd finally

managed to say. His voice sounded a little hoarse, but he was at least able to get the words out.

"Uh-huh," Pete said from where he lay by the fireplace. "You mean the one where there's no actual contact?"

"It's the one the movie stars do," Judd said as he felt Lizette move away from his shoulder a little.

"Sometimes," Lizette said as she took a steadying breath, "actors get very involved in their roles and forget who they really are."

"I'm not getting that involved in being a rat," Pete said as he stood up.

Judd had to admit he wasn't asking himself how a Nutcracker would feel about anything, either. He had enough trouble just knowing how Judd Bowman felt.

Lizette stepped out of his arms and Judd let her go. In that instant, he knew exactly how Judd Bowman felt. He felt as though a truck had run him over, and he wanted to beg it to come back and run him over again. He couldn't breathe.

"I think we've gone far enough in the story for today," Lizette said as she stepped even farther away from Judd. "We'll meet again tomorrow—"

Charley cleared his throat. "But tomorrow is Thanksgiving."

"Oh, yes." Lizette blushed. "I mean on Friday. We'll meet to practice on Friday. And I hope all of you have a nice Thanksgiving."

Judd was starting to breathe normally again.

"But we were going to ask you," Amanda whispered as she came up beside Judd and put her hand in his.

Judd let his fingers curl around the little hand.

"We *were* going to ask her, weren't we?" Amanda asked as she looked up at Judd.

"Yes, pumpkin," Judd said as he tried to get himself to focus. He felt as though he'd been bucked off a stallion and hit his back hard coming down. He looked down to see what Amanda wanted.

But Amanda was no longer there. She'd slipped her hand out of his and gone over to Lizette.

"We want you to come eat Thanksgiving with us," Amanda said loud and clear. "And I'm going to help make the potatoes. Cousin Judd said I could. Bobby gets to help with the vegetables."

"Oh, that's very sweet," Lizette said as she looked over at Judd with a question in her eyes. "But I'm sure you'll be—"

Judd could see the excitement start to dim in Amanda's eyes. If he'd had his wits about him, he'd have given her some excuse about why they couldn't invite Lizette. He knew it did a man like him no good to start dreaming about a woman like Lizette. He could never give her all that she deserved. But he couldn't put his comfort ahead of Amanda's happiness, either.

"Please come," he finally said.

"We're going to have dinner and then go to the candle service at church. Bobby and I get to take the candles we made up front. Cousin Judd said we could," Amanda added.

"I'm sure you both have beautiful candles," Lizette said as she put her hand on Amanda's shoulder.

"I made one for you, too," Amanda said softly.

"Oh," Lizette said, and then she looked at Judd.

Judd figured that was when she decided. He noticed she lifted her chin a little for courage.

"I'd love to join you for dinner," Lizette finally said. "And church, too."

Judd hadn't realized he was holding his breath again until he let it out. So, they were having company for Thanksgiving dinner after all. And then they'd all be going to church.

"I'm doing vegetables," Bobby said as he stood up from the floor. "Mrs. Hargrove told me how."

"Green beans in mushroom soup topped with fried onion rings," Mrs. Hargrove said from the sidelines. "It's the simplest vegetable recipe I know, and it's good."

"I could bring something," Lizette offered.

Judd noticed the color was coming back to her cheeks.

"I think we have everything we need," he said.

"You're sure? I could make a pie," Lizette said.

"You can?" Charley said as he stood up from his narrator chair. "What kind of pies can you make?"

"Well, most kinds," Lizette said.

"If that don't beat everything," Charley said to no one in particular. "She can make pies."

"I like apple," Bobby said. "Can you make apple?"

Lizette smiled. "I'll need to run over to Miles City to get some apples, but I need to go later today anyway to get some flyers printed for the Nutcracker. I want to post them around."

"You use real apples?" Charley asked. "It's not that canned filling?"

"Oh, no," Lizette said. "There's nothing like real apple pie."

"Hallelujah," Charley said.

"I could make one for you while I'm making pies," Lizette offered.

Charley nodded and sighed. "I'd sure be happy if you did."

Judd figured Lizette had already made him happy even if she never made a pie.

"I've heard an apple pie is the way to a man's heart," Mrs. Hargrove said softly as she stood next to Judd.

Judd remembered Mrs. Hargrove was in a match-making mood. He wasn't so sure he wanted the whole countryside to know his heart was taken by Lizette. When the word got out about the pies, Judd figured he'd be one of a long line of broken-hearted men hoping for a kind word from the ballet teacher.

"Lemon's more my pie," Judd said.

"Oh," Mrs. Hargrove said in surprise. "I meant Bobby's heart."

Judd smiled. "Of course."

Judd wondered how he'd made it to adulthood without understanding women.

"Although, now that you mention it," Mrs. Hargrove said thoughtfully. She smiled at Judd. "That was a very unusual stage kiss."

"I'm new to the stage stuff."

Mrs. Hargrove smiled. "You're learning fast."

Judd nodded. He was a marked man and Mrs. Hargrove knew it. His only consolation was that the older woman seemed to be kind. He hoped that she also knew how to keep a secret. Judd wasn't sure he could stand for the state of his heart to become a topic of common gossip around Dry Creek.

Chapter Eleven

Lizette put the lemon pie on the table. She could as well have laid a snake down in front of the man.

"But you made apple pie," Judd said.

They'd already finished their dinner of roasted turkey and mashed potatoes and green been casserole, and it was time to have pie. Lizette had kept the lemon pie in a box in the refrigerator while they ate because it needed to stay cool. She hadn't realized until now that Judd must have thought it was another apple pie in the box.

Lizette had made two apple pies for Bobby. She'd delivered the extra pie wrapped in tin foil so he could freeze it for a later meal. She'd also made an apple pie for Charley. Charley and Bobby had been delighted with their pies. Judd, however, looked horrified.

"You said you liked lemon pie," Lizette reminded him. She tried to keep her voice calm. He was looking at her with questions in his eyes. What could she say? She'd made the man the pie because, well, "I had leftover crust."

There. That should satisfy him that she wasn't attempting to lure him into a relationship. The pie was simply a pie.

Lizette took a knife like the one she'd used to cut the apple pie and cut several small pieces of the lemon pie. "I made three pies with the crust I had, and there wasn't enough dough left to make another apple pie because it takes double the amount of crust, so I made a single-crust pie. Lemon."

"Oh." Judd seemed relieved even though he didn't put his plate forward for more pie like the kids were doing. "I wouldn't want you to go to any extra trouble. I mean, I like apple pie, too."

"Besides, it's really for everyone," Lizette continued. She used a pie lifter to put a piece of pie on Bobby's outstretched plate and then on Amanda's plate. "I'm sure the kids like lemon meringue pie."

Amanda nodded from her side of the table. "And chocolate. We like chocolate pie, too, with the white stuff."

"Maybe next time, sweetie," Lizette said as she put the pie lifter on the plate next to the lemon pie.

Amanda swallowed. "But what if my mother comes back before you make the pie?"

"I'm sure she'll wait long enough for you to eat a piece of pie," Lizette said, making a mental note to get the ingredients for a chocolate pie the next time she drove into Miles City. It wouldn't hurt to make a crust and keep it in the freezer so she could whip up a pie at a moment's notice.

Actually, while she was making crusts, maybe she should make several crusts. The people of Dry Creek seemed to like their pies. Well, except for Judd, of course. He was still just looking at the lemon pie.

Amanda nodded as she took up her fork. "My mom likes pies, too. She always made us a chocolate pie for Christmas."

Lizette watched as Amanda set her fork back down without taking another bite. The girl's lower lip was beginning to tremble.

"What if my mom doesn't get back in time for Christmas?" Amanda asked.

"Oh, sweetie." Lizette pushed her chair back from the table and stood up so she could go around to Amanda and give her a hug. Judd was already there by the time Lizette reached the little girl's chair.

And that was the way it was supposed to be, Lizette told herself as she stood and watched Amanda reach up to go into Judd's arms. Lizette supposed it was the kitchen table that had confused her. The table was square and had a place for each of them—Judd, Amanda, Bobby, and herself, Lizette. The table had made her feel like she was part of their family.

But Judd was the one the children turned to for comfort. He was the one who was standing in for their mother.

"Don't worry," Judd said softly to Amanda as he held her close. "I've already asked the sheriff to look for your mother, and he said he'll do everything he can to track her down."

"Maybe she's hiding from our dad," Bobby said from his place at the table. "Maybe she doesn't know he's in jail."

"Maybe," Judd agreed.

Lizette admired the way Judd was so honest with the children. He didn't pretend that they were asking questions they had no right to ask. He didn't gloss over the fact that their father was in jail and that their mother hadn't returned when she'd said she would. He didn't promise them things that he couldn't deliver, either.

As a child, Lizette remembered her mother always being so cheerful about their difficulties that she had never really told Lizette what was going on. Lizette had never even known what disease her father had died of until just before her mother was diagnosed with cancer. Lizette had wondered if her mother finally realized all of the things she hadn't told Lizette over the years and was trying to make up for it by telling her everything she could before she died. Lizette wished her mother had started really talking to her years before she did.

"You must miss your mother very much," Lizette said.

Amanda nodded, her head against Judd's shoulder. "She's not going to be here for her candle."

"Amanda made her a candle," Bobby said quietly from where he still sat at the table. "I told her there was no need to make one. Mom won't be home in time to light it in church tonight."

"We can light it for her," Judd said.

"But she won't be able to say what she's thankful for—" Amanda lifted her head away from Judd's shoulder and protested. "You have to say what you're thankful for when you light the candle. That's what Mrs. Hargrove says."

"I know what your mother's thankful for," Judd said. "The two of you."

"Will you say the words?" Bobby asked. "Amanda and me want to light the candle, but we want someone else to say the words."

Judd nodded. "I'll be happy to say them for your mother."

Amanda had stopped crying by now. "Do you think she'll be able to hear when we say the words? No matter where she is?"

Lizette held her breath. She wondered if Judd would lie to the children.

Judd thought for a minute. "If she doesn't hear them, I'm going to remember them so I can tell her what they were when she gets here."

Amanda nodded. "I'm going to remember them, too."

Lizette vowed she would remember them as well, even though it was absolutely unnecessary. She knew she wouldn't have much of a chance to talk with the children's mother when she came back into town, and if Lizette did get a chance to talk to her, Lizette thought she'd probably have something else to discuss with the woman.

For starters, Lizette knew she'd like to ask Judd's cousin how she could have left her two children for such a long time. Didn't she know they would worry? Lizette knew if *she* was lucky enough to have children like the ones in front of her now, *she* wouldn't be able to leave them with someone else.

"This pie's real good," Bobby said. He'd taken a bite of the lemon pie.

Amanda squirmed to be let down from Judd's arms, and he settled her back in her chair.

"Let me taste it," Amanda said as she took her own bite of the lemon pie.

Lizette couldn't believe that was it. One minute the children had been in tears, and the next they were smiling because of pie. Even Judd was looking happier than he had a few minutes ago.

"Lemon pie has always been my favorite," Judd said as he helped himself to a piece of the pie. "Maybe that's what I'm going to say I'm thankful for tonight in church. Lemon pie."

Amanda giggled. "You can't be thankful for pie. You have to be thankful for people. Mrs. Hargrove says that's the most important thing."

Lizette felt a sudden dart of alarm. People? She was supposed to be thankful for people? "Can't we be thankful for other things, too?"

Amanda thought for a moment and then nodded. "But they have to be big things."

"And you can't be thankful for dragons," Bobby

added. "The Curtis twins told me that. One year they told everyone they were thankful for dragons, and everyone said they were cute. Some of the women even pinched their cheeks. I don't want to get my cheeks pinched."

"I could be thankful for my dog," Judd said. "He's turned out to be a fine watchdog for a stray."

Amanda nodded. "A dog would be a good thankful."

Lizette wondered if she could be thankful for a whole town. She was beginning to feel like she had a home among the people of Dry Creek, even though she hadn't expected to feel that way when she moved here.

"I don't know," Judd said as he helped himself to another small piece of lemon pie. "This is awfully good pie. Maybe I could be thankful for the pie *and* my new dog."

Judd smiled at Lizette before she started to eat the piece of pie on her plate. "I haven't even said a proper thank-you yet for the pie. It's excellent. I don't think I've ever had such good lemon pie."

"Lemon pie's not that hard to make," Lizette said. "You just have to use real lemons."

"Any pie is hard to make in my opinion," Judd said. "I'm not much of a cook."

"I wouldn't say that. The meal today was wonderful."

When Lizette had arrived, Judd had a dish towel wrapped around his waist and he was mashing potatoes with an old-fashioned masher he said he'd found in the pantry. There had been things left in the house, he explained, from when the Jenkins family lived here.

Lizette figured that the curtains had been one of the things left in the house by Mrs. Jenkins. They had to have been hung over the sink by a woman. They were white threadbare cotton, and they had tiny embroidered pansies on the bottom of them. The pansies were lavender, pink and yellow.

The kitchen was a comfortable room that had seen its share of family meals over the years. Lizette had noticed that the doorway from the kitchen to the living room had a series of old cuts in the side of it and two new cuts. The wood of the old cuts was gray, but the color of the newer cuts was golden.

Judd had noticed her looking at the cuts. "Kids' growing marks. I thought I should add Amanda and Bobby. It took me long enough to figure out what the other cuts were there for—I figured some fancy exercise machine or maybe someone just standing there who had a new knife and wanted to try it out. But the marks were too deliberate for either of those."

Lizette had smiled. She knew enough about Judd's childhood to understand how bewildering it must have seemed to mark a child's growth. It was a homey thing that spoke of love and attention.

Lizette wondered if she could list as her grateful the fact that she was a guest in this house today for Thanksgiving dinner. She had expected to have a cup of canned soup in her studio. Of course, some of the other families in Dry Creek had invited her home with them for Thanksgiving dinner. She'd refused all of the other invitations. She didn't want to be with a family that was whole. In a family like that she would be extra. But in this little makeshift family she felt like she had a place, even if it was only for the day.

"I have lots of eggs," Judd said. He'd finished his piece of pie, and he pushed the plate away from him. "If you want any eggs for your baking, just let me know. You're welcome to all you need. I got some chickens after the kids came, so we have lots of eggs."

"Thanks. That's helpful." Lizette figured it was the Montana way to give small gifts like that to your neighbors. "And if you want any baked goods, let me know. Doughnuts. Pies. Anything."

Lizette figured that would be the best gift she could give any of the men around here. After she'd agreed to make doughnuts for the one cowboy, she'd gotten five more orders for closer to Christmastime. It was apparently going to be a merry Christmas in the bunkhouses around here.

"You don't need to pay me with baked goods," Judd said as he stood up from the table. "You're still welcome to the eggs."

"Well, I have to do something for you," Lizette said as she stood up, too. "You've invited me to dinner and offered me eggs and—"

Judd walked over to the kitchen sink. "If you're set on paying me back, you can help with the dishes. I'll wash if you dry."

"Yes, but doing dishes isn't enough."

"You haven't seen how many dishes we have,"

Judd said as he turned the faucet on and let the water start to run in the sink. "And I'm including the pots and pans."

In the end, Lizette didn't dry many of the dishes. Bobby and Amanda both wanted to help dry dishes, so Lizette found her job involved more reaching the tall shelves to put the dishes away and handing clean towels to the two children and scratching Judd's back.

"Maybe you should see a doctor," Lizette said the second time Judd asked her to scratch between his shoulder blades. "Maybe you have a rash."

"That's the place," Judd said with a sigh as her fingers gave a gentle scratch to the area next to his right shoulder blade.

Lizette let her fingers settle into the lazy circles the man seemed to like. "Maybe there's some cream that would stop the itch."

"No, it'll be fine," Judd said lazily, and then seemed to remember something. "Not that it's a rash. I'm a perfectly healthy specimen. No rashes. No long-term medical problems at all. Good teeth."

"He's got a funny toe," Amanda whispered as she leaned over to Lizette. "Have him show you his funny toe."

Judd figured he might as well give up and declare himself a freak of nature. He sure didn't know much about how to make a woman want to date him. Not that there was much chance that Lizette would want to date a man like him anyway, even if his health was reasonably good. No, she'd go for someone ten years younger, someone more her age. Someone about the age of Pete.

"I think Pete has a rash though," Judd offered. "Nothing serious. Something to do with the cattle."

"It's not mad cow disease, is it?"

Judd groaned. He wanted to scare Lizette away from Pete, not away from the whole town of Dry Creek. "No, I think it was just a little poison ivy he got in one of the cattle pastures on the Elkton ranch."

It was this past summer when Pete had stepped into some poison ivy, but Judd didn't think he needed to be that specific. The hardware store had been buzzing with the news the whole week last summer. Apparently poison ivy was rare in these parts of Montana. But, for all Judd knew, the cowboy still had the occasional itch from the experience.

"I don't have any poison ivy on my place," Judd added just to be on the safe side. "No rashes. No poison ivy. No mad cow disease."

"Yes, but—" Lizette stopped scratching and leaned sideways so she could smile at him. "You do have that funny toe."

Judd didn't know what had possessed him to try to tell the kids the story of the little piggies. He'd seen a woman in a supermarket once playing the game with her baby's toes while they sat on a bench beside the bakery. Judd had been so taken with the singsong way the woman had recited the nursery rhyme that he'd stayed and listened to her for half an hour.

When the kids were so scared that first night they were at his place, Judd had remembered that nursery rhyme. It was the only thing he knew to do to quiet little kids, and Amanda made him tell the rhyme again and again even after she stopped being afraid. Unfortunately, she wanted to use his toes to represent the little piggies, and not her own.

"Amanda thinks my little toe is too big," Judd finally admitted.

Amanda nodded emphatically. "It's not the little-piggy toe at all. It's supposed to go wee-wee all the way home and it's not wee at all."

Lizette smiled. "So it's not broken or anything?"

"Nope, just too big," Judd said.

Lizette smiled at him again, and suddenly Judd felt ten years younger. Maybe he could hope, after all. Maybe she hadn't noticed he was that much older than she was. Maybe she didn't care if he had a big little toe. Maybe she wouldn't even care that he didn't know much about family life and was a poor prospect as a husband and an even poorer prospect as a father.

Maybe—Judd stopped himself. He would have been safer thinking that he could turn his little toe into a squealing pig than that he could turn himself into someone worthy of Lizette.

Judd brought his dreams to a complete halt. He didn't know much about family life, but he had learned a few things from the kids while they'd been staying with him, and one thing he did know—it didn't pay for a man to have dreams that outreached any realistic hope he had of grabbing hold of those dreams. He'd miss the kids when their mother came back, but he could live with that pain.

What he couldn't live with was getting himself to thinking he could make a home of his own with Lizette. When that dream came crashing down, he'd feel the pain for the rest of his life.

No, it was better to stop the dreaming in the first place.

Chapter Twelve

The steps to the church didn't look as hard to climb at night as they had been on Sunday morning. Maybe it was because Lizette knew there were friendly faces inside. At least she knew what was going to happen this time when she went through those double doors at the top of the stairs.

The kids had given her and Judd complete details on what to expect. They'd mentioned that everyone sat in the pews and different people went up to set their very own candle on the table next to the pulpit. Then the person would light their candle and tell everyone what he or she was thankful for during the past year. Then the person went back to their pew and sat down.

Essentially, Lizette told herself, it was up, candle, thanks and down. She could handle that even in unfamiliar territory like a church.

Lizette had to admit to herself, however, that she no longer felt as much like a stranger as she had expected. The people from the church weren't as critical of her as she had imagined they would be. No one seemed to care if she wore a hat when no one else did or if she had to read the words to the hymns from the songbook when everyone else knew the words by heart.

So, she told herself, she should relax. Besides, tonight there wouldn't be any lessons on how people should treat each other, so there would be nothing that could cause her any awkward tears. She didn't want to risk ending up on Judd's shoulder again. Not after that kiss.

That kiss had been superb acting. She had felt the Nutcracker's passion all the way down to her toes. But it was the mistake of a novice to imagine that the person acting a role next to you onstage actually meant those feelings for you. That's what made a play a play. It was pretend. Lizette thought of all of the actors who had played Romeo and Juliet over the years. Did they get married to each other after the play? No. What happened on stage was pretend.

Lizette must have given herself that speech a dozen times over the last few days, yet she still felt the need to remind herself.

Apart from that kiss, Judd had given absolutely no indication that he was interested in her in any way except as a dinner guest and ballet instructor. In fact, usually he just frowned at her. She didn't know why she was having these fluttery feelings about him, but it had to stop. She didn't want to embarrass herself by making him worry that she was getting romantic ideas just because he'd thrown himself into the part of the Nutcracker with enthusiasm.

And the kiss—well—what man wouldn't be pleased to know he was a prince instead of a wooden kitchen utensil used to break apart nut shells? Didn't she remember that football players kissed their teammates after winning a particularly important game? Of course, she didn't think they kissed them on the lips, but that was only a matter of location. The principle of the victory kiss was the same.

No, she had no reason to take Judd's kiss personally. She was a professional. She knew how people threw themselves into acting.

Lizette looked over at Judd. They were standing at the bottom of the church stairs as they had before, only this time it was dark and it was hard to read any expression on Judd's face. She did notice that he wasn't frowning though, and that was a good sign with Judd. Now that she thought about it, she didn't think he'd frowned at all today. Except, of course, when he'd first seen the lemon pie she'd made for him.

"You've got your candle?" Judd turned to Lizette and asked.

Lizette nodded. Amanda had already given her the candle she had made for her to use tonight. It was a short pink candle, and Amanda had put glittery sequins all over it, because, she said, it reminded her of the ballet costumes.

"I've got mine, too," Amanda said as she held out her blue candle. She had decorated it with the same kind of sequins and sparkles that she'd used on Lizette's.

"Mine are here," Judd said as he patted the pocket of his coat.

Lizette had already seen the two candles he carried. One was the candle the kids had made for him and the other was the one they had made for their mother.

Lizette had smiled when she had seen the candle the kids had made for Judd. They obviously couldn't agree on what kind of candle Judd would like, so the candle had been dipped in red coloring on one side and green coloring on the other. The two colors mixed in places and made long rivulets of dark purple. The one thing the kids had seemed to agree on was cow stickers, and they had put them all over the candle. The candle they had made for their mother was a tall yellow taper with stickers of two long-stemmed white roses on the side of it.

Bobby hadn't shown any of them his candle. "It's green," was all he would say.

Judd and Lizette seemed to take a deep breath at the same time and they looked over at each other and nodded. Then they each took the hand of a child and started to walk up the steps to the church.

The church was transformed at night. Last Sunday morning the light shining into the sanctuary from the windows had made the place look homey. The light had also clearly shown up the nicks in the back of the pews and the scuff marks on the floor by the entry.

But tonight, there were no nicks or marks showing. There were light sconces on the side walls and a dim glow came from each one. There was also an overhead light that gave a muted light. Instead of the imperfections of the room, the yellow light made everything look richer.

Lizette glanced over at Judd. It also made everyone look more handsome.

"Do they have a ballet here, too?" Amanda whispered in a hushed tone as they stood at the back of the church.

"No, sweetie, those are choir robes," Lizette answered as she followed the direction of Amanda's gaze.

Two women were standing near the piano and they had on long robes made of midnight-blue satin with white collars. They were leaning over to read some music that the pianist was playing. From where they stood, Lizette could hear the soft hum of the women's voices as they sang a song.

"Oh, welcome," Mrs. Hargrove said as she and Charley walked down the aisle toward them. "I'm so glad you came."

"We wouldn't miss it," Judd said as he shook the hand Charley offered. "We have some special candles to light. Besides, I wanted to talk with the sheriff if he's here."

Judd still hadn't talked with the sheriff, and he wanted to know a little more about when the kids' father was coming up for trial. Not that Judd expected to go to the trial. He just thought he should know unless anyone said anything in front of the kids.

"Sheriff Wall had some kind of business that took him out of town," Charley said. "Asked me and my son to give the Billings police a call if anything went wrong around here."

"Does he usually leave someone in charge when he's gone?" Judd hadn't realized how much he'd counted on calling the sheriff if trouble did come up with Amanda and Bobby's father.

"There was never any need for him to leave someone in charge," Charley said. "I think he's just worried because—" Charley glanced at the children and lowered his voice until only Judd could hear "—well, we don't usually have something in town that a criminal wants that much. But now—well, the sheriff said he'd feel easier about leaving the two of us to keep an eye on things, especially until they got the man transferred over to the Billings jail. My son doesn't get into town much except for church, but I'll be around to keep a lookout."

Judd frowned. "Is there a delay with sending him to Billings?"

Charley shrugged. "They needed to wait for an opening. The jail in Billings is full at the moment. So they're keeping him in Miles City."

"There's nothing wrong with the jail in Miles City, is there?"

Charley chuckled. "Nothing some extra heat wouldn't cure. The county doesn't like us to keep folks there in the winter because we can't afford to heat it the way it should be. It tends to be on the cold side."

"But it's secure?" Judd asked.

Charley nodded. "It might not be comfortable, but it's built like a fort."

Judd nodded. He supposed there was no need to worry. The Miles City jail should hold the man, and that was all he cared about.

Mrs. Hargrove smiled down at the children. "Why, look—you've both got your candles."

Judd prepared himself for Amanda to press her face into his leg from shyness, and he had his hand halfway down to reassure her when he realized there was no need. Amanda didn't even look back to see that he was there. She just smiled up at Mrs. Hargrove and started walking down the aisle between the pews.

"We want to get a good pew," Amanda turned around and said to Judd and Lizette.

Judd wondered what made a pew a good pew, but it looked as though Amanda had definite opinions on the matter. If she didn't, Bobby had almost reached her and would no doubt add his advice, as well.

Apparently, going to this church had done something besides make Judd uncomfortable. It had made the children confident in Dry Creek without him.

"I guess they don't need us," Judd said to Lizette now that both children were ahead of them.

Judd looked down to smile at Lizette and was glad he had gotten the words out of his mouth before he did. He'd never seen Lizette in soft light before. He'd seen her in the bright daylight of the ballet studio and the ordinary light of his dinner table. He'd even seen her just minutes ago in the darkness outside as they walked up to the church. But he'd never seen her in soft muted lighting like this.

She was beautiful. Softly beautiful. Stirringly beautiful. She was—

"Whoeee." Pete's voice broke Judd's concentration before he even knew the cowboy had walked up behind them. Not that the cowboy was paying Judd any attention. The man was looking at Lizette like she'd stepped off the pages of a magazine ad for a tropical paradise. "Aren't you something?"

Lizette smiled at the man.

Judd resisted the urge to growl like a guard dog. Well, he tried to resist the urge. No one noticed he didn't quite succeed except for Mrs. Hargrove.

"If you need an antacid, let me know," the older woman said as she looked at him and patted her purse. "I carry a small pharmacy in here. After a big turkey dinner like today, you won't be the only one who needs help digesting it all."

"Thanks, but I'm fine."

Judd told himself he was fine. He was certainly just as fine as Pete.

And Lizette must realize it. She was looking at him now instead of at Pete.

"Maybe Mrs. Hargrove has something in her purse for that rash of yours," Lizette said with a sympathetic tone in her voice.

Judd grimaced. "I don't have a rash." He looked over at Mrs. Hargrove and then at Pete. Their eyes were all bright with curiosity. "I just asked her to scratch my back while I was washing dishes. I just had a little itch. That's all. No rash."

"Hmm," Mrs. Hargrove said with a smile. "Well, I don't think I have anything to treat that with."

"I think I feel an itch working its way up my back right now," Pete said as he stepped closer to Lizette. "Maybe you could scratch it for me?"

"We've got candles to light," Judd said as he took Lizette's arm and steered her down the aisle.

"Here we are," Amanda whispered from the pew she and Bobby had chosen.

Judd almost groaned again. The two of them had chosen the half pew that was off to the right side of the piano. He figured the pew could hold two adults comfortably. But when you added the two children, they would all be very tight.

The kids were geniuses, Judd told himself ten minutes later. The only way he and Lizette could fit in the pew with the children was if he held Amanda on his lap and Bobby sat next to the piano. That meant he and Lizette were in the middle and pressed close together. It was perfect. Judd could watch the light dance around in Lizette's dark hair as she moved her head, and he was also close enough to smell the faint lilac perfume that she wore.

He was a happy man.

"Can I go up with my candle now?" Amanda asked as she squirmed down off of Judd's lap.

Judd looked around. Several people had taken their candles up, but it didn't look like anyone was standing up right this minute. "Sure. Do you want me to come with you?"

Amanda shook her head. "I can do it."

Judd had to blink his eyes when he saw Amanda walk up in front of the whole congregation and put her candle on the table. A few weeks ago she wouldn't even speak to him, and now she was telling everyone why she was grateful.

"I'm glad I get to be the Sugar Plum Fairy," Amanda said after she put her candle on the table. Then she skipped back to the pew where the rest of them sat.

"You did real good, sweetie," Lizette said to the girl as Amanda crawled back up on Judd's lap.

"You sure did," Judd added. It was Lizette who had worked the change in Amanda. Judd had known how to protect the child, but he hadn't known how to make her so excited about something that she needed to talk about it.

Several more people got up to take their candles to the front of the church. Pete was one of them. He had a plain white candle stuck in the bottom of a tin cup, and he said he was thankful he'd gotten to have Thanksgiving dinner with his mother up by Havre.

"Ah, isn't that sweet?" Lizette murmured.

Judd grunted. He'd been unaware that Pete had a mother.

"And I got to bring her a geranium plant that was blooming," Pete continued. The cowboy held his hat in his hands, and Judd couldn't tell if the other man was sincere or just saying what the women wanted to hear. "She appreciated the plant now because her arthritis is bad and she can't be out much."

"Ah," Lizette sighed. "He's good to visit his mother."

Judd didn't point out that for all they knew the cowboy only ever spent one holiday with her. One holiday didn't mean he visited his mother regularly.

Judd was frowning by the time Pete sat down in his pew. Judd knew he was being uncharitable and it made him irritable. The truth was, Pete probably did know more about family life than *he* did.

Mrs. Hargrove stood up next. The older woman carried a candelabra with several candles in it. She said she was lighting candles for those in her family who couldn't be here. "And one of them should be," she added. "And will be by next Thanksgiving if I have anything to say about it."

"Amen," Charley said from his place in the church, and several people nodded.

Judd noticed that the middle-aged man who sat next to Charley didn't nod like everyone else in the church did. He didn't even smile or look the least bit thankful. That must be Charley's son. Judd wondered if the poor man had any idea what his father and Mrs. Hargrove were planning for him. Probably not. But the man looked like someone who could take care of himself, and Judd had enough of his own trouble to worry about.

Bobby went up with his candle after the Curtis twins had finished.

"I'm thankful that my Mom is okay even if I

don't know where she is," Bobby said bravely after he added his candle to the table. Judd noticed Bobby had wrapped a yellow ribbon around the candle. It must have been the ribbon his mother accidentally left when she left the children with Judd.

"Shall we go up now?" Judd whispered in Lizette's ear.

Lizette nodded and stood up when he did.

Judd set Amanda down on the floor so she could walk with them.

Sometimes a man had more to be grateful for than he could share with other people. Having Lizette come up front with him and the kids beside him made him feel humble and proud all at the same time. When they were together in church, Judd felt like he belonged somewhere and to someone. He wondered if church did that to other people.

"I'm grateful that the town gave me a place to set up my ballet studio," Lizette said as she set her pink candle on the table. "It's made my mother's dream come true. I wish she were here to see it."

Judd wished he'd had a chance to meet Lizette's mother. She must have been a special woman to raise someone like Lizette all by herself.

"I have two candles," Judd said as he reached into his pockets. Both Amanda and Bobby were on his right, so he handed their mother's candle to them. "The first candle is for Barbara, Amanda and Bobby's mother. If she were here today, I think she'd tell you that the thing she is most grateful for is her two wonderful children."

Bobby and Amanda carefully set their mother's candle on the table.

Judd pulled the other candle out of his pocket and set it on the table. "As for me, I'm grateful for—" Judd stopped. He meant to say he was grateful for the dog that had wandered onto his farm last spring. And he *was* thankful for the dog. He'd never had a pet before. But he suddenly wanted to be more honest with the people of Dry Creek who were watching him. So he cleared his throat and began again. "I'm most grateful for feeling like I'm part of a family today."

There, Judd told himself. He'd been open and vulnerable and no one had stood up and called him a liar or anything. In fact, what he could see in the dim lighting was that most people were nodding their heads like he was right to be grateful for that. Judd stood with the kids while they waited for Lizette to light her candle.

The rest of the people in the Dry Creek church lit candles. Some of them mentioned being thankful for good health. One or two were thankful for the year's good crops. Still others were grateful that family members were all able to be together for the holiday.

When everyone had finished taking their candles up to the front of the church, the two women in choir robes sang a song about amazing grace. Judd figured they had that about right. He'd never seen much kindness or grace in his life, but he was beginning to think that the people in this church knew something about grace that he didn't. Maybe he should take the kids to church here until their mother came to get them.

He'd like for them to know about this amazing grace that was in the song.

He sighed. He guessed if he was going to do this church business, he should do it right. Maybe he could order a tie from the catalog. While he was at it, he'd order a suit, as well.

Judd looked over at Lizette. He wondered if she'd wear that cute little hat to church again if he wore a tie. At least as long as the kids were with him, Judd was pretty sure she'd sit with them in church.

And Sunday was only a couple of days away. Maybe it wouldn't be such a hardship to go to church after all.

Chapter Thirteen

It was the Monday morning after Thanksgiving, and Lizette was making progress on plans for the Nutcracker. She'd seen Mr. Elkton in church yesterday and he'd offered her the use of the barn he owned on the outskirts of Dry Creek for the performance itself. She'd been assured by Mrs. Hargrove that enough people would come to see the Nutcracker performance that they would need to have more space than Lizette had in her dance school.

"Plus, we can set a refreshment table up at one end of the barn for those lovely pastries you mentioned, and we'll need some punch, of course," Mrs. Hargrove said. "Don't you worry about it being a barn. The building hasn't been used as a barn for ten years or more. We keep it clean just for events like this. We'll have our Christmas pageant there on Christmas Eve, so we'll just get things ready earlier and have the Nutcracker in the barn, too."

Lizette planned to have the ballet this coming Friday evening, December 3. She'd walked over to the barn after church yesterday and checked to see if the floor was smooth enough for ballet movements. It was.

Plus, the barn was charming. There were several windows on each side of the barn, and the sunlight showed off the square features of the structure. There were rafters and square trim around the windows and the large double door. The wood was all golden as if it had been polished.

It was easy to believe that there had been other performances in the building. There was even a small sound system that had been wired around the rafters so that the music she used for the Nutcracker would be easier to hear.

"We're getting to be a regular cultural center here in Dry Creek," Mrs. Hargrove continued. "What with the ballet and then the Christmas pageant. I can take my Christmas tree over to the barn anytime you want and Charley can move the fireplace he made over so we'll be all set for the ballet. And with the hayloft, there's even stairs you can use for when Clara goes up to her bedroom to sleep." Mrs. Hargrove stopped all of a sudden and shook her head. "There I go again. Making everyone's plans for them. I'm working on controlling my organizing spirit this Christmas."

"Don't worry about it with me," Lizette said. "I'm happy to have a little guidance."

Mrs. Hargrove nodded. "Well, I suppose you do need someone to show you the ropes for the first time. It'd be a pity if we didn't have everything ready for our Dry Creek ballet premiere. At least I think we should call it a premiere in our advertising, don't you?"

"Advertising?" Lizette had a sinking feeling. She'd been focused on practicing and getting the costumes ready. "It's probably too late for advertising. I wasn't thinking. Newspapers usually need more notice. The performance is Friday."

"Edna will free up some place in the Miles City section of the paper," Mrs. Hargrove said. "It won't be much, but that's only one way to let people know. We can also put up posters."

"I don't have much money for printing and things like that," Lizette cautioned her. "I thought this would be a small performance since it's our first one."

"Don't you worry about a thing," Mrs. Hargrove said. "And, believe me, we won't have a small turn-out."

Mrs. Hargrove should run for president, Lizette thought a few hours later. And not just of the USA. Mrs. Hargrove could run the world. She had arranged for Edna to do a review of the Nutcracker at a special dress rehearsal the cast would do Wednesday afternoon. That way people in the area would know about the Nutcracker and Lizette wouldn't have to pay for an ad. And, if that wasn't enough, the older woman also talked with Glory Curtis, the pastor's wife, and got an offer from the woman to create full-color posters to hang both at the hardware store and at several locations in Miles City.

"She's an artist, you know," Mrs. Hargrove confided to Lizette when she hung up the telephone. "She used to work as a police sketch artist—that's what she was doing when she first came to Dry Creek—and now she's gaining quite a reputation for her portraits."

"That's an unusual occupation for a pastor's wife. A police sketch artist?"

"Oh, well, she wasn't married to Matthew then," Mrs. Hargrove said. "Although she's always been an independent-minded woman, so it wouldn't make any difference to either of them if she was working for the police still—except for the fact that Matthew didn't like the thought of people shooting at her."

"Well, no, I suppose he wouldn't."

"I tell my daughter, Doris June, that a woman can be and do about anything in Dry Creek these days. She's always so worried about her career, but there's nothing to say she can't have a career right here."

"I hope your daughter does come home soon." Lizette had heard about Mrs. Hargrove's plans to have her daughter come home and marry some local man from Judd. She hated to think that the older woman would be disappointed, but Lizette thought it was likely. "It must be hard when your daughter doesn't do what you want her to do."

"Ah, well," Mrs. Hargrove said. "A mother can hope."

Lizette was glad she was able to make her mother's dream come true even if her mother wasn't here to enjoy the fact with her. Sometimes, when the day was done and the streets of Dry Creek were quiet and dark, Lizette talked to her mother and told her all about what was happening with the Baker School of Ballet.

Sometimes, instead of pretending to talk to her mother, she actually called Madame Aprele and told her about what was happening. The odd thing was, she didn't exactly tell either woman the whole truth.

Lizette didn't want to disappoint them, so she made it sound as if the school was a real school and not just space in an old store. She made her students sound like real students and not just a few people she'd managed to talk into dressing up in costumes. She certainly wouldn't tell either of them that her premiere performance was going to be held in a barn or that both her Mouse King and her Nutcracker were hopeless at ballet.

One thing she could tell them, though, Lizette thought cheerfully, was that she was having someone from the local paper come to the dress rehearsal to write a review of the performance. That should make them both feel that her school was doing well.

Judd never thought he'd worry about the problems of being a Nutcracker. "If he's wearing a red military coat and black boots, you know he'd never agree to having some little girl stand in front when he's battling a mouse."

"Rat," Pete corrected him. "I'm a rat."

Pete was standing beside the fireplace that they had just moved over to the barn from Lizette's dance studio.

"When he's battling a large rodent," Judd corrected

himself. "A Nutcracker just wouldn't do that. He's got more dignity."

Judd had gotten a better picture of the pride a Nutcracker would have when he'd seen the poster Glory Curtis had drawn. The poster showed the Nutcracker standing tall with the little girl, Clara, at his side. Glory had used both Judd and Lizette for models in the poster, and even though the sketch was in pencil, Judd swore it was the best likeness anyone had ever made of him, and the girl looked exactly like Lizette.

Judd figured people would know him as the Nutcracker for miles around. He didn't want people stopping him in the grocery store and demanding to know what kind of man he was for letting a girl stand between him and danger.

"But Clara owns the Nutcracker," Lizette protested. She was draping an afghan over a wooden rocking chair that Charley would sit in as the narrator. "She's only protecting what is hers."

Judd had nothing to say to that. Actually, he didn't want to say much to that. It made him feel pretty good.

Pete, however, had something to say. "It's only a nutcracker. Who'd be fool enough to risk getting a rat bite just to save a wooden utensil? You could get rabies."

"He's her prince, that's why," Lizette said as she tucked the back of the afghan into the arms of the rocker and then stood back to look at her work. "There. That's straight."

Pete grunted. "It doesn't do any good to have a prince if you're dead because of rabies."

"Don't worry," Lizette said as she moved the rocker closer to the fireplace. "You'll do a good job of fighting him in the beginning and look very impressive."

"I could still switch and be the Nutcracker," Pete suggested.

"Not on your life," Judd said. He knew Pete wasn't so much dismayed at being a dead rodent as he was envious of Judd for getting to kiss the ballerina. Well, actually, he hadn't kissed the ballerina since that first time, but he figured one of these days Lizette would forget about the stage kiss and go for a real one.

"It's too late to make changes," Lizette said as she put a picture frame on the mantel of the fireplace. "We have the dress rehearsal at two o'clock tomorrow afternoon—I know it's not our usual time, but Edna needs to come then in order to get our review done for the paper."

"She's not going to take pictures, is she?" Pete asked.

Lizette shook her head. "I don't think so. She said there's not much room for the review even."

"Good," Pete said.

"You'll be able to get off work, won't you?" Lizette said to Pete.

Pete nodded.

"I know you don't have to worry," Lizette turned and said to Judd.

"One of the good things about owning your own

place," Judd said as he helped Lizette place a small rug in front of the fireplace. "I'm free as a bird when it comes to my schedule."

Judd hoped she appreciated that he was a man with prospects. It didn't seem like she even noticed.

"I'll start with a quick rehearsal of the kids a couple of hours earlier, so I won't take either of you away from your work any longer than necessary," Lizette said as she straightened up after placing the rug.

"I can spare the time. I don't answer to anyone," Judd said as he brushed his hands on his jeans. Lizette wasn't even listening to his declaration of independence, so Judd gave it up. "As long as you've got plans for the kids, that'll give me a chance to run into Miles City without them. I want to check with the courts about their father. I'm wondering if anyone has asked him for more information about Barbara."

"You should have plenty of time to go to Miles City and back," Lizette said. "And if we finish early, I'll just put all of the kids to work cutting up those dried plums for the pastries I'm making."

"Really?" Pete brightened up. "The boys in the bunkhouse have been asking what kind of pastry these sugar-plum things are."

"It's like a cream-filled croissant with raisins, except there's a different kind of cream and the raisins are plums and it's not really croissant dough."

"But you don't need to go to the ballet to get one, do you?" Pete asked.

Lizette laughed. "I'm afraid so. I know you're hoping the others won't come, but that's the only way to get a sugar-plum pastry. Unless there are leftover ones after the ballet."

"There won't be any leftovers," Pete said.

"If you need any last-minute things from the store in Miles City, let me know since I'll be going in there anyway," Judd offered.

"I haven't thought of what to use as a cloth on the table where we'll be serving the pastries and punch," Lizette said. "Maybe you could buy some white silk fabric at the store—some of the washable kind would work best."

"I haven't seen any fabric stores in Miles City," Judd said. He didn't add that he wouldn't know silk if he saw it. He was more of a denim and flannel kind of a guy.

"Oh, I'm sure they must have a store that sells bolts of fabric," Lizette said. "You'll just have to ask around."

Judd decided he would have to take her word for it. She was probably right anyway. It was the kind of thing a woman would know.

Besides, Judd thought to himself, at least buying some silk would give him a good reason for going into Miles City apart from his vague unease. He was beginning to wish that Amanda and Bobby's father was already in the jail in Billings. Maybe there was something Judd could do to speed up the process if he went into Miles City and talked to whoever was in charge at the jail. Surely they could find room in the Billings jail if they put their minds to it.

Judd didn't know why he was feeling nervous. Everyone he had asked said that the jail in Miles City was built like a rock. A body had more chance of freezing to death inside their cell there than of actually making an escape.

Of course, Judd wasn't sure he was worried about the jail.

For all Judd knew, his unease might not even be about the kids' father. It might be about the upcoming ballet. Judd figured he knew his part as well as he was ever going to know it, and he was smart enough to realize that Lizette had organized everything, so he more or less stood still while she went twirling and dancing around him. He was more of a post than a dancer. Still, he was uneasy about the whole thing.

He'd never in his life performed in front of an audience. When he was riding in the rodeo, there had been an audience, but there was nothing required of the performers but to stay on the back of a horse. It was different than the ballet.

In this ballet, he was supposed to be the prince. Him—Judd Bowman. He knew that Lizette didn't have many contenders for the role, but still. He'd never figured he was a prince kind of a guy. He was more like the guy out in the stables who took care of everything while the prince was inside talking to people and impressing the princess.

If Judd had known that the Nutcracker was more than a utensil, he'd have thought twice about volunteering for the role. Even now, if any man but Pete stepped forward and said he wanted to play the role, Judd would be tempted to let him.

A man could just pretend to be something he wasn't for so long in life. Judd figured his limit would be Saturday. He hoped he would get through the ballet with no problems. Then he could go back to counting out his nails so he could finish working on that fence of his like the solitary guy he was meant to be.

There wasn't anything wrong with building fences, he reminded himself. He needed those fences, and that's what he'd started out to do that day he'd come to town with the kids. This whole ballet business had just been a distraction. He needed to get back to business. Besides, the whole world would be a better place if people had more fences.

Chapter Fourteen

It was only six o'clock, but Lizette was wide awake. She was lying in her bed in the back of her dance studio and looking at the hands of the clock on her nightstand. For a moment, she thought her alarm must have gone off, but it hadn't. It wasn't scheduled to go off for another hour.

Lizette had just had a dream about mice escaping into the audience and the Nutcracker's hat falling off his head. The reason she was awake was that she was having performance jitters. She hadn't had those in years. The odd thing was that she wasn't even worried about the dancing. She could dance Clara's role in her sleep, and she'd simplified everyone else's steps so they would look fine even if they forgot everything she'd taught them. Clara did all of the true ballet dancing.

No, she wasn't fretting about the dancing; she was worried about more basic things—things like the tin soldier dying in the wrong place or the mice giggling in the middle of their fierce attack.

Or the Nutcracker forgetting how to stage a kiss and giving her the real thing. Not that she was worried about thinking the kiss would mean anything. She'd given herself that speech enough times the last time it happened that she didn't think she'd fall for that illusion again. Even if their lips did happen to meet, she would know it was just an acting kiss.

But it could still fluster her so that she would forget some steps in the performance. Since she was really the only one dancing, that could be a problem. She was going to have to remember to tell Judd again that their stage kiss didn't require any physical contact. The audience couldn't see if their lips touched or not. They were supposed to air kiss beside their lips, not on their lips.

Maybe she should draw him a diagram, Lizette thought as she stretched and threw back the covers.

Ohh, it was cold. Lizette had the heat on in her room at the back of the studio, but she had kept it low. Until she knew how much money she would be making each month, she didn't want to spend too much extra on heat. That was an incentive to get more students if nothing else was.

Lizette reached under the quilt that covered her bed and pulled out the sweatpants and sweatshirt that she'd put there last night. Her neighbor Linda, at the café, had taught her that trick. When it was cold out, you took your clothes for the next day to bed with you and they were warm when you got up. Of course, Linda recommended putting them just under the top blanket instead of between the sheets. That way, she assured Lizette, the clothes didn't get wrinkled.

Lizette pulled the sweatpants on.

She then quickly pulled on the sweatshirt, telling herself she should just go over and take another look at the stage they had made in the barn. She wanted to see what everything looked like in the muted light of morning. This lighting would be the closest to the subdued light they'd have on their actual performance and Lizette didn't want to miss any chance to see how the shadows would fall. She wasn't sure how the shadows could help her, but knowledge always made one better prepared.

After all, she told herself as she walked to her stove and turned the tea kettle on, her very first ballet production was going to be reviewed this afternoon. She hadn't realized quite how important that was until she had talked with Madame Aprele a few days ago and told her about the upcoming review.

Of course, she hadn't told Madame Aprele that the review was going to run in a section of the paper called "Dry Creek Tidbits" or that Edna Best, the woman reviewing the ballet, obviously didn't recognize the Nutcracker and was, by her own admission, more comfortable covering the bait and poundage reports during fishing season.

Lizette saw no reason to dismay her former teacher when the basic facts themselves were encouraging. Her ballet performance was scheduled in a large local community center, her dress rehearsal was Wednesday at two o'clock, during which time a reviewer would be present to critique the performance, and the Snow Queen was predicting a good audience turnout for the actual performance.

Madame Aprele was ecstatic with the news, and Lizette told herself she should just focus on the good things that she had told Madame Aprele.

It took Lizette ten more minutes to wash her face and fix her hair. She thought about putting some makeup on just to help keep her face warmer, but decided against it. Then she put her wool coat on and wrapped a knit scarf around her ears and neck. She had put a tea bag in her cup of hot water a few minutes ago, and now she poured the tea into a thermal mug so she could take it with her to the barn.

The air was cold outside. There was no fresh snow, but the snow from yesterday was still on the streets of Dry Creek. It had been tramped down and was starting to be slippery.

The day promised to be gray, and Lizette wondered if she'd gone out too soon. The hardware store was still closed, as was the café. There was a bathroom light on in the parsonage next to the church, but there were no other lights in the houses along the street. Most people had sense enough to stay in bed until the sun had a chance to warm up the day.

Lizette decided maybe she had the heat too low in her room. It barely seemed any colder outside than it had been inside. She would be glad to have the tea to drink while she looked around the stage.

The windows in the barn were covered with frost, and thin strips of snow sat on top of the door rim. The main double door was wide enough for a farmer's wagon to pass through it. The walls of the barn had been painted the usual red, and the trim was white. A wide slab of cement stood in front of the door to help with the mud.

The place might be humble compared to other performance centers, but it was large, clean and sturdy. It even had a heating system. Apparently Mr. Elkton had installed heating in the building after the town started using it for their meeting center. Of course, it took a long time to heat up the huge building, so he had suggested she turn the heat on low several days before the performance.

Lizette had turned the heat up to fifty degrees yesterday, and she was looking forward to seeing what the air was like inside the barn.

"Oh," Lizette muttered as she looked at the barn door. When she'd turned the heat on yesterday, she'd also locked the front door to the barn. She had brought the trunk over that held the props and costumes and she thought the sight of all those might tempt someone to experiment with them. And maybe it had, because now the door was most decidedly unlocked. It wasn't unlatched, but clearly someone had gone inside since Lizette had been here yesterday.

Of course, Lizette told herself as she opened the door and stepped into the barn, she supposed that half of the adults in Dry Creek had keys to the barn. One of them might have wanted to check to be sure the heat was on.

Lizette turned on the overhead light. She was

enough of a city woman to want the lights instead of the shadows until she figured out if anything was missing.

The Christmas tree was there, right in the middle of the area they had decided on as the stage. The cardboard fireplace stood next to the wooden rocking chair. The old Christmas stockings that Mrs. Hargrove had hung on the stairs leading up to the hayloft were still tied in place. Folding chairs lined the edges of the barn and a table was sitting at the far end of the barn where they were going to put the pastries and punch.

No one had moved anything big.

It was the bathrobe, Lizette decided after she looked around. All of the costumes and props were still in the trunk except for the heavy bathrobe that the narrator wore. Maybe Charley had come to get it for some reason. Or Mrs. Hargrove might have decided it needed a good washing and taken it with her. It certainly was nothing someone would steal.

Lizette told herself it really didn't matter as she walked over to the small panel that ran the sound system. A bathrobe was the one costume that she could easily replace. She bet there were a dozen old bathrobes around that the men of Dry Creek would donate if she made the need known. Especially if she promised the bathrobe owner wouldn't have to actually dance in the ballet along with his robe.

Lizette selected the Nutcracker audiocassette, inserted it into the panel, and turned the volume on low.

Pete Denning kept saying that he was willing to

do whatever she needed to help with the ballet, and he could probably find a bathrobe in that bunkhouse where he lived that looked as warm and comfortable as the one Charley had been using. Of course, the reason Pete was so helpful was because he was hoping she'd go out with him when the ballet was over.

If Pete had kept the role of the Nutcracker, he would have studied up on the proper way to give a stage kiss.

So far, Lizette had been able to gently refuse his requests for dates, explaining that it was not proper for her to date one of her students. Pete had offered to quit right then if she'd go out with him instead. Fortunately, Lizette had talked him out of that idea, as well. But he was bound to ask her out again after the Nutcracker was finished, and she didn't know what she would say.

The sounds of Tchaikovsky's music filled the old barn. It truly was beautiful, soaring music Lizette thought to herself. Whoever had set up the speaker system had done a professional job. Several speakers hung from the rafters and several more hung either beside the hayloft or on the other side of the barn by where the refreshment table stood.

If the barn were a few degrees warmer, Lizette would be tempted to take her coat off and dance awhile. If nothing else, the sounds of Tchaikovsky would bring enough culture to the people of Dry Creek to reward them for coming to the ballet.

Lizette drank the last swallow of her tea before she walked back to the door and opened it a crack. She looked across the road and saw that a light was now on in Linda's café. Good, Lizette thought, she would forget about the cereal in her cupboard and have a proper breakfast in the café this morning. After all, it was an important day. A critic from the press was going to come and review her performance.

The blinds were half-drawn on the café windows and there were no customers other than Lizette. The floor was a black-and-white pattern and the tables and chairs had a fifties' look about them. A large glass counter filled the back wall. Linda had added a counter recently to sell more baked goods.

There was a phone call just as Linda was bringing Lizette's order out.

Linda set Lizette's plate of food down on the counter and answered the phone.

"Some telemarketer," Linda had said thirty seconds later as she put the phone back on the hook and picked Lizette's plate up again. "Asking about a taxi in Dry Creek. Anyone from here to Wyoming knows there's no taxi in Dry Creek."

"Why would they call the café anyway?"

Linda shrugged as she put Lizette's plate in front of her. "We're the only business in the phone book with Dry Creek in our name. People get confused."

"Well, just as long as it's not Edna Best from the newspaper."

Linda snorted. "Edna was born out this way. She'd be the last to call for a taxi."

Lizette figured it probably was a telemarketer then. In any event, she wasn't going to worry about it. She had a plate of golden-brown French toast in front of her, and it was sprinkled with blueberries and raspberries.

Linda went to the kitchen and came back with a bowl of oatmeal for herself along with an apple and a small glass of orange juice.

"These frozen berries are the best," Lizette said.

"I'm trying out a new brand," Linda said as she sat down across from Lizette.

The two ate in silence for a few minutes. Then Lizette fretted aloud about the newspaper critic. "A review can make or break a production."

"Don't worry. Edna will be positive. She's probably never even been to a ballet."

"Still, it doesn't hurt to be prepared."

"Well, she's liked her coffee strong and black as long as I've known her. Having a full cup will go a long way to giving her a positive impression since it's so cold outside," Linda said as Lizette finished up her French toast. "I'll fix up a big thermal jug for you to come get around one o'clock. And I still have a few of those chocolate chip pecan cookies you made. We'll put those on a plate for her. That should take care of Edna. Did I tell you my afternoon business has picked up since I've started selling cookies to go with the coffee?"

Last week, Linda had offered Lizette meals in exchange for baked goods to sell in the café. So far, Lizette had made individual apple coffeecakes and the cookies.

"I'm thinking I'll try some pies next," Lizette said

as she pushed her plate away. "Maybe cherry and apple with a special order possible for chocolate pecan for the holidays."

Linda sat across the table from Lizette with her glass of orange juice in her hand. "I can sell all the baked goods you give me. You can make money in addition to your meals. We might even make up a batch of fruit cakes."

"The people of Dry Creek sure do like their baked goods."

Linda nodded as she picked up her apple. "They need to eat more fruits and vegetables, but you'll never convince these ranch hands around here. If it's not meat or bread, they think it's not food. I'm surprised you haven't started getting marriage proposals. I guess they're all giving you a month or so to settle in before they start to pester you with their pleading."

Lizette laughed. "If they like good cooking, I would think they'd be stopping at your door instead. I don't know when I've had such good French toast."

"It's the bread," Linda said. "I use sweet bread. Besides, I've refused them all so many times they've stopped asking."

"Don't you want to get married?"

Linda finished chewing her bite of apple. "I was engaged once. That was enough."

Lizette didn't think the other woman could be over twenty-two. "What happened?"

"He decided he wanted to be a music star instead," Linda said as she leaned back in her chair and put the rest of the apple on her plate. "Life here in Dry Creek wasn't good enough for him."

"Oh, I'm sorry."

"Don't be. The funny thing is that he's making it. I've started to hear his songs on the radio. He's even doing some big tour in Europe."

"But he could have taken you with him!"

Linda smiled. "He offered a while back. I just didn't want to go. Who wants to be the wife that keeps him back? And then there are the fans. I didn't want to share my husband with them. No, I'm better off here in the café."

Lizette noticed that the other woman's voice was too bright and brittle to be convincing. "Well, if there's ever anything I can do, let me know."

"Thanks," Linda said as she stood up. "But there's nothing anyone can do. We make our choices in life and then we live with them."

"But have you talked to him since or written him a letter or anything?"

Linda shrugged. "What would I say? Sorry you're becoming a star. I miss the old you. No, he's gone on and I've stayed the same."

"Well," Lizette said as she, too, stood up from the table. She noticed the sun had fully risen. It was a new day. "Maybe there will be a nice young rancher move into town and you'll come to like him."

"There is Judd Bowman," Linda said as she stopped walking to the back of the café and turned to face Lizette. "He seems nice enough."

Lizette swallowed. "Yes, he does."

"Hmm," Linda said as her eyes started to twinkle. "He does seem a little preoccupied lately, though. I'm not sure I could get his full attention."

"He's just worried about the ballet."

Linda grinned. "Is that what he's worried about?"

"Well, he's probably still worried about his cousin and the kids' father, too."

"I don't know—all I hear him muttering about lately is Pete Denning and how he gets all of the attention in those classes of yours. If I didn't know better, I would say he was jealous."

"I try to give all of my students my full attention," Lizette said. "It's just that some of them are—"

"—more difficult," Linda supplied helpfully. "More independent. More disturbing."

"Yes," Lizette said. She was glad someone understood. "Judd is all of those."

Linda nodded. "Good."

"I don't know if it's good. It does make the ballet more difficult."

"But doesn't it make life more interesting?"

"Maybe," Lizette admitted. "But right now I have a critic to prepare for and plum filling to make."

"The kids can help with the plum filling, and Mrs. Hargrove and I will help you with the custard. I've never made a cream filling, but Mrs. Hargrove will know how."

"You have those kettles with the thick bottoms," Lizette said. "That's the key right there."

"How many pastries do you figure you'll need?"

"Mrs. Hargrove figures we'll need twenty dozen."

"Two hundred and forty!"

Lizette nodded. "She says we're going to bring in crowds from all around."

"I'd better get my salads made for lunch right now then, so I can clear the kitchen for the custard. Mrs. Hargrove will be over any minute."

"Be sure she remembers to come over to the performance area in time to get ready for Edna." Lizette refused to call the place a barn. From today until the night of the ballet, it was a performance center.

"She'll be there. I think she's excited to be the Ice Queen."

Lizette smiled. "She's the Snow Queen. She's in charge of the snowflakes."

"Then you have nothing to worry about," Linda said.

Lizette repeated the words to herself as she left the café. She had nothing to worry about. The people of Dry Creek would be kind critics. They were looking for entertainment, not perfection. Everything would be just fine.

Chapter Fifteen

Nothing was fine. Lizette's watch was missing. Which meant the schedule was all off. The kids were still at the table cutting up dried plums, and they should be in their costumes if they were going to practice before the dress rehearsal. Plus, Linda had just come over with a message saying that Pete had been out working with the cattle and had run into a bit of a problem, but that Lizette wasn't to worry. He would be there in no time.

It wasn't until Linda mentioned that Pete was late that Lizette looked for her watch. She couldn't believe she hadn't known how much time had passed. She'd been busy diagramming the steps to a stage kiss and it had taken her longer than she had anticipated. That's why she hadn't noticed she didn't have her watch with her. She'd left it on the cardboard fireplace before she'd gone over to the café for breakfast.

"I'm sure it was there," Lizette said as she started walking over to the stage area.

"Maybe the mice took it," Amanda offered. She had followed Lizette over from the table. The little girl had a dish towel wrapped around her neck for an apron and a piece of twine holding her hair in place. She was licking a spoon that had plum mixture on it. "Or maybe the big rat that lives in the fireplace took it. He's scary."

"The mice were over there with us cutting up dried plums and the rat better be in his pickup driving here." Lizette checked to see that the mice really were still at the table before she looked around again. There weren't any cracks big enough for a watch to fall into, and the furniture in the stage area didn't have any pillows or other hidden areas. "Maybe someone came in and borrowed it."

"More likely someone stole it," Linda replied. "You could report it to the Billings police. Charley is probably at the hardware store by now, and I know he's itching to call something in now that Sheriff Wall is out of town and has designated him and his son as the men to watch Dry Creek."

"I don't think anyone would steal it," Lizette said. She'd only paid twenty dollars for the watch. It wouldn't be worth it for anyone to steal it to resell it.

Linda shrugged. "Well, Mrs. Hargrove is making some bread dough for hamburger buns for me—I'm running low on buns again. But she's going to be here any minute."

Lizette nodded. Judd wasn't back from Miles City, either. He was going to stop at the jail and talk to whoever was in charge there and then he was going to locate four yards of white silk material for her. He should be back any minute, as well. And, when he did get back, she wanted to go over her diagram with him and explain once again that there is no physical contact in a stage kiss.

"So what time is it again?" Lizette asked Linda.

"My watch isn't accurate, either," Linda said. "I was working with it to use it as an oven timer, so I'm not sure if it's twelve forty-five or one forty-five."

"Oh, it can't be one forty-five," Lizette said. "Edna Best is supposed to be here before two and—"

The sound of a car honking came from outside the door.

"That must be Pete," Lizette said hopefully. Or maybe Judd. Or Mrs. Hargrove. Anybody but Edna Best. They weren't at all ready for the reviewer to be here. They weren't even in costume.

"I'll go get that coffee," Linda said as she looked out the window and turned to the door. "And remember, she's one of us. She won't go hard on you, and she's early, anyway. Maybe you should send her over for a cup of coffee."

"Hellooo," a woman's voice called from the outside.

Lizette took a deep breath and put a smile on her face. Then she walked to the door of the barn and opened it up. "Welcome. You must be Edna Best."

The woman nodded. She was a short, plump woman wrapped in a hooded parka. "I wasn't sure where the performance was."

"We have some posters up in the hardware store,

and we're making a sign that says 'Nutcracker' to point people to us," Lizette said, realizing she had also forgotten that they needed programs for the evening of the ballet. She hoped that Edna wouldn't ask to see one. That would show her right away that they were amateurs.

"Most folks will know where it is anyway if we say the Elkton barn," Edna said as she stepped inside. "The only question they'll have is about the cost. I didn't see the cost mentioned anywhere in the notes I have so far."

"Cost?" Lizette said. "We weren't planning to charge."

"Of course you've got to charge," Edna said as she looked around inside. "Maybe not much, but enough to pay your expenses. I know props and costumes don't come cheap."

"Most of the costumes are mine, and my former ballet teacher is lending us the props and some more costumes. I'm planning to send her money for postage when I return them to her, but that's not much of an expense."

"Ah," Edna said as she took a small notepad out of her black purse. "That might be a lead. 'Big-city ballet teacher does favor for local teacher.'"

"I don't think Madame Aprele would want to be the feature in your story," Lizette said. "She doesn't like to be written up in the media unless it's for her dancing."

"Madame Aprele?" Edna said as she wrote the name in her book. "That's an interesting name. She's not in the witness protection program or anything, is she? I hear they let you make up your own name. We had a rancher some years ago down by Forsyth that turned out to be in the witness protection program. He never wanted to be in the paper, either. We weren't even sure if we should put his obituary in the paper when he died. We did, of course, but we wondered."

"I don't know if that's her real name," Lizette said as she tried to steer the reviewer toward the folding chairs she had set up earlier around the stage area. "I've always called her that, and I've known her for more than fifteen years."

Edna let herself be led.

"I'm sorry it's not warmer in here," Lizette said. "Linda's going to bring some coffee and a cookie over for you shortly."

"I heard she's been serving cookies lately. When the guys in the newsroom found out I was coming out here, they all told me to bring back cookies if I could. I hear she's got a baker making cookies for her."

"That's me," Lizette said. "I bake a little in my spare time."

"Now that's the hook for my story," Edna said as she settled herself into a folding chair next to the chair Lizette had been sitting in when she was diagramming the stage kiss. "Baker Turns to Ballet for—" Edna paused. "Why would you say you turned to ballet from baking? For inspiration? For profit?"

"It's been my dream," Lizette said as she tried to figure out a way to get her kissing diagram back before Edna noticed it sitting on the chair next to her.

Maybe the best approach was the most direct, Lizette thought as she reached over to pick up the diagram. "Let me just get this out of your way. It's nothing—just some stage directions."

Lizette willed herself to stop. She always talked too much when she was nervous. "Nothing. It's nothing."

"I had no idea you had stage directions in a ballet," Edna said as she looked up from her notebook and frowned. "I told the guys in the newsroom that I didn't know enough to cover this story."

"Oh, don't worry," Lizette said. "I can tell you anything you want to know."

"They only sent me here because I'm a woman."

"Well, I'm glad you came anyway," Lizette said as she sat down beside Edna. "Just ask me any questions you want. I can tell you everything you need."

Edna's face brightened. "That's kind of you. Not everyone takes the time to explain things. First, tell me about these stage directions. What were you mapping out? The battle with the mice?"

Lizette wished she could lie, but she couldn't. "The kiss."

Edna's face brightened even more. "Who's kissing who?"

"The Nutcracker kisses Clara."

Edna frowned. "Isn't the Nutcracker, well, a nutcracker? And isn't Clara a little girl? I did some research on the Internet just to get the basic plot. I only got the start of the ballet, but—"

"When Clara kills the Mouse King, she turns into

a young lady and the Nutcracker turns into a prince. That's when they kiss."

"My, how romantic!" Edna said as she wrote in her notebook. "People around here love a romance. So, tell me, who plays the Nutcracker again?"

"Judd Bowman."

"He's the guy out on the old Jenkins place, isn't he?"

Lizette nodded.

"So the stage directions are for him? On how to kiss?"

"Well, sort of. You see a stage kiss is different than a real kiss—"

Lizette heard another set of tires in the distance. Now, that should be the sound of one of her dancers coming.

The door opened and Linda came inside along with a gust of snowy wind. "There's a regular convention out there."

"Is it Pete or Judd?"

"Neither," Linda said as she brought the thermos of coffee over to Edna. "It's a taxi."

"But there are no taxis here," Lizette said, even as she began to wonder if—

There was the sound of a honking horn and the slamming of a car door outside. Lizette walked to the window. The heat had been on long enough that a small corner of the window was now clear of frost. It was a large enough piece of window that Lizette could see a woman, covered from head to toe in black wool and black scarves. The only color anywhere was a lavender feather boa that the woman had flung around her shoulders.

Madame Aprele was outside.

Lizette hurried to the door even though she wanted to hurry in the other direction and find a place to hide. She opened the door. "Madame. What a surprise! A pleasant surprise!"

"Oh, Lizette." Madame Aprele turned toward Lizette with relief in her voice. Then she started unwinding all of the black scarves and walking toward the open door. "I'm glad I found you. This man was trying to tell me that this barn is the town's performance center. What kind of an old fool does he take me for? I'm so glad you're here so you can show me the way to where you're doing your dress rehearsal for that reviewer. I came to lend my moral support. Newspaper people can be so difficult."

By the time Madame Aprele stopped talking, she had unwound all of the scarves from her head and was fully inside the barn.

"Dear me," was all she said as she looked around.

"Madame Aprele," Lizette said as she held out her arm for the many scarves. "I'm touched that you came all of the way from Seattle. If you'd like me to take your scarves, I can."

Madame Aprele gave Lizette the black scarves. "You're rehearsing here?"

Lizette nodded as she held out her elbow for Madame Aprele to take. "Yes, and I'll take you down for a front-row seat right next to Edna Best, the woman who is going to review us."

"You're rehearsing in a barn?" Madame Aprele asked. "When do you move it to the performance center?"

"The barn *is* the performance center," Lizette said as she started walking Madame Aprele down to the chairs next to the stage.

"But what about the cows?" Madame Aprele said as she sat down in the chair next to Edna Best.

"You have cows in the ballet, too?" Edna asked as she wrote something in her notebook.

"No, there are no cows," Lizette said as she stood beside the two seated women. "Now, if you'll excuse me, I need to get my dancers ready. Madame Aprele, let me introduce you to Edna Best, who's going to review our performance today. Maybe you could answer any questions she has?"

Both women nodded to her and then to each other.

Well, Lizette thought as she stepped away, she'd done all she could. Even if one of her dancers didn't show up, she could deal with it now. All of the things in her nightmare could happen and it wouldn't even faze her now. Madame Aprele had come and seen that she was a fraud.

Her mother's old enemy and her new friend had seen that all of the things Lizette had said about her little dance school were nothing more than the longing in her heart that it be so. The performance center was a barn. Her dance students were over at a table eating a mixture of dried plums and sugar. None of them were in costume. And the only reason any of them were even her students was because they wanted to wear those costumes. The reviewer who was going to write about the ballet, although she was kind, had never even seen a ballet performance before.

There was no way for it to be worse than it was.

Lizette squared her shoulders. She had absolutely nothing to fear now. Let the ballet begin.

Chapter Sixteen

Judd Bowman wished silk had never been invented. Or women. Or both of them. If he hadn't decided to track down some white silk cloth for Lizette before he stopped at the jail to check about Neal Strong, the kids' father, he wouldn't have wasted two hours of valuable time that he could have spent out looking for the escaped prisoner alongside the sheriff's department.

Neal had escaped yesterday afternoon.

Someone had decided that there was room in the Billings jail for Neal and had gone to Miles City to get him in a patrol car. On the way there, Neal complained that he needed to use a restroom. Unfortunately, no one checked to be sure Neal's handcuffs were secure before they escorted him to the restroom. When a backup patrol car came to investigate why there was no response to a radio message, the officers found one of their own unconscious on the floor of the restroom, and Neal, along with the officer's gun, nowhere to be found.

Judd demanded to know why no one had called him last night with the news, only to be told that they were trying to reach Sheriff Wall in Colorado to inform him of what had happened.

Judd pressed the gas pedal on his pickup a little farther down. The police in Billings thought Neal was more likely to head for a drug dealer or the border than his children, but Judd wasn't so sure. He wasn't going to take any chances.

Judd relaxed a little when he saw Pete's pickup in front of the barn where the ballet rehearsal was going to happen. The cowboy would see to the kids' safety if their father was around.

Judd looked at the clock on his dashboard. Speaking of the ballet, he was late. He hoped the extra yards of white silk he'd bought would be enough to make Lizette forgive him.

It hadn't been easy to find silk in Miles City. Judd had had to buy it from a secondhand store owner who called someone he knew who had some white silk left from an old customer who had been using the stuff to make parachutes—or maybe it was bags for parachutes. Neither store owner could remember. They did remember it had been extra-strong silk, guaranteed to hold a hundred pounds, or maybe it was two hundred pounds. They couldn't remember how much.

Judd assured them the silk only had to be strong enough to hold a punch cup, and that he would take it as soon as the other man could get it there. He only hoped it wasn't nylon instead of silk. No one was really sure on that point, either.

Lizette was still waiting to begin the performance. Linda and Mrs. Hargrove had helped clean the faces of her younger dancers and slipped their costumes over their heads. Charley had fussed about his missing bathrobe so much that Lizette had given him a big towel to wrap around his shoulders. Then Pete had walked in a few minutes ago with a bruise on his cheek, muttering something about a stubborn cow. Lizette had asked him what happened, but he shrugged and said he'd tell her later.

"The show must go on," Pete said with a grin as he took his Mouse King costume off the chair where Lizette had laid it and started toward the stairway leading up to the hay loft. "I'll be right back."

"Oh, you can change down here," Lizette said. She hadn't wanted to send the children up to the cold hay loft to change, so she and Charley had hung a blanket in a corner of the barn.

But Pete was already halfway up the stairs with his tail dragging behind him.

Lizette herself was in her ballet slippers and her yellow dress.

"I can fill in for the Nutcracker," Mrs. Hargrove offered. The older woman had changed into her billowing Snow Queen costume and was chatting with Madame Aprele and Edna Best. "I think I have his lines memorized from watching him practice with you."

Charley was sitting in his rocking chair next to the Christmas tree. "The whole thing?"

Mrs. Hargrove nodded.

"So you'd do the Nutcracker kiss?" Edna Best asked as she pulled her notebook back out of her purse.

"Oh, no," Mrs. Hargrove said, and then chuckled. "I see you're still looking for that headline."

Edna smiled and shrugged. "Nothing ever happens around here. I was hoping maybe I could get a news story in the regular part of the paper as well as a review in the Dry Creek Tidbits section."

"Surely it's news that a ballet is going to take place in a barn," Madame Aprele offered helpfully. The older woman no longer seemed as shocked about everything and was actually giving Edna some valuable pointers on how to review the ballet. "In Seattle, that would be a headline."

"Barns are not news around here," Edna said. "We have so many of them."

"Well, you'll have to wait for Judd to get here to stage the kiss," Mrs. Hargrove said. "Although I must say, he seems to have a mind of his own about how a kiss should go on."

"That's why I drew him a diagram," Lizette said. "He just needs to see how to do it."

Charley snorted. "Whoever heard of a diagram for a kiss?"

There was a thud up in the hayloft that sounded as if Pete was taking off his boots.

Edna was writing notes. "Could you tell me more

about what's lacking in the way the Nutcracker kisses?"

"Oh, I didn't say anything was lacking," Lizette said. She hoped the boot thud meant that Pete was almost in his costume. "And I don't really think you should be quoting me on this. I mean, I'm not an expert on kissing or anything. It's just for the ballet scene."

Lizette decided there was really no need to wait for the Nutcracker to arrive before they began the production. "Charley can just read the Nutcracker's lines."

"I can do the Nutcracker's kissing, too," Charley said firmly. "In my day and age, we didn't do any of this stage-kissing stuff. That's just for Hollywood types."

"How do you know? You've never kissed a Hollywood type," Mrs. Hargrove said.

"Now, how do you know who I've kissed and who I haven't kissed?" Charley said with his chin in the air.

"Well, I've known you all your life."

"That doesn't mean you know all about me. I could still surprise you yet."

"Don't think I couldn't surprise you, too," Mrs. Hargrove retorted.

My goodness, Lizette thought, what was wrong with the two of them?

Someone cleared his throat loudly from the sidelines. It must be Pete coming down the stairs, Lizette thought as she looked up.

"Speaking of surprises," Pete said calmly as he stood very still.

Pete hadn't changed into his costume, although he did have another bruise on his face. Still wearing his work jeans and a flannel shirt, he was standing at the top of the stairs with his arms in the air. There were shadows, but there was enough light to see the gun that was being held to the back of Pete's head as well as the man behind him holding the gun.

There was silence for a moment.

"There's my bathrobe," Charley finally said.

Lizette felt two pairs of little arms circle around her legs.

"That's my dad," Bobby whispered as he tightened his grip on Lizette's legs.

"You've been hiding up there all day?" Lizette said. She tried to make her voice sound normal and conversational. She didn't want the children terrified any more than they already were. "No wonder the door to the barn was unlocked. After all that time, you must be hungry."

"I'm not hungry. I have a headache. I've been trying to sleep, except you have that awful music playing and it's making my eyes cross."

The man did look pale, even in the shadows.

"That's Tchaikovsky!" Madame Aprele protested. "He's famous. He's never given anyone a headache!"

"I prefer a fiddle," the man said. "Something with some spirit."

Madame Aprele opened her mouth to say something and then thought better of it and closed it again.

Lizette agreed there was no reason to argue music with a man holding a gun. "I'll be happy to turn the music off, and then maybe you can go back and lie down and have a good rest."

The man snorted. "Nice try, but I think I'll stay right here where I can see everybody. Like you, old man." He pointed at Charley. "I see you reaching inside your coat pocket for something. You got a gun in there?"

Charley held up his open hands. "No gun. I was reaching for an antacid. Stress is killing me."

"Well, you keep your hands out of your pockets." The man nudged Pete to start walking down the stairs. "You all keep your hands where I can see them. We have a situation here."

"We don't need to have a situation," Lizette said as she put her own hands out in full view. "If you just put the gun down, no one needs to get hurt."

"You'd like that, wouldn't you? You always were looking out for yourself first," the man said. "I remember you from the gas station. No room for a poor man like me to ride with you when anyone could see you had enough room. Someone like you thinks they're better than me. Well, you're not better than me now. Not when I've got the gun."

"I don't think I'm better than anyone," Lizette said. "I just want everyone to be safe."

There was an awkward silence as everyone thought about being safe.

"You must be Neal Strong," Edna finally said. She had her hands out in front of her, as well. "I've heard about you. Something about a wrongful arrest."

"You bet it was wrongful!"

"Well, maybe you'd like to put down the gun and tell me about it. I'm a reporter with the newspaper. If we work at getting your story out there, maybe there's a chance for you."

"The only chance for me is this," Neal said as he nodded toward the gun he held in his hand.

Pete and Neal had reached the bottom of the stairs, but no one started to breathe normally.

Even with no breath left in their lungs, they all gasped when the door to the barn started to open.

Judd held himself perfectly still. He'd come up to the door earlier and heard some of what was happening inside. He'd run over to the café and asked Linda to call the police in Billings and tell them their man was armed and in the big barn in Dry Creek. Then he'd run back to the barn door.

"I know I'm late," Judd said as he stepped into the main area of the barn. He had the white silk under one arm. "I had a hard time finding the silk and—"

Judd broke off his words, hoping he sounded genuinely surprised. "Well, who's this?"

Judd already knew who the man was, but he didn't want to give Neal any reason to be suspicious that Judd had notified the authorities.

"I'm the kids' dad," Neal said as waved his gun around. "You must be that cousin of Barbara's? You look a lot like her."

Judd felt his smile tighten. "You've seen Barbara?"

Neal nodded. "Tracked her down. I told her she had no right to leave the kids off somewhere. I'm their dad. I say where they're supposed to be."

Judd knew he shouldn't argue with the man, but he didn't like the scared look Amanda was giving him.

Judd took a casual step closer to the kids. "Bobby and Amanda are with me for now. They're no trouble. No need to bother yourself with them."

"You and Barbara would like that, wouldn't you?" Neal sneered. "You're two of a kind. Bowmans both of you. You're spoiling the kids."

So that's what family is, Judd thought. Hearing your name coupled with someone else's in a sneer and not even minding it because it meant someone else was in the thick of it with you. What do you know? He did have a family.

"They're good kids." Judd took another step closer to Amanda and Bobby. He figured the gun could go off at any minute, but if it did he had some things to say to some people before he died. "I'm not nearly good enough for those kids of yours, but if they were mine, I'd be proud of it. They're part of my family and I love them both."

Judd half expected the gun to go off when he said he loved the kids. Maybe Neal Strong didn't hear him. The words echoed in Judd's own ears, but that might be because he'd rarely even said he *liked* anyone in his life. He'd certainly never admitted to loving anyone. Love had never been for a man like him. Judd wasn't sure what love was, so he couldn't say for sure that's what he felt when he looked at those two kids holding on to Lizette's legs, but it must be. He was willing to die to protect them. That had to be something close to the love that made a family a family.

All three pairs of eyes—Lizette's and the two kids'—looked up at him.

Judd blinked. He wondered what was happening to the air around here that a man's eyes could tear up just looking at someone.

Judd took the final step that brought him next to Lizette and the kids.

"Now ain't that touching," Neal drawled as Amanda and Bobby left Lizette's legs and wrapped themselves around Judd.

Judd resisted the urge to bend down and lift the children into his arms. Instead, he gently guided both children to the back of his legs so that there would be less of them to be targets if Neal was as unsettled as he looked.

Judd forced himself to shrug. "It's still cold in here. They just like to wrap themselves around something warm. That's all."

Neal snorted. "You don't fool me. I don't let go of what's mine all that easy. Just ask Barbara."

"I've been wanting to talk to Barbara," Judd said casually. "Do you know where I can reach her?"

Neal just laughed. "You ain't getting nothing out of me."

"I'd be willing to pay," Judd said smoothly.

"I've got money."

"I wasn't thinking of cash," Judd said. He hoped the police speculation that Neal had been going through drug withdrawal was correct. "I've got some white stuff out in the pickup that might interest you."

"What is it?" Neal said.

Judd saw the look in Neal's eyes and knew he had him. Hook, line and sinker. "Not something you'd want me to announce right out here in the open."

"Bring it in."

Judd shrugged. "If you were interested in it, I'd throw in the pickup, as well. You might want to get out of here before anyone knows you're here."

Neal took a few steps closer to the door, turning as he walked so that everyone was still in his range of vision.

"I need your keys."

Judd tossed him the keys to his pickup.

"Where's the stuff?"

"In the back of the pickup, alongside the hay bales I have in there. I'm not sure what side it's on."

"What? You can't be too careful with the stuff, man."

"I'm sure you'll take care of it." Judd watched as the man walked even closer to the door.

"Is it good?" Neal asked when he had his back at the door.

"Pure as snow," Judd said as he watched the other man open the door and slide outside.

Judd counted to two. He figured it would take the man that long to get off the steps. "Everybody out the back window."

Pete was already with him on this one and had opened the back window already. The cold air swept across the barn, but no one noticed.

Judd rushed over to the door and locked it from

the inside. It would take the man a while to find the key that had let him into the barn in the first place.

"The little ones first," Madame Aprele said as she lifted Amanda into Pete's arms.

Pete lifted the little girl out the window. Then he lifted Bobby.

Charley brought over a chair for the women, and one by one they climbed up to it and then slid out the window with the men's help.

There was a banging on the door to the barn just as Lizette slid over the window's edge.

"What did you have in your pickup?" Pete finally turned to Judd and asked. "I didn't figure you for a user."

"I'm not. I told him what the white stuff was. It's snow."

"Oh, man, he's going to be mad," Pete said with a grin on his face.

The gunshot echoed throughout the barn.

"Charley, the kids need a guard," Judd said as he and Pete overruled the older man's objection and lifted him out the window. "Get them all someplace safe."

Another gunshot echoed. This one sounded as if it struck metal, which meant Neal had hit the lock.

"Now you," Judd said to Pete.

But the cowboy was already building a barricade of metal chairs. "The others need a few minutes to get away from the window. There's no cover out this way."

Judd moved chairs, too. "I can be as distracting as any two men. No sense in both of us being in here."

Pete flashed him a grin. "I'm the Rat King. I don't run away."

Judd only grunted. He was a family man now. He didn't run away, either.

Something crashed against the barn door, and both Pete and Judd dived behind their shelter of metal chairs.

"Where are you?" Neal demanded as he swung the door wide open and stepped into the barn. "You think you can fool me. I'll show you."

It was silent for a moment. Then Neal said, "I see where you are. Think you can hide behind a pile of old chairs—now who's the fool?"

Judd grabbed one of the chairs. Neal would have to come close to them to actually have any hope of shooting them, and when he did, Judd intended to bash him over the head with one of these chairs. It wasn't much, but with God's help it might work.

Now, where did that thought come from? Judd wondered. It must be all this church he had been going to that gave him this nagging sense that he should be praying.

A loud creak sounded from the middle of the barn floor. Neal was walking this way.

Oh, well, Judd told himself, if he was going to die on his knees anyway, huddled behind a twisted mess of metal, he might as well figure out if God had any interest in him.

"Come out with your hands up!" The sound of the bullhorn made everyone jump.

Judd blinked. For a moment there, he'd thought that was God's voice answering his first feeble attempt at a prayer.

"What's going on?" Neal stood in the middle of the room and demanded.

"Come on out now with your hands up!" the voice on the bullhorn repeated. "We've got you surrounded."

"Ah, man," Neal said as he started walking toward the door. "All I was trying to do was get a good night's sleep."

Judd and Pete waited for the door to the barn to close before they stood up.

"Well," Pete said.

Judd nodded as he held out his hand to the other man.

Pete shook his hand. "Well."

Judd nodded.

Then they turned to walk out of the barn together.

Chapter Seventeen

Lizette wondered how she'd be able to hold the ballet without a Nutcracker. The Friday edition of the Billings newspaper had arrived on the counter in the hardware store, and the men hadn't stopped laughing since. On the first page was Edna Best's lead news story about the shoot-out in the Dry Creek barn. Gossip had circulated that story before the paper could, so the only real news was that the police officer who Neal had hit over the head was doing fine.

No, it was the sidebar to the story that was gathering everyone's interest this morning. The sidebar led to a human interest piece Edna had also written on the ballet that was tucked away on page twelve. The headline read, "Ballet Instructor Teaches Local Rancher, Judd Bowman, How to Kiss Like a Movie Star—Diagram Included."

Lizette's heart had stopped when she read the headline. Her ballet performance was doomed. Judd would never show up.

Even more important, her friendship with him was doomed. He wouldn't want to be seen with her if people teased him about it, and no doubt some of those ranch hands at the hardware store were already thinking up clever things to say if they saw Judd and her together.

One thing Lizette knew about Judd was that he was a private person. He'd told her he hadn't talked to the people of Dry Creek for the first six months he'd lived here. She figured that was his way of warning her that he wasn't the cozy kind of person most women look for in a male friend. She had received the message and decided to ignore it. She didn't care if he was cozy or not. He was Judd.

She liked Judd and she wanted him to just be who he was. She'd wanted to get to know him better. She'd hoped maybe their friendship could grow into something more—maybe even the kind of love that people get married over.

But those hopes were all gone. Judd was probably home now planning how he could avoid the town of Dry Creek—and her—for the rest of his life.

It was hard to dream of a future with someone who never wanted to see you again.

Lizette couldn't exactly blame him, and she figured if he wasn't going to show up for the rest of her life, then he wasn't going to show up tonight either, so she'd best stop being sentimental and get on with the problem at hand. It was time, she told herself with a mental shake, to go with Plan B. Her heart hadn't been broken. Cracked maybe, but not broken. If she pulled herself together, she could think of a way to salvage the ballet performance tonight. That was what she wanted, wasn't it?

It was funny how the answer to that question was not as clear as it had once been.

In fact, after looking at the gun in Neal Strong's hand two days ago, Lizette had done a lot of thinking about what exactly her dreams were. She'd never been as scared for anyone else as she had been for those two children who were clinging to her legs.

Maybe it was time that ballet wasn't her only dream.

Madame Aprele had been staying in Mrs. Hargrove's spare room and helping with the last-minute preparations for the ballet performance. She could play the Nutcracker part if need be.

Lizette herself, she realized, had more important things to do right now.

There weren't many places in Dry Creek where a person could sit in silence and think. Lizette told herself that was why she headed for the church. It was as good a place as any, she reasoned, to take the things in her life and add them up so she'd know what she had.

Lizette wasn't halfway across the street before she heard the sound of a vehicle starting up behind the church. Somebody had already been there to see the pastor. Lizette wondered if a person was supposed to make an appointment. She'd have to ask.

Glory Curtis, the pastor's wife, was walking down the center aisle when Lizette stepped inside the church.

"Oh, hi," Glory said.

Lizette noticed the other woman didn't seem surprised to see her. "I don't have an appointment or anything."

Glory smiled. "You don't need an appointment. Most folks just know that my husband has office hours from nine to noon every day before he goes over to work the counter at the hardware store."

Lizette had heard the pastor partially supported himself by working in the hardware store. "I don't need to talk to him for long."

"Take your time."

The pastor himself didn't seem to be in any more of a hurry than his wife had been.

"I've never been to see a pastor before," Lizette confessed.

The pastor nodded. "Sometimes when people have been through a traumatic event like having a gun pointed at them, they want to talk to someone. That's what I'm here for."

"I should be able to handle it myself. It's just that it sort of shook me up."

The pastor nodded. "Shook you up in what way?"

It seemed that the gun pointing at her had shaken her up in more ways than Lizette had thought. Her worries and concerns poured out of her. She'd even signed up for more meetings with the pastor. They were going to study the book of John together.

When Lizette left the church an hour later, she realized she'd completely forgotten about the ballet that was happening this evening. Even more amazing, she didn't start worrying when she did think about the ballet. She and the pastor had prayed, and God, she reasoned, would provide a Nutcracker.

The barn smelled like Christmas. Mrs. Hargrove and Charley had spent the afternoon bringing pine boughs down from the mountains and spreading them around the barn. The other scent was the warm smell of the sugar-plum pastries that Linda had baked this afternoon in the café ovens.

Lizette had gone back and forth between the café and the church doing last-minute things and being increasingly grateful for her friends. The Nutcracker performance might not live up to its ballet potential, but it was certainly living up to its friendship potential.

"Here, let me help you with that," Madame Aprele said as she walked alongside Lizette and offered to carry one of the trays Linda was lending them to display the pastries.

Lizette gave her the lightest of the trays. "If nothing else, people will like the pastries tonight."

Madame Aprele chuckled. "It'll all work out fine. You always used to make yourself sick worrying before any of your performances as a child. Remember, I used to say ballet is for fun."

Lizette grimaced. "It wasn't for fun in our house."

"I know," Madame Aprele said as they both stood on the cement area outside the barn. "I blame myself for not thinking of a way to bring your mother back into the ballet herself. Then she might not have demanded you do it for her."

"Oh, but she—" Lizette stopped herself. She'd never thought about the fact that her mother could still have danced. She might not have been able to do it professionally, but she could have danced in the productions at Madame Aprele's. She could have danced the ballet for fun.

Lizette opened the barn door and stood to one side so the other woman could enter.

"With your mother, it was all or nothing," Madame Aprele said. "If she couldn't be the star of the show, she didn't want to be *in* the show."

Lizette nodded as they walked down to the end of the barn where the refreshment table was. "She used to say the same thing herself. Well, almost the same. She'd say if I wanted to dance, I should dance the main part."

Madame Aprele nodded as she put her tray on the table. "Ballet was never for the joy of it with your mother."

Lizette nodded as she set her tray down, as well. No, ballet was never for the pleasure of it with her mother. She wondered what her mother would do if one of her principal dancers didn't show for a ballet the way Lizette was expecting would happen tonight. Jacqueline would never forgive the dancer who didn't show, Lizette knew that much for sure.

For the first time in her life, Lizette didn't want to be like her mother.

Chapter Eighteen

The first group of people arrived in a noisy caravan of pickups from the Elkton ranch bunkhouse. It was snowing slightly, and the men stomped their feet on the cement outside the barn to knock any loose snow off their boots before they removed their hats and went inside the barn.

The Christmas tree in the stage area was lit with hundreds of tiny lights and all of the ornaments that Mrs. Hargrove generally hung on her tree. There were angels and red birds and golden sleighs. Someone, Lizette thought it had been Charley, had put a small wooden nativity set under the Christmas tree.

Lizette had all of the dancers, except for the Mouse King and the Nutcracker, up in the hayloft so that the audience wouldn't see their costumes until it was time for the ballet to begin. She had hung a blanket in a corner of the loft so they had a changing room, and all of the children were in their costumes. The children had peeked over the edge of the loft and whis-

pered about how many people were in the audience.
Even Mrs. Hargrove and Charley were standing near
the edge of the loft.

They all saw Pete come in with his friends.

"We're up here," Lizette called, and Pete looked
up to where she stood at the top of the stairs leading
to the hayloft.

"I'm coming right up," Pete said as he left his
friends.

"We still have a few more minutes," Madame
Aprele said as she, too, walked to where the others
stood and put her hand on Lizette's shoulder. "The
children said Judd was coming. That he just had an
errand to run in Miles City, and that he'd be back in
time."

Lizette supposed she should be grateful that Judd
had brought the children into town at least. "We'll
have to go on without him if he's not here."

Mrs. Hargrove nodded. "There's still time for him
to get here."

Lizette wondered if she could demand that everyone give her their copy of the diagram she'd drawn of
how to stage a kiss. In all of the confusion, she'd left
hers on the chair next to Edna. The reporter probably
didn't even realize Lizette didn't want the diagram
published. It had just been an image to go with the
text Edna had written. There were now thousands of
that image between here and Billings. Some of them
were going to be in the barn tonight.

Lizette looked over the rail of the loft and saw at

least two ranch hands who had a piece of newsprint in their hands. It had to be the diagram.

There was probably no chance that Judd hadn't seen it, Lizette thought.

"Do you get a newspaper at your house?" Lizette turned and asked Bobby.

The boy shook his head. "Cousin Judd listens to the radio."

Maybe there *was* a chance, Lizette thought. Fortunately, no one on the radio was likely to have heard about the Hollywood Kiss Diagram, which was what Edna had referred to it as.

Fifteen more minutes passed and Judd still hadn't arrived. The barn had filled with a good-size crowd, and everyone seemed to be having a good time.

Lizette had decided she wouldn't sell tickets to the ballet, but Linda had offered to put a bucket near the refreshment table where people could make donations to cover the costs of the production. There was a line now for the coffee, and it looked like most people held a dollar bill in their hand to put in the bucket.

"I'll go down and get the music ready to start," Lizette said. It was five minutes until the time the ballet was scheduled to begin. She looked over at Madame Aprele and smiled. "You'd best get in the Nutcracker costume. When I come back up, I'll wait a few minutes and then give Linda the signal to dim the lights and push the play button for the music."

Lizette walked down the stairs and onto the barn floor. Half of the chairs were filled with people drinking coffee or punch and waiting for the ballet to begin.

The other half of the chairs would comfortably seat the people who were still in line for their beverage.

Linda had suggested they serve the drinks before the ballet and then serve them again after the ballet when they brought out the pastries.

"Hi," Linda said when she saw Lizette walking toward the refreshment table. "We'll be finishing up here in a few minutes."

Lizette nodded. "Judd's not here yet, but he might not make it. When everyone gets settled down here and back to their seats, just dim the lights and then a minute later start the music. The dancers will come down the stairs then and we'll begin."

The chatter in the barn had a warm feeling to it, Lizette thought as she walked back to the stairs. People smiled and greeted her like an old friend instead of a performer, and she liked that.

Lizette climbed the stairs to the hayloft and gathered her dancers around her for a final word of encouragement.

"This is for fun," Lizette said to them all as she nodded to Madame Aprele, who was holding the Nutcracker's hat but still hadn't changed into the entire costume. The older woman had more hope than Lizette did. "I don't want you to worry if you make a mistake. Everything will be fine."

"I'm not going to make any mistakes," Amanda said. She had her costume on, and the wings glittered pink and gold in the light that came into the loft. "I'm a Sugar Plum Fairy, and we don't make mistakes."

"We try not to make mistakes," Lizette agreed. "But sometimes we do."

"Like Cousin Judd," Bobby said. "He's making a mistake because he's late."

Lizette put her hand on the boy's shoulder. "It's all right. It will be okay even if he doesn't get here. We'll all understand."

Lizette hoped that message would get to Judd through the children.

"Uh-uh." Amanda shook her head. "Cousin Judd needs to be here. He's the Nutcracker. Who's going to do the kiss if he's not here?"

Lizette exchanged a glance with Madame Aprele. The older woman would play the part of the Nutcracker. But— "Maybe there won't be a kiss this time around."

"I'd be happy to do the kiss," Pete said as he stepped out from behind the curtain in his Mouse King costume.

Lizette noticed the ranch hand had not flirted with her since he'd arrived. He wasn't even flirting now.

"On Judd's behalf, of course," Pete added. "As a friend."

"Oh, well—" Lizette stammered. "No one needs to do a kiss."

Pete stepped closer to the edge of the loft and looked over. "I think they're going to demand a kiss."

Lizette stepped closer to the edge of the loft just in time to see the barn door open.

"Well, look who's here," Pete said with relief. "I knew he'd make it."

It was Judd walking through the door, along with a woman who was wrapped in a long black coat with a gray wool scarf wrapped around her face so that none of her hair or skin showed.

Lizette tried not to be jealous of the fact that Judd was walking with his arm around the woman and leading her to one of the chairs in the back of the barn. Who Judd put his arm around was none of her business, Lizette told herself, even though he was carrying a huge bouquet of roses that he gave to the woman when she settled into her chair. Judd called Linda over to the woman before he looked up to the hayloft and saw Lizette and Pete.

The chatter in the barn grew more excited as Judd walked over to the staircase leading up to the hayloft.

"Cousin Judd!" Amanda squealed when she saw Judd coming up the stairs. "You came!"

"Of course," Judd said as he stood at the top of the stairs.

"You need to get into your costume," Pete said as he slapped Judd on the back. "We've got a ballet to do."

Linda dimmed the lights to signal the audience was ready. Judd was already walking over to Madame Aprele, who held out his costume to him. Then he headed for the curtain to change. "If you want to start, I can slip down in a few minutes."

Lizette nodded. "You don't need to be in the first few minutes, anyway. We thought we'd have the family sing a carol in front of the tree to start."

This, Lizette thought, was what a family Christmas felt like even hundreds of years ago when the Nutcracker was written. It was gathering your friends and family together beside a tree and celebrating a wonderful time of gifts and love.

The carol the family sang was "Silent Night." Mrs. Hargrove led everyone in the barn in softly singing the song and the sound filled the whole structure with warmth.

Lizette slowly danced ballet steps to show how a young girl would see the wonder of that night long ago when Christ was born. The audience was hushed. Lizette had not known until these past few days what it meant to be truly silent on that holy night.

After the carol finished, Charley started to read the story of the Nutcracker.

The Nutcracker came on the stage just when the presents were given to the children, and Lizette realized what she should have done. She should have taken a moment to warn Judd about the kiss. He must not know that everyone had been talking about the kiss he was going to give her tonight.

Lizette danced the part of Clara's excitement over her new gift, hoping to come close enough to whisper in Judd's ear. Unfortunately, none of the steps got her close enough to say a few words to him that all of the others wouldn't also hear.

She'd have to wait for the battle scene, she thought. There would be enough noise with all of the mice attacking that no one would hear her talking to Judd.

What was wrong with the Nutcracker? When they had practiced, Judd had held back as though he wasn't part of the mice attack. He'd let the children attack him, but he hadn't gotten into their play. Now, he attacked with abandon, lifting one mouse up in the air until the mouse giggled and then going after another until even the tin soldier forgot which side of the battle he was on and all of the children swarmed around the Nutcracker.

Lizette didn't have a chance to talk to Judd, so she just kept dancing. She twisted and turned and made it look like the whole stage was alive with ballet.

Then Charley started to read about the attack of the Mouse King, and Pete burst out of the fireplace with a roar that briefly overpowered the music.

Now, Lizette said to herself, as she tried to dance closer to Judd to explain that he didn't need to kiss her. There wasn't a kiss in every Nutcracker production, and there wouldn't be one in this one. The people of Dry Creek would have to get their romance elsewhere this Christmas. Her friendship with Judd was more important than the ballet, even if this ballet affected the future of her ballet school in this little community where she was making her home.

"Psst," Lizette hissed as she danced as close as she could to Pete and Judd.

The Mouse King and the Nutcracker were engaged in a magnificent battle, and the audience was shouting encouragement to them both. There was enough noise that she could deliver her message to Judd if he'd only look her way.

But the Mouse King had the Nutcracker in his grip, and Charley was clearing his throat.

"The shoe." Judd twisted his neck and finally looked at Lizette. "You need to throw your shoe."

Lizette figured she'd have to talk to Judd after she saved his life.

Lizette's shoe hit Pete on the shoulder, and he went down with a groan.

The music swelled up and Charley threw sparkling confetti in the air as if it was a party.

Judd moved closer.

Finally, Lizette thought as she danced closer to him, she'd have a chance to tell him about the kiss.

"You don't need to do the kiss," Lizette whispered as she came close to Judd.

Judd had already taken his hat off, and he wasn't frowning at all. In fact, Lizette thought he looked downright happy. Which meant only one thing. He hadn't heard about the story in the newspaper.

"Oh, yes, I do," Judd said as he moved even closer to her until she had no room left to dance.

"But—" Lizette said before Judd bent down and kissed her. It wasn't a stage kiss, of course. He hadn't taken any of her earlier suggestions. The funny thing was that she didn't care. She had his kiss.

Yes, she thought to herself, this was what Christmas and mistletoe and family were all about.

Lizette was only dimly aware of the applause.

"We're not finished," she murmured as she settled even closer to Judd, if that was possible.

"Not by a long shot," Judd agreed with his lips close to hers.

"We still have the Sugar Plum Fairy."

"That, too," Judd agreed as he smiled into her eyes and then kissed her again.

The applause overpowered the music. Lizette thought there was some stomping, too.

"Oh, yes," Judd said as he slowly pulled himself away from her. "I almost forgot—"

Judd looked to his side where Linda stood with the hugest bouquet of red roses Lizette had ever seen.

"These are for you," Judd said to her as he took the roses from Linda and handed them to Lizette.

She almost cried. Everything was perfect for the moment. But when someone said something about that diagram, she didn't know what he would do.

Judd then turned to the audience and said quite clearly, "And for those of you who are wondering about the secret to a Hollywood kiss, that's it. Bring her roses, boys, that's all there is to it."

The audience loved him. Lizette could see that. Odd that she still had the urge to cry.

"That was a smart move," she said to Judd. She couldn't look him in the eye, but she could look at his chin, which was close enough. "They won't tease you now. It was brilliant."

"Brilliant had nothing to do with it," Judd whispered as he tipped her chin up so her eyes met his. "I'm hoping to kiss you a lot in the days ahead, and I don't want someone stopping to draw a diagram of it every time I do."

"You do? Hope to kiss me?"

Judd nodded. "A man's got to have hope even if he's got no reason to."

Lizette smiled. "You have reason."

Judd grinned and kissed her again.

Lizette danced the next scenes as she had never danced before. Madame Aprele was right about ballet being fun. The Snow Queen must have thought it was fun, too, because she almost frolicked during her scenes.

Then there was the Sugar Plum Fairy. Amanda glowed as she stood at the edge of the stage area and started her dance. Lizette had had more time to teach Amanda dance steps than any of her other students, and the little girl was actually doing ballet.

Lizette had given Amanda a solo part, and so Lizette had danced to the sidelines to wait while Amanda completed it.

Madame Aprele was standing next to Lizette. "She's got promise, that one. She's a natural."

Lizette nodded. It was good to know she had at least one student who was in it for the ballet instead of the doughnuts.

"There will be more," Madame Aprele said with a nod to the audience. "You'll find more students out there."

The applause at the end of Amanda's solo was as loud as the kiss applause, and the little girl glowed under the shower of encouragement until one woman at the back of the seating area stood up to give her a standing ovation.

"Mama," Amanda squealed, and forgot all about

being the Sugar Plum Fairy as she ran down the aisle to her mother.

Lizette swore there wasn't a dry eye in the whole barn by the end of the ballet.

Chapter Nineteen

"We're going to need more napkins," Linda announced as Lizette managed to walk through the crowd of well-wishers in order to check with Linda on how things were going. "Next time we should forget asking for contributions for coffee and just sell handkerchiefs. We'll make a fortune. Even I was teary-eyed."

"Who wouldn't cry when Amanda saw her mother?"

"And you and Judd," Linda said as she reached for a napkin. "That sent me over the edge."

"Well—" Lizette wanted to admit that it had sent *her* over the edge, too, but the man was nowhere around and so she wasn't sure she should be thinking what she was thinking, so she didn't want to say anything.

"I mean, when he gave you the second kiss, I knew—that's the real thing." Linda dabbed at her eyes. "Judd's just so romantic. My boyfriend used to be that way, too."

Lizette couldn't help but think it would be a lot more romantic if Judd had actually hung around to talk to her after a kiss like that. At first she thought he was with the kids and their mother, but she'd looked over there and he wasn't with them, either. She'd heard that Judd's cousin had been in a hospital in Colorado until Sheriff Wall went there to convince her it was safe to come back. Judd had met her in Miles City and brought her out to the performance. After such a long day, maybe Judd was just tired. Maybe he'd just gone home without a word to anyone.

"Ah, there he is," Linda said.

Lizette turned to look in the direction of Linda's gaze.

So there was Judd, coming in the door with Pete right behind him. They were both still in costume although they had put on their hats and their coats, so they looked a little odd.

Lizette could see Judd scanning the crowd and looking for someone until his eyes found hers and the scanning stopped. He started walking toward her.

"If you'll excuse me," Linda said as she started to walk away from Lizette. "I think three might be a crowd right about now."

"Sorry," Judd said as he stopped in front of Lizette. "I had to give Pete a key to my place and I'd left the key in my pickup."

"Pete?"

"Yeah, I told him he could stay at my place for a few days until the teasing dies down about his tail."

Lizette smiled. "I didn't think of that."

"Yeah, this having-a-friend business is a commitment, you know," Judd said as he reached out and touched Lizette on the cheek. "Not that I'm opposed to commitments anymore. I want you to know that. In fact, there's one commitment I'll welcome if I get a chance to make it."

"What's that?" Lizette said.

"This one." Judd bent his head to kiss her.

Epilogue

From the Dry Creek Tidbits column appearing in the March 17 issue of the Billings newspaper:

The bride, Lizette Baker, and the groom, Judd Bowman, were married in the church in Dry Creek last Saturday, March 14, at two o'clock in the afternoon. The groom's little cousin, Amanda Strong, was the flower girl and her brother, Bobby Strong, was the ring bearer.

Both children (who take lessons at the Baker School of Ballet along with eight other children) executed perfect pirouettes on their way down the aisle as a special gift to their ballet teacher.

The bride and groom gave special thanks to the pastor of the church, who had baptized them and received their confession of faith several months prior to their marriage.

Doughnuts were served at the reception along with a five-tiered wedding cake, both made by the bride, who offers her baking services at the Dry Creek Café.

Readers of this column who want to send congratulation cards to Mr. and Mrs. Bowman can send cards to the Bowman Ranch, Dry Creek, Montana (the groom assured me there is no need to refer to their place as the Jenkins place any longer and I believe he's right. It's now the Bowman family's place.)

Readers of this column will also remember that the bride and groom were engaged shortly after demonstrating the Hollywood kiss that was diagrammed in this column. Their kiss after the wedding ceremony rivaled the one many readers saw at the Nutcracker ballet performance before Christmas.

The bride was quoted as saying, "Finally, we have that kiss just right."

The groom offered to keep practicing.

* * * * *

Dear Reader,

I hope you enjoyed reading about Judd and Lizette. When I was telling their story, I thought about what it's like to go to a church for the first time. Their feelings of awkwardness can be seen each Sunday as someone visits a church and isn't sure of what their welcome will be. During the Christmas season, you may see people in your church who do not seem to feel comfortable. Hopefully, you can help them feel like they are among friends.

Sincerely,

Janet Tronstad

We hope you enjoyed reading
this special collection.

If you liked reading these stories,
then you will love **Love Inspired**® books!

You believe hearts can heal. **Love Inspired**
stories show that faith, forgiveness and hope
have the power to lift spirits and change
lives—always.

Enjoy six new stories from
Love Inspired every month!

Available wherever books and
ebooks are sold.

Love Inspired

**Uplifting romances of faith,
forgiveness and hope.**

STEP